THE DAGGER OF ISIS

LESTER PICKER

DEDICATION

For Jennifer, Aidan, William and Terran

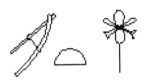

I am Meryt-Neith, Queen of the Two Lands, loyal wife of King Wadjet and mother of King Den, son of King Wadjet, son of King Djer, son of King Hor-Aha, son of the god-King Narmer. I swear before you, Anubis, that these scrolls are the True Telling of My Life. I was a good niece, a good wife and good mother. I was the caretaker of our beloved Kem until my son, King Den, came of age. I beg you to be lenient toward the sins of my sister, Nubiti, so that she may enjoy the rewards of the Afterlife. I await your judgment.

Anubis, I am Nubiti, half-sister of King Wadjet and daughter of Shepsit and King Djer. Before your scales I swear that my heart is light as a feather. Before you lay the scrolls of my life as told to my scribes. Please do not judge Meryt-Neith's actions harshly. Allow my sister to visit with me in the Afterlife. My words are Truth.

Concerning Egypt I will now speak at length, because nowhere are there so many marvelous things, nor in the whole world beside are there to be seen so many works of unspeakable greatness.

- Herodotus

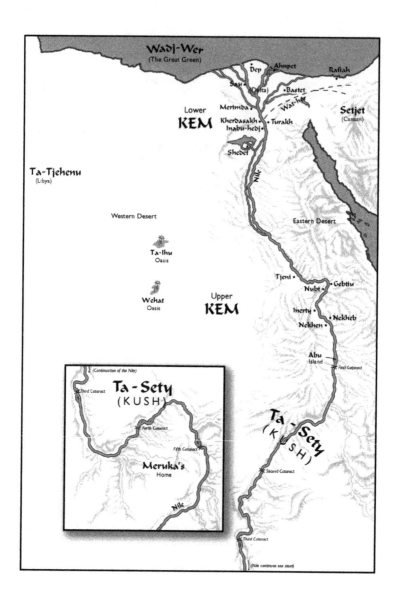

SCROLL ONE

Mery

I ran through the meandering garden path as fast as my young legs would allow me, giggling, despite myself. At the very last second I ducked under the drooping fronds of a thicket of exotic trees brought to the palace from far away lands, frightening yet magical places that Amka had described to me many times. As I ran around a section of the royal garden that contained tubs of tall green rushes and red water flowers, I flushed four colorful glossy ibises. They futilely flapped their clipped, purple wings as if to take to the air, their feet skimming the sandy ground, their long, silvery beaks jutting out comically from their skinny necks as they shrieked in fear.

The heels of my tiny sandals flung pebbles high in the air as I ran. I felt the joy of the dry, warm desert wind whipping against my body, my side braid gently tapping against my shoulder. Oh, if only those joys had not been so fleeting, like ghostly spider threads blown about by a breeze.

"Mery, wait! Don't run so fast, you'll hurt yourself!" Abana yelled after me in frustration. But I was far enough ahead to pretend not to hear. Instead, Abana lifted her coarse linen robe and scurried after me, a game she knew she was destined to lose.

Still giggling so hard that my cheeks hurt and my breath came in gasps, I scurried on all fours like a dung beetle so Abana could not see me and I made my way to my secret hiding place, the one place where I knew I would be safe from nagging adults and the prying eyes of the rekhi, the poor common people who waited outside the royal compound every day seeking favors of my uncle.

When I finally heard Abana's voice turn in the wrong direction, I smiled, crawled out from my hiding spot and stood up. I gasped. Directly in front of me stood Rami, one of the keepers of the royal menagerie, his feet filthy from the caked dung of the giraffes and water buffaloes under his charge. He stared at me and then at my breasts, in such a way that it sent a sudden chill through me. Then, slowly, he smiled, his rotten teeth bared, his face covered in dirt and marked by rivulets of sweat.

Ever since I was a toddler I would come to the royal menagerie to see the elephants, giraffes and lions, and always I was afraid of Rami, who Abana despised because of his poor rekhi hygiene. Now I shuddered and ran away from him as fast as I could.

In just a few moments I was at the administrative section of the palace. At the first gate, two guards dressed only in pure white loincloths greeted me. Playfully, they crossed their spears.

"And who are you, little woman, that you think you may pass to visit with the mighty King?" one of them asked in as gruff a voice as he could muster.

"It's me, Mery," I said, still out of breath.

"Oh, that's easy for you to say," the second guard

yelled out, pointing his finger at me. "But perhaps you're an evil spy of the Ta-Tjehenus, dressed in the skirt of a girl just to fool us. And perhaps not even a girl any more," he added, pointing good-naturedly to the new additions to my chest.

"Yes, perhaps you're here to harm our King, Horus' brother," the first guard chimed in. "You'd best be on your way or we'll be forced to battle you to the death."

"I am no spy!" I answered, hands on my hips. "But, that man over there might be," I said, pointing behind them with my finger. As soon as they turned around, I crawled under their crossed spears and ran to the King's large meeting room, the guards calling after me that I had tricked them for the last time.

"Next time it'll be death on sight!" was the last thing I heard them yell, barely containing their amusement.

I burst into the meeting room panting so hard I had to bend down to recover my breath. The coolness of the airy room quickly chilled me and I was surprised to see two tiny bumps rise at the tips of my breasts. They felt uncomfortable and I crossed my arms over my chest and stood up, to the smiles of my uncle, King Djer, and three of his advisors.

"Well, I hope we are not disturbing your interruption!" my uncle said, laughing. Amka, my uncle's shaman and Vizier, and also my tutor, blushed with embarrassment. He rose up immediately.

"I am sorry, Djer. I do try to teach her not to be so impulsive, but…"

"Nonsense," my uncle interrupted, waving his hand at the men. "Go. We are done anyway. My little Mery and I have more important things to discuss. Go, go, go." Amka gathered up his scrolls and the men quietly left. But I could tell from Amka's hard stare that I had not heard the end to my display of impertinence.

As soon as his advisors left the room, Uncle Djer opened his arms and I ran into them. I loved his big embrace, and the way his clothes always smelled of frankincense and myrrh. "And where is Abana?" Uncle

Djer asked as soon as he let me go.

"I… uh.."

"Aha, you have played her for a fool once again, I see," he said, winking at me. At that we both laughed. To my left, my Aunt Herneith, walked into the room, her posture erect, her simple, sparkling white robe accented by a breastplate of pure gold and Ra's light sparkling off her lapis lazuli jewels. Her eyes were lined in black kohl and the lids filled with shades of green malachite and dark gray galena.

"I just came from the garden," my aunt said casually as soon as she entered. "And, my dear King, you'll never guess who I came upon."

"Who is that, my dear?" my uncle responded.

"A handmaiden hunting feverishly for her lost charge… the King's niece, no less." She tried to hide her smile, but as I ran to her she laughed a hearty laugh and threw her arms around me. "Mery, you are incorrigible!"

"Mery, your aunt and I called you here for a reason," my uncle started as soon as my aunt let me go. "Have a seat, my sweet, and we will begin." My uncle's formal style, as if he were speaking with his advisors, surprised me. I detected that something was amiss. He glanced toward my aunt.

"Mery," she said, sitting erect in her wood and cane chair, looking every bit the Royal Consort, "word has come to us from Abana that this very week you have become a woman."

I was mortified. I sat rigid in my chair, my eyes averted from my uncle's glance. I hardly knew what to say. I felt my cheeks flush. I could only hope that the cloths between my legs did not bulge and that my new breasts were not doing something else strange to betray my discomfort. I instinctively closed my legs tight.

"Dearest Mery," my aunt said, coming to sit by my side and taking my hand into hers. "Do not feel embarrassed. To become a woman is something to be proud of. Indeed, we will celebrate this passing with a party in your honor… women only," she said winking at me.

Still, I sat next to her, mute, although I appreciated having her next to me to lean on. "Is it your uncle? Are you embarrassed?"

I did not know what to say, so I just shrugged my shoulders. "He has something very special to tell you," she went on. Just then Bes, my aunt's short-haired cat, sauntered in, meowed, and jumped onto my lap.

My uncle cleared his throat. I glanced up and saw that this conversation was as much an ordeal for him as for me. In a strange way, that pleased me. But Uncle Djer also looked paler and older than I had seen him before. I wondered if he felt ill.

"Mery, now that you are a woman, it is time to assign Abana to another child in the court."

Against my will my head shot up to confront my uncle, brother to Horus and the most powerful man in all the lands, even those outside our beloved Kem. Abana! I had never known a day without her. She was my nursemaid since birth, my constant companion, except for the hours I spent each day being tutored by Amka.

"But, I don't want to lose Abana! She is like my mother. I…" Bes tensed, ready to jump from my lap.

"Mery, my lotus," my uncle continued, shifting in his chair. "I love you as I do my own son. Your mother was my flesh, my blood sister. And your father and I fought together side by side against the Ta-Tjehenus when he was killed before my very eyes defending me. I would do nothing to harm you, you know that, do you not?"

In that instant I missed my mother so intensely my heart pained. Although the gods brought her to the Afterlife a week after my birth, I still believed I could recall her talking to me, and lovingly nursing me. There were times, lying quietly in bed, my eyes opened to the heavens, when I even saw my mother's eyes looking deeply into mine as she held me gently in her arms.

I paused before answering. "I know that, uncle,

but I will miss my Abana very much." I felt a lump forming in my throat and could not stop the tears from flowing down my cheeks. "Can I... may we at least visit from time to time?"

"Of course. Perhaps when her next young charge is put to sleep at night. But, the gods tell us that for every loss there is also gain," Uncle Djer continued. "Your aunt has a wonderful present for you." He turned to look at Aunt Herneith.

"Uncle Djer is right, Mery. Now, instead of a nursemaid, you will need your own personal healer." I felt my eyes widen at this sudden prospect. None but the most esteemed in the King's eyes had their own healers. It was a sign of high placement in the Royal Court and an honor to be bestowed only by the King and Queen, and never lightly.

"I have chosen for you Ti-Ameny as your personal healer," she continued. "May the two of you grow old together," she said, holding her hands above my head in a sign of blessing.

Even I was amazed at how quickly my mood changed, from one of despair to one of exhilaration. I jumped from my seat, spilling Bes onto the floor, and hopped from my aunt to my uncle. "Really? Is this really true?" I asked again and again, turning from one to the other. I adored Ti-Ameny above all the healers serving the royal families. She was a student of Amka, so I often saw her as she came in to question him while I was practicing reading and writing the picture-words. Ti-Ameny was also a respected priestess of Isis. For a few minutes the three of us discussed Ti-Ameny's god-given skills as a healer and midwife and what her appointment would mean to both of us.

Finally, Aunt Herneith took my two hands in hers and sat me down. We looked across a low table toward Uncle Djer. "Your Uncle has something else to discuss with you," she said and nodded toward him.

"Perhaps we should discuss this other matter at another time," he began, looking uncomfortable and suddenly old. I looked up just in time to see Aunt Herneith shaking her head disapprovingly.

"Well, then, alright, there is another matter of importance to discuss with you Mery. You know that I am King of the United Lands, Master of Upper and Lower Kem," he started. I nodded in understanding. "And that our family comes from an unbroken line of kings, starting with King Narmer."

"May his name be blessed for all eternity," I muttered, as we all learned to do as youth whenever God-King Narmer's name was spoken.

"From King Narmer came who?" my uncle asked.

"From King Narmer and Queen Neith-Hotep came King Hor-Aha, then you, King Djer, I said smiling at him. "Next will be King Wadjet, your son."

"Correct, little one. Amka has taught you well. And keeping our Two Lands united is a very, very difficult job. One that requires the Royal family to collect taxes, to foster trade with our neighbors and to stand united against our enemies, both inside and outside the Two Lands. Are you following me?" I nodded, not really understanding, but also anxious about where my uncle's lecture was headed.

"Good, because governing the Two Lands means having people around me who I can trust, like your Aunt Herneith." I looked up again and smiled at her. She squeezed my hand and I felt her hand moist with perspiration.

"Our son, your cousin Wadjet, will someday be King of Upper and Lower Kem, as you have noted," he continued uncomfortably. "He, too, will need people around him he can trust, people who will tell him the truth that their eyes have seen and their ears have heard."

I thought of my cousin Wadjet then, his chubby, but kind face, the way he teased me when I was younger. I had not seen Wadjet for more than a year, ever since Uncle Djer sent him to Lower Kem to lead an army unit to chase out the fierce Ta-Tjehenus, who periodically raided us from the barren desert lands to our west. Many times Amka had shown me the maps of the Two Lands and the origins of our enemies, so I had a vague idea of where Wadjet was each time messengers brought back news of his skirmishes. Every day the entire court offered prayers to the gods and goddesses for his safe return. I also remembered the very last time I had seen him when, resplendent in his white tunic and soldier's breastplate, he chased me through the Royal gardens, finally catching me and tickling me until I could stand it no longer. Many at his farewell banquet marveled at his ability to lead troops while he was only in his early twenties.

"Now, Mery, the one person a king must trust most of all is his wife. It is from his wife that he seeks the most important advice." I fidgeted with impatience, still unsure why Uncle Djer was telling me all these things.

"Sit still," my aunt whispered to me, but loud enough for Uncle Djer to hear. "I am sure that King Djer, brother of Horus, descendent of God-King Narmer, will make his point shortly."

Uncle Djer cleared his throat. "Well, I was coming to it," he muttered, embarrassed. "The point, my dear Mery... the point is that we... your Aunt and I and Amka... have chosen you to be the trusted wife of Wadjet." I think I remember him then leaning back in his chair, satisfied with himself and smiling.

The room disappeared from my sight at that moment. I think that I forgot to breathe, because in a moment I suddenly drew in such a sharp breath my aunt turned in her seat to look into my eyes. Marriage! And to Wadjet, who was an old man already, perhaps twenty-five years old! I must have blanched the color of death.

"Mery, what is wrong?" my aunt asked me, taking my shoulders in her hands.

I'm still a child, I remember thinking. I yet wanted to run free in the gardens, to feel Mother Nile's cool waters caressing my naked body, to feed and play with the animals that our traders brought back to us from the dark recesses of Kush. Yes, my monthly flows had begun and Abana had told me what this might mean. My closest friend, who had started her womanly flow almost a year ahead of me told me of her family's plans for her eventual marriage. But those talks were but fleeting parts of our play. Marriage was a faraway thought in my head at that young age.

I stood up suddenly and angrily turned toward my aunt and uncle. I felt the blood pounding in my head and neck. "I hate you!" I shouted at them, crying uncontrollably. "I hate you both! You can keep Ti-Ameny. You are trying to ruin my life. I will run away with Abana and live in... we will live..." I tried my best to come up with some far-off land that would shock my aunt and uncle, but in my angry state I could not think of anyplace that Amka had taught me about, other than my beloved Inabu-hedj. I could see a smile beginning to form on my uncle's face, which only infuriated me more. I turned and ran from the room.

"Mery! Wait. Come back here," my uncle called after me.

The last thing I heard was my aunt saying, "No, let her go," just as I ran through the wide mud-brick portico and back out toward the gardens. This time no one stopped me as I ran, sobbing, to my secret hideaway. I ducked under the overhanging branches to the tiny, secret clearing tucked under the protective hedges that was my own special refuge.

Marriage! Could what I just heard really be true? In my own mind I was still but a child, despite the two bumps that had magically appeared, almost overnight, on my chest. I lifted my knees to my chest and wrapped my arms around them, not feeling at all like a woman, at least not like the beautiful women who strutted around the Royal Court, dressed in their finest white linen robes, gold chains studded with precious jewels adorning their necks and wrists, cosmetics perfectly applied and smelling from delicious unguents. Yes, I had started my monthly bleeding, but I yet did not feel like I understood even an inkling of the many secrets that women must surely know, secrets that I suspected they shared with each other with but a glance or a nod of their perfumed necks and oiled hair. I rested my chin against my arm and tried to think of the predicament that was suddenly thrust upon me. My tears had already dried, but the dry sobs had turned into hiccups.

Ti-Ameny. That was it! It was Ti-Ameny who would teach me the mysterious womanly arts, I thought. I was suddenly as sure of that as I was about my aunt's choice for me. Of all the healers Ti-Ameny was most in demand. But the King inexplicably had not yet assigned her as a personal healer to anyone within the court, and now I knew why. Everyone seemed to love her dearly. She lightened a room by her very presence and it did not matter whether or not men were present. Ti-Ameny's ka was as strong and independent as that of the fiercest warrior. They must have intended her for me for many years. I felt a great weight lift from my shoulders in that instant and though I remember well my youthful fears of what was to come, of how much I did not yet understand, I still felt hopeful and full of the energy and the promise of youth.

I silently prayed to my mother and thanked both her and my father for interceding on my behalf, for I had no doubt that they always watched over me from the Afterlife. Even this private spot, Aunt Herneith once told me, must have been revealed to me by my mother, for she, too, was a great lover of animals and would often stroll among the Royal menagerie. Here is where I felt closest to my mother, who I had never met. It was here that I could talk to her when I felt saddest, when other children would ask where my parents were, when I longed to hold her tightly and instead hugged my own bent legs. Now I felt myself smile, imagining my mother laughing with me, dancing around the palace celebrating my betrothel, holding me and swinging me around, and my mood was buoyed up greatly.

And so I learned a powerful and painful lesson that

very moment, one that has served me well throughout my life; that the wings of hope are too often borne aloft by the winds of despair. For right then, curled up as I was in my shaded hiding place, I heard a whispered voice calling to me. And not the delicate whisper of Abana as she stroked my hair just before I fell asleep, nor the heavier whispers of my uncle as he explained to me during festivities why he greeted so warmly someone he had told me just days before he despised. No, the voice of this whisperer was carried on the dead fish tide. His breath reeked of decayed fish such as we experience each year when the Inundation recedes and fish lay flapping on the fertile mud plains until they die and rot.

"Don't be afraid, child, it's me, Rami. Remember me?" he asked, as if I could ever have forgotten him and his frightening manner. He was on all fours, crawling into the tiny clearing that I had carefully tended over the many years I had sought refuge in the royal gardens. I felt trapped, like one of the animals he looked after in the menagerie. I wanted to run, but his stubbly face loomed right in front of mine now. He barely squeezed himself into my hiding place. I quickly put my feet down and backed as far away from him as I could.

"No, no Mery, don't be afraid. I'm here to help you. Yes I am. I… I heard you crying and I've come to help. I swear to Horus," he said, making the sign to the heavens.

My breath caught in my throat and I suddenly felt mute. "You…" I started and hiccupped. "I… I do not need help."

"But surely something bad… no, something difficult perhaps. Yes, yes, something difficult has happened, for whenever I see you coming here to hide it's always with you in a mischievous mood, never sad and crying. No, never." He smiled at me and I counted only six front teeth and even they were worn down from eating rekhi bread that was peppered with desert sand.

"You have been spying on me?" I said, catching my breath and trying my hand at frightening him into letting me pass. Instead he curled up into a sitting position directly in front of me.

"Spying? Me spying? Oh, no, no, no," he answered, his forced smile still on his lips. "I don't have time to do all my chores, let alone spy on anyone. No, no, never." Immediately behind me we heard the deep rumbling of one of the lions. "It's just that you remind me of my daughter, who now lives with the gods in the Afterlife, or I hope she does since we couldn't afford a decent burial for her, nor many foods or her bed to take with her on her journey. Not much, not much at all."

"How… how did she die?" I asked, intrigued.

"Oh, how indeed. Yes, she died all right. Drowned. Dead. Not more than a few steps from Horus' temple. Two days we searched for her body. Two cursed days they were. By then, may Hathor be kind to her, she was little more than the leftovers of a crocodile's meal." Rami looked away from me and for a moment I let my guard down.

"That is awful," I said, trying to sound as adult as I could. "How old was she?"

Rami thought for a few seconds. "She would've been your age. Just a few days before her death our village had celebrated her becoming a woman."

"As have I!" I jumped in. Almost immediately I realized my error. He turned toward me and the dappled light of Ra piercing through the branches gave his face the appearance of a monster from the underworld.

"Ah, so you have, little Mery, so you have." He stared at my chest and a lump formed solidly in my throat, so great was my fear. My heart raced.

"And there's so much for a young woman to do," he continued. "So much to learn, so much to think about. So very many burdens. Yes, yes, so many." He paused for a moment and looked away. Then, looking uncomfortable in this tight space, he shifted to a squatting position and turned toward me.

"Have they yet talked of your marriage? Surely they must have, for you're a princess of high worth to the royal family. Not that it's any of my business. No, I'm just a lowly servant of the King's menagerie," he said, shaking his head.

"But, you, princess, you will soon marry and then what? Have you thought about that, Mery? Have you thought about what it means to be a wife, to please a man the way a woman is bound by ma'at to please him?"

I had been so absorbed by Rami's evil magic cast upon me, I had not noticed that his left hand had fallen between his legs and his fingers were now wrapped around something. At first glance I thought it was one of the snakes from the menagerie, but as he turned more in my direction, I saw what it was that he grasped. It was swollen and red.

"Yes, Mery, look at this, look at it good, for this is what ma'at is all about. This is what you must do for your husband. Soon, yes, yes, very soon you'll need to… here give me your hand and I'll show you how to gently coax the milky seed from a man and please him… oh, yes, please him in untold ways." Rami swayed to his side and pulled hard on his member. It was not that a man's private organ was new to my sight, but I had never seen one so engorged, as if it were possessed of an angry spirit of its own. No matter how hard I tried, I could not take my eyes off of it. I feared that it might strike out at me like a desert viper if I turned away for even an instant.

"Yes, that's it, look. Watch how I stroke it. See how it stretches toward you, its ka wanting to please you. Let me have your hand, Mery and together we'll make it very, very happy."

When he reached for my hand with his dung-stained hand, I suddenly came to my senses. The stench of his breath mixed with the sweat of his heated body and I felt the sudden urge to vomit. Instead, I screamed.

In an instant he lunged at me, grabbing me hard and forcing me down into the sand. He grabbed my robe and tore it from my body in one swift motion. He touched my breasts with one hand and held my mouth shut with the other as I struggled in vain against him. All the while, his knees worked feverishly to split my legs apart, to do something to me, I was sure, something vile with his angry member. I fought him as long as I could, for what seemed like an eternity. I tried to scream again, but his filthy, foul-smelling hand – oh, Ra, his stench haunts me still!- covered my mouth and nose and I felt as if I would suffocate. I felt in my ba that it would be but a moment before I lay unconscious and subject to his evil desires.

And then, it was over. Suddenly I could breath and I gasped repeatedly. I looked up to see Rami flying off me, as if the talons of Horus himself had snatched him from me. I watched, uncomprehending, as he was propelled out of my hiding place and out into the light of Ra. I quickly sat up and watched him fall hard, face down, on the garden path.

"Princess Mery, are you alright?" Akori, the captain of the King's palace guards called in to me, his booming voice full of concern. I grabbed my robe and hurriedly threw it around me, whimpering and shaking as a leaf. My head throbbed and without answering I crawled out of the place that had been a haven for me throughout my childhood, and to which I never again returned.

"I... I... I am good," I said weakly, sensing that it was important for me to regain a semblance of control. I held my head high, although my legs shook so badly I was afraid I would collapse. Tears streamed down my cheek.

"Thanks to Ra," Akori said and nodded to his soldiers. Two of his guards held Rami by his arms and twisted them so that he was forced to kneel on the garden path, shaking, sweat dripping from his dirty face. He whimpered like a child, begging to be spared. A crowd of my relatives and some gardeners had gathered and murmured amongst themselves, some pointing with revulsion toward Rami. Then I watched a tiny figure break from the crowd and run directly toward me. Despite tears blurring my vision, I knew at once it was my older cousin, Nubiti.

Akori motioned for Nubiti to come closer and quickly whispered something to her. She then turned and grabbed me tight into her arms and it was as if a dam had burst. Tears flooded from me and my entire body convulsed with fear and shame. With one side of my head nestled against Nubiti's warm breast, she shielded me from the sight of Akori's swift action. The last thing I remember before passing out was Rami's head rolling past us on the garden path, its lips parted, his bared teeth already caked with sand and mud.

SCROLL TWO

Mery

The Royal Court was in a frenzy of activity. Despite the heat, servants ran from the grain fields and the orchards to the palace, then from room to room, making ready for visitors to the grand celebration. They arranged flowers, prepared food baskets, and moved in specially commissioned furniture for distant relatives I had never before seen and for exotic dignitaries from lands to our south and east. It appeared to me like a beehive, but with two queen bees in charge, my healer, Ti-Ameny, and Amka, my uncle's Vizier and my personal tutor. Yet everyone instinctively knew the gods would never permit two queens in one hive. The crosser those two became from stepping on each others' toes, the better the servants became at hurriedly getting their jobs done and scurrying away. Perhaps that was Amka's strategy in order to get the job completed in time, but I knew that my dear Ti-Ameny was far too expressive to reign in her emotions no matter what the nobler goal.

As for my emotions at the time, I can still recall my childish fears, although I hardly would have agreed to call them childish back then. But the truth is that I was but fifteen years old, a woman, yes, but barely beyond a child. As the wedding plans progressed and became steadily more complex, many is the time that I wished I could have run to Queen Herneith's lap, close my eyes and retreat from all my cares in the warmth of her embrace, my nose buried in her neck, smelling the faint remnants of her distinct perfumes and unguents on her soft skin.

"Come here," I recall her once saying to me as we discussed a complex wedding ritual that had me perplexed and anxious. She held open her arms to me as she stood on the shaded portico overlooking Mother Nile. Oh, how we hugged in that moment, her soft womanly breasts gently pressed against my chest.

"You miss her still, do you not?" she whispered.

I hesitated, knowing full well what is was she referred to, yet also not wanting to acknowledge it. "I do not think of them anymore," I answered brusquely. "I try not to think of them, of her." I could feel Herneith smiling. She stroked my hair.

"As your dear Uncle would say, Mery, despite your perfume you smell of dung."

I turned away from my aunt, then, and leaned over the balcony, thinking of how difficult it was at times to push away thoughts of my mother. Yet ever since that horrible day with that rekhi in the garden, I did not want to revisit the pain and longing of being motherless.

"You know, I do not think we have ever spoken of this, Mery," Aunt Herneith started as she turned toward me and leaned her hip against the brick railing.

"Your father, he died as your Uncle Djer watched, helpless to do anything. He was killed by a Ta-Tjehenu's sword in his back."

"So I've heard," I sighed. "Uncle Djer has told me many times."

"Yes, he has, yet this he has not told you for it

concerns his dear sister, your mother." At this I turned toward my aunt. "He loved her greatly, Mery, as only a brother and sister born of the same parents and raised together can. Of death in battle my husband can plainly speak; of a broken heart he cannot, for even today it pains him beyond measure that his sister walks the Afterworld and is not here by his side. I have seen him on lonely nights stand in this very spot while Ra's silver light reflects his tears."

This revelation surprised me, for I always sensed a reluctance on the part of my Uncle to discuss my mother at all.

"They were always close. Your uncle protected his younger sister as your grandfather, Hor-Aha, commanded he do. He handpicked your father to marry her, but only after examining his sister's heart for her approval.

"That is why it is said that their marriage was ordained by the gods. They loved each other very much, Mery. When the news of your father's death reached your mother, she... she grieved, yes, but like none other I had ever seen, or have seen since." Herneith turned toward Mother Nile and gazed across her mighty waters.

"She was but a ten-day from your birth. All the preparations had been made. She calmly retreated to her rooms and waited. Some say Amka helped her birth pangs to begin, of this I do not know for he would never reveal such a thing to me. But she soon gave birth to you, quietly, without even a whimper. Then she held you... even now it is hard for me to speak of this, my sweet Mery." Aunt Herneith lifted the drape of her gown to dab her eyes.

"In all these years, Amka and I have never spoken of this, although we both were present to witness this miracle. Now that you are about to marry, I will confide in you." Herneith looked out over the water, her eyelids red. "She held you so lovingly all I could do was observe, spellbound. It was the early morning hours and suddenly Ra's rays lit up the room and through a smattering of clouds Ra shone his golden beam of light onto your tiny body and upon your mother's face. That was it, just the two of you illuminated, as if none of the rest of us mattered at all.

"You did not cry. Instead you reached up your tiny little hand so gently to her face and even though you could not yet see with your own eyes, your ka and hers met for those brief moments. I could hardly breathe. Amka, too, stood with his mouth open. Together the two of you sat, locked in each other's embrace, speaking without words, sharing the secrets of your hearts."

My eyes were closed as my aunt told me this story, yet I could see my mother as clearly as if it were she who stood before me. I could clearly recall my mother's love. It had not been a dream after all, a child's wish, that I had felt all these years. Tears now ran down my cheeks, yet I was grateful to Herneith for confirming this.

"She handed you to me then and I swear to Horus I knew right then that she would never hold you again. Amka told me that something in her insides must have torn open, like happens to so many of our women at childbirth. But once, months later as we strolled along Mother Nile as I held you, he confided in me that he believed her ka could not live without her husband, that despite her love for you she could not bear the pain of raising you knowing that your ba was born of two so beloved and he not there to share in this love. In a few days time she was gone."

Over the next few days I thought much on what Herneith had told me. After my initial sadness I found that I drew strength from thoughts of my mother and the love she felt for my father. I then began to realize that despite the difference in our ages, Wadjet and I might yet enjoy a love as deep. At least that was my heartfelt hope.

A few days alone with my thoughts were all I had, for the wedding details pressed upon me once again. At those times I was secretly grateful that Ti-Ameny, Amka, and the King and Queen made most of the important decisions.

And so it was that the King, after conferring with Amka, had decided to hold my wedding to Wadjet in Inabu-Hedj, rather than further south, at the Temple of Horus in Nekhen, the sacred birthplace of King Narmer, may his name be blessed for all eternity. This was not a lightly made decision and Amka, in turn, had conferred with Tepemkau, the Chief Horus Priest in Nekhen before finalizing the plans. The revered Horus priests, for Amka was one himself in addition to being the King's Vizier, wanted to reserve the ancient temple in Nekhen for Wadjet's eventual coronation and not diminish its value by making it available for lesser functions like his wedding.

King Narmer himself was crowned Master of the Two Lands in the holy city of Nekhen so many years ago, and to this day the palette of Unification was still displayed in the temple, proudly describing the events surrounding Narmer's most famous military victory, his defeat of King W'ash of Lower Kem. I remember as a toddler seeing the palette for the first time, its immense size as tall as I was, its black and green coloration adding to the mysteries carved into its surface. In that same temple, King Narmer's son, Hor-Aha, my grandfather, was crowned, as was his son, my uncle, Djer.

Yet the Horus Temple in Nekhen itself was modest and far smaller than the much newer and airier Horus temple here in Inabu-hedj. In that way it was as if time had stood still for Nekhen, both a blessing and a curse, for while they retained the most holy of Temples exactly as it had always been, as a result their town would never grow larger for it could not accommodate enough priests to serve a growing population.

Since Narmer unified our lands, Kem had grown mighty, both due to the expanded commerce within its borders and the trade with our outside neighbors. Each town along Mother Nile seemed to attract artisans of a particular craft. So one was known for exquisite pottery, while another was famous for its beer or elegant weaving or fine jewelry making.

Ever-longer caravans of donkeys continually left from towns along the Nile traveling east and south to exchange our fine clay pots and exquisite jewelry and even our many beers for wood and spices, clothes and all manner of exotic wares from our neighbors. As the fortunes of the merchants and the nobles increased, our towns grew in size and influence. Each year new goods were imported to our lovely Kem, from places that were further and further away. Exotic woods with strange patterns in them came from Lebanese craftsmen, fragrant spices arrived from the lands east of Babylon, all manner of colorful cloth came from Kush and from the southern lands beyond, and furnishings trimmed in precious metals from Babylon itself.

In the capital city of Inabu-hedj our markets were easily double or triple the size of those in other cities. Just walking down the sandy main streets, one could find every manner of food and wares. Rows of merchants stood before their stalls, hawking their products. People shopped under the tattered burlap awnings that covered each stall, picking at the wares and loudly haggling over prices. The wide roads, the spacious Royal palace and the elaborate houses of the nobility and wealthy merchants made Inabu-hedj the location of choice for the royal wedding. Quarried stone has begun to replace mud bricks in the construction of the homes of some of the wealthier residents, giving Inabu-hedj a gleaming white presence such as no city in Kem has ever seen. And, with twenty thousand inhabitants, we were the largest city in Kem by far.

I, for one, had been praying to Isis every day that the wedding would be held in my precious Inabu-hedj and so was thrilled by King Djer's decision. Although Amka certainly knew of my predisposition to Inabu-hedj, he maintained that it did not enter the deliberations at all, which I assumed he was saying to defend his and the King's male prerogatives.

Oh, and those prerogatives! Ti-Ameny had spent

the last three years instructing me often in the womanly arts, many hours of which involved trying to help me understand what it was that men desired from their women. Some of her teachings seemed simple enough to understand, mostly descriptions of the sex acts, which were not surprising since I had many times seen animals copulating in the royal menagerie or in the fields surrounding the palace, or else heard the pleasure moans and gasps of many couplings within the palace walls.

However other of her teachings baffled me greatly. I had few opportunities to learn about men from my friends, almost all of who were other girls. My male cousins were put to work while still in their youth learning the various crafts and skills deemed necessary for noblemen or warriors, so that I was deprived of their knowledge just as my body changed and I needed their explanations most. So I remembered one particular exchange I had with Ti-Ameny after she had been with me for nearly a year.

"I do understand that his organ must get hard and I do understand that he wishes to place it inside me, but that is not my question," I said, frustrated.

"Alright, explain to me your question again," Ti-Ameny said patiently.

"Ahhh," I sighed in annoyance. "What I am asking is how does he signal his intention to do this thing? Does he just show it to me, or point to it? Is it already long and stiff, or is there some secret signal given between husband and wife that begins this... this process?"

To her credit, Ti-Ameny never laughed at my silly questions. Her patience was well known to everyone in the Royal Court. "This is the hardest part to explain," Ti-Ameny started. We were seated in the courtyard of my new quarters, which the King had built just for me in the palace once I entered womanhood. Colorful birds, attracted to my private gardens that I had designed with my uncle's architect, flitted from branch to branch, chirping and trilling in all manner of sweet song. The male gardeners had learned to stay out of earshot whenever Ti-Ameny and I were engaged in conversation and when they saw us approaching they nearly stumbled into each other gathering their tools to leave.

As on most days, Ti-Ameny was dressed in her pure white linen robe, with a swag of neatly pleated and pressed fabric running across her abdomen. Her jewelry was always simple, yet somehow noticeably elegant, as if her jeweler made each piece for her alone, knowing what would accent the goodness of her ba. She wore the honorary gold armband of the King's retinue on her left bicep and a delicate gold-chain necklace made for her in the King's own workshops. Her sandals were of the finest woven rushes, inlaid with colorful orange carnelians and deep blue lapis lazuli. Her hair was carefully pinned up with ivory combs and fell in deep, dark curls onto her shoulders. Her eyes were always shadowed in a pleasing green, and delicately lined with black kohl. With her diminutive stature, I never tired of looking at her.

"Well, of course there are obvious differences between men and women," she began. "Whatever the gods placed in their bas to make them bigger and stronger than women, also appears to make them more prone to displays of anger. But it also appears to make them sexually desire us constantly. They are known to think about pleasing their organs and spilling their seed… I'd say most of the time!" At this she laughed, and I suspected she was recalling experiences from when she was a priestess at the temple of the goddess Isis. In recent months several of my female relatives had mentioned her renowned sexual experiences during her youth, ones that made her the very healer to seek out when sexual problems emerged between a couple. Both men and women could be seen consulting with her, often in hushed tones in the corridors of the palace.

"So, you needn't worry. It really doesn't take much for a woman to excite her mate. I will soon teach you how to bring Wadjet into heat such as I suspect he has not experienced so far in this life. But, to answer your question directly, sometimes men announce their desire in the way they look at you, or the way they kiss you at bedtime, or by the way their stiff organs propel them into heat beyond their control. All of these things we will discuss, my princess, very soon. It is in how you respond to Wadjet's desire that will determine much of the joy and success in your relationship with him."

She shifted now in her seat, turned sideways and looked me in the eyes. "But, there is another part to this story that we haven't discussed... yet," she said, smiling. "And that is the pleasures you are entitled to feel while Wadjet receives his pleasure from your coupling." I stared at Ti-Ameny, wide-eyed I am sure.

"You look at me in wonder, but it is true, my young princess, that Kemian women are unique among the women of our surrounding lands. I have been with men from far away places, like the Akkadians and Sumerians, even a few of the darkest Ta-Sety men you will ever see. To them, sex is only a way for the man to be satisfied. Their women are much disrespected, I must say, and are treated as mere beasts of burden conveniently able to bear children. But Kemian women are treated differently, whether inside the home or out. We have many rights not granted to women in other lands. We are expected to enjoy the acts of sex, too."

I was often puzzled at much of what Ti-Ameny said, but none more than now. I had so many questions I hardly knew where to begin. But begin I did and for the next few hours we strolled through the elaborate gardens that I had designed to encourage and reflect ma'at, stopping every so often to giggle, or so I could absorb the scandalous things she passionately described about our bodies, but that I scarcely believed could truly be so. Even then I remember that our conversations often brought strange, pleasurable sensations to my body. On those evenings I retired to bed feeling a wetness and exquisite sensitivity between my legs. That was three years past and now we had reached the point where all her instructions were about to be tested.

Not that Wadjet and I had not tried out some of Ti-Ameny's suggestions in the intervening years, for I had learned early on from the seers in the temple of Isis that my ba was an adventurous one. We did kiss whenever we could be alone and, if we were seated, it took just a few thrusts of my tongue to notice Wadjet's ample one-eyed beast struggling to poke out from his loincloth. There were even times when we were alone on an evening stroll, when we would stop to sit and I stroked his organ until, with a series of groans, he shot his warm seed with great force onto my arm or robe. The first few times such a waste of seed distressed me greatly, but I saw that it pleased him and no ill fortune seemed to derive from it. The supply miraculously seemed inexhaustible.

Once, on a still evening, as her current gently lapped against the shore, we strolled along Mother Nile and stopped to sit on a stone bench that was secluded among some trees and bushes. I had already decided to try something adventurous that night that I had just learned from Ti-Ameny. After we kissed tenderly for a long time, and my tongue had aroused Wadjet's passions, he tentatively touched my breasts. Just as he began to excite my nipple, I slipped off the bench and gently held his pouch and placed his member in my mouth for the very first time. He gasped so loudly I feared being discovered by one of my Uncle's guards. But, in his passion Wadjet thrust his penis too deeply and I choked and forgot Ti-Ameny's lessons on how to prevent that from happening. Wadjet laughed good-naturedly that night, and throughout our time of courtship he was always patient with me, for which I will always be grateful. We never crossed the line and engaged in the forbidden act of intercourse before marriage, one that would have shamed us had I become pregnant. As I fondled him and learned what pleased him over the following months, he did the same with me, caressing my most sensitive parts and leaving me gasping with pleasure. With the wedding upon us, I frequently spent nights wondering how it would feel to have Wadjet penetrating those sensitive parts.

With preparations for the wedding entering their most hectic phase just a month prior to the wedding, I was summoned one afternoon to King Djer's quarters, where I waited for nearly an hour as I heard him repeatedly try to end a meeting of his advisors. I knew how he hated those meetings, for he was old and had been reigning as King for most of his life. I paced the portico outside my uncle's rooms, admiring his garden with its many shallow pools surrounded by trees and flowers, servants dutifully absorbed in feeding the colorful fish and birds or trimming the water weeds that were planted in buckets throughout. Ra stood high in the azure blue sky and not a cloud was in sight. I looked out over Mother Nile, its waters still flowing full after the annual floods, the life-giving soil it left behind a dark, rich brown. Each whisper of wind carried the scents of flowers and herbs and the trills of birds, so that my mood was buoyed up as I waited.

"Does my niece think I have all day to wait on her as she makes poetry in her heart to Mother Nile?" I heard a gruff voice roar behind me.

"Oh, no, Uncle. I... I was just waiting for your meeting to be over." Then I saw him break into a smile and he held out his hands to me. I was torn by my desire to run into them and jump upon him, as I had always done. But now that I was in my fifteenth year and to be a married woman, I held my head stiff and walked toward him as regally as I could bear. Still, we hugged each other warmly, he rocking me back and forth gently while stroking my hair.

We sat out on the balcony under a canopy of reeds, alabaster bowls filled to overflowing with fresh fruits placed beside us. My Uncle's girth had expanded since my youth and he hardly gave the appearance of a warrior king as he munched from a handful of grapes and nuts and periodically pierced a piece of cheese with his alabaster fork. No matter, for to me every deben of him I loved dearly like I would have my own father. Together we watched the fishermen balanced on the gunwales of their boats, effortlessly tossing their nets into Mother Nile's swift current and a few moments later pulling in their abundant catches. The iridescent scales of the fish reflected Ra's rays as they flapped frantically on the decks.

"And how go the plans for the wedding?" Uncle Djer asked, still looking out over the sparkling waters that he alone commanded. The desert dust created a haze that partially hid the red hills across the muddy river. With that I proceeded to tell him of the intricate web of his government ministries, personal relationships and bruised egos I was learning to negotiate in order for all the wedding plans to come together. Wadjet had assigned to me a supervisor from his retinue who was an expert in arranging government celebrations, but at this point I was at a loss to know how all the details would eventually merge. Uncle Djer laughed frequently at my tribulations, especially when I described Amka and Ti-Ameny's conflicting responsibilities.

"Ah, Mery, I assure you everything will come together as planned. There are none in the Two Lands who look out more for your welfare than Amka and Ti-Ameny." Then, shifting his body in his seat, Uncle Djer looked directly at me. "Mery, there are other things of which we must speak, serious things." From the gravity of his voice I said a quick, silent prayer to Isis that, thinking I was motherless, he was not about to have a talk with me regarding sexual matters. I turned my gaze toward my sandals.

He groped for the right words. "You know, Mery, our people often speak of King Narmer..."

"May his name be praised..."

"Yes, yes, we all know the correct responses. May his name be praised for all eternity. May his name be recorded in the scrolls of life. Yes, yes, yes." He paused, appearing agitated, thinking of what to say next.

"It is a difficult thing, Mery, when a great man- or a great woman for that matter- dies and all we are left with are memories of his ba. Even sadder is the fact that almost no one who now walks the Two Lands ever knew King Narmer personally. Amka and I are perhaps the only ones left. All the others hear are stories, tales that become so twisted they only bear the most distant resemblance to the truth. Most who live here in Kem," he said swinging his arm in an arc over Mother Nile, "were not even alive when he died." Uncle Djer looked away, tossing the few grapes he held back into his bowl.

"It is of the mighty Narmer that we must now speak, little one, for as surely as his spirit now roams his beloved Kem, watching over us all, he would be exceedingly proud of you and Wadjet." I sat up straight in my chair, feeling a mixture of fright and excitement, for never in my life had Uncle Djer spoken to me in detail about his grandfather.

"And, you knew him," I said cautiously.

"Yes, I knew him," he continued, looking sad, "but only when he was already what you would consider ancient, and very close to his journey to the Afterlife. The gods had rewarded his good deeds with a life of nearly sixty years by then. My father, your grandfather Hor-aha, used to bring me to him to visit, or that is what I thought my father's purpose was at the time. Sometimes King Narmer would recognize me as his grandson and future heir, other times he imagined that he looked at a reflection of himself in a mirror and he would talk to me as if he talked to his child ba. Or sometimes he mistook me for his long-dead Vizier, Anhotek. At those visits I would be frightened and run to my father's side." I smiled at Uncle Djer's recollection.

"Yes, I look back on that time, my little lotus, and wonder why Horus afforded me the honor to sit on his lap and touch his mortal flesh, to be loved by such a one as King Narmer." Uncle Djer shook his head and reached for his cup of barley beer. He sipped from it for many minutes, the white alabaster translucent in Ra's rays, before he spoke again.

"Now I realize that my father's purpose in having me visit Narmer so often was different, far wiser. By insisting that I form a bond with my grandfather..." Again he hesitated. "Damn, I hate this!" he suddenly shouted, pounding his fist on the arm of his chair. He stood and paced between the balcony wall and me.

"I'm sorry, Mery, I don't mean to frighten you. It's just that I find it difficult to put these important thoughts into words. I'm not very good at speeches." He paced a few more steps.

"Reading the scroll parchments, the ones written by King Narmer and his beloved scribe Anhotek, where they describe all they did to unite the Two Lands, one can only marvel that two such god-men walked the very ground we trod in our beloved Kem, even here in this very palace." Goosebumps immediately played down my back and I shivered despite the heat.

"Ma'at was never stronger than in the old days, perfectly balanced, so that the forces of chaos were kept in control. The Horus priests' magic was the strongest it had ever been. Their daily prayers keep Ra rising each day, even as the forces of chaos press in upon us, always.

"In Narmer's times the swamp dwellers of the north threatened us. The Ta-Tjehenus, may their names be stricken from the book of life, raided us from the west without mercy, killing our people, raping our daughters, stealing our food. Famine was upon our land. Yet King Narmer's vision of a united Kem was far stronger than those forces could ever be, for his vision of a greater Kem was given to him by our gods, who waited for generations for the man with a pure and mighty ba, a man with his inner character, to arrive in our land. That is why he accomplished what none were able to do before him."

Uncle Djer patted the stool in front of his chair and I rose to sit before him. He grasped both my hands in his and I could feel the warmth and power in them.

THE DAGGER OF ISIS

"Mery, the scrolls record deeds performed by Anhotek and his assistant, Meruka, so magical they defy description. Desert vipers tamed, death spells cast or broken, treacherous acts of betrayal unmasked." I felt goose bumps raise along my arms and neck.

"Yet all of this was made possible only by the vision that formed the very substance of King Narmer's ka, a soul whose vision foresaw Kem's greatness; a vision of the Two Lands living under one rule for all eternity. And that is why Hor-Aha, your grandfather, made such a strong effort to connect me with Narmer.

"You see, when a vision such as Narmer's is first given by the gods to a mortal, it is tenuous, like vapors that rise from Mother Nile and quickly dissipate into the heavens. Men become distracted by everyday tasks that spell survival. They soon forget these godly visions. We are only two generations removed from Narmer and so my father knew how important it was to stay connected to that vision for as long as possible, until our Kem was truly stable, united by a succession of strong leaders under compassionate rule." By now Uncle Djer was excited, pacing and speaking as much with his hands as his voice. Then he stopped directly in front of me.

"And, that, my dearest niece, is where you come in." My uncle's words made me spring upright in my seat.

"Where I come in? What..." I heard a rushing noise in my ears.

"It is King Narmer who ordains your marriage, little one. I have never discussed this with you before, but of this I am certain. He has visited me in my sleep and told me so." My ears buzzed with a rushing sound, as if Mother Nile's floodwaters surged through them. I felt dizzy and cast my gaze away from my uncle.

"You seem surprised, yet there is nothing I can do to lessen the importance of this revelation, although your dear aunt begged me to introduce this to you gradually. Both you and Wadjet are blood descendents of King Narmer and your holy union is destiny. It will strengthen

Kem for generations to come."

My heart weighed my uncle's words and I found it difficult to breathe, for as true as my uncle's words sounded to my young ears, I also suspected even then what a burden they would prove to be. King Narmer was the most revered of all our kings and until this day we worship him as a god-King. As a younger child I often felt estranged from my uncle for days after someone would remind me, usually in awe-struck whispers, that King Djer had known and actually touched King Narmer. I felt self-conscious of my dear uncle's hugs then, knowing that those same arms had once encircled a god.

And so it was that Uncle Djer's words that day had a greater effect on my growing out of my youth than even my monthly flows. And from that discussion on we had an understanding, a deepened bond, as much conveyed in silence as in words, that my role was to be more than wife, more than mother, even more than the eventual Queen. I was part of a living legacy, a continuation of a godly thread that ran from my grandfather's father, through him to Djer and on to me and Wadjet, and then to our children's' children. As equally that god force resided in me as in Wadjet, a fact that was sanctioned by my uncle that day. I left his quarters shaking, whether in fear or in anticipation I am not certain, but knowing in my heart that Amka would soon need to teach me everything about King Narmer that was contained in the holy scrolls in Nekhen.

For the next few days I wandered about my quarters heavily burdened by grave thoughts. I slept lightly, thinking that every leaf brushed by the wind was a harbinger of King Narmer's imminent arrival in my dream world. No such thing happened, not yet, but I was listless and not as attentive as I should have been to planning the wedding.

It was on the morning of the third day after my talk with Uncle Djer that Ti-Ameny announced to me that my cousin, Nubiti, wished to visit with me. It had been weeks since I last saw her, and my heart lifted at the news of her visit. I asked Ti-Ameny to immediately show her in.

"Little sister!" Nubiti shouted at me from across the room, smiling, as she opened her arms to me. We hugged warmly and began immediately to gossip in urgent tones, as I led her toward my bedroom, where we would not be disturbed.

"Tell me everything that's going on," she insisted. "If you leave even one morsel out, I'll never speak with you again!" We laughed continuously as I explained to her all my dealings with court officials, using the humorous nicknames we had devised for them over the years. I felt grateful for the diversion.

Finally, after an hour of mostly me talking, I remembered my manners and offered her some water. She hesitated.

"Do you have any of that fine beer that Amka gets from the priests in Nekhen?" Nubiti asked. Although my cousin was Wadjet's half-sister, Nubiti and I had been close ever since that terrible day when that low-class rekhi pig, Rami, attacked me in the garden.

"Do you really drink beer?" I asked, showing more surprise than I had intended.

"In private I do," she said, laughing. Although I laughed with her, I wondered how I would ever mature from the unsure child I felt I now was to the mature, twenty-one year old woman who sat beside me. Although Nubiti's language was coarse, in the way of the Delta culture, I still admired her vitality. I quickly ordered one of my servants to fetch us a pitcher of Nekhen beer, but to be sure to keep it from Amka's prying eyes.

"I hear that your wedding plans go well," Nubiti volunteered. I knew that Nubiti and her mother, Shepsit, kept close tabs on all that went on in the palace. It could not have been easy being King Djer's Second Wife, yet it appeared to me that Shepsit wore the title as well as any woman could. I knew from comments made by Aunt

Herneith that she did not trust Shepsit. Yet, at the same time, she was always respectful of the difficult role the Second Wife played in our state affairs.

Ever since King Narmer married a woman from Lower Kem to mortar his rule over them, every King was obliged to take on a Second Wife from Lower Kem. Tradition had decreed that the princes of Lower Kem choose the woman the King was to marry and ten years prior to my birth, they chose Shepsit. It took years before my uncle agreed to consummate their marriage, but finally they created Nubiti. I had a sense from my aunt that she was relieved that Shepsit had not had a boy to rival Wadjet.

Yet by the less refined way she spoke and by her appearance there could be no doubt in anyone's mind that Nubiti was from Lower Kem. She was short and heavy set, with very large breasts, a decided contrast to my slim body and small breasts, like most women in Upper Kem. She wore her black hair down to her shoulders, perfectly framing her heavy brows and brown eyes. I remember that once Aunt Herneith remarked that Nubiti and Shepsit reminded her of old acacia trees, strong, stout and solidly planted.

For several more minutes we discussed the wedding plans. Finally, Nubiti stood to leave. "Well little sister, you've done well for yourself. Wadjet! Think of it. Soon you'll be married to the most important man in the Two Lands."

"Second most important," I responded.

"Only for the moment, dear sister, for my father, Djer, is an old bull now and surely won't reign many more years. But you... you've snatched the best prize in Kem. I envy you for that."

This surprised me, for I would not have thought there was anything that Nubiti, who I admired greatly, would be jealous of, let alone something that involved me. Yet I could also see that in this case her feelings were natural enough.

"Nubiti, you have always treated me like your

sister, of this I am most grateful. I have often thanked Isis for the blessing of your presence to guide and protect me. But there is one thing of which I am most perplexed. I have not felt brave enough to ask this of you until this moment." I felt my cheeks inflame from my sudden boldness. But Nubiti merely laughed.

"Well, child, don't just stand there. What plagues you?"

"Why haven't you married yet? I… what I mean is you are so… womanly," I said, moving my hands through the air to describe her shape.

"What, these?" she said, crudely cupping her own breasts. "Only Delta men seem to appreciate them. The only reaction these… these melons get from Upper Kemian men… and women… is curiosity. Sometimes fear, I think, for their eyes widen as if they've seen an evil mut."

"That… that is not quite what I meant," I stammered, embarrassed. "You are smart and gracious and you always know what to do at festivals. Surely men would be honored to have you as their wife."

"I'm touched that you feel that way, Mery. Truth is that my mother hasn't yet found a man she feels is suitable. I know you miss having a mother and father, but in some ways you've been most fortunate having instead a loving aunt and uncle to watch over you. I love my mother, but as Second Queen she's a difficult matron to please and that's all I'll say on the matter."

I nodded, feeling deep pride that by confiding in me my cousin and I were truly sisters in spirit. We silently hugged each other.

"Well, I've got to go now," she said pulling away. "Ti-Ameny gave me some tasks to do for the wedding. In the meantime, keep Wadjet straight," she said, winking at me and laughing. My face must have revealed that I did not understand what was meant by that remark.

"You know, keep it straight," she repeated, holding up a bent finger. Still I did not comprehend her meaning.

"Oh, for the sake of Isis!" Nubiti laughed. "His penis, the way it bends so to the right... you know, keep it straight," she said, now straightening her finger. I was so startled I could hardly breathe. I felt the blood drain from my face and suddenly my knees felt weak.

"How... how do you know of such a thing?" My hands were tightly clasped together. The smile immediately left Nubiti's face.

"Oh, sister. I... I thought you knew. Oh, by the gods how stupid I am!" She paced before me. "I... Djet and I, when we were younger we played together," she said, using Wadjet's more intimate name. "We were always close, you know, being the only two siblings in the court. We... when we came of age, we played at sex, too, as... as children do. We laughed at how his organ curved to the right, as if it were an eel trying to escape from a fisherman's net. Our friendship... I thought Djet had mentioned it to you."

I was torn between feelings of betrayal and my affection for my beloved and for Nubiti. I stood there, wringing my hands, tears filling my eyes. Nubiti closed the space between us and put her arm around my shoulder, pulling me in tight.

"Sister, don't let this come between us. Worse yet, don't let it come between you and Wadjet. It was innocent play between half-siblings." She now turned to me and placed both her hands on my shoulders.

"Let me give you some sisterly advice, Mery. I wouldn't mention that you know of our sex play to Wadjet at all. If he hasn't yet told you, he may have his reasons, such is the way men are." She looked into my eyes, yet I could not return her gaze, for I saw something in her face that I had never before seen. Chills ran up my spine.

"Here, give your big sister a hug," she offered, holding me tight. "It'll be all right. I've told you this secret and there'll be times when you'll do the same with me. Remember my words, the Royal Court can be a cold and evil place at times. Sisters must stick together, Mery. Remember that lesson well. You must always trust your big sister."

SCROLL THREE

Nubiti

"Pregnant? You're absolutely certain?" mother asked, clutching her hands to her breast in her typical dramatic fashion.

"Yes, I'm certain," I responded, restraining my own anger. "She hasn't had her monthly bleeding for two months now. She's been throwing up, she hardly eats. Ti-Ameny and Amka have examined her and confirm it." I stood before Shepsit dressed in a fine linen robe, having just returned from the Royal Palace.

Shepsit paced before me, agitated. "Oh, dear!" was all she said as she twisted her hands anxiously.

"May Isis damn her, with her stuck-up talk and her... her newly found royal bearing!" I blurted out angrily, kicking mother's woven rush footstool out of my path with my foot. "How could that harlot become pregnant so quickly? Women sometimes try for years and she does so in just a few months. That little whore!"

Mother knew better than to try to reason with me when I was this mad. A handmaiden suddenly poked her head through the portico entrance to see what the commotion was about.

"Leave!" I shouted, pointing directly at the frightened girl. "When the Queen needs you she'll call." I turned back towards mother. "These Upper Kemian servants are stupider than jackasses. In the Delta servants know their place."

I slumped into one of the chairs at the edge of mother's bedroom, so that I could look out at the green fields and red hills while she fretted and I stewed. Shepsit continued to pace, lost in her own thoughts. Perhaps it was my mood, or perhaps the rare cloudy day, but mother looked older and frailer. Wrinkled skin hung around her elbows and bags sagged below her eyes. Deep lines were etched above her upper lip. Her lustrous black hair now lacked its previous silkiness and was streaked with coarse gray strands. She appeared tired, worn. My heart skipped a beat, for I suddenly realized that soon I would be thrust into her role as Lower Kem's symbolic presence in the Royal Court.

"And how do Djer and Herneith take the news of an heir?" mother asked sarcastically, stopping directly in front of me. I looked up as calmly as I could manage, not wanting to further inflame my own passions.

"Obviously, they're pleased. Herneith visits Mery every day since she's received the news. Djer boasts of his son's fertility at meetings of his council."

"That pig!" my mother said with disgust. "May Anubis find his heart heavy as stone."

"Careful mother. That's my father you speak of."

She threw a quick glance at me to make sure I was joking. "He contributed his seed and that's all. If I didn't see him at festivals, years would pass without our speaking two words. The mighty King Djer. May his brother Horus' talons pierce his arrogant heart!"

Again she paced before me, her brow creased from thoughts and scheming, of that I was sure.

"This is disturbing news, indeed," mother continued. "I hoped we'd have more time to set our plans in motion. If it's not one thing it's another that the gods place in our path. By all rights you should be married to Wadjet and having his child." At that, I turned my head away in frustration at our thwarted plans, looking to the red cliffs beyond the fields. Farmers and their children hand-tended their crops and thick smoke from potters' kilns rose from the base of the cliffs.

"You turn away, Nubiti, but…"

"Mother, don't start down that path again. It's well trodden already."

"Don't you insult me like that! Everything I've done since I agreed to marry that southern swine Djer has been for you." I didn't bother to remind my mother that she'd hardly agreed to marry Djer, she was forced into it by her Delta prince relatives. At first she thrived on the attention and high rank. All she'd done since my birth was for her benefit and none other. Nor was I blaming her for her own frustration, for to live as Second Queen was a curse not easily borne by any woman.

Mother turned on her heel and walked away from me. I paused to take a deep breath. "Look, mother, we've been allies since I've come of age. Djer's decision to bypass me as Wadjet's wife was a slap in our faces, a… an embarrassment acted out before all those in power throughout the Two Lands. We became jokes. Unification, ha! My father's commitment to unification is as shallow as the waters at Urimbe. He had the perfect opportunity to unite the Two Lands… truly unite them, by marrying Wadjet to me, his half-sister." Mother leaned against one of the mud brick pillars and tilted her head back.

"Yes, it's a pity, really. Now his slap has resounded throughout Kem, and I'll tell you, daughter, it's been heard in the Delta by some very powerful people." She sat with a sigh in the chair nearest mine, her lips pursed in anger.

Mother has always been a force not to be taken lightly. Those few who have underestimated her passions over the years have suffered grave consequences and stories to that effect have circulated through the palace during my growing up years. Many is the time I overheard discussions about my mother, spoken in hushed whispers, followed by the gossipers making the sign across their brows to ward off the evil eye. More than one referred to mother as Shepsit the Sorceress.

Until that day, when I brought her the news of Mery's pregnancy, I'd never seen any indications of Shepsit's sorcery, only her vituperation and bile. Yet on that day, as she sat in that chair, stiff as the Lebanese wood from which it was made, I was granted a glimpse of my mother's powers. And it began with the maid again poking her head in the archway.

"I thought I told you to disappear!" I shouted at her. The poor girl shook and tears ran down her cheeks.

"But, my… my Queen," she pleaded, looking at mother, "it's important. I've been sent to…"

"Well, out with it!" mother insisted.

"It's the King, Queen Shepsit. He… he's gravely ill."

And so it was that events of unimagined importance unfolded over the next few days and months, events that held the forbidding possibility of changing our fate, and that of the Two Lands itself. Through it all, through days of secret meetings and sleepless nights of planning and plotting, I was reminded of my mother's anger that day and how she had damned the royal family and my father, in particular, with her curses.

We both rushed from mother's chambers and were immediately carried by porters across the Royal compound to King Djer's palace. A crowd had already gathered and our porters had to shout ahead to get them and their donkeys to part so we could gain admittance. The porters stopped at the palace stairs and a phalanx of armed guards refused us entry. The entire palace was off limits to anyone but the Royal family.

"We are the Royal family, you idiots!" I protested. The commotion soon brought out Ti-Ameny, who whispered to the leader of the guards and soon we were walking into the spacious, light-filled entrance to the palace.

"It is grave," Ti-Ameny began. "He was struck by pains in his chest during a meeting with his Council. Fortunately, Amka was there and was able to minister to him."

"How bad is grave?" mother asked coldly. Ti-Ameny was momentarily taken aback by mother's tone. She first looked around her before answering.

"He is pale and he has difficulty breathing. I have seen this before, many times. His heart will soon be weighed on Anubis' scale." I shuddered, thinking of mother's earlier curse.

Despite my mother's angry swearing against my father throughout my life, curses that were sometimes justified but often exaggerated, I felt a strong pang in my heart over Ti-Ameny's dire prediction. I know that my father often slighted my mother with his actions. Whether he intended to do so I couldn't properly judge from mother's reactions alone. He married her and then shunned her, that much was obvious. He created a child with her and then mostly ignored us. But, although I saw him irregularly, when I did Djer was always friendly to me, although distant and formal. I never looked at him as my father. He was not like the fathers I saw throughout the court, mostly loving men who doted on their wives and children. The only time I saw Djer treat a child warmly was when he was with Mery. My heart ached now with that memory.

"Is he in pain?" I asked of Ti-Ameny.

"I think not. Amka has given him an herb that keeps his senses dulled."

"Can we see him?" I persisted. Ti-Ameny shot a look at my mother.

"Not at this time," she replied slowly. "Herneith, Wadjet, Mery and his advisors are all there. The room is crowded. I'm sure you understand," she said casting her glance from my mother to me.

We went back to our rooms to await word of Djer's condition. Shepsit asked me to stay with her in her bedroom, so her servants brought in a bed for me to sleep on. But it was hardly needed for I paced anxiously, sometimes leaning over the balcony brickwork or peering toward Mother Nile shimmering under Ra's disk below us.

It is said by the Horus priests that if a person survives a dire illness through the night he has a greater chance of returning to health. So when we awoke we waited for word from the palace. Just after Ra rose into a cloudless sky, we received that word; a series of blasts from the ram's horn. During the long night, King Djer had begun his journey to the Afterworld.

Within moments we heard wailing throughout the Royal Court. Women in the courtyard rent their finest garments in grief. Handmaidens ran through the alleys, screaming, spreading the news of the King's death. Men fell to the ground, beating their chests in anguish. Horus priests from the temples of Inabu-hedj, as well as priestesses from the Temple of Isis scurried earnestly to their temples to receive offerings and chant prayers during this propitious time. Looking out from mother's balcony, I could feel ma'at's tender hold on our land begin to quiver and slip away. The life balance of the Two Lands was in mortal danger. A chill ran through me as I contemplated images of the evil mut spirits gathering, their foul bodies slithering just outside the Two Lands, probing for openings into our world and seeking opportunities to create the death and chaos for which they were created. I imagined Apep the serpent god sounding his horn, summoning the mut demons from every crevice in the underground. My hands sweated and I trembled with fear.

The next seventy days were a terrible time, in

Upper Kem at least, for I'd heard from mother that
many of our relatives in Lower Kem had secretly
celebrated Djer's death. Despite four generations of
unification, my Delta people still felt slighted by those
from Upper Kem who lorded their power over them.
Since I was old enough to remember, visits with my
relatives were always filled with back room whispering
and late night plotting. And mother, may Isis bless her,
was always in the thick of it.

Three days after my father's death, a delegation of
senior Horus priests arrived by boat from Nekhen to
prepare the king for his journey, for only they were
allowed to touch the body of the brother of Horus.
Wedding and birth celebrations and parties of any kind
were cancelled throughout the Two Lands. Wherever
one walked, women gathered in small groups and spoke
in hushed tones, frequently accenting their remarks with
the hand sign across the brow made to ward off the evil
eye. Cripples waited in the heat, in long lines, to bring
offerings to the priests and priestesses in the temples.
Children were quickly scolded for wandering out of their
parents' sight, so great were the people's fears of mut
spirits seeking to create illness among our youth.
Caravans no longer wound through the desert and
business dealings were put on hold.

With the King dead, ma'at, that delicate balance
between the forces of good and evil that we so depended
upon for our very existence, was endangered. People
awoke hesitantly each morning, frightened that Ra may
not have risen in the sky. Every stumble, every child's
scraped knee was viewed as an omen. Shamans
throughout the lands were busy interpreting such events,
as well as the confused dreams of the rich and powerful.
Even the dead of the wretched rekhi couldn't be buried
properly since the King's ka was in limbo. Instead, much
as our ancestors did many generations ago, they were
placed on their sides in simple shallow pits in the desert,
with only a few jars of food and possessions to serve
them in the Afterlife.

That's why I wasn't surprised when one of Mery's handmaidens arrived and summoned me to the palace one afternoon. I hurried there, not having seen my cousin for two or three ten-days. Both my mother and I were starved for information. The rumors within the palace were that she took the death of Djer very hard, but even with that I wasn't prepared for the scene that greeted me.

As I came into her wing of rooms, nothing initially seemed unusual. Her servants scurried around, sweeping out the ever-present desert sand, dusting the mud brick columns, trimming the abundance of potted plants and removing bowls of spoiled fruits and replacing them with fresh ones. But, when I entered Mery's private bedroom, I was startled. Wadjet wasn't present, probably engaged in one of the endless meetings over succession that must have occupied his attention. Mery's clothes were tossed on her bed. Her sandals lay in the middle of the floor, one overturned, as if she'd kicked them off and forgotten them. A piece of apple, now browned and soft, lay near the bedpost, large black flies hovering around it.

"Mery?" I called tentatively. Something stirred in the corner of the room and I immediately turned toward the sound. Mery was curled like a baby, a light shawl covering her slight body. As I approached her, the smell of vomit was strong.

"Oh, Nubiti!" she moaned. "It hurts. It's the baby, my baby." As I squatted toward her, Ti-Ameny entered the room. Our eyes met for the briefest of moments, but I read in them the severity of the situation.

I gently took Mery's hand in my own and she immediately grabbed it in both hers and pulled it toward her face. Tears wet my hand. Her body felt hot to the touch. Ti-Ameny moved to my side.

"My princess, you must allow Nubiti and I to move you to the bed," she whispered, as she took Mery's arm firmly and eased her from the floor. Mery groaned and clutched her abdomen. As we led her, sobbing, to

THE DAGGER OF ISIS

her bed, the tapping of Amka's wooden staff suddenly announced his arrival.

"Why was I not summoned immediately?" he demanded angrily of Ti-Ameny. She silenced him with a look that would have halted a lion in full charge. Once we had made Mery comfortable, Ti-Ameny made room at the bedside for Amka. He quickly went to work with his characteristic efficiency, feeling her pulse and looking into her eyes and throat. In all the years I'd known him, he hadn't changed one bit. His bald head accented his dark, penetrating eyes. His skinny frame made his large hands and hooked nose look almost comical.

When he was done, he asked me to leave the room, while he and Ti-Ameny performed a more intimate examination. I stood outside waiting. One of Mery's servants approached me to inquire how she was, but one of my stern looks in her direction soon disabused her of the notion that she'd dare address the Second Queen's daughter without being summoned.

In a short while, Ti-Ameny came to get me. "It is bad," she began. "She has miscarried." I noticed spots of blood on the front of Ti-Ameny's robe. "She has been terribly depressed at Djer's death. Not even Wadjet has been able to console her. They had a special relationship, she and the King. Amka believes the baby had to escape her body because her sadness was too much for any child's ka to bear."

At that moment confused emotions overcame me in quick order. As a woman, and as Mery's older sister, I felt a small part of the pang of loss that Mery must be feeling. Yet, just as quickly my mind grasped the sheer enormity of this turn of events and the good fortune it potentially held for me. I wanted to race out to tell Shepsit about our unimagined opportunity. Yet, I held my place and didn't let my face betray me. I went back into Mery's chambers and in front of her two most important ministers I held her close and spent the next few hours comforting her as her handmaidens changed her sheets and washed her frail body and tiny breasts.

Amka left and returned with an herb dissolved in wine to calm her and she eventually slipped into a deep, but restless sleep. I used that as the excuse I sought to leave her bedside.

Shepsit hugged me and squealed with delight when I told her the news of Mery's miscarriage. Once we'd calmed down, she brought out an urn of fine wine from her closet to celebrate quietly, since libation was forbidden during the King's mourning period. Due to the mourning there was little we could do at present other than plan, so we spent the better part of what remained of the day discussing the several directions that were suddenly open to us. But first, we drank a toast to Apep, the god of the Underworld, and the most powerful god of the Delta, who had brought to us this unexpected fortune. We drew and redrew plans, for mother was far more cautious than I. As Ra set in the sky, we discussed what must be done next. With that accomplished, we both slept well.

Just beyond another ten-day, Djer's funeral finally took place. The Horus priests had commandeered the temple in Inabu-hedj for their secret rituals and for seventy days they prepared Djer's body for his journey. Once they began, no one could see or touch the priests. Food was delivered and left outside the temple walls. Rumors circulated wildly each of those days. Some claimed the guards heard King Djer moaning throughout the preparations. Others claimed that Djer's ka was seen walking the temple grounds. Anyone allowed to wander near to the temple heard the priests chanting and singing for hours at a time, sometimes at Ra's ascension, and at other times during the deepest parts of the night.

For me the time between Djer's death and burial was a luxury. I spent days dictating my words to my trusted Delta scribes, planning and making lists of things I had to do to further our ambitions.

Days before the funeral, crowds began to gather in the town such as I'd never seen before. Even the Sed Festival crowds, estimated at up to fifty thousand in a good year, were dwarfed by the masses congregated for Djer's funeral. The King's guards believed that the population of Inabu-hedj had swelled from twenty thousand inhabitants to more than one hundred thousand.

On the morning of the funeral, I awoke to the sounds of rams' horns being blown from the Temples of Horus and Isis. Although we were hundreds of cubits from the closest temple, almost immediately I heard chants and prayers of welcome to Ra resonating in the thick morning air.

No one in the palace ate anything that morning for, like Djer himself, we'd be symbolically journeying with him to the Afterlife. He would be laid to rest in his mastaba, the lid of his coffin closed and the tomb sealed. Then he'd continue without us to his meeting with Anubis and, if his heart were found to be lighter than a feather, he'd be allowed to partake of the storerooms of meals that accompanied him. I'd never heard a priest state how long the journey to the Afterlife took, but as a symbol of our mourning, no one but children and the elderly would partake of a morsel of food until later that day.

But it was far more than a day without food for Mery. So deep was her grief, neither Ti-Ameny nor Amka could persuade her to eat much. When I saw her a few days after the funeral, she was gaunt, her eyes unnaturally sunken, and her skin as pale as papyrus paper. But mostly it was her ba that seemed to be affected, since she was merely a listless shell of her former youthful, energetic self.

Ti-Ameny used my visit to meet with Amka in an adjoining room and so I situated myself in a spot where I could observe them while talking with Mery. I watched as they poured over papyrus scrolls that Amka took from various clay jars. Amka animatedly pointed from scroll to scroll and Ti-Ameny nodded in obvious agreement.

"Our beloved Djer's now in the Afterworld," I

ventured hesitatingly to Mery. She didn't respond, but stared quietly out toward Mother Nile.

"It is so soothing," she offered after several minutes. "Mother Nile flows and flows and flows." She sighed and rested her head on the balcony wall. "I wonder what it would be like to gently slip under her waters," she whispered so softly I had to lean forward to hear her.

"Mery, you mustn't say that! It is forbidden!" I admonished.

"I only mean that it would probably be so pleasant, so peaceful, to surrender to her life-giving waters... to be nourished by her sweet embrace." She closed her eyes and appeared to drift off to sleep.

"He's dead, isn't he?" she added with a start, still resting her head on the balcony wall, as if she had not the strength to support it.

"Yes," I responded.

"The funeral procession... they tell me it was marvelous to behold." This last comment intrigued me.

"But Mery, you were there."

"I suppose I was." She hesitated for many seconds, as if her mind were mired in quicksand. "I do not remember it. It was more a dream than a real happening." It was then that I realized that Amka's medicines must have put her in a dream state to enable her to be at her husband's side through the ordeal. I silently thanked Isis that such weak afflictions of the ba had never affected me, despite the disappointments that my mother and I had faced over the years and her quickness to criticize my behaviors.

More the pity that Mery was so weak, for Djer's funeral was an event that would mark people's lives. Forever more, rekhis and royalty alike would refer to that day as a milestone, a day against which all others would be measured. I once heard one of my maidservant's daughters say many years later that she turned twelve in the year of Djer's death, not even mentioning that the year was also marked by her marriage and first pregnancy and a birth from which she nearly died.

For me, Djer's death represented another milestone, for the outpouring of love for my father also taught me a valuable lesson, one that I wouldn't share with my mother. My view of my father was terribly skewed. I hadn't realized how protected I was within the walls of the palace, nor how one-sided was my mother's feelings toward my father. Seeing thousands upon thousands of common Kemians weeping openly for their King shocked me. During the funerary procession I forced myself to stare straight ahead, not knowing how to handle the emotions of the throngs that mobbed us. They tore their garments, threw flowers and grabbed onto our chair platforms to walk a few yards with us telling us their tales of Djer's mercy and fairness before they were pushed away by the King's guards. Djer was loved, more than I thought possible.

That night, as I sat upon my bed, I swore an oath to Isis to cast a wider net in gathering information, an oath that would later prove critical to my successes. My mother would be one source of information. She would no longer be my main source.

One other oath I swore to myself, never to allow myself the weaknesses of Mery's ba. I would always remain strong and unyielding, focused on my vision. I knew I was better than Mery and time would vindicate our cause, the ascendancy of Lower Kem over haughty Upper Kem.

I slipped contentedly under the light linen sheet of my bed and for the first time in many ten-days I felt a sense of hope, of a future full of promise. I was elated. I envisioned my eventual role as Queen of the Two Lands, wearing the gold crown and jewels and the finest gowns designed by Kem's best craftsmen. Their skill made me appear thinner and hid my large breasts. People sought favors from me and bowed low as I was carried through the streets. Suitors gazed upon my curves with obvious lust.

The feathery sheet caressed my sensitive skin and I shivered as it touched my nipple. I grabbed my breasts and squeezed them tightly. Turning on my side I felt that my Wings of Isis were moist and slippery and I squeezed my thighs to intensify the pleasure between my legs.

I thought to just fall asleep, but the delicious feel of my inner pleasure was not to be denied. Not tonight. Ever so gently I caressed my inner thighs, teasing my sensitive skin and increasing my excitement. When I finally touched the pleasure spot between my wings, I gasped, for it felt delightful beyond imagining. I rubbed it tenderly now, rocking slowly back and forth. When I could stand it no longer, I reached for the blanket that sat on the chair next to my bed. I rolled it tight and placed it between my thighs. I rubbed against it, at first slowly, then faster and faster until the sensations brought me to the very edge and I slipped beyond my mortal bounds. My eyes rolled back in my head and I groaned aloud as I flew aloft with Isis, wave after wave of pleasure flowing through my body. Completely spent, I slept soundly as I hadn't done in many ten-days.

Slowly, Mery began to recover from the spell she was under, in no small part due to the role I played, and played well. Both Amka and Ti-Ameny were impressed with my virtuous behavior and told me so many times and even Wadjet nodded his approval from time to time. It was easy for me, for I felt little for spoiled Mery and even less for her whining and pitiable weakness. For my efforts I was amply rewarded. I had access to Mery's heart and to all the goings-on in the Royal court and, most especially, the Royal bedroom.

During this delicate time Shepsit quietly began to implement her part of our secret plans. It was important that I appeared to be uninvolved in these plans so I could deny my role if the plans collapsed and the plotters found out. Instead I was devoted to Mery. Mother told me of every detail of her manipulations, which were deftly handled. I say this with respect for mother, for we didn't seek anything we felt was not due our people to rectify the wrongs heaped upon us by the haughty Upper Kemians.

The first step was to have me named a priestess in the Temple of Isis, on its face a simple and entirely expected request, since Isis was a much-loved goddess throughout the Two Lands. My mother herself, in her youth, had served as an acolyte in the Temple of Isis near her childhood home in the Delta. With the assent of Ti-Ameny, beloved by her sisters at the Temple, and with the approval of Irisi, the Head Priestess, the appointment was made and I spent six of my monthly cycles within the walls of the Temple receiving training. I'm under oath never to reveal what I learned from my sisters there, but I can say that the lessons were wide, deep and swift, like Mother Nile herself, from whom we draw much strength. And so I quickly advanced to a full priestess and led daily prayers, accepted donations and counseled common women.

I'm not certain whether it was my advanced age of twenty-one years, or the training I'd received in the sexual arts by my Priestess sisters, but at this point in my life I spent much time thinking of suitable mates, an issue that I soon raised with my mother.

"Who do you have in mind?" Shepsit asked me as she poured me a cup of fine beer, imported from Canaan.

"I'm still considering the options," I responded, "but I fancy Herihor."

"Herihor?" Shepsit asked, placing the pitcher on the table. She sat down beside me, lifted her cup to her lips and took a long drink. "Herihor you say? For my life I cannot place the name."

"He's an officer in the King's Guard, under Panahasi."

"That old goat!" mother replied.

"He is not!" I protested.

"Panahasi, not Herihor," mother said seriously. "Yes, I do imagine I know who this Herihor is. No doubt he's that tall, good-looking one… the one with the big scar running down his cheek."

"Yes, that's him," I said, leaning forward in my chair, smiling. "He earned that scar in a battle with the Ta-Tjehenus."

"Our allies," mother said acidly. I could feel the bile suddenly flow into my mouth, and I braced myself for what I knew was coming. Her face immediately took on the look I had come to dread, that of critic, of condescension, of disapproval. She stood and paced a few steps to the portico overlooking Mother Nile and stood against the brick wall, her white robes revealing her still slim figure. After a moment of silence, she turned back to me.

"You've made a good choice, daughter of my womb," she said quietly, shocking me so greatly, I felt sure I had misheard her words.

"Really, mother? Or do your words hide your true beliefs?" I stood and walked next to her.

"No, my darling, they are true words. You have good taste in men. He's a handsome and strong man... and smart. He would father formidable children with you. Any woman would be proud to have him as her life partner." She held my hand in hers for a moment, then turned her gaze back toward the water.

"And so, why the sour face?" Shepsit drew herself up to her full height.

"My dear Nubiti," she began and I knew that my initial fears would come to pass. "The fact is that you aren't just any woman."

And with those simple words my life changed forever. Within a year, I was married to Sekhemkasedj, the son of one of the wealthiest merchant families in Upper Kem and already the administrator of the King's largest agricultural estate, one that employed more than a thousand laborers. Our marriage was by far the most prized penetration of Upper Kemian society by a noblewoman from the Delta and would undoubtedly advance our status within the Royal Court. We'd soon be able to appoint our Delta allies to powerful positions in

Upper Kem.

Shepsit and I believed our plans were advancing far better than we had anticipated. It was as if Djer's death had unlocked the floodgates to our good fortune. As mother and I were soon to find out, those waters kept flowing in our favor and it couldn't be long before the crown of Queen of the Two Lands sat comfortably on my head.

SCROLL FOUR

Mery

"By the might of Horus," Wadjet said excitedly, "I have never seen a child suckle like that! If he is not careful, there will nothing of your breasts left for me!"

I loved it when Wadjet took pleasure in our new baby, and even more when he noted the pleasures he received from my body. "Don't worry, if anything he has swollen my breasts to twice their size. I look like a Delta wife. There will be plenty left for you, my dear." With that, Zenty had finished nursing and fell asleep with my nipple still protruding from his tiny, milk-lined lips. I studied his face for the thousandth time. It was something I could never get enough of, its perfection, the peacefulness of his ba, the gentle curve of his soft lips, the downy feel of his hair, the smell of my milk so sweet upon his breath. I had never imagined such absolute love could exist in my heart.

"Well, he certainly has thickened your nipples," Wadjet said, laughing, as he reached down to take Zenty from my arms. "Thank you for that, my little Zenty," he said, calling our son by his birth name, which meant 'of the desert,' a tribute to King Narmer and his love of the Eastern desert.

"I'm tired," I whispered, half-asleep already. "If you wish to make love tonight, you had better call Abana now to put him to bed."

Wadjet surprised me. "No... I mean, yes, I want to make love to you, but I also want time alone with our son. Ra's silver disk is full and I'll walk with him along Mother Nile to see how far she has receded. You go to sleep and if I am in need when I return, I will wake you gently, my dear." Wadjet bent over to kiss me goodnight and I immediately fell into a deep sleep, such are the demands that I had learned new babies make upon their mothers.

During that night, my parents visited me. This never happened when I was a child, but had begun to occur after I birthed Zenty. Now I relished their dream visits. My mother whispered in my ear what a good-looking baby I had made and my father beamed with a warrior's pride. Uncle Djer was in the dream, too, standing behind my father, smiling. Our eyes met for an instant and I felt proud in my own heart and very content. It was then that I became aware of Wadjet nestled behind me, his hand on my breast halter and his lips kissing my neck, gently awakening and arousing me. I reached my hand behind my back.

"And what is this weapon you bring to bed with you?" I teased, grasping his hard organ and squeezing it, as I knew he liked me to do. With that I turned towards him and felt his lips upon mine. His breath smelled of mint, freshly brushed with a crushed acacia twig.

"Not fair, you brushed," I said, turning my head aside.

"Your breath is fine, my love." He turned my chin toward him. "Kiss me more." I felt his tongue slide into my mouth and at once I felt a twitch inside me. My breasts immediately leaked through my wrappings.

I gently cupped Wadjet's bag in my hand and slid down toward his now stiffened manhood. I slowly slipped its head into my mouth, and teased its underside with my tongue, as Ti-Ameny had long ago instructed me to do. I felt a special pleasure in the fact that his penis was no longer as curved as it had been. Ever since his circumcision, part of his purification rituals in preparation for his ascension to the throne of the Two Lands, his penis had lost its sheath and had straightened a little. Once the swelling and pain went down and we could return to our normal sexual pleasures, I realized that for the first time since I had known him, I alone would know his manhood intimately. No longer would Nubiti, nor any other woman, be able to share a laugh at my expense about such a personal matter as the shape of my husband's private parts.

Wadjet moaned with delight and reached for my own source of pleasure, already wet with anticipation. I arched my body toward him so that he could caress me with his fingers. We spent many delightful minutes thus occupied, before Wadjet whispered to me.

"Mery, all I want is to be inside you. I cannot stand it much longer."

I turned on my side to answer my love, holding his face in both my hands. Ra's silver disk made shadows play across his scar, so that it appeared darker and thicker. I gently ran my fingers over this face that I had grown to love so deeply and I softly touched his scar with my lips.

"Amka says that we must wait just a few more ten-day cycles, my love. I, too, want nothing more than to have you inside. Here, I will finish you off," I said, sliding down again and putting him back into my mouth. I rubbed his shaft vigorously with my hand.

"Then at least you will have your pleasure, too," Wadjet whispered, and he turned me onto my back and began to caress my most intimate parts with his lips and tongue while I did the same to him as he straddled me from above. Despite my weariness Djet's skilled tongue quickly brought me to the height of my excitement as my body tensed and I surrendered to its exquisite pleasure. In just another moment Djet's warm juices squirted forcefully into my mouth and he soon collapsed on his side next to me. We slept well that night, although half the night would be more accurate in my case, for a nursing baby is demanding, indeed.

These are the happiest days of my life, without doubt. Wadjet is secure in his reign over Kem and ma'at is strong once again throughout the land. Hap-Reset, god of the annual floods, had blessed us with copious flooding the past few years during Akhet and Isis' fertility made the mud as life-giving as ever. The harvest last year was excellent, resulting in abundant food stores in all the Royal granaries and even in the growing number of public granaries built by the King for use in times of famine. So far all signs pointed to another year of blessings and farmers throughout the lands looked forward to the waters receding and planting their crops. But, most dear to my heart, Zenty grows strong and Wadjet and I love him with the fullness of our bas. If I spent an entire day merely gazing upon our baby's perfect features it would be a day of complete joy and fulfillment for me.

Due to the abundance, parties abounded throughout Kem, whether planned well in advance or thrown together as a last-minute excuse to celebrate friendships or business deals. One such party to which we were invited was for the wedding of Akori, one of Wadjet's finest soldiers. As was the custom for the Royal family, we arrived at the bride's parents' house only after the party was at its liveliest. Scantily dressed professional dancers gyrated to the music of the sistra, drum, trumpet and flute and surrounding them were men and women in various states of inebriation trying their best to dance to the beat.

Amidst generous applause and good wishes, we were led to an elevated platform where the choicest table and two comfortable chairs of honor were placed.

Before us the large round table was laden with luscious foods. There was a basket of fresh fruits, small loaves of bread, roast fish and quail, ribs of beef, honey cakes, many types of cheeses, bean paste and red wine. Since I was still nursing my appetite was vigorous and I hardly knew where to begin. Even considering Amka's prohibitions against consuming wine or beans while I was nursing, I did not suffer from any lack of choices before me. No sooner had I placed a slice of quail in my mouth then the guests began circulating to our table to bow before us and talk to Wadjet of public works projects and business deals, public service appointments for their kin and some problem about the proliferation of rats due to the abundant grain. Women came to me to ask about Zenty and to share stories of their own children. Many of the women had their hair curled and arranged just so upon their heads in the latest fashion in Kem's larger towns. Some wore wigs. Little cones of perfumed wax sat atop their hairpieces, releasing their varied fragrances as the evening progressed and the wax melted.

Beautiful servants, tastefully dressed in linen robes, walked among the guests carrying jars of wine and trays of delicacies, including a bean paste prepared by a visiting Babylonian chef. Few people indulged and when I sampled the concoction I immediately knew the reason.

"Dear Isis, this is awful," I whispered to Wadjet, as I discreetly spit out what I could into my alabaster cup.

"That's the Babylonian way," Djet said smiling. "We like plain fresh foods and much variety at our tables. They prefer fewer foods but much more heavily spiced."

"Well, they can keep their spices," I said, taking a bite of my bread to dull the assault on my mouth.

"And so it is," Djer said, turning to me and laughing. "They buy much more of our food than we buy their spices. Our ministers are happy... as is our treasury."

Singers began to serenade the guests with sad songs of moral failures and lessons learned too late in life. But few of the guests paid attention and instead kept the wine and beer maidens busy. An hour or so after we arrived the wife of one of the army captains vomited from excess drink, to the amusement of her circle of friends. Even Wadjet began to get silly. Before he, too, embarrassed himself I feigned tiredness and the fullness of nursing breasts.

It had been eighteen months since King Djer's death and my miscarriage. No day went by that I did not at one moment or another recall Djer's loving kindness and that of my Aunt Herneith, too. I also prayed daily for the ka of my lost baby, for I did not want him to forget us or that we would join him soon enough in the glories of the Afterworld. I felt certain that Djer had taken him with him to the next life and that he was raising him, both of them ready to greet us when our journey was ended. Yet I often wondered what my baby was like, what he had been named, how obedient he was in service to his King.

Our lives in the Royal Court had settled into a stable routine. Nearly every day Herneith would visit Zenty and me, unless she was away representing the King with the governors of the nearly fifty nomes that now made up the administrative units of the Two Lands.

It was concerning one of those expeditions that Herneith returned to Inabu-hedj days earlier than expected. Her retinue of boats docked below the Royal compound to much commotion. Ra had already set in the sky and it was unusual for a Royal delegation to return after dark, when mut forces roamed so freely. Wadjet rose from our bed, put on his loincloth and walked to the balcony to witness the unloading activity below, now occurring by torchlight. Soon Djet's servant appeared at our doorway and summoned him from the room.

"No, stay here and talk, Djet. Invite mother in. I will throw on my robe," which I did as soon as he left. In a moment Djet returned with Herneith's arm hooked through his. She looked far older than her years, her hair completely gray and her shoulders already stooped from life's tribulations.

"I am afraid I come with bad news," she began, as I hurried to pour her a mug of cool water. She took a gulp before continuing. "We were sailing north to arrange the construction of a granary in Khirdasa, as the council suggested and you, my son, commanded. We knew that we followed Irisi's boat by a little less than a ten-day."

"Irisi? The High Priestess of the Temple of Isis here in Inabu-hedj?" Djet asked, pointing toward the hill where it proudly stood.

"Yes, she was recruiting acolytes and also visiting with priestesses of other temples, as she does each year after Akhet, when Mother Nile's floods subside and navigation is not so difficult. Every place we docked, women were excited to have seen her. She gave them her blessings everywhere she went. In any event, when we docked at Khirdasa, two Isis priestesses ran up to me, crying, rending their clothes, to tell us that Irisi was dead!"

I gasped, for Irisi was one of the most beloved priestesses in all of Kem. Her name itself meant that her ba was fashioned by Isis, as everyone who knew her earnestly believed was true, for her outer beauty was only equaled by her beauty within. I recalled my special meetings with her before my wedding, receiving her blessings and her advice on dealing with men. "How? How did this happen?" I asked.

"She was walking in the desert, according to these priestesses, and was bitten on the calf by a viper. She was alone, walking to a meditation spot, so the priestesses suspected nothing amiss when she hadn't returned. They found her that evening just as Ra was setting. Poor Irisi must have died a horrible, painful death."

The room was silent, as we each tried to grasp the meaning of this terrible circumstance. All I could think of was the story of Isis saving her son, Horus, from certain death by a viper's bite, only in that case the snake was actually Isis' awful brother, Set, in disguise. Why had Isis not intervened and saved Irisi, her priestess sister?

Suddenly there was a rustling noise and low voices could be heard coming from the corridor outside our bedroom. Soon Amka announced his presence and was invited in, followed by Ti-Ameny, whose eyes were red from crying. As soon as she entered, she saw our somber moods and seemed surprised to see Herneith there.

"You know, then?" she asked of no one in particular. Everyone looked toward Wadjet.

"Yes, Herneith just informed us. She has just returned from Khirdasa with the news."

"From Khirdasa?" Ti-Ameny asked, confused.

"Yes, the Queen was on her way north on the King's business. We are all shocked." Wadjet motioned for Amka and Ti-Ameny to sit with us. "Tell us, Ti-Ameny, how will this affect us? What must we do?"

Ti-Ameny hung her head down for a moment to compose herself. "It is complicated, my master," Ti-Ameny began. "The priestesses here in Inabu-Hedj are forlorn. They have rent their robes and mourn Irisi deeply, for they loved her beyond measure. She was like a mother and older sister as one to them. Many were orphans when she took them in as acolytes." Ti-Ameny coughed.

"Here, have some water, my dear," the Queen offered, standing to serve her. Ti-Ameny was visibly embarrassed and rushed to take the mug from her superior.

"The difficulty is this, my master. Irisi was barely thirty years old and had not yet trained a replacement. Until her replacement is named, ma'at, especially for women and children throughout the Two Lands, is disturbed. Women will begin to whisper of their fear of miscarriages or marital difficulties. The priestess community must feel whole to intercede with Isis on behalf of women's problems. The power of Isis flows through the High Priestess." The Queen and I nodded in agreement.

"And so, what would you have the King do?" Wadjet asked.

"I suggest we do nothing right now. Once the mourning period is over, we... you, my King, will have to name a successor."

"With your help, I hope," Wadjet replied to Ti-Ameny.

"We will give you good counsel, as is always our intent," Amka suddenly interjected, tapping his staff on the mud brick floor for emphasis.

And so it was that an extraordinary series of events took place over the next one hundred days, events that would shake the foundation of King Wadjet's rule and would portend even greater changes in the years to come, changes that would eventually threaten the very existence of the Two Lands. Yet nearly all of those who participated directly in these events had no idea at that time of their import for our collective future. Nearly all, but not everyone I later learned, to my great and eternal pain.

Just one ten-day after Irisi's mourning period ended, Nubiti visited me. Wadjet was involved in settling a judicial dispute that had been brought to his attention by the Horus priests and so I was alone with Zenty, playing with wooden toys and telling him stories of his grandfather.

I hugged Nubiti warmly and we exchanged pleasantries and then sat with a pitcher of weak beer to catch up on our lives, as was our custom. I looked upon Nubiti as a sister. I could talk to her freely about anything, no matter how personal, especially now that she was trained as an Isis priestess and steadily learned the skills and secrets shared with her by her sisterhood. We often discussed a troubling or embarrassing marital issue and, for my part, I could always count on Nubiti to give me wise counsel.

For her part, I had come to learn that Nubiti's marriage was not an easy one. Sekhemkasedj was much devoted to his business ventures. Managing a complex agricultural estate for the King took a great deal of time. Crops needed to be planted according to a rigid schedule, harvests needed to be supervised lest workers steal some of it, crops had to be readied for export and supplies needed to be provided for the various Royal craft shops. The extended Royal family required constant supplies of fine barley beer and good wines, linen from the King's flax fields, and all manner of fresh produce. The King' estates controlled every part of the process, from planting crops and raising animals to manufacturing the clothing we wore. Sekhemkasedj traveled to Kush or Canaan and once even as far as Punt on trade missions. When all was said, poor Sekhemkasedj was away from the house for long periods of time, leaving Nubiti by herself, although she had the good fortune of a close relationship with her mother, a joy I envied but had never known.

"Zenty's such a precious child," Nubiti offered. He sat in her lap and they played, Zenty placing his hand in her mouth as she pretended to eat it. He giggled so hard he began to hiccup.

"Oh, yes. I think there is not a child in this land as loved as he is. Djet dotes on him. He takes him with him wherever he can, to the point that I sometimes worry about his safety. But I know that Djet is careful with him. And we are so blessed to have Abana caring for him."

"Yes, dear old Abana. She's raised many in the Royal family."

"She certainly raised me, although I admit I was a handful for her. She is slower now, but until Zenty is able to run around she will be a good influence on him and will scold him when needed, for neither Djet nor I are good at that. Like I said, we are blessed."

Nubiti paused her playing and turned Zenty around to face me. At once Zenty threw out his arms and I reached over to grab him. I smothered him in kisses and he squealed in delight. "And when shall we all be blessed with Sekhemkasedj's progeny?" I asked, perhaps too boldly. In fact, Nubiti silently debated her response.

"Ahh, that question's on many peoples' minds, most especially Shepsit's," Nubiti said, laughing. "Poor Sekhem works too hard. He doesn't appear to have time for, shall we say, life's more enjoyable pursuits," she winked. Together we laughed.

"There's something I need to discuss with you, dear sister," Nubiti said hesitantly. "Reluctantly, but if you… if you'll take this as something I'm only sharing with my sister, then you'll understand my intent."

"You know there is nothing between us that should make you hesitate. We tell each other everything!"

"I know, but with your position now as wife of the King I don't want anything we share to look like I'm asking for special favors."

"Special favors? Nubiti, you know that I would do anything for you, absolutely anything and I would never consider it a favor."

"Well, I'd never want it to appear that way. I couldn't tolerate the court thinking that my status was affected by the special love between us."

"Dear sister, tell me what is on your mind."

"There is talk of my being named High Priestess of the Temple of Isis here in Inabu-hedj."

I hesitated for a moment to absorb the news and probe it for political difficulties, as Wadjet had coached me to do, but nothing seemed obvious to me. Yet, I thought it odd that I had not yet heard my sister's name mentioned on any of the lists for Irisi's replacement that now circulated through the Court.

"Oh, Nubiti, that is wonderful news!" I replied.

"Not to some," Nubiti responded.

"But, why not? How could anyone object?" By now Zenty was becoming restless, so I called for Abana to take him to join his playmates in the Court nursery.

"It's complicated, Mery. You haven't grown up as the daughter of a Second Queen. Every whisper carries danger, every action by the King could shift the foundation beneath your feet."

Nubiti was right. Herneith's and King Djer's desire to protect me from the conflicts within the court had also served to keep me naïve to its inner workings. I knew that I would need to become more adept at these matters to be a good wife for Wadjet, but Djer's death, my miscarriage and Zenty's birth had all served to keep me from my vow to become a student of the court, let alone a serious player.

"There are objections to my appointment," Nubiti continued. "While I'm well enough liked by my priestess sisters, I've not been there nearly as long as some others."

"But, shouldn't the appointment be based on skills rather than length of service?" I asked.

"You and I agree to that, but others don't." Nubiti stood and paced before me. "The real issue, Mery, is that I'm from Lower Kem, viewed as no more than a street dog to those who control this process."

"Oh, no! Do not say this, Nubiti," I pleaded. "The Two Lands are one people now, ever since King Narmer, may his memory be blessed. Wadjet seeks to make this ever more true during his rule. This I know."

"More true? Perhaps, but not completely. The High Priestess is a powerful position and a Lower Kemian has never held it. People are upset at the possibility of my being appointed."

"Such as who?" I demanded

"I can't say, Mery. That'd be gossip and I don't want to draw you into this mess."

"How will I ever learn about this court… this… this intrigue, if you do not help me with it, Nubiti?" For a long time she stood where she was, staring at the mud brick floor. Finally, she sighed deeply and sat back down.

"You're right, little sister. I'll help you, as best I can. Your welfare is always my first concern. It's the Horus priests of Nekhen who stand in my way. I imagine they fear a Delta princess named to head the most important

Temple of Isis would dilute the power they hold. Besides, it's never been done before and we're a people of unchanging tradition. Many within the Royal family share these views."

For a long time I sat, pondering what would be the right thing to do. "I will do my best to help you secure this position," I offered Nubiti. She leaned on the balcony, looking toward the mighty river, lost in thought. After a moment she spoke again.

"You know, the priestesses believe that fat Hapi, with his pendulous breasts, sends Inundation down Mother Nile, but it's Isis who determines its duration and the amount of fertile silt it carries. Fertility is her essence." She turned and smiled at me. "Mery, I don't want you to fight my battles. Besides, you're Djet's wife, but even that power has its limits."

I hesitated a long moment, hesitant about telling her the secret entrusted to me. "As his wife, yes, but perhaps not as Queen Consort." Nubiti's expression changed immediately and I saw her pale for an instant before she recovered.

"Is... is this true? You are to be named Queen Consort?"

"Yes, but you are now the only one to know, other than the King and Amka. They have discussed this with me ever since Den was born and I have been meaning to talk with you about it. Now I understand it is soon to happen, although I know not exactly when."

"That... that's wonderful news, Mery," Nubiti said, smiling and coming over to hug me. "But, I've already taken too much of your time boring you with my petty problems. Anyway, we both have challenges that we'd do well to face together. We've got to confide in each other sister. Shall we make a secret pact to continue to do so?"

"Of course," I replied eagerly. "I promise to tell you every juicy detail, just as I always have." With that, Nubiti smiled and left.

In an hour, Wadjet came into our quarters and ordered that the mid-day meal be brought to the veranda. Within minutes, the servants began bringing in freshly baked bread, many varieties of cheeses, fresh fruits and nuts and even sliced duck. While they set up I nursed Zenty and gave him back to Abana for his nap.

"I swear in front of all the gods that there is nothing more that I hate than minding these endless disputes between the nomes," Djet began as soon as we were seated. He took a long draft of beer. "In this nome the governor wants to raise taxes, in that he wants to lower them and put an end to tax rebellions. Somehow the King is supposed to solve all the problems they face, especially if it involves riches from the treasury. There are times when I feel I spend all my time on these petty disputes."

"And what does Amka say of this?" I asked, knowing full well that Djet would have already spoken about the issue with his trusted advisor.

"We have already discussed this and have a plan in mind."

"Which somehow involves me."

"Why would you assume that?" Djet asked, a wry smile on his face.

"Mid-day meal on the veranda? That serious look on your face? Good barley beer in the middle of the day?" Djet sat there, just staring at me for a full minute.

"You are an evil mut spirit, my dear," he said smiling broadly. "You know my thoughts even before I speak." He placed my hand in his and with the other took another draft of beer before continuing.

"Amka believes that we have waited long enough and should move quickly to name you Queen Consort. However, power without responsibility would not be wise, so we have been debating for a month over what authority to invest in your title. Kem has now grown to nearly fifty nomes. The governors each want more of the King's ear, but that is impossible due to the many demands our lands now face. So, we would like you to take on the role of an emissary to the nomes, sort of a… a Minister of Nomes."

To say I was shocked would be to make light of my reaction. I put down my bread and sat back in my chair, wide eyed.

"You needn't say yes right away," Djet continued. "We... that is, Amka and I, would work with you first, train you, explain to you the personalities of each of the governors."

"But, I have no experience with governing at all!" I objected. "I would be made a fool and compared to a donkey throughout the Lands."

"You would not be expected to govern, my dear, but rather act as my ears, listening to the various complaints and requests and suggestions for strengthening the nomes and the Two Lands that come from the governors. Once gathered, you would distill these issues, these requests, into something that makes sense, so that the King's Council could act on them.

"Since King Narmer's time, the number of nomes has expanded greatly. Right now most of what we hear comes from rumor and gossip and frequent disputes. We need a Council just for the governors and our thought is to make you head of it. You are a wonderful listener, my love, and your heart is light."

As I sat listening to my husband, I found the thought of being entrusted with such responsibility dizzying. Yet despite the joys I found in raising little Zenty, I also knew that my usefulness to my husband and to Kem demanded more of me. Uncle Djer had tried to explain this to me when he told me of King Narmer's dream visit and that my destiny was to be Queen and to always be at my husband's side, supporting him, aiding his rule, keeping ma'at strong for our people. It was true that I had become a good listener as I matured and, if anything, such a role would serve to immerse me quickly into the intricacies of the Royal Court.

"And you would train me, you and Amka, as you have suggested?"

"Absolutely!" Djet said, smiling.

"Well, I will think about it and get back to you," I replied, echoing Djet's very words when I made a request of him that might, for example, impact the treasury or require a traveling escort. Djet looked crushed.

"Will you share with me what your hesitation is?" he asked. "Perhaps if you tell me what it is, I can resolve the problem now and we shall all be happy."

I hesitated for a long time, not being experienced in such negotiations, but having witnessed them performed by masters such as Amka. Finally, I stood and walked past Djet to the veranda wall. Surrounding the palace, the evidence of Mother Nile's floods during Akhet abounded. The farmers' plantings during Proyet was all around us. Lush crops of barley and flax carpeted the land as far as I could see. The rich smell of Mother Nile's fertile mud rose to my nostrils.

"There is something that bothers me," I said. "It concerns Nubiti." Immediately, Djet shifted in his seat to face me fully and his smile disappeared from his face.

"If this is about her being named High Priestess, it will never happen," Djet said sourly. "Besides, such decisions do not involve you, Mery. They are made by the priestesses themselves."

"I... I did not mean to thrust myself into such powerful discussions," I countered as meekly as I could. "But Nubiti is my sister and..."

"She is your half-cousin, Mery."

"By birth, yes, but sisters by our connected bas," I said firmly, for it was not the province of a man, not even the King of Kem, to intrude, or even to comment on sisterly bonds. Such was the tradition in Kem, written into our very laws.

To his credit, Djet immediately recognized this. "I did not mean that as it came out," he backtracked. "But it does not change my position. This is a matter best left to those who are in the position to decide."

"Has Amka, then, become a priestess of the beloved Isis?"

"What kind of silly question is that?" Djet shot back. "You say that it is up to the priestesses to decide. But I have heard it from good sources that the Horus priests of Nekhen, led in this instance by none other than Amka himself, are blocking her appointment." Djet shifted uncomfortably in his seat. His silence spoke for him. After a moment he lifted his mug and drained it in one long gulp.

"And what are you suggesting?" he asked of me angrily.

"Please my dear, do not be angry with me. If this is what happens when one assumes power to help the King, then I would rather be nothing but your wife and would continue to consider it the highest honor in all the land. You may keep your Queen Consort and all other titles." By now my eyes watered and my voice became shaky, for never in our relationship had Djet and I argued.

Djet rose and came to me then, wrapping me in his arms. He leaned his head forward and whispered in my ear. "Mery, my lovely Mery. I am sorry if I have offended you. That's not my intent. There have been many pressures on me lately. My father, may his name be praised, used to tell me that being selected by Horus to lead our people is as much a curse as a blessing. Since he has lived in the Afterworld I have found his words to be true, indeed." He turned me around to face him.

"What you ask is not unreasonable. I will speak with Amka to determine why the Horus priests are so determined to prevent Nubiti from serving as High Priestess. If I deem it to be petty, I promise to do what I can to intercede. But I cannot promise you the result you want, for there may be issues involved that even I do not yet understand."

"Thank you, my dear," I said and reached up to hug him tightly. I felt light as a feather, for not only had the King respected my position, my husband had proved once again that he loved me. I smiled widely.

Djet then did a strange thing to me, something he

LESTER PICKER

had never before done. He reached around himself and unwrapped my arms and held them firmly as he pushed me away from him.

"Mery," he began and I sensed immediately that his words would hang heavy on my heart. The wrinkles in his brow radiated the seriousness of his message. "The path we now embark on is not a stroll in our gardens. Far from it. It is bound to be like a treacherous rocky path in the mountains of the Eastern desert. By becoming Queen Consort and taking on these responsibilities, and I assume by your negotiating you have agreed to these things, you are taking on a far greater role.

"You now become my advisor. In your coronation as Queen Consort you will be commanded by Horus, who is a hard master, not merely blessed by sweet Isis. I will value your opinions in governing the Two Lands. But you will be witness to some of the worst parts of a man's ba. You will take part in decisions that govern war and peace, life and death. Our very decisions may send hundreds of men to their deaths and we can only pray that Horus and the gods have guided our mortal actions. But it is a heavy load we must carry."

"Are you afraid that I will not be able to measure up to your expectations?" I asked, hoping against hope that he might suddenly realize the absurdity of his request and free me of this terrible burden that now caused me to tremble in fear.

"No, my dear Mery," he answered, letting go of my arms. "Quite the opposite. I only fear that you will become too adept in these matters. I fear that these responsibilities will change you in ways that we might both regret. I shake at the thought of losing the only person into whose sweet, sweet softness I can allow myself to melt." I looked up to my love and saw his eyes filled with tears.

SCROLL FIVE

Nubiti

"Let's not panic," I said, as mother wrung her hands and paced back and forth in her quarters. She was lately stooped with age, her brow wrinkled, but her dark eyes shone brightly, as they did when she faced her greatest challenges. She was dressed in fine linen, with a braided gold rope belt tied around her middle and gold earrings with orange carnelian studs accenting the gold necklace that hung around her neck. Her ivory hair combs lay scattered on her makeup table, left there by her servant when I arrived. "All it means is that we must move our plans faster."

"The crow cannot fly faster than the wind takes it," she replied dejectedly.

"Do I have to remind you of your own advice?" I yelled at her. "The gods create the winds and you shouldn't underestimate their ability to change its direction," I continued firmly. "Since I've been a little girl you told me that all problems have solutions. But if you continue to bare your neck like a dik-dik to a lion, then you'll always be a victim."

Since I told her that Mery was to be named Queen Consort, mother was dismayed. "I know you're correct," she said, "but it's hard to see anything positive in these developments. It seems never to be enough, no matter how risky or aggressive our actions."

"And that's why there are two of us, mother. One sees what the other is blinded to. Having Mery's confidence is our hidden weapon. We know of Royal plans before they take effect. Wadjet's simpleton wife will be his own worst enemy. I already have some ideas on our next steps."

"Steps beyond poor Irisi's murder?" mother asked, her voice heavy with sarcasm.

I froze in place at that last comment. Slowly I turned to face mother, both my fists squeezed into a tight ball, my face reddened and the veins in my neck pulsing hard. "Think twice before you utter such ill advised remarks!" I spat. "This isn't a game of senet, mother. Far from it. We deal with issues of life and death now. Our game pieces are kings and queens, princes and princesses, viziers and entire nomes. We play for control of the Two Lands itself!"

Mother was agitated now. In three steps she crossed the divide between us and took my chin in her hand and searched my eyes.

"What have I created?" she asked. Her question only made me angrier.

"Created?" I stood before her and saw only a frustrated woman whose hopes of power had been squashed like vermin under the feet of powerful, pathetic men.

"The time has come to decide, mother. You're either in this with me, the two of us together, side-by-side, or we abandon these plans right now, this instant and resign ourselves to oblivion throughout eternity. You agreed that it was essential that I become High Priestess and now you whine like a baby."

"But I did not condone Irisi's murder," she pleaded.

"Stop it! Stop it right now!" I shot back. I pulled myself erect to my full height. "Choose. Do you wish me to be Queen of the Two Lands or not? But do not dare say yes without also knowing that it means by all means at our disposal... all means... for this is nearly an impossible task we face. Irisi will be well provided for in her Afterlife, but in this world we still remain deprived of our rightful due."

For a long moment I mulled over in my mind the choices I now confronted. But the vision remained the same, that of me on the throne, sitting a step behind the King. In this mother's and my fate were joined. If Lower Kem were ever to achieve equal footing with Upper Kem, then I must be the one to do it. Our vision was far more important than the lives of one or two who might stand in our way.

Mother stood before me and stared directly into my eyes. She searched my ba for a long time and found it true. "Yes, you will be the Queen of the Two Lands," she said. "I will do as you command."

"Yes, you will," I smiled in return. "Yes, I can see you will."

And so we agreed that the next step was for me to convince Sekhem to speak with Remmau on the King's Council and make his wishes known to have me appointed as High Priestess. Since Sekhem steadily provided Remmau's family with every manner of goods from the King's farms, and not all of it legitimate, we knew that we could count on this favor.

I left it to mother, however, to deal with one difficult part of the negotiations. In two days, she arranged a meeting with Amka in the library at the Temple of Horus, where he spent part of every day studying the papyruses of Upper Kem's greatest scribe and shaman, the great Anhotek, Vizier to King Narmer himself. It was a practice that my mother had often ridiculed as a waste of time for she had little regard for the medical practices of Upper Kem.

The library was impressive. I had visited it twice as a youth. The building was detached from the temple itself, but it stood in a corner of the temple complex, its brown stone block walls rising two stories on three sides. One wall was an additional story and beams from Lebanon cedars were placed along the slope and criss-crossed with dried reeds to provide shade for anyone studying within. The vaulted wall was lined with shelves and packed with clay jars laid on their sides. Stuffed into each jar were several papyrus scrolls. From each jar hung an ivory tag listing the contents within. Each scroll was tied with a goat hide lace that also held a label.

The other walls, too, were lined with shelves and clay jars and were further subdivided into sections. One section was dedicated to medicinal information, while another concerned itself with the intricacies of the laws of the Two Lands, although my mother often pointed out that they were truly the laws of only Upper Kem that were unfairly imposed upon us after Unification. My eyes were always drawn to the section of drawings of plants and animals, especially the colorful birds. I don't remember the other sections, as I found the library intimidating as a child.

"And what brings you here, my good Queen?" Amka asked as soon as she entered the light-filled building. He immediately arose from the long table in the middle of the room in front of which he sat, scrolls spread out before him and bowed low to her.

"We're both busy people, Amka, so I suggest we not bore each other with ceremony and platitudes."

Amka smiled broadly. "You know, Shepsit, you are a most formidable woman," he said while wagging his finger at her. "Of what, then, shall we speak?"

"And why play the fool, Amka? You know full well why I'm here. I wish Nubiti to be named High Priestess of the Temple of Isis."

Amka calmly reached for his wooden staff, always within an arm's reach, and slowly paced away from mother. When he reached the vaulted wall, he turned back to her.

"Do you know what these scrolls contain?"

"I'm not a child, Amka. I'm in no mood to be quizzed."

"No, no, I quite realize that, Shepsit and I did not mean to be condescending." As mother described it, Amka was dressed in his most simple tunic of coarse linen, as if he were a mere penitent, which irritated mother. But he also wore the King's wide gold armband around his right bicep, a potent sign of the King's might and Amka's most elevated standing as Vizier. None but the King held more power in the Two Lands.

"Here, then, is my point. Contained in these scrolls," he said, sweeping his arm around the room, "is the wisdom of hundreds of years of Upper Kem rulers, including the mighty King Narmer, may his name be blessed." In my mother's inner eye, she made the sign warding off the evil mut, a common gesture whenever we lower Kemians heard Narmer's name, a tyrant who we hardly regarded as a hero. "It also contains the medical knowledge passed down from Upper Kem's greatest healers. But here, Shepsit," he said sweeping one entire wall, "here are the laws of our land. Every law, every decision made by judges, by viziers, and by the Kings themselves."

"I didn't come here for a history lesson, Amka. What's your point, for we've got serious business to discuss?"

Amka sighed, infuriating my mother. "I will get right to the point, Shepsit. Here in Upper Kem," he said emphasizing the words Upper Kem, "we live under rule of law."

"Are you implying that we live like animals in Lower Kem? Is that what you dare suggest to your Queen?"

"Second Queen, Shepsit. But I am sure I need not remind you of that," he replied, his voice dripping with sarcasm. "And, no, I do not believe that Lower Kemians are like animals. Far from it, for some the most skilled shamans in the Two Lands have come from the Delta. But make no mistake about it. I also believe you are not a people of words and you do not value order as do we. Your legends are told from father to son, mother to daughter. Your laws are decided on the whim of your local leaders, with no regard for precedent. When one is in power he rules against his enemies and then when the enemies rise to power, they rule against the former. Your people never mastered the holy picture words that have come to define Upper Kem. Our legends are written down, our prescriptions for treating illnesses are stored here, committed to paper or parchment. Every tradition, every law is written down for future generations to learn."

"To what end?" mother snapped.

"To what end? So that all may consult these scrolls to find out what to do in any given situation. Laws must be consistent or chaos rules, not judges."

"That's absurd, for if there's an answer to everything, then all learning has stopped. There's no possibility for change."

"Change is most often contrary to ma'at. Change must be approached cautiously."

"Which brings us back to Nubiti's appointment. You will doubtless argue that the High Priestess has always been from Upper Kem. Yet that ignores the fact that Narmer changed tradition by conquering Lower Kem."

"Uniting the Two Lands," Amka corrected. Mother sneered at him.

"I'll argue with you over titles, not words, Amka. I've come to strike a bargain."

"A bargain? Who am I to bargain for such a thing?"

"Don't be coy with me. You're the leader of the Horus priests that oppose…"

"The High Priest in Nekhen is their leader, Shepsit."

"Stop flinging the dung, Amka! You're the King's ears in matters of the Horus priesthood and the High Priest wouldn't piss in the sand without your approval." Amka remained silent.

"So, what I am offering is this. We won't stir the pot regarding Mery's appointment as Queen Consort so long as you advise the King to appoint Nubiti as High Priestess."

"And the 'we' that you refer to, who might that include?"

"Oh, Amka, that was a shallow play indeed. You know full well that the nomes in Lower Kem are pots that always simmer, just waiting for a talented cook to build up the fire so they boil over. And with the Queen Consort about to coordinate administration of the nomes… well, let's just say that her initiation into affairs

THE DAGGER OF ISIS

of state could go smoothly or… or less smoothly."

"And how would you know of the Queen's proposed duties? The King has not yet assigned them."

"Surely you of all people know that the walls of a palace are thin indeed, Amka." With those words, Amka stood still, silently looking at the mud brick floor before him. Suddenly he looked up at his staff and then at mother.

"Made of parchment, we say," Amka responded, laughing for the first time.

"I guess parchment does have a use after all," mother added, joining into the laughter. Thus it was that a hard-won deal was struck that day and in three moon cycles I was installed as High Priestess of the Temple of Isis in Inabu-hedj.

My installation ceremony was a relatively simple affair, restricted by our traditions to my sister priestesses and our acolytes and taking place under the full silver disk of Ra that governed our monthly cycles. Again, I am forbidden to disclose the details of the ceremonies, but they took place over three days, for three is a sacred number to our calling. Of course, we fasted on the first day, to prepare our bodies for what was to come, although throughout the day we drank from Mother Nile's cool waters, and not by drinking from pitchers and mugs, but by immersing ourselves fully until we were one with her ever flowing ka. That day was also spent in rest and quiet meditation, for the next days would bring each of the priestesses to the limit of her capabilities.

The second day of my initiation as High Priestess began before dawn, when I was awakened to greet Ra's disk. We offered prayers to Bes, the fat little god who protected families, to Bastet, the mother cat god who protected all mothers of Kem, and to Tawaret, the hippopotamus god who protected mothers in pregnancy and childbirth. All these gods we welcomed into the Temple of Isis. With each one we celebrated the special qualities that women throughout the Two Lands possessed.

It was on the evening of the second day that began the most- how can I say this without appearing trite? - the most intensely spiritual experience I'd ever witnessed, let alone participated in, and I say this altogether admitting that I'm the daughter of Shepsit, that most cynical of women. The priestesses of Isis are known throughout the land for their ceremonies, ones that penetrate the humdrum of a woman's daily life and bring her into the passionate embrace of Isis' loving arms. But no ceremony ever witnessed by outsiders could compare with the initiation of an Isis High Priestess, for in this single event the sisterhood achieves its perfection.

Some call it an orgy. If so their language is understandably limited. They rely only on the sounds emanating from within the innermost chambers of the Temple, secret chambers that mirror the womb, the innermost temple of a woman's body.

Some say the initiation is an unending feast. They, too, are limited in understanding, for though we assimilate the procreative fluids it is not to nourish our bodies, but to celebrate our roles as women, the creators of life. Some even say it is simply a night of revelry, of unadorned dance, pleasant music, laughter and fun. Need I say that they, most of all, know nothing of what transpired that night and all the next day.

Yes, we danced and sang. We chanted and drummed. But to describe it as such is to call the King's gold breastplate a fine yellow trinket or the height of sexual passion a pleasant feeling. The dancing, the fury of the drumming, the indescribable sexual joys that we ourselves experienced and then bestowed upon a few chosen men were never before seen in the temple. One of the priestesses who had participated in Irisi's initiation told me later that my event eclipsed Irisi's, a comment that gave me untold satisfaction.

And a word about those fortunate chosen men, too, for they reveal much about the kindness and nurturing of Isis herself. Fortunate is a relative term. Any man walking the streets of Kem would have sacrificed his own riches to have days and nights spent immersed in the delights of Isis priestesses. But these men hardly walked the streets of Kem. No, these men were known to the priestesses as outcasts, beggars, dirt beneath the feet of even the rekhi. One was formerly a soldier in the army, blinded in battle by a mace that crushed half his face. One had both legs bitten off below the knee by a crocodile that was in the midst of devouring his baby son who he tried to rescue. Others had similar horrible fates befall them. But for those few nights of pleasurable relief from the agonies of their bodies they gladly swore an oath of silence.

My initiation was an experience I'd never had before in my life, a deep, intense feeling of being at one with the goddess, feeling Isis flowing within me as I flowed within her. The incessant, furious drumming and chanting, the intertwining of our heated, womanly bodies, the uninhibited dancing and sexual pleasures drew me up, again and again, to the heights of ecstasy, to fly with Isis. To this very day I look back with a mixture of awe and sadness at my initiation; awe at the epitome of spiritual and bodily ecstasy, sadness that I never again was able to achieve such heights.

On the eve of the very next full silver disk, I served in my first official capacity as High Priestess of the Temple of Isis at Inabu-hedj. Ironically, I helped install Mery as Queen Consort.

Mery's installation was almost as elaborate as King Wadjet's coronation. It was also as different from my initiation as any two events could be. For if there is one word that can be used with any event that the Horus priesthood is involved with it is pompous.

People came from all over the Two Lands to glimpse the King and Queen, the long procession of Horus priests and Isis priestesses, and the parade of dignitaries that stretched for miles and took hours to pass. The governor of every nome attended. Emissaries from

Canaan, Punt, Babylon, Kush, Lebanon and even further carried presents of every manner and description for the Royal family. The King generously provided each with gifts of fine gold jewelry from his workshops as a token of our trade friendships. At one point I stood next to the emissary from Punt, a slovenly man with a long, unkempt beard and hideous, dirty braids in his hair, who commented to me that there was more gold worn on the bodies of those in the procession than in the treasuries of all the lands surrounding Kem. It was true that people lining the parade route had to often shield their eyes from Ra's rays reflected off the polished gold breastplates that passed before them.

Mery, I must admit, looked radiant. She sat upon her carry chair, immediately next to and slightly behind the King, looking every bit the part of the Queen Consort she was about to become. When she disembarked at the Temple of Isis she handled herself impressively, having been coached by Amka's and my assistants for days. She stood erect and her gaze swept the multitudes impassively. She even raised her hands for a blessing of the people, for which they sang her praises.

Mery was outfitted in an elegant pure white robe, woven of the finest linen produced by the King's workshops, once again ironically under the supervision of Sekhem. Every yard of the fabric was inspected to guarantee that there was not the slightest imperfection. The Queen's seamstresses had sewn every pleat, every drape to conform flatteringly to Mery's petite figure. The drape of the gown intentionally hinted at Mery's dark and enlarged nipples, a symbol of her maternal aptitudes.

At this stage of Mery's installation she wore few jewels, other than a gold ring, a gold and carnelian bracelet, and a thin armband that signified she was the First Wife of the King. Her face was radiant, lined with black kohl around her eyes and a subtle shade of green malachite on her eyelids. Her lips were painted in a bright red. Her hair was worn up in a bun, with gold thread woven through and through.

Mery's procession accompanied her up the steps to the Temple, where I greeted her. One of my sister priestesses held a beautifully decorated ceramic bowl of water and I dipped into it a cloth woven with gold thread, knelt down and washed Mery's feet. Thus cleansed, we retired into the Temple. All others, King Wadjet included, waited outside, for none but the sisters of the priesthood are allowed into its innermost chambers.

The ceremony itself was a simple one and I blessed Mery in the name of Isis and wished her well. The highest-ranking priestesses offered their own blessings for Mery's fertility, for a strong family, and for long life. All this, even the foot washing, I found easy to do. It was the next part of the ceremony that I found the most difficult.

Outside the Temple, a platform had been erected, onto which Mery now proceeded. There she was met by the Priestess of the Temple of Neith who had journeyed from Sais to perform Mery's naming, for as Queen Consort she would need to be rebirthed with a new name. Like many within the royal family since Narmer's time, Mery had chosen to add the goddess Neith to her name. Whether this was partly the influence of Herneith or Amka I wasn't certain, for Mery was vague about how she came to this. The Horus priests were known to usurp the name of Neith to forge some artificial, self-serving bond to the Delta. They couldn't have known how much we detested their taking on the name of the most revered woman deity in Lower Kem.

And so, with tens of thousands of Kemians and foreigners watching, Mery took on the name of the goddess Neith. The priestess bestowed upon her a golden bow and arrow, symbols of Neith's prowess as a huntress and warrior. She gave her an ancient weaving shuttle, proof of Neith's skill as a weaver and dutiful wife. Next came an intricately carved shield, depicting Neith as a mother suckling her child, the crocodile god Sobek. All these acts, although I resented them deeply, I took as one does a foul medicine. It was the next one that made me choke on bitter bile.

The priestess raised the double crown of Upper and Lower Kem and placed it upon Mery's head, all the while declaring her the Queen Consort. She called out her new name, Mery-Neith, to the crowd below. A huge roar went up and people jumped up and down in the streets. Lyres and drums and rattles sounded. Professional dancers grabbed ordinary people in the streets and the Horus priests ordered that wine and beer be dispensed freely. The soldiers began to force some semblance of a parade route back into the crowds and soon Mery was escorted back down the temple steps and onto her waiting carry platform where a beaming Wadjet greeted her.

I recall wishing Mery well as she passed by me, but my stomach churned with disgust. I caught a glimpse of my mother scowling, along with several of our relatives and I wondered whether Amka, the King, or any of the priests and priestesses from Upper Kem understood what we felt at that moment. Watching their faces I could only hope that they were guided by a misreading of our feelings about our beloved Neith and not by a more malicious intent.

Afterwards, mother and I discussed the implications of Mery's naming in great detail and our belief was that, despite her new name, our plan was proceeding even better than we could have expected. One benefit to Mery's coronation was that our allies from Lower Kem attended without raising any suspicion. We were able to meet with them regularly for a period of months as they traveled back and forth to help with the planning for the ceremony and the endless discussions afterward with the King or with the various wealthy merchants with whom they had dealings, or wished to.

I reunited with many of my aunts and uncles, cousins and relatives in high positions in Lower Kem, reunions that were filled with wine and good foods, singing, dancing and much laughter. But there were also late night meetings held in whispered voices long after the other guests had left. By the time Mery's celebrations were over, we had ever more tightly woven our cloth of alliances, along with secret methods for communicating with each other.

One of the advantages that came with the position of High Priestess was the necessity to travel to the many temples to meet with my priestesses to discuss liturgy, taxes, budgets and recruitment. It was two months before Akhet was expected when I was able to arrange a trip to the Delta. Mother Nile was at her lowest point of the year and while sailing downstream in Upper Kem was easy, negotiating the tributaries of the black lands of the Delta was exceedingly difficult. Besides the many muddy traverses we encountered, we were also forced to deal with hoards of incessant mosquitoes that seemed as large as water bugs. Amka had provided us with a lotion that worked for short periods of time, but it smelled so bad we all swore it was mainly concocted from a foul brew of aged piss from virile warriors and fermented crocodile manure.

It was on our third day after entering the Delta, after the mighty Mother Nile split into five smaller rivers, that we entered the area that surrounded Dep, the capital of the Delta. I had last visited Dep when I was a child and had only vague recollections of its beauty. We approached by a small tributary that led directly to the city. As we rounded the final bend, the walled city loomed before us, its architecture so different from what I saw in Upper Kem, but also far smaller in stature and less grand. The city wall itself was made of large mud bricks, but instead of running smoothly along its top, it was notched every ten feet or so to accommodate lookouts and warriors, who had last used it several generations before in their losing battle with King Narmer's army.

In fact, a large monument was erected in the field approaching the city's walls commemorating Narmer's victory, a monument scrupulously avoided by the locals, for it callously showed Narmer murdering our King and beheading our allies. And, of course, there was no corresponding monument to our own King W'ash, who bravely defended the besieged city.

But it was another feature of Dep that made it stand out, despite its more primitive architecture, a feature that no grandiose structure in Upper Kem could ever hope to duplicate. As we approached the massive city gates themselves, Wadj-Wer appeared before us in all its magnificence. The Great Green's waters shimmered in Ra's light, its waves gently rolling onto the white shore in the distance. The most pleasing smell of salty water filled our nostrils and I felt for the first time what it meant to be truly home. Wadj-Wer was the largest body of water known to Kem, and no fisherman had yet discovered its boundaries, let alone its source. Gently, predictably, each day its waters rose and fell, rose and fell. Yet fishermen were often lost to its terrible storm fury. Mother Nile herself flowed into Wadj-Wer's salty receptacle and so we understood that it belonged to the gods themselves and we were blessed to live on its shores and take sustenance from its abundant fish.

We were greeted in Dep by King Wadjet's governor, who pointedly walked us to Narmer's battle monument immediately after the midday meal, tediously describing Upper Kem's victory over King W'ash as my sister priestesses nodded submissively. After that we chatted amiably the entire afternoon, but just before the evening meal he left us to attend to other duties. After prayers at the local temple, I excused myself from my priestess escorts and retired to my room in the back of a dormitory that adjoined the temple.

In the late hours of the night, someone shook me awake. As I bolted upright, I could see in the dim moonlight a man holding his finger over his lips. I hurriedly draped a robe over my bare chest. He quietly placed a footrest before the window and he deftly slipped out and dropped to the ground below. I followed and two men grabbed my elbows and guided me to the ground. Without a word they escorted me through winding, overgrown paths that meandered through a marsh and in thirty minutes we were greeted by crashing waves and a fleet of three fishing boats waiting on the sand. Before we exited from the marsh onto the beach itself, they looked about cautiously. One of my escorts made a sound like a wild bird. In seconds it was answered by a man in a fishing vessel.

In a burst of speed, my escorts ran with me across the sand and heaved me brusquely into the middle vessel, which was covered with a tarp of goat hides. Despite the darkness, I could sense the presence of others, although they made not a sound. I was careful to stay quiet, although I felt sure they could hear my racing heart. In seconds we were pushed out to sea, the oars rhythmically clicking against their wooden swivel locks.

After we had traveled for a time, the captain of the vessel called softly to the men who sat under the tarp with me. One of the men lit a small fire in a brazier with sparks from his flint and the first thing I saw was a low table with delectable foods laid out upon it. On the opposite side of the table I was surprised to see Khnum, the High Prince of Lower Kem. Beside him sat Bakht, his shaman and healer.

My body shivered gazing upon Bakht's dark, pitted and scarred face, for Bakht was a master of the dark arts and his scarring came from his initiation into levels of his craft that reportedly no mortal before him had yet reached. He wore his hair combed back into a braid, tied at the end around the tooth of a hippopotamus. He wore a necklace of enormous crocodile teeth. From his left ear, running down his arm and continuing along his ribs and back was the most ornate and sinister tattoo I had ever seen. The rumors I had heard told tales of his kidnapping a fierce shaman from the darkest reaches of Kush and forcing him to apply that hideous tattoo over days of drinking and burning foul herbs. In the dim light it took me a full minute to recognize the tattoo as Apep, the snake god-monster of the dark shamans, emerging from the Underworld, spreading his wings as his body slithered upward. I quickly turned aside my gaze.

"Welcome, Priestess," Khnum greeted me with a serious expression on his face. "I apologize that our first meeting in the Black Lands must, of needs, be under such inelegant circumstances. Perhaps you know Bakht, my loyal servant."

"I know of him and am honored to meet both of you. This has been a most interesting late night stroll," I quickly added to avoid dwelling on Bakht.

"A necessity, I fear," Khnum answered, "for the King's ears are everywhere. Here we may speak freely. Everyone here has sworn his life to our purpose."

"The plan has advanced," I offered, looking both men in the eyes.

"Yes, and our congratulations on your being named High Priestess. You and your mother have worked your end of the plan well."

"You've heard of Queen Shepsit's negotiations with Amka that led to our latest achievement?"

"It's the details we lack." I spent the next few minutes recounting for them the highlights of what my mother had relayed to me.

"And so, we seem to have gotten what we wanted. The stage is set for the play to begin."

"Amka, too, has gotten what he wanted," Bakht suggested, speaking for the first time. His deep voice reflected no emotion.

"True, but we've achieved the greater victory," I quickly interjected with a forced smile. Bakht smiled back broadly. He glanced at Khnum, who nodded imperceptibly.

"Dear Priestess, and I speak cautiously here for in the future I hope to address you as Queen of the Two Lands. Never underestimate Amka and the Horus priests. They are a mighty presence, whose wisdom descends from the time the god-mortals walked the land. It wouldn't surprise me to find out that it is we who have won the shallowest victory."

"But I hold the title of High Priestess of the Temple of Isis," I countered, no longer sure of my footing.

"Ah, even the best general sometimes confuses battlefield victories with winning the war, only to watch the unyielding sword of his enemy descend swiftly toward his neck when the fighting is done." In that one moment, I knew that I had an invaluable ally in Bakht, and I assumed Khnum, allies who might even rival Amka in wisdom.

"How do you see Amka gaining by my being named High Priestess? My appointment's for life. It may never be withdrawn."

Khnum spoke up. "On the surface it seems that Amka and the King don't gain, but Wadjet and Mery have now consolidated power through their marriage and the new titles it brings. Even more important, they believe they have you confined in a package, as tightly wrapped as a child's gift at Wepet-Renet. They can watch you with their spies and focus their efforts at confining you and your duties. They can continue to dole out gifts of gold and long, worthless titles, and tombs next to the King. That's how they gain powerful allies among the wealthy and powerful of Upper Kem and, I must admit, even Lower Kem."

"Even assuming you're correct," I asked, knowing full well in my heart that they were, "we already have plans for our next steps."

"Men plot and the gods laugh," Bakht said calmly.

"And your point?"

"First, we agree that you and Queen Shepsit, along with your own network of spies and informers, understand the Royal Court far better than we do. But, at some point you'll need us to provide certain… ummm, force from the outside to mobilize against the King and his generals, be it distracting skirmishes or perhaps… and we hope it never comes to this… in outright war."

Inwardly my heart buzzed with excitement, for I'd

never had direct contact with men of such high placement and obvious power and skills. I also recognized how valuable it was to have advisors beyond my mother to witness and interpret events, to help plan strategies and execute tactics.

"And, speaking of Mery," Bakht continued, "what've you heard about her Council of Nomes?"

"I haven't followed her performance closely. We're gathering more information."

Bakht and Khnum exchanged glances once again. Khnum spoke. "Well, we've been given detailed debriefings of their meetings, as well as reports from our spies as to the information that Mery has passed on to Amka and Wadjet."

"And who spies for you at the Royal Court? Is it the same woman who is in mother's service?" I asked, curious.

Bakht smiled again. "Dear Priestess, sometimes it's far more valuable to be able to deny the obvious with a light heart than to have it weighed down with too much knowledge. In this case it's better that we have two networks working independently of each other." I nodded in agreement.

"In fact, we hear that Mery has been disturbingly effective in ferreting out certain patterns in our collective behavior," Khnum went on, reaching forward for some grapes. "Go ahead, help yourself Priestess," he said pointing to the fruits, nuts, bread and bean pastes that were distributed in crude pottery dishes over the table. I was taken aback by the stark contrast between Upper and Lower Kem even in such a small matter as this. In Upper Kem the reddish pottery was elegantly made, thinly crafted and finished with artistic black rims. Here the pottery, even for a Prince, was rough and squat and lacked any artistic merit. I dipped a piece of brown bread into the first paste and enjoyed the pungent garlic and spices on my palate.

"She's created a papyrus map of the nomes and has plotted on it the various locations of both internal tax rebellions and also skirmishes with Ta-Tjehenu tribes from the west. It does not present the Delta in a very good light," he said, tossing a rotten grape over the side of the boat. "Unpopular taxes by the King are followed by an internal rebellion. Force used against a popular Delta leader is followed by a Ta-Tjehenu attack on a border village marketplace. These attacks are, admittedly, coordinated by certain, shall we say, known entities," he said half-smiling, "all designed to keep the stew simmering, waiting for the right opportunity. But these many actions, when put together, may well betray secret relationships best not exposed to Ra's light."

"And Mery has figured this out?"

"Not entirely, only that there's a pattern and that its heart lay in the Dep nome. She's presented these findings to Wadjet and Amka." I was too shocked to hear of my cousin's surprising competency in these affairs of state to ask anything further.

"She's also been proving her worth to the governors in other ways," Bakht went on. "Apparently, unlike Amka who ran these meetings before, she doesn't defend every action of the King and cut off their complaints. Instead she listens to them, both their complaints and suggestions. She even encourages dissent. She's begun to involve them in making decisions about granary storage buildings for use in times of famine. You can only imagine how that will mortar the power of the governors and strengthen their allegiance to the King and Queen Consort. All in all, very disturbing developments, which begged a meeting between us tonight."

"Why tonight?"

"We've heard that Wadjet has brought in one his generals to plan a march into the Delta as a show of the King's force of rule and to exact select punishments as examples to others."

"Which general?"

"A rising warrior who has distinguished himself in skirmishes with the Ta-Tjehenus to the west and the

Philistines in the east, a man named Herihor."

"Herihor, you say? I know him. He is a great warrior." My heart beat faster at the mention of his name. "How soon is this action to take place?"

"Hard to say," Khnum answered. "From activity that our informers observe, we assume it's just in the discussion stage. An incursion like that would take a great deal of planning and coordination and become known to us well in advance. In any event, it wouldn't prove to be popular to the tribes of Lower Kem and may even backfire, so we are counting on the fact that it will only happen if Wadjet, Amka and their Council feel they have no choice."

"We've stopped any subversive activities we sponsor from here, to give the other parts of our plan a chance to mature," Bakht added.

For a moment I thought of the many challenges we faced, but also the rich resources that were suddenly available to me, more than I'd ever imagined, having been confined to the Royal Court with my mother as my only advisor for so many years.

"And that's good to do," I finally commented, "to give us time to mortar our base in Upper Kem. Yet, I think it'd be wise to keep up the pressure on Wadjet and Amka. To do less would be a lost opportunity."

"What would you suggest?" Bakht asked, looking from me to Prince Khnum.

"You have strong relations with the Philistines to the east, right?"

"Yes, with some of the chieftains there, but not the entire people. They are a very splintered group and spend as much time fighting among themselves as they do trading or fending off the Babylonians."

"I see," I responded. "But trade between Kem and our eastern neighbors some would argue is the most important we have. We get our wood, spices, the finest wines and most of our jewels from them. It's an orderly trade route, isn't it? I've seen endless caravans coming and going from Inabu-hedj."

"Ah, and so the plot thickens, my priestess. Well done. I see where this all leads," Bakht exclaimed, leaning back on his cushions and laughing.

"So, enlighten me," Khnum said, turning first to Bakht and then to me.

"I think that our most devout and compassionate priestess here recognizes that the tolls the Upper Kemian traders pay to pass through the Philistine lands might be inadequate to the sacrifices those poor people make to maintain the routes. And if the King of Kem is not willing to pay higher tolls, then what choice do those poor people have but to exact payment through, shall we say, relieving the caravans of a fair percentage of their burdensome loads?"

With that Bakht and Khnum fell onto their sides laughing. "And you...," Khnum tried to say, pointing to me, "you are just like my cousin, Queen Shepsit, only... you're... you're..." but he could not finish his thought without laughing more.

SCROLL SIX

Mery-Neith

"You are far too strict with him!" I said, turning from Abana to Zenty who toddled, still sobbing, to my open arms. I wiped his tears with a cloth.

"I tried to learn from you," Abana quickly replied. I could see that she struggled to calm her breathing.

"What in Ra's name are you talking about? I am hardly strict with him at all, compared to you."

"That's not what I meant," she answered, exasperated. "What I mean is that I learned from raising you that I should've been far stricter." For a moment I hugged Zenty to my breasts, but from above his head I could see my dear Abana shaking. Suddenly she seemed so old, her voice wavering.

"Was I so bad, Abana?" Zenty had stopped crying and was already squirming in my arms. I kissed his cheek and he smiled and ran off to play with his carved wooden animals, as if nothing had just happened.

"You were headstrong," she said, "and you're still headstrong. People…" She stopped herself and turned from me to face Zenty.

I realized Abana had been trying to tell me something. I took a deep breath. "People are talking," I started carefully, "but not to my face. I depend on you, dear mother, to tell me what others have not the courage to."

Abana's face was red from embarrassment. She opened her mouth as if to speak, baring her few remaining teeth, which were terribly worn from eating rekhi bread that contained too much sand.

"Go ahead, you know you can always speak your mind to me," I said to urge her on. I knew she would probably offer me no revelations, no information that I did not already know from Ti-Ameny. But I also knew Abana from the time she was my own wet nurse and I understood that if she did not speak her mind now, she would carry the poison of her nervous heart in her ba for days. I did not want Zenty exposed to that poison if I could possibly help it.

"It... it's that you... oh, I'm not good with putting thoughts into words," she said in her heavy Rekhi accent, as she wrung her hands. At that moment Zenty came running up to her and she knelt down to pick him up, instinctively checking his undergarment for accidents. Suddenly she appeared to gain strength and it was then that I realized that without a child in her embrace, Abana's ba was not full. She and Zenty hugged each other as she rocked him from side to side.

"People whisper that you've changed," she began. "I, too, notice this. You take on too much... too much for a woman, more than Queen Herneith ever did. It's not ma'at."

"Ah, I see how this bothers you."

"No, you don't," Abana shot back. "You're too busy. Always in meetings, traveling here and there on the King's business, doing man's work. Everyone talks about it."

So it was that I learned from Abana that the work I was doing for my husband, the brother of Horus, had become the gossip of the Royal Court. I accepted Abana's concern without comment and after she had expressed herself more on this subject we hugged warmly. I did not bother to explain to Abana the reasons for my work for she viewed life only from within her own narrow circumstances. She worked in the Royal Court, but she was rekhi through and through. I never felt that was a hindrance, for her uneducated self brought us many blessings as she focused all her attention on raising the royal children. The only travel she ever did was with Zenty and me on the Queen's barges and even then she not once ventured off the boat when we stopped at various villages for she was paralyzed with fear at such times that mut spirits and demons from the Underworld would devour her. She watched Zenty with special zeal at such times.

As soon as Abana left to take Zenty to the garden pool I freshened myself, brushed my teeth again with a fresh acacia twig and mint leaves, and crossed the palace to Wadjet's meeting rooms. By now Ra was high in the sky and the heat was oppressive. The winds were still and so servants stood around the rooms waving papyrus reed fans and the newer ostrich feather fans that our merchants were now importing from Kush.

The guards saluted me as I approached and as soon as I entered the room all the men rose and bowed. Only Herihor stood ramrod straight and saluted me, his forearm crossed over his muscled chest.

"The King will be with you shortly," Amka said softly. "Have a seat here if you wish."

I sat on a rush chair and observed the meeting, being held in the largest of the meeting rooms. The room was open on three sides. One side overlooked Mother Nile, flowing swiftly below us past Inabu-hedj, Ra's light shimmering on her surface, and behind her the Eastern desert and its red and blue mountains. The second side provided a view of the Kings vast agricultural lands, while the third side faced the Western desert and the mountains that came close to our walled city.

Wadjet and Amka were in the midst of questioning Herihor on some military preparation and he, in turn, would periodically ask his subordinates for their opinions. It was rare for Herihor to be in the palace. More and more frequently in the past two years he was out on some military mission, stopping Ta-Tjehenu raids along our western border, recruiting soldiers, or training patrols out in the remote eastern desert. Often two or three full moons would pass between his visits here within the white walls of Inabu-hedj.

As I watched, I could not help but notice the respect his men had for him. He treated them with equal respect, listening carefully to their opinions, yet pushing them to challenge their own beliefs.

But it was Herihor's ba that commanded one's attention. He was taller than most men in Upper Kem, much taller than those of Lower Kem and he carried himself erect, even when he sat. His upper body and arms were highly muscled from the intensity of his training and on his left bicep he wore a wide gold band with Wadjet's serekh cast in it and below that the symbol of Sobek, the crocodile god. I once watched a young woman gasp when she first laid eyes on him, for across his cheek, from his left eye to his lower lip, ran a raised welt from the knife of a Ta-Tjehenu warrior. There were similar, albeit smaller scars in various other parts of his body.

Yet it was his eyes that made the greatest impression. They were dark, deep set, and framed by heavy, black brows that added an aura of power and mystery. I realized I had been staring at him too hard when I saw him turn his gaze to me and I quickly averted my eyes to the floor.

"We have made great progress today," Wadjet said to the group as he stood up. "We will finish our preparations tomorrow. I have kept the Queen waiting long enough and from what I hear from the Governors, she has lately become a more formidable foe than the lot of you." To the resulting peals of laughter I smiled, but after hearing of the gossip within the Royal court from Abana, my husband's good-hearted joke stung me. I vowed to myself to use my heart's eyes to witness my actions more carefully to see if I was behaving in a manner that would please both my husband and my personal goddess, Neith.

With everyone gone but for Wadjet and Amka, I wanted to ask what the meeting was about, but I knew that Wadjet resented it when I inquired after official matters of Kem. Instead I asked vaguely how his meeting went.

"It went far better than I had imagined it would," he responded, "don't you think, Amka?"

"No, I expected that Herihor would come prepared. He has a knack for planning that rivals his prowess on the battlefield. That is a rare combination, indeed. We are fortunate that Horus provided you with such talent at times of unrest." Amka sat with a sigh on the chair next to me.

"Well, more on the meeting in a moment, my dearest. Here, have some wine and cheese," he said, pointing to the plate that Amka placed between us. I reached for a slice of bread and dipped it in honey. I noticed that Wadjet just sat with his hand on his cheek.

"Does your tooth still bother you?" I asked.

"I'm sure it does,' Amka interrupted, "for your husband, aside from being King, is the most stubborn man in the Two Lands. If he allowed me to pull that poisonous tooth or if he would at least take the medicine I offer him every day, he would be most improved. Instead he plays the martyr."

"Oh, Horus, why do you torture me with a shaman who nags me worse than a wash woman? You must think me crazy if you believe I would willingly subject myself to the agonies of a tooth pulling. And I would take your damned medicine if it were not so foul tasting!" Amka leaned his forehead against his staff and grunted. "Anyway, I want to hear more about the

Council of Nomes." Amka slowly turned his seat to face me directly.

"I believe the King will be pleased with the latest developments," I began. "The Governors have put together a list of projects in their individual nomes that they would like to see the King develop."

"From your treasury, of course," Amka added wryly, tipping his staff towards Wadjet.

"Of course," Wadjet responded. "But, then again, we have had some very plentiful years. The treasury is strong."

"In any event," I continued, "the Governors have even prioritized the projects, understanding that we create a stronger, more united Kem by doing so. They have weighted the projects to the north, to allow Lower Kem to catch up, as it were, with Upper Kem. And in so doing, I have come to find which of the governors are trustworthy and which are decidedly not."

"For example?" Amka asked.

"I believe that Wahankh is trustworthy. His ba radiates honesty."

"Wahankh of the Inabu-hedj nome?" Wadjet asked.

"Yes. I have come to believe that because his nome encompasses the King's city he sees firsthand how serious we are about uniting the Two Lands. Due to his proximity he also gets to attend more functions of the Royal Court as the representative of Lower Kem."

"That may be so, dearest Queen," Amka said, "but I beg you not to go too far in your trust. Anhotek's scrolls cautioned that the people of Kush often hunted gazelles by disguising themselves in the skins of zebras." I nodded in agreement.

"And what about those you deem not trustworthy?" Wadjet asked.

I sighed through pursed lips. "That's more complicated, for I do not yet understand all the alliances. But Pamiu of the Dep nome I do not trust at all. He is a liar and a coward, not daring to say things to my face."

"His mother must have played a joke when she named him 'tomcat.' Does he still avoid Council meetings?" Amka asked.

"Oh, yes. Ever since I began drawing up maps of rebellions that seemed to focus around Dep, he has been absent at most meetings... always with good reasons, of course."

"Of course," Amka echoed. Turning to the King, he said: "We have our spies keeping an eye on him. The pot simmers in Dep, although Prince Khnum appears to be keeping himself out of it. But I believe there is a connection between Dep and the caravan attacks in Palestine, although I cannot yet prove it."

"Yet," Wadjet said, nodding to Amka. "Back to the Council, what types of projects are they planning?"

"Well, aside from the usual roads and granary storage projects, two nomes have joined together to create a pottery district, to allow the Lower Kemians to advance their pottery design and firing to the standards of Upper Kem."

"But why join together to do this?" Wadjet asked. "Isn't pottery-making unique to each nome?"

I did not know how to answer this without appearing boastful. Fortunately Amka intervened. "I believe the Queen is being too modest. My informants tell me that the Queen, in her desire to create harmony among the nomes, and to protect your treasury I might add, encouraged them to work together. She suggested that you might fund a larger project if they joined forces."

"Well, the best site, one with steady winds to generate higher kiln heat, was on a rise that actually bordered the two nomes," I interjected, "so it was not hard to persuade them to my vision." Wadjet looked from me to Amka and then burst out laughing.

"By Horus' holy name, I'll be damned!" he roared. "You are amazing, my dear! Truly amazing. Is she not, Amka?"

"We made a wise choice in appointing her head of

the Council," Amka said, as he tapped his staff on the ground a few times for emphasis.

"Good, then... very good. Things seem to be in order here." Wadjet reached to grab a cup of beer, brought it to his lips, then quickly put it back down without drinking. I knew his tooth pain was bad.

"My dear, why not take some of Amka's medicine now?" I ventured.

"Yes, as soon as we're done. But first I must tell you about our military plans," he said, looking discreetly at Amka.

"You are aware of the attacks on our trade caravans in Palestine?" Amka asked, as he rose and walked a few steps. His staff made a tapping sound on the brick floor.

"Yes, vaguely," I replied

"Well, the long and short of it is that the caravans of our traders, both Kemian and foreign, have been attacked by Palestinian tribes," Amka continued, as he paced back and forth. "I guess attacked is too strong a word. They have been stopped and convinced that it would be in the best interests of the caravan owner if he would agree to part with some of his wares in return for safe passage through their barbarian lands. Interestingly, they do not extort the King's caravans, only private traders."

"That is odd," I said. "Why the difference?"

"Amka here, as well as several of my other advisors, think it is so as not to affront the King directly," Wadjet said.

"It applies pressure on the King's rule, while avoiding a direct confrontation," Amka added.

"But why? Who is behind this madness?"

"Ah, and in that lays the horns-of-the-rhino conundrum," Amka said, emphasizing his comment with a smart tap of his staff.

There are times when I admit that Amka's wisdom is buried too far beneath stories and aphorisms. I stared at Amka, uncomprehending.

"You know..." he babbled on, "you grab at the horns to protect yourself from being gored and with a shake of his head the beast throws you off, and all the while underneath his armor lies an evil heart."

"She is asking you what the point is, Amka!" Wadjet interrupted. Poor Amka looked as if he had been gored.

"I... I simply mean... well, there are several of us that believe..."

"The point, Amka, the point," Wadjet said, holding his hand to his painful jaw.

"The point is that the Palestine tribes may be doing the bidding of another, more sinister, force. Eventually we will find out who is behind this."

"If anyone," I suggested.

"Yes, if anyone," Amka added. "They could be acting alone, but I've never known them to be so bold. But in any case we are mounting a military campaign against these vultures who pick at our traders."

"Yes, I have chosen Herihor to lead it," Wadjet said. "I have decided to accompany the army, to send a clear message to the barbarians that we will not tolerate extortion."

"Is that wise?" I asked. "I mean to go yourself?"

"It is a choice I could have made either way. However, Amka believes that doing so will indicate a new policy to our neighbors, one that says that trade is so important to us as we grow and prosper that we will no longer separate the King's trade from private trade. If you attack any of our imports or exports, it is as if you attack the King."

"And that is a powerful new policy that we believe is best delivered through the firm hands of the King of the Two Lands himself," Amka said, bowing slightly and tipping his staff toward Wadjet.

And so it came to pass that within one moon's cycle, Zenty and I watched from the palace as two thousand men from the King's army, with Herihor in the lead, marched from Inabu-hedj. Zenty was so excited, he jumped up and down on the balcony wall as I held him tight, waving and yelling 'Aba, Aba' toward his father's litter. Three times as many support servants followed the soldiers, leading donkeys heavily laden with food, clay jars of water and military supplies. They streamed from the city as the Royal family and thousands of residents watched and cheered from the parapets and streets. As the soldiers passed by, spears held upright, people threw flowers at their feet, so that the streets were ankle deep in trampled petals, creating a confused scent of perfume and men's sweat.

Priests from all temples in the surrounding nomes sent representatives to the gates to bless the King and his men. When the King's litter approached the priests, it halted and the carriers placed the litter on a raised platform. There Amka and the Chief Horus priest from Inabu-hedj personally blessed the King. Then the priests kneeled and received a blessing from Horus' brother, Wadjet. As Wadjet rose, the crowds shushed each other, until silence fell upon the streets, except for a single donkey braying in the distance. Wadjet wore a breastplate made of pure gold and his warrior battle dress of thick leather. His scabbard held his sword, which he handed to Herihor who now stood beside him. He wore a helmet of leather, with a gold half-mask that covered the upper part of his face, save two slits for the eyes, so that the rekhi would not have to turn away from Horus' countenance as they bowed low before him.

Once the King completed his blessing, the column of soldiers resumed their march. The last of the crowd that the soldiers passed were their wives and children, girlfriends and parents. There were cries of anguish as children, held tight by their mothers, reached out their tiny hands to be held one last time by their fathers. Yet the soldiers had to ignore them and look straight ahead. Many silent tears ran down the cheeks of those brave warriors that sunny morning.

Many not so silent tears I shed, too, and I would be lying if my account told that I had no troubles with Djet leaving me, for he had never before left me to go on a prolonged military expedition. Djet had to spend far too much of his time and patience listening to my worries over our parting and drying my tears, this I admit.

"We have been over this... more than once or twice," Djet said to me the evening before his departure.

I felt melancholy and throughout the day I had sulked and was not good with Zenty. Abana, who always worried about fevers and mut spirits, told me at one point to lay down and she had a servant bring me an herbal tea.

"I know, dear. I... I do not understand why I yet feel so badly," I replied, pacing away from my beloved. My heart beat hard in my chest.

Djet walked over to me, his body casting long shadows in the candlelight. Outside Mother Nile flowed quietly under the light of Ra's silver disk. Inabu-hedj seemed quieter than usual and all I could think of was the thousands of wives and girlfriends who felt, as I did, that a part of their hearts were about to be ripped from them. I thought of my own father, then, and it was as if Horus sent a bolt of lightning to illuminate my heart.

"That is it!" I said, turning back to Djet. The thoughts now raced through my heart. "Yes, yes, that must be it!"

"What?" Djet asked, catching my enthusiasm and putting his hands on my arms. "What is it?"

"Oh, for the love of Isis, that is it!" I reached up to touch Wadjet's face. "It's my father... and... and perhaps it is yours, too." I smiled with this new realization as it settled comfortably upon my heart.

"You are speaking in riddles, Mery."

"I know, I know. Here it is, then. I have been so fearful that you will be killed in battle, as was my father. I never knew him except in the dream world. And I sometimes feel as if I hardly know you, I mean really know you. I love you so much, Djet. I love the new life the gods have helped us create. I wish to grow old together, side by side."

"Oh, Mery, we will. And we shall have a daughter

next, to care for us when we are doddering old fools."

With that, Djet took me in his arms and hugged me so tightly I could hardly breathe. "Ow, not so tight!"

"But I'm not." Djet replied quizzically, and then I knew that Djet's father, my beloved uncle, also encircled me, as did my own father and mother, and Herneith. I knew then that Djet would not perish by the sword, for my uncle would watch over and protect him as he was not able to do with his own brother.

After days of feeling glum, my ba felt light and as soon as Wadjet came to bed I insisted on easing his tensions by massaging his back and shoulders with flax oil. As I rubbed his buttocks, I noted his organ slowly begin to grow and snake out between his thighs. I felt in a mut mood, and so I continued to massage him, moving down past his bottom to his tight bag. He drew his breath in sharply as I gently massaged that sensitive place, alternately teasing his engorged staff. He moaned in excitement before rolling over, wanting me to climb onto him.

But, although I was tempted, I resisted, knowing how much he enjoyed my putting his member in my mouth. Djet propped himself up on his elbows.

"No, Mery, come, get on top of me," Djet begged.

I pushed him back down, for tonight I wanted this to be only about his own pleasure and told him so. With his penis firmly in my hand and my tongue already darting over his swollen head, he did not argue.

For the next few minutes, I expertly toyed with him, for I was taught by none other than an Isis priestess. I brought him close to the edge, then playfully did not allow him to reach his final pleasure. He moaned and groaned and recited Horus' name over and over again, begging me to end his exquisite agony. Finally, when I knew he could take it no longer, I took in as much of his organ as I could and as I withdrew slightly Wadjet arched his body and shot his seed into me so forcefully I could not handle it all. As I held fast to his organ, together we watched its final spasms spurt all over my chin and hair. He fell back onto the bed and we laughed as I wiped his sticky seed from my body.

Knowing that I sent Wadjet off a satisfied man, I felt fulfilled. I watched for hours as the long line of men and their beasts of burden snaked out into the desert, heading east along the main trade route. Zenty was overjoyed watching the parade of soldiers and supply caravans and he marched around the balcony imitating his father and the soldiers, much to the delight of our relatives. Finally, the expedition passed beyond the mountains and could be seen no more.

The season of Proyet was fully upon us, so the farmers did not dally watching the procession, but went immediately back to their fields, still planting and tending the young crops of emmer wheat and barley that by now had created a soft green carpet that covered the land from the banks of Mother Nile to the base of the nearby mountains. Looking west the carpet was divided into different sized patches, tiny ones privately owned by rekhi and larger ones owned by merchants who hired rekhi to care for their holdings. But, looking north and south the fields were an uninterrupted carpet of green, for they were the lands owned by King Wadjet and supervised by Nubiti's hard-working husband, Sekhemkasedj.

Wadjet had left the Court with clear instructions about what was to be done in his absence. Amka was the administrative ruler whenever Wadjet traveled, and with good cause. Tiny Amka, for he was indeed short and pitifully thin, had served King Djer for fully half his reign and so had the advantage of experience in addition to the wisdom he had cultivated as a respected Horus priest and revered shaman. Amka's knowledge of law and history was legendary. He could quote a ruling back to King Narmer's father, King Scorpion. He could cure all manner of disease. But above all he was able to read people better than anyone in the Royal court and as such was invaluable. If there was one piece of advice that Queen Herneith had given me that I treasured above all, it was to suggest that I form a tight bond with Amka. And so we had.

As the weeks passed one after another during Wadjet's military campaign, Amka continued to tutor me in matters related to the Royal Court and politics. I had long ago memorized every nome in Egypt, who governed there and the unique political qualities of each ruler and region. Now I learned of the alliances we had throughout our history with the black Ta-Sety tribes to our south.

We also spent hours discussing the many gods that our people worshipped, for it is true that the rekhi and the privileged each have their own pantheons and that is good for it takes the entire collection of gods to keep ma'at strong in the Two Lands. As a Horus priest Amka spends much time worrying about these matters.

Every week, we would receive a small delegation of Herihor's soldier messengers. As soon as they had washed the desert sand from their bodies, they would visit me and Amka, telling us of Wadjet's mixed progress. Apparently there was much hand-wringing going on, with the Palestinian tribes each denying their involvement in the extortion activity and pledging their undying allegiance to the King. Poor Wadjet was trying to untangle the mess and get to the bottom of the situation, while Herihor and his troops stood by, hopelessly frustrated.

On one such occasion, as Amka and I awaited the arrival of Herihor's messenger's, I noted Amka talking to one of his assistants and instructing him in a mundane administrative matter.

"It intrigues me that you are able to focus on other matters, when I am so nervous to receive news of my husband. I suppose it is yet another difference between men and women," I noted, sighing.

"Perhaps it is," Amka responded, discharging his assistant with a nod. "But there's nothing of note... " Amka blushed and turned from me as if to retrieve his staff.

"What is nothing of note?" I asked, piqued by his embarrassment, which I found amusing.

"It is nothing," he said, tapping his staff nervously.

"Oh, no, it is not nothing that we waste our time debating, you old goat," I said, smiling at him. "I know when you withhold, for who else has observed you for twenty years? You know something about what the soldiers will report and you are hiding it."

Amka fidgeted for a moment. "Abana is right, you are too headstrong for a woman. And it's not that I know something, it is that I know there is nothing."

"For Ra's sake, you are being... oooh, this is so frustrating!" I stomped my foot, now angry at our circular dance.

"What I mean to say is that I know the soldiers will have nothing special to report, nothing different from last week."

This intrigued me. I sat down, staring at Amka. "Is this always the case?" I asked. "I mean, all these weeks, do you always know what they will say to us... to me?"

"Yes," Amka said firmly, trying hard to keep his head high. I did not know what to make of his response and I sat there, perplexed.

"Mery," he began, calling me by my childhood name for the first time since my marriage. "Perhaps this is as good a time as any for a lesson, so listen well. Leaders hate surprises. A good leader knows in advance when a surprise is coming. A great leader learns to manipulate circumstances to his advantage so as to avoid surprises altogether. A truly great leader is the one who surprises others, keeping them dancing to his tune." I caught a twinkle in Amka's eyes and found myself absorbing his words and nodding.

Many are the times that I think back to that day, sitting with Amka, and not only because I did follow his advice throughout my life. No, I recall that day because of the surprise we both received just hours later, the surprise that changed my life forever and with it that of all Kem. For on that very day, just as Ra almost set in the western sky, we received news that my beloved, King Wadjet, brother of Horus, lay dead upon the sands of the Eastern desert.

SCROLL SEVEN

Nubiti

"Dead! You say dead!" I stared at my mother, disbelieving. "Are you certain? Absolutely certain?" I asked in amazement.

"Yes, I'm certain. The news came from a reliable source. I'm sure that not even Mery knows yet. She'll probably find out later today. My messengers took a secret route through the mountains to save time." Mother's eyes glistened with tears, even though she smiled broadly. "I... I hardly know what to think." She began to pace before me, one hand entwining the other.

"The possibilities... they're enormous," she continued. My own mind spun with the import of the event. Wadjet, dead!

"But we are now without the protection of Horus," mother blurted out, suddenly sending a chill down my spine. I spun on my heels to face mother.

"And when've we ever been under the protection of Horus' wings?" I asked venomously. "Horus forsook our people long ago. Now these Upper Kemians have even stolen Neith from us. Her-Neith, Mery-Neith, it's a damned abomination! Neith has always been the goddess of the Delta." I held fast to the back of a chair and thought for several moments, then stepped forward and took mother in my arms.

"No, mother, I see now that it's quite the opposite. It's the Land of the Lotus that has now lost its patron god and we, you and me and our people, we've been given a blessing like... like never before. Our prayers to Apep have been answered. Bakht has worked his magic. The plans we hatched here and the ones we began in Dep have born fruit." Tears of joy ran down my cheeks.

I thought back to my furtive meeting with Khnum and Bakht and realized that it was my suggestion that we kindle discord among the Palestinians that led to Wadjet's military excursion there. My heart skipped a beat and for an instant I felt the bile of guilt rise in my throat.

"Did you... did we...?" mother began.

"Don't be a fool!" I shot back. "Of course not. Murdering him would've been too risky. Sometimes the gods themselves enter the drama and then who's to predict which side will benefit? In this case, the good fortune falls to us."

The house was empty of all but my servants. Sekhemkasedj had left before Ra rose, as was his habit every morning. I would not see him again until after Ra set, whereupon he would be so exhausted he would fall into bed, half clothed, a filthy habit that disgusted me. In fact, due to the pressures put upon him and the over abundance of food on the King's farms, Sekhemkasedj had grown considerably in girth since our marriage to the point that it sickened me to look at him waddling around the house breathing like a pig or snoring so loudly his cheeks shook with each tortured breath. Yet his position within the Royal Court did allow us certain advantages, not the least of which was the fine house in which mother and I now met. Built only a stone's throw from the palace, it was large with separate servant quarters. It overlooked the King's southern fields, so that Sekhemkasedj could distract himself with work even when at home.

"Alright, let's gather our wits about us and figure out the best course of action. We've got no time to lose," mother said, pacing. "Let's consider the facts that the gods have laid out before us. First, Wadjet is dead," mother continued, holding one finger down with her other hand.

"That gives us seventy days of mourning to maneuver," I offered, knowing full well that we had to act while Wadjet's death was fresh.

"Yes," mother retorted, "but we must act fast. By the time Wadjet is prepared for his journey to the Afterlife, Amka's plans will have become actions. Once that happens we'll all have to live with that reality for years, perhaps a lifetime. We've got to help those gods who share our vision and not Amka's."

Just the mention of Amka's name, and the Horus priesthood he represented, brought chills up and down my spine. Horus was a formidable god and the Horus priests know how to summon his help in times of crisis.

"We'll need to enlist Bakht's help with the Apep priesthood," I said.

As if reading my thoughts mother added. "I'll dispatch my most trusted messenger to Khnum with the news, which means that Bakht will know first." Immediately I recalled the forbidding tattoo that adorned Bakht's body and I imagined the mighty essence of Apep slithering up from the underworld.

"You shiver, I see," mother noted, "as will Amka and his charlatan priests, for while they've grown fat and lazy as vultures over the Two Lands, Bakht and his priests have maintained their discipline in secret."

Mother looked at the mud-brick floor as she paced. "So, we have the King dead and the mourning period soon to begin. Zenty is but a year old and unable to reign. Herneith is too old and frail to reign…"

"By all rights she couldn't anyway. She's Queen Mother and Mery now is First Queen," I noted.

"True enough, but Mery is twenty years old."

"Narmer ascended when he was younger than that."

"May his balls be devoured by Apep!" Mother responded angrily.

"Anyway, being a woman Mery can't be named King. No, we must... wait, give me a moment to think..." I put my hands to my temples and paced along the room's perimeter. Ra's light danced across my white flaxen robe as I passed by the columns that formed the archways to the garden.

"Yes, yes, I think I've got it!" I exclaimed after a few moments. Mother turned quickly and rushed back to where I now sat. "Here it is then, here's what we must do."

For the rest of that day, as Ra ended his journey and Herihor's messengers arrived at the palace with their terrible news, mother and I formulated the skeleton of our plan. True, there was much flesh to add to its bones, but even I, far less experienced in matters such as this as was mother, understood its brilliance. Mother had reminded me many times that the winds of change may bury men alive or expose to them treasures beyond imagining. Only those who prepare can survive or, the gods willing, even prosper.

Reduced to its simplest, we came to realize that day that we controlled many of the pieces in this unfurling game of state. Unrest here, an unfortunate death or two there, strategically placed spies and well-made alliances could alter the map of Kem forever. That, and the intervention of the gods to whom we prayed.

There was no way we could realistically make a determined move to take command of Upper Kem immediately, and anyone from Lower Kem who might suggest otherwise, and there were some, was a fool. Nor were we at a point where we could have a caretaker King named from the nomes of Lower Kem. No, our only hope was to view our challenge as a game written on large papyrus sheets, a game that required rewriting all the rules, redrawing the map of Kem to our purpose. Mother thought it grandiose, perhaps even foolhardy when our discussions began, but by the end of the day I saw in her eyes the flicker of promise. As we sketched in one detail after another, that flicker caught fire within our bellies. The death of just one key figure at the right time would sow confusion in the ranks of the ruling elite. The addition of a tax uprising or an attack by our allies would distract the army.

The powerful crave ma'at. Change is unacceptably frightening to them. If nothing else, our eventual rule after a period of chaos would bring welcome stability throughout the Two Lands. The sheer audacity of our strategy alone would catch the power structure of Upper Kem by surprise. For trade, treasure and family the merchants of Upper Kem would welcome us when the time came.

Yet it was not a rebellious plan that we hatched. No, our plan was a gradual one, insidious, subtle, each act seemingly unconnected to the next so that, in the end, the powerful of Upper Kem would not know what had really happened. Even Amka, assuming he was alive and would eventually catch on to our strategy, would be powerless to reverse it. If the gods favored our plans, we could be in power within ten years, perhaps five if they admired and rewarded our boldness. Even the grandest and strongest structures cannot withstand the relentless gnawing of insects, and in Upper Kem the vermin were the plague of corrupt civil servants and wealthy noblemen who would do our bidding.

The key was communication among the small group comprising our cabal. We would need to strengthen our network of spies and informers. We would have to bring on wealthy individuals who could fund our efforts and who saw the potential for their own gains as we rose to power, for it would take much gold, silver and jewels to bribe and reward our way down this path.

It was late in the night when mother and I finally celebrated our initial victory, the death of Djet and the birth of a plan. We dined on fresh baked bread, drank fine Babylonian wine and ate an assortment of fruits, meats and cheeses. We lit candles to our patron goddess Neith and then prayed to Apep for him to aid the strength and cunning of Khnum and Bakht. With mother gone back to the palace, I went to bed, apprehensive, yet contented that we had finally begun the arduous journey down the road to a victorious Lower Kem.

Sekhemkasedj snored loudly on the opposite side of our large bedroom. I had long ago appealed to him to allow us to sleep separately, for my duties as Chief Priestess often kept me out late. We hardly ever had sexual relations any more, since Sekhem worked so hard. He had also gained much weight over the years and was usually as uninterested in sex as I was in having it with him. Yet tonight I was too tense, too excited to sleep.

I went to the side of his bed and reached under the sheet. I found his tiny organ and began to massage it with my hand. He snorted mightily, and turned away from me, but did not wake yet. I persisted and put my hands between his thighs and grabbed his balls and squeezed. He awoke with a great start.

"What...? What in Horus' name...?" he sputtered, sitting upright.

"It is only me, dearest," I whispered. "I know you had a hard day and I have not been a good wife to you lately. Allow me to make it up to you, if only in this little way." I grabbed his penis and began rubbing the head between my fingers.

"I was asleep," he protested weakly.

"And so you shall be again shortly," I responded, knowing all too well how true that probably was. But I was determined not to go to sleep frustrated this time. As soon as he hardened, I climbed on top of him.

It was difficult to get the right angle for my

pleasure, so big was Sekhem's girth. But, by putting a blanket under him and bending back just so, I soon began to enjoy the sensation of having a man in me once again. Just as I was beginning to climb the mountain, Sekhem suddenly cried out and shot his seed. In seconds, he closed his eyes again and with me still thrusting above him, started snoring. Disgusted with him, and with my own weakness of the flesh, I dismounted him. Back in my own bed I finished what I had started.

As soon as Ra emerged over the horizon, my servant, Hentu, awakened me as I had instructed her. As she prepared my bath, I rehearsed in my mind what it was I needed to do that day. Hentu showed no signs that she knew of anything amiss in the palace. I smiled, for I knew that Amka would call a secret meeting upon hearing of Wadjet's death and would spend the entire night creating a plan for how to handle it before announcing the tragedy to the Two Lands. His predictability was my ally.

I dressed, drank my herb tea and then walked the short distance to the palace. Two of my acolytes walked alongside me, waiting for me to assign them their daily tasks. I admired their lithe bodies and eager, unquestioning attitudes. They were both from Upper Kem, which I knew would work in my favor when I drew them, unwitting, into our scheme. For now we walked the dusty street among the rekhi who scurried by us, chasing their goats or carrying wares to and from the market. Two feral cats fought in an alley over the carcass of a mouse.

As we approached the palace, I closed my eyes and drew in two sen-sen cleansing breaths, for I knew that by tomorrow, the scenes on the street would radically change. For an elderly king to die was dreaded, but normal, and even then the rekhi and privileged alike would live in fear until the new king was crowned. But Wadjet was young and all Kemians would view this time as terribly auspicious. With ma'at so fragile, no one would conduct business other than purchases of life sustaining food and medicines.

When we arrived at the palace, the guard contingent had been doubled. I turned to my acolytes. "Kainefuru, Nyla, hurry to the temple," I said in my most serious voice. "Tell Peshet to assemble all the priestesses immediately. Isis whispers to me that something terrible may happen. We must pray for Kem."

Both girls held their breath and blanched. They turned to face each other in fear. "What is it, mother?" Nyla asked.

"I can't say for sure, but I sense that when I cross into the palace the blessings of Isis will be required. Tell Peshet to have runners available to send messages to our temples. Return here quickly for further instructions. Hurry girls!" With that they hiked up their robes and ran off and I entered the palace.

As I walked toward Mery's wing, I saw a group of men leaving one of the meeting rooms and huddling in the corridor, weariness in their expressions. Just as I came abreast of the group Amka walked through the doorway, nearly bumping into me.

"Oh, I'm sorry Nubiti!" he apologized, backing away from me. He leaned heavily on his staff. Heavy bags drooped from his eyes.

"Have you heard the news?" he asked.

Mother and I had prepared for this conversation. "What news?" I asked. "I have just come to visit with Mery."

"That is fortuitous," Amka replied, "for Mery will need you. The King is dead." I gasped loudly.

"Dead? Surely this is a poor attempt at humor," I said, doing my best to rise to the occasion.

"It is true," Amka responded. "We only found out last night. This is a terrible tragedy and it will have great implications for Kem."

"But... but how did he...?"

Amka leaned forward and placed his forehead on his staff. He looked far older than his years. "He died from body poison," Amka said.

"Poison?" My thoughts raced with visions of Khnum and Bakht conspiring behind my back.

"Body poison," Amka sighed. "He had a purulent tooth and the stubbornness of his ba was his undoing. He neglected to take his medication and he refused to have his tooth pulled and so the poison spread throughout his body. This type of thing is usually confined to the rekhi. The army tried to march him home, but he died while still in the Red Land, on the caravan route. We... we are shocked, for he was otherwise a healthy man."

"By the goodness of Isis, Amka, what are we to do?" Fortunately, tears now streamed down my eyes.

"It is interesting that you ask that, Nubiti, for the Council has formulated plans to guide us through this delicate period. I was about to summon you and your mother to the palace to ask for your help."

"Anything, Amka. We... we'll help in any way we can."

"Good, but we must also hear this from your mother, Nubiti, for as the Second Queen she alone can speak with any authority for Lower Kem. This is a difficult time for us all. When the King is dead, mut spirits roam the land creating danger and ill will. Now is not the time for divisions between our people. She must actively conduct affairs that keep the lid on Lower Kem."

"I agree, Amka. Mother will, too, I'm sure." I felt a chill run through me, for the next step of our strategy was being handed to us on a platter. "But, this is terrible news, indeed. Does Mery know yet?"

"Yes, of course." Amka looked at me for a moment. "You know she is no longer a child, Nubiti." I stared back at Amka, surprised at his comment.

"She is still my little sister," I retorted. "Nothing can ever change that bond which Isis mortars between two women. Whether in love or hatred the sisterly bond endures."

Amka nodded. "True enough, although I do not pretend to understand such bonds. This I do know. Mery would welcome your presence. Ti-Ameny is with her now. Go."

As soon as I entered Mery's chambers she burst into tears and ran into my arms. "Oh, Nubiti," she sobbed, "I... ohhh..." and she cried out, wailing. I had to hold her to keep her from falling to the floor.

"Shhh, my sister." I shuffled her to a nearby chair and sat, rocking her gently until her sobs lessened. In a moment, I could feel her asleep, interrupted every so often by a shudder as she breathed in deeply.

"What's happening with Zenty?" I whispered to Ti-Ameny.

"He is with Abana. We have not told him yet what has happened, although he will not understand it, anyway." Ti-Ameny was without makeup. Her basket of medicines was open on a small table next to the bed. "I have given her a quieting herb. She will sleep most of the time."

Ti-Ameny helped me carry Mery to her bed and we covered her with a linen sheet. For several minutes we both stood over her, watching, as she tossed fitfully.

Out of the corner of my eye, I noticed Ti-Ameny shudder.

"These are unpredictable times," I offered.

"Unpredictable? They are dangerous times," Ti-Ameny countered. "Wadjet's ka walks between two worlds and I fear that he carries the fate of the Two Lands with him."

"What do you fear?" I asked.

"Fear? I fear plague. I fear deaths in childbirth. I fear Mother Nile withholding her floods. I fear dissension. I... do you not have fear in your heart?"

"To be honest, Ti-Ameny, I haven't had time yet to think. I only learned of the King's death." With that Ti-Ameny turned toward Mery and stroked her hair lightly.

"I'll begin a period of solemn prayer with our

sisters in the temple," I told her. "Wadjet was a good man and his heart was light, but it wouldn't hurt for Isis to intervene, would it?" Ti-Ameny nodded and I took my leave to go back to the temple. No sooner had I left the palace then my two personal acolytes joined me. They had just heard the news.

Each had rent her robes and had streaks of kohl running down their faces. I, too, tore a seam of my gown. The streets of Inabu-hedj were in commotion. People wailed as they heard the terrible news, tearing at their clothes. Mothers ran about looking for their children and husbands. Merchants busied themselves closing their stalls. People strode by each other without looking at faces, for fear of the evil eye. A woman scurried by, her face partially hidden by her shawl, her one exposed eye covered with two fingers that warded off the evil eye of others. Goats bleated as they were herded quickly back to the courtyards of their owners. Dogs barked incessantly.

My two acolytes dropped to their knees, each one grabbing the hem of my robe. "You were right, mother, something was amiss. Isis sent you a message. You are a seer."

We rushed together to the temple where a crowd of perhaps two hundred women awaited outside, each one carrying an offering seeking the protection of Isis. When I arrived a great noise arose, but not one of joy, rather one of great anguish and sorrow. Women reached out to touch me and I tried to offer comforting words and an understanding touch to each group I passed.

Once inside I instructed the priestesses on what to do and soon we had alters set up throughout the temple. Acolytes and priestesses brought groups of women into the temple to burn incense and to chant the loving prayers to Isis. Mothers asked for protection for their children, barren women requested blessings for their husbands and families.

The other priestesses encouraged me to offer words of comfort to the crowd and so I mounted the steps of the temple. Women shushed each other as I stood before them and in a moment silence fell.

"Women of Inabu-hedj, visitors, my sister priestesses," I said, holding my arms open and turning to encompass them all. Heads bowed down. A few women held their hands up toward me, as if to grab my words from the air and gather them into their hearts.

"A tragedy's been thrust upon us. I just learned that Wadjet, our King is dead, and so soon after the death of his father, Djer, may his name be blessed."

"But you were warned of this before it happened!" a woman yelled from deep inside the crowd.

I looked to my priestesses and saw a few with prideful smiles. So, the word had already spread from my two personal acolytes to the priestesses and now to the crowds of women who had arrived at the temple before me. I instantly saw how this unintended consequence of our plot might benefit us.

"Yes, it is true that Isis visited me before this tragedy and warned me that something evil was to transpire and so I was able to fulfill my duty to the poor Queen, who's in deep mourning.

"I ask that all of you gathered here say a prayer and give offerings to Isis, mother of us all, guardian of women throughout the Two Lands. Join our sisters in praying for the King's ka as he journeys to the Afterlife. Pray that Anubis and Thoth find Wadjet's heart to be lighter than a feather so that he may journey to Osiris' side and live abundantly and watch over us for all eternity." I paused, pulled the hood of my robe over my head and turned my head to the skies, eyes closed.

"And don't forget to include Queen Mery in your prayers, for her ka is but an empty shell as her beloved husband journeys between worlds." Women whispered the prayers taught them by their mothers and soon a cacophony of ritual wailing engulfed the crowd. I stood before the women and offered prayer after prayer for their safety and comfort while their King was in the cold, dark ether of Nun.

The rest of the day was spent in prayer, even late into the evening. I slept for a few hours with my sisters in the temple that night, only to be awakened in the early morning by one of mother's trusted messengers. I dressed quickly and followed her to the palace. But instead of going to mother's quarters, I was taken to Amka's.

Amka's space in the palace was sparse, consisting of no more than one large room with a meeting table for ten, a corner with a few rush chairs with comfortable stuffed cushions, and a study table where Amka always seemed to have scrolls opened. In fact, he usually slept at the Temple of Horus compound, on the other side of Inabu-hedj. Although I had never personally seen his quarters there, I was informed that it consisted of no more than a wooden bed, straw mattress and four walls in what was generously described as a storage closet. On the rare occasions when he had business late into the night at the palace, he was known to nap for an hour, never more, right on his desk, looking for all Ra's creation like a corpse. He lay flat on his back, hands folded across his chest, unmoving until, as if awakened by some unseen god, he simply awoke, stood up and resumed business completely refreshed.

By time I arrived, it was immediately apparent that mother and Amka sat in their chairs in decided discomfort. Mother pretended to sip at a medicinal tea that Amka's assistant had prepared. I knew that she despised the bitter taste of his concoctions and she suspected he therefore intentionally served them to her.

Amka struggled to stand as I entered. "No, please Amka, stay seated," I said, holding out my hand to him. He held it lightly for a moment and motioned me to an empty chair. I sat and his assistant poured me a mug of tea.

"I was just telling the Queen that King Wadjet's body should arrive in Inabu-hedj tomorrow or the day after," Amka began. In his weariness I could see pain in his eyes, although he would hardly allow himself the luxury of grieving when so much needed to be done.

"The most important thing now is that we must agree to the details of a pact between us that would allow for an orderly transition," he continued, looking intently at mother as he spoke. To her credit, mother stared back at him without the slightest trace of emotion.

"So, lay out your plans to us," mother said with an inflection of bitterness, "for I'm sure that you and your Council have plotted every detail of what's to transpire." I admired how readily mother took on the role of the bitter Second Queen with Amka. I smiled inwardly at our ability to play the great Horus priest for a fool.

Amka took a sip of tea and very deliberately placed his mug on the small table beside him. "That is not the purpose of this meeting," he said. "Our plans so far have more to do with the proper preparation of the King's body for the Afterlife and deciding which of his devoted servants will accompany him on his journey... the list of volunteers is far longer than the available burial sites. The fact that the King is so young and his death unexpected means that his tomb is not nearly completed. The logistics leading to his burial in seventy days is... well... daunting would be a good word." Not until that very moment had I considered the enormous responsibilities that rested on Amka's narrow shoulders.

Amka sat back in his seat and took a deep breath. "Nubiti, your mother and I have always been direct with each other, and I hope we can always be such, so here it is. These are very delicate times. The fate of all of Kem floats in the fog of the netherworld with our King, until he is buried and the new King named and ma'at restored. We need to negotiate an agreement, one that will be agreeable to Upper and Lower Kem, and then you will need to have Khnum buy into it..."

"But, I... we..."

Amka held up his hand to me and smiled. "Nubiti, stop, for your mother and I know full well how transparent is the veil of secrecy. Mother Nile herself would envy how swiftly flows the messages between us and our allies… on both sides," he added, tiredly circling his hand to include us all.

"I ask you now how you would propose to restore ma'at to our land. I would like to listen, to understand what you propose." He grabbed his staff and used it to pull himself upright in his chair, looking for all the world like a stuffed goose, his long beak protruding from his emaciated face, perched atop his scrawny neck.

Mother looked at me and drew in a breath. She stood and walked behind her chair, holding firmly to its back rail. "What we want is simple, Amka. Zenty is but a child, a baby really. He won't be in a position to rule for perhaps fifteen years at best, maybe even twenty. Since before Narmer there has never been an instance of the heir being so young at the King's death."

"True, but that makes the need for caution all the more prudent. Ma'at hangs by a spider's thread," Amka said. "How exactly do you suggest we proceed?"

"Name an interim King, one who is acceptable to the nobility in both lands."

Amka sat unmoving, looking at mother for a full minute, his heart weighing the many options that mother's suggestion entailed. "Interesting, Shepsit. Full of problems, but interesting nonetheless."

"What in our world is without problems?" mother replied. "Some solutions are just more difficult than others." There could be no doubt that Amka understood the veiled threat.

"Agreed," Amka replied, "so let us consider each one separately. First, how would you propose we choose this interim King?"

"I'll confer with those in Lower Kem able to make such a decision. We'll come forth with a list of three names that are acceptable to us."

"When?" asked Amka.

"Within a moon cycle," she answered. Amka now rose and paced away from us, to a tiny window that sat by his study table. He leaned against his staff and peered out the window for several moments.

"I'm sure you have already considered that we have a First Queen in Mery, with a recognized heir to the throne. If we appoint an interim King, he and Mery would have to be wed."

Mother and I had discussed this and even though we knew that Amka and his council would never accept that proposition, we felt it would strengthen our eventual position if we at least offered it.

"Well, of course she'd marry him," mother said stiffly, trying to maintain her composure. "But Mery'd keep her position as First Queen, with Zenty still the heir."

"And what about future heirs?" Amka asked.

Mother hesitated. "No matter what future heirs result, Zenty would be the oldest and first in line to be King." We all sat quietly, as Amka digested mother's proposal.

"I do not believe your proposal would be acceptable to the royal family," Amka finally replied. "A king from Lower Kem? No, I think not, Shepsit." Amka still leaned against the wall next to the window. He looked exhausted from lack of sleep.

"Acceptable to the Royal family? That excuse is nothing but hippo dung, and you know it!" mother yelled. "They'll follow whatever the Horus priests and the Council advises and that means what you advise. If it's heirs you worry about, then the marriage could be one of convenience only."

"And you, Nubiti, what do you think?" Amka asked, turning only his head in my direction.

Finally it was my turn, just as mother and I had rehearsed. "With all due respect to my mother, I don't think her idea very practical." Amka immediately straightened and turned fully to face me, his eyes alert. He walked toward his chair and sat down with a groan.

"I don't think that my daughter..." Amka raised his staff to silence mother.

"Pray explain your thoughts, my dear," Amka said to me.

"I'm sorry, mother, but to my way of thinking, naming a king from Lower Kem would fly as well as a hippopotamus," I began. "There's no precedent to this and we're a people of rigid traditions. It's an idea fraught with problems." Mother shuffled nervously.

"And so, what is your suggestion?" Amka asked

"I haven't thought it out completely, Amka, but I have an ill-formed idea in my head ever since Wadjet's death. I was going to discuss it with mother first, and if she was in agreement propose it to you. I suppose now's as good a time as any." I picked up my mug, inhaled Amka's foul brew and sipped it, trying not to gag.

"Keep Mery as the titular First Queen. Just appoint three noblemen from Lower Kem to your Council of Advisors and have the lot of you rule as a council of regents, until Zenty comes of age. That way we have at least some input into rule." I sat back, trying to conceal my obvious pleasure in offering such a reasonable solution.

Amka rocked back and forth, his forehead resting on his hands that, in turn, gripped his staff. Finally, he arose slowly and nodded to each of us. "Well done, the both of you," he muttered and I wondered at that moment what he meant by that, whether he was sincere or had seen through our ruse. In any event, within minutes we were in mother's quarters at the rear of the palace. It was only after we entered mother's private bedchamber that she dared speak.

"That son of a whore!" mother said, pacing in her typical agitated manner. "That miserable stuck-up runt. He acts as if he's the King." I allowed her to take a few breaths to calm herself. "Do you think that miserable excuse for a man suspected our act?" she asked.

I grunted. Thoughts of our meeting ran through my mind. "I can't tell for sure, but let's assume he did. If our little act worked we'll hear in a few days regarding our choices for the Council. If not we'll be forced to jump ahead to the next steps in our plan. In any event, I've got to arrange a meeting with Khnum and now we've been given free reign to do it."

My heart skipped a beat thinking of the treacherous path that lay ahead. But it was a journey already begun. Only bold actions carried any hope of Lower Kem regaining its prominence. And with the simple acts of Zenty and Mery suddenly and tragically dead, the route to succession would finally be open to us.

SCROLL EIGHT

Meryt-Neith

Amka tells me not to whine, that it is healthy to grieve, only not too much. Well, how much is too much? Does one's heart suddenly say enough and all sorrow ends, as a priest would snuff out a candle?

I suppose it is Amka's deep faith that allows him to offer those platitudes. He believes with all his heart that we walk this life for only the briefest of time, but that we spend the rest of eternity in the glorious Afterlife, so to him life and death are merely transition times. But to me my grief seems overwhelming and everlasting.

My dear Wadjet has been dead for six ten-day cycles already and almost every day Zenty, my precious little Zenty, asks for him. Amka has explained to him that his father is preparing to live in the glorious Afterlife and he makes it sound so attractive Zenty asks if he can please go with his father.

I know that Amka is right. He seems always right in the end. The rekhi have no time to grieve. Their loved

141

ones die and they quickly bury them in shallow graves in the desert and then go about their work, for without honest work they starve. What gives me the luxury to grieve until my heart is magically healed? Still, I find that I cannot spend enough time with Zenty, playing his toy soldier games, telling him stories, sometimes just picking him up as he naps and holding him as I rock us both to ease my pain. I smell his skin and the unguents in his braid and for brief moments I am transported to the times that Wadjet and I held him and admired with gratitude the blessing that the gods had bestowed upon us.

There is much to be done, even during this period of mourning. As the Horus priests prepare Wadjet's body for his journey, Amka, Ti-Ameny, Herneith, Nubiti and Shepsit and I must decide on who will accompany him. The list of volunteers is a long one and the requests are heartfelt, but we have decided on no more than twenty of his most faithful servants and friends. Amka promises that the poisons he will administer will cause no pain.

But there is another list we consider daily, one that has been vexing us greatly. It is the one provided by Shepsit and Nubiti, with the names of nobles from Lower Kem that they propose be placed on a governing council for the Two Lands. That was the purpose for Amka's visit.

"It is not that the list is without merit," Amka stated as he paced before me while we sat outside in a shaded corner of the veranda. "Nor are the people they recommend incompetent, no indeed. All are known to us and well respected."

"And so?" I asked.

"I will speak with you candidly, Mery," he said, then stopped before me, pushed his chair back and sat down. I could see from his expression that this was to be a serious discussion.

"Mery, I knew your father and ministered to your mother. I helped to birth you. I have faithfully served

142

your husband and your uncle. You know that I am not one prone to overstate matters. But, I tell you now that we face the most serious crisis of my lifetime. Oh, yes, you look surprised, but I would dare to say that this is the most serious crisis to face our lands since King Narmer, may he be exalted forever."

"But, why would you say that? Nubiti's suggestion seems to me to be reasonable. Even you agreed. You just said those they nominated were well respected officials."

"Tssk," Amka hissed through his teeth. Then he leaned back and took a deep breath. "I felt obliged to listen to Shepsit and Nubiti, for to shut them out without a hearing would have been unwise. Allowing your enemies… "

"But they are not my enemies," I objected.

"Yes, well… at the very least we must view them as rivals. And allowing your rivals to air their differences always reveals useful information, my dear." I cringed at Amka's condescending tone, although I realized that he still was able to teach me important lessons.

"In any event," he continued, "there is a far larger issue involved here, Mery, and that is the purpose of this meeting."

"Go ahead."

"On the surface the waters appear smooth, but underneath they roil with malice." With that he sat quietly and, I assumed, smugly in his use of yet another of his obtuse sayings. I willed myself to sit as quietly as did he, but after a moment or two I could stand the silence no longer.

"I assume that by smooth waters you refer to Shepsit's list of names, but I am at a loss to figure what you mean by malice."

"They are one and the same. When poison is masked by wine's sweetness it is all the more dangerous."

"Oh, in the name of Ra, you sometimes infuriate me with those… those… ridiculous sayings of yours!"

Amka smiled at me, then, which served the

purpose of making me even angrier. "Mery, do not allow this part of your ba to surface. A ruler must force herself to be calm even in the face of others' anger or subterfuge or even in the face of her teacher's infuriating sayings." At that we both smiled.

"We Horus priests use sayings to help others remember the greater truths. As you gain more experience in rule you will realize that it is usually not the specifics that matter, for there are always differences from one situation to the next. The important thing to keep in mind is the general principle, and our sayings are our way of teaching those principles."

For a moment I looked back at Amka's teachings and realized that even as a child one of Amka's many sayings would pop into my thoughts when I confronted a seemingly new situation. "I understand your point," I said to him. "I will try to be more patient. Now explain to me how Shepsit's list roils the waters."

Again Amka stood, for he often thought best while he paced to and fro. "The list is irrelevant, although it is much to her credit to offer it as a means to distract us from the more disturbing path I assume she wishes us to walk. What she is suggesting, Mery..."

I could see that Amka was distressed. "Bear with me as I explain this. Using a governing council sounds like a workable solution. Zenty is too young to rule, you are a woman, the Delta is restless, the Palestinians to our east and the Ta-Tjehenus to our west seek to gain advantage. So Shepsit and Nubiti suggest that the Council of Advisors, which has served us well for generations, now take on the role as a regency council until Zenty comes of age."

"And it does sound reasonable to me," I offered.

"And that is why it is so dangerous. It sounds perfectly reasonable. Except for the fact that it is fifteen or twenty years until Zenty comes of age and far too many things might happen before then. But, there is a far, far greater issue at stake here. One that has secretly caused the leaders of the Horus priesthood a great deal of anguish since Shepsit's and Nubiti's bold suggestion."

Amka turned to face me. He placed both hands on his staff and leaned toward me. "Never in the history of Upper Kem, or Lower Kem, has it… have we been without a King. Never. Ma'at has been turned on its head. Certainly since Unification, every King has had an adult son to ascend to the throne. The leaders of the Horus priesthood predict enormous disasters might befall us. Ma'at is built on order and our society is built on ma'at.

"The multitude of rekhi live to support the merchants, priests and scribes, who serve the few nobles who, in turn, serve and are all led by the God-King, son of Horus." Amka bent down and quickly picked up a handful of sand that he sprinkled on the mud brick floor. With his staff he sketched a rectangular block, then a smaller block atop that, then a still smaller one atop that. With that he stepped back and looked from his sketch to me and back again.

"This," he said pointing his staff at his drawing, "is how it has always been and must always be for a people to have a stable society. A land governed by a council will degenerate quickly into squabbles and dissension, bribes and cabals, with no one able to decide, to lead with vision and purpose." With that he drew a larger block atop the structure and even I could see its instability. Suddenly, I could see the truth within Amka's fears of Nubiti's suggestion.

"And with that instability, dear Mery, will come chaos. Evil muts will converge upon us from all sides and from the Underworld. Enemies will be emboldened to attack. Our glorious Kem will surely crumple and be reduced to petty, warring tribes. We will be no better than the Ta-Tjehenus."

Tears filled my eyes as I looked up from Amka's sand drawing. "And… you… you believe in your heart of hearts that this was intentionally proposed by Shepsit and Nubiti for just such a… a diabolical purpose?" I swallowed hard fearing his answer.

Amka gave but the slightest of nods, as if he feared that saying anything at all would let loose the floodgates of pain and sorrow, not only for my recent loss of my husband but for the deeper, more painful loss of my political innocence. Nubiti was my sister, my confidante and, at times, my mentor. To think of her conspiring with Shepsit made me feel sick to my stomach.

I knew that Amka wanted to say more, to discuss with me the status of the deliberations of the leaders of the Horus priesthood. Yet I could bear no more for that day and I dismissed him until the next morning.

Once he had gone, I felt an urgent need to see Zenty and to hold him close and so I sent for Abana. As soon as Zenty saw me he ran into my arms, his sidelock bouncing on his right shoulder. I knew I would need to be careful or I would squeeze the life from his tiny body as I rocked him back and forth to gain strength. I breathed in his sweet smell. In a moment he wriggled free and ran after Basty, his favorite cat. The poor thing allowed herself to be picked up and carried in the most awkward of positions, the front part of her body hanging far down, with Zenty's arms locked tightly under her rear legs. Once Zenty sat on the floor, Basty tried to get away, but Zenty quickly grabbed the cat and flipped it over to stroke its belly.

"Oh, do be careful Zenty. You don't want to hurt poor Basty," I said, coming to sit down next to them. Beams of Ra's warm light shined on us. Together we petted Basty until she began purring loudly, much to Zenty's delight.

Once Abana had put Zenty to bed, I sent for Ti-Ameny, for I felt the need of a woman with whom I could talk and share my sorrows. For nearly two hours we talked, at one point walking along Mother Nile. I poured out my miseries to Ti-Ameny, my feelings of betrayal, my fears of being able to carry the burdens of my station with dignity. And, as always, Ti-Ameny listened without judgment, asking me questions to elucidate my feelings and fears, so that by time I was ready for sleep, I felt as if a great burden had been lifted from my ka. Before she left, Ti-Ameny walked over to me as I sat in my chair, gently cupped my head in her hands and hugged me tenderly to her chest, rocking me ever so slightly from side to side. It felt so heavenly to nestle into her soft breasts, to smell her delicate unguents, to forget my troubles for a few delightful moments and I wondered if what I missed as a child, to have a mother who would hold you close to her breasts, was something I would ever be done with.

A few days later, as I drank my morning herbal tea and nibbled on smoked duck dipped in honey, Amka arrived at my quarters and requested that I accompany him to one of the meeting rooms in the main palace. To my surprise, Tepemkau, the Chief Horus Priest of Nekhen was waiting for us and stood and bowed low to me. The meeting room Amka had chosen could not have been by chance. It was a room within a room, guarded from prying ears and eyes by thick walls. I noted that Amka had stationed two guards at the entrance.

Once we sat down around the smallest table, Amka wasted no time. "My Queen, I thought it best to invite Tepemkau here to participate in our discussion, for his visit to me yesterday, after you and I last met, had to have been guided by Horus himself." I could feel the hairs on my arms rise. Amka nodded to Tepemkau.

"My Queen, the Horus priests… umm, you are aware that they are the eyes and ears of the King in all godly matters related to the Two Lands."

"Spies, in simple language," Amka interjected. Tepemkau blushed deeply.

Tepemkau looked confused, unsure if Amka was joking. "The King is the head of the Two Lands, but a head must have eyes to see and ears to hear and a nose to sniff things out."

"I understand. Go on," I offered, trying to ease Tepemkau's discomfort. As the Chief Priest he was unused to dealing directly with a queen.

"We... by that I mean our priests, are hearing that Shepsit and Nubiti are working hard throughout Kem to advance their idea of a regency council. They are employing Sekhemkasedj to speak with his business contacts. They have given permission for the nobles of Lower Kem to speak loudly in favor of this proposal. Nubiti is secretly using her Isis sisters to place this idea into the hearts of influential women throughout the lands. We fear that unless we act quickly, this idea will take hold and we will be powerless to suggest, or rather to enact, an alternative... to the ascension. The one that we favor, that is."

"An alternative?" I looked toward Amka. "To ascension?"

"I have not had the opportunity to speak with her yet," Amka said. "We were to do so yesterday, but the time passed with other urgent matters."

"Yes, of... of course," Tepemkau stuttered. "I, uh, was not prepared..."

"Here it is, then," Amka said, tapping his staff and standing. "Later I will have the Chief Priest detail for you what Shepsit and Nubiti are up to. But here is the most urgent matter. What the Horus priesthood is suggesting, the alternate plan, is that you ascend to the throne."

Amka said this so matter-of-factly, at first I thought I misheard him. "Who would ascend to the throne?" I asked.

"You," he replied, holding fast to his staff. I was about to laugh, but when I turned from Amka to Tepemkau, I saw that he held his breath. I knew then that I had heard Amka correctly and that this was no joke. I jumped from my chair, my heart racing so hard I had to clutch my chest. My breath suddenly came in short gasps.

"Wh... what are you saying?" I stammered. "Are you possessed by mut spirits? Both of you... are you mad?" I backed away from them, frightened. The hairs on my neck stood up and I felt a cold sweat creep over my body.

To his credit, whether by experience or inspiration from Horus, Amka sat silently, saying nothing, his eyes closed in what appeared to me to be a peaceful repose. Tepemkau just sat there, rigid as a pole, his eyes wide with fright. This gave me time to compose myself, as I paced along the far wall. Finally, I strode back toward Amka and stood before him.

"Amka, tell me what this is about, what this madness is about. I cannot become King, we... we all know that. I am a woman. I am a mother. You know the history of our people far better than do I. You... and you..." I said pointing at Tepemkau, "know the history of our gods better than anyone else in the Two Lands. I... I have never heard of a woman King. It... it is contrary to ma'at. It is... no one will accept this!"

I took a few steps away from Amka, then turned back. "I will not accept this. This is... oh, I don't know... this is absurd, it is folly!" Again, Amka remained silent. "Which is why I do not understand how you, the Vizier and my teacher, and you, the Chief Horus Priest of Nekhen can dare to suggest this!"

I now felt my heart racing and my legs begin to give out from under me and so I sat with a thud in the rush chair beside me. "Explain this to me for Horus' sake!"

For a moment quiet reigned. There was no breeze in the air and the only sounds that were heard were those of the birds in the garden that chirped merrily. As if waking from a dream, Amka slowly released his fingers from his staff and took a long, deep sen-sen breath.

"You are right, my dear Mery. You were always an eager student," he began, his voice barely above a whisper. "I have searched all the sacred papyruses and there is no mention of a woman being King of Upper Kem. There are stories back into our deep past that tell of women shamans leading small tribes that used to roam the land, but even our oldest scribes have not heard in our oral tradition any story of a female ruler of Upper Kem or even a nome of Upper Kem." Amka sounded like a defeated man.

I was so perplexed with this conversation that I thought I must be dreaming or else affected by one of the herbs Ti-Ameny had given me after Wadjet's death. I felt jittery, like I wanted to run from the room.

"And yet, our history is equally clear that rule by one man, and one only, is the way of ma'at, the path to stability and prosperity and might. So you might imagine the difficulties our current situation has presented to the Horus priesthood, for the Kingship derives from Horus. The King is Horus' son, the god-King incarnate."

"How, then, can you even consider...?" I started to ask.

"The answer comes from the gods themselves," Tepemkau responded. "Did not Isis help Osiris to rule? Did she not gather his parts together after he was dismembered by Seth so that his reincarnated self could live forever in the Afterlife?"

"Yes, and more to the point, my dear Mery," Amka continued, "is your namesake, Neith. She births Ra in the sky every morning and receives him in the evening. She was the first god to emerge from Nun, the ether, the Void of Nothingness. From her sprang all the other gods, including Osiris and Isis and their son, Horus." I listened, frightened yet fascinated, for Amka helped me to revisit my childhood lessons but now with the added perspective of an adult.

"As a practical matter women manage large households, run temples and own their own businesses in Kem. And there is another issue, Mery, one that is so deep in the teachings of the priesthood of Horus that I can only begin to give you a taste of it's meaning, for it is not taught except to the most worthy and experienced priests." I noted that Tepemkau nodded to Amka to continue.

"Men and women each have qualities of the other within their kas. Even their bas reflect this duality, for sometimes a woman becomes as angry as a man and at other times a man can be as gentle and nurturing as a woman. Nowhere is this more of a reflection of the gods than in Neith, your namesake. Yes, she is the Creator goddess, but also the warrior huntress, the fiercest protector of women and children. That is why many of her statues show her holding a shield and a bow and arrows. So..."

"I see your point," I interrupted, "but even if I may possess certain characteristics of the male ba, it does not make me able to be King. Nor, even if I were able, would I want such an exalted position."

Amka turned then to Tepemkau, the bags under his eyes so drooped he radiated a profound sadness. He bowed his head for just a moment, then looked directly into my eyes. He sighed deeply and said simply the words that changed my life forever. "Mery, you do not have a choice in this matter. None of us do."

And so it was that over the next many days, Amka and Tepemkau persuaded, cajoled, argued and educated me to the need for my ascension to the throne of the Red lands of the deserts and the Black lands of Mother Nile's Delta. There are many events in my life that I can barely recall, significant ones that by all rights should be nearly as clear to me as the day they occurred. Even the incident with that foul-smelling rekhi when I was but a child is nothing more than a vague recollection, more a feeling than a vision. But of those days spent with Amka and Tepemkau, days filled with argument and deep teachings, of resistance and meditation, of understanding and finally acceptance, it is as if my senses were heightened to their highest. I recall every moment, every passage from the holy texts they read me, every facial expression on those two. I can still feel my heart filled with emotions, the depths of which I had not to that point experienced.

And there was yet more, for during those days I truly lost my innocence. In that period I learned the truth about my sister, Nubiti, and her scheming mother and it changed me in ways that I could not have imagined. It hardened my heart. With Amka's help I learned how to build a wall around me to shield my vulnerabilities and I began to do so. It required of the three of us that we create a new model of communication and that I rethink how I would use the people around me to support my differing needs as a woman, mother and ruler.

I left immediately afterward with Amka and Tepemkau, Abana and Zenty and Ti-Ameny on a three-day voyage up Mother Nile to Nekhen. I loved those times with Zenty, sailing and rowing under Horus' blue skies, passing verdant fields planted with flax and wheat, the distant red and blue mountains rising to meet Horus from the desert floor. We floated on Mother Nile's back, with nothing to distract me from fulfilling Zenty's needs. We told each other stories and laughed so much together my stomach sometimes hurt. One of the King's guards fished with Zenty every day and the first time my little one happily caught a perch he cried mightily when the guard slit its head and gutted it. Even that ended as a joyful experience, for Zenty ran to my arms, crying, buried his head in my chest and cuddled until he fell asleep under Ra's disk. Oh, how I treasured those times together.

Yet those times also allowed me time to think and the more I did, the more frightened I became, and the harder my heart beat within my chest. Djet was not here with me. I felt his presence looking out upon us from the Afterlife, but my rock, the man trained to lead Kem since his birth, no longer sat upon the throne. Could I walk even a step in his sandals? Just the thought of that caused me to shiver in fear.

Once we arrived in Nekhen, the pace of life changed and I hardly had time to think even for a moment. In the oldest and holiest of temples in all of Kem, the Temple of Horus, Tepemkau had arranged a series of events that would ultimately lead to my ascension as King, albeit as a regent until Zenty came of age. There were rituals and cleansings, readings and incantations, medicinals and spells all designed to reveal to the Horus priesthood my suitability for my ascension to the throne.

There was a humorous aspect to these preparations, albeit the subject of long and serious discussions among Tepemkau, Amka and Ti-Ameny. That subject was the issue of my circumcision, for it was the custom of all who served Horus, whether priests or Kings, to be ritually cleansed and circumcised. For days the three debated what circumcision might mean in the case of a woman and the debates often became arguments and even shouting matches.

"Yes, I can see the priests demanding that this must be done. They have always been the ones to circumcise the new King," Tepemkau mused.

"With deep respect, Tepemkau," Ti-Ameny said, nodding her head ever so slightly. "But I don't give a donkey's ass what your priests want. Not one of them will touch the Queen. Besides, in your infinite wisdom of the woman's body, can you explain to me exactly what it is you would circumcise?"

Tepemkau blushed a deep purple. He was about to attempt an answer, but Amka spoke up.

"Yes, yes, yes, you each have a good argument. Tepemkau, may I suggest that... at least my position is that the Queen is, shall we say, already circumcised... as a practical matter, I mean... if... if you understand my intent?" Tepemkau stared at the floor and nodded vigorously.

Then Amka turned to Ti-Ameny. "Perhaps you could... what I mean is in order to appease those priests who are more insistent, of course... perhaps you could make a light cut... no?... or maybe bring a drop of menstrual blood which... with the proper ceremony, of course, we could say represents something similar to the blood of circumcision, if you understand..."

"Done," Ti-Ameny said with considerable distaste, but she was not going to pursue a point she had already won.

In the end, unwilling to challenge Amka and Tepemkau, the priests determined that I was already

revealed as the leader of Kem and that the gods had
played out the events of recent years to just such a
purpose. Further, those priests who were also seers
promised that I would have an uneventful reign, that
Kem would prosper greatly under my regency and that
Zenty would become the greatest King to ever rule.

Ti-Ameny, too, had predictions, for as a priestess
of Isis her gift of seeing was revealed when she was still
but a child. However, Ti-Ameny was reluctant to share
her visions with any of the Horus priests, most especially
Amka. The two fought almost constantly while we were
in Nekhen and it was only many years later that I found
out the true reason for their conflict. Ti-Ameny's visions
were troubling, far more so for what she learned about
herself than for what they revealed about my rule.

That many of the Horus priests' rosy visions
would prove untrue would come later, in tragedies
beyond my imagining, but for now those predictions fed
upon themselves and word spread quickly throughout
the land that I was to become regent as soon as Wadjet
was buried. The reaction in the Royal Court was
immediate and the opposition led by Shepsit and Nubiti
was furious. My refusal to give them an audience during
this time only fueled their anger.

Six days after my return to Inabu-hedj, Wadjet was
buried in a simple ceremony. Fewer than twenty-five
thousand people came to the funeral. Amka and the
priests felt that keeping the numbers down would be
prudent, especially as Inabu-hedj was right at the border
with Lower Kem. By now I was accustomed to Wadjet's
passing so that the part of the ceremony that pained me
most was watching his loyal servants buried with him in
a series of unadorned tombs surrounding his funerary
enclosure. But I was also comforted knowing that they
would accompany him to the Afterlife and serve his
needs throughout eternity and thus bring honor to their
descendents.

With Wadjet's body now joined with his ka, Kem
was finally free to go about its business. Against the

background of this renewed energy, Amka called together his Council of Advisors and informed them of the plans to have me serve as Regent. I arranged an emergency meeting of the Council of Nomes for two days after Wadjet's burial, but I did not attend that meeting. Instead Amka and Tepemkau told the governors of my regency and implored their support during these unsettled times.

"We find it both peculiar and interesting that none of the governors from Lower Kem asked a question or challenged the decision," Tepemkau reported afterward.

"What do you make of that?" I asked Amka.

"It is a dangerous situation," Amka suggested, "for it confirms in my heart that Shepsit and Khnum have already set their plot in motion with the representatives and demons from Lower Kem."

"How should we react?"

Amka sat silently for a moment. "We have anticipated this and our recommendation is for you to immediately send Herihor into Lower Kem with a division of soldiers on some pretext, just as a show of your power, perhaps coupled with some land grants for Khnum to divide amongst his most loyal princes. It is a matter of fruits and mace heads."

"But I cannot yet order Herihor to do anything, not until I am made regent."

Amka turned to Tepemkau. "My Queen, we are planning that as we speak," the elderly priest said. "Our desire is to do this immediately, before Shepsit's and Nubiti's pot boils over."

"When?"

"On the tenth day following Wadjet's burial."

I looked at Amka, thinking that he would correct the Chief Priest's obvious error. Instead, Amka just sat there, saying nothing.

"But... but that is a mere seven days away!" I said, incredulous.

"There is no time to waste," Amka said. "We will begin the purification process with you this evening. It will last until the day prior to your ascension."

"But..."

"The timing is fortuitous," Amka continued, "for you had your womanly flows eight days ago. Also, as we've already discussed, you do not require circumcision, which would take several ten-day cycles to heal. In this case haste is on our side, for then Shepsit and Khnum will be caught off guard and will not be able to react quickly enough. We have told no one of this decision."

My purifications went uneventfully, all supervised by Ti-Ameny. Each day I was given a concoction of herbs with which I was to internally cleanse my female parts. Each herbal brew was linked to a favored god or goddess. However, on one matter I had a change of heart. I convinced Ti-Ameny to make a tiny cut, just enough to draw blood, in the skin above my pleasure center, so that the holy men, defending my honor and legitimacy, could claim I was indeed circumcised.

Amka and Tepemkau rehearsed parts of the ceremony with me every day, sometimes twice, so that by time seven days were up I knew every detail of what was to happen. On the day before the coronation ceremony Amka and Ti-Ameny presented me with three benben seeds, crushed into a tea and mixed with honey. I innocently drank the concoction and within an hour felt the most violent cramps I had ever before experienced. Thankfully, Ti-Ameny was by my side and rushed me to the bathroom, where I stayed for the next six hours. As quickly as I defecated, Ti-Ameny forced me to drink copious amounts of water, although I could not understand the sense in that since I was certain I would die anyway. But as quickly as the cramps had started they suddenly ended and my insides were thus fully purified.

Before Ra's rising on the morning of the ascension I was awakened and given a strong herbal tea prepared by Ti-Ameny under Amka's direction. They explained it would relax me enough to withstand the demands of the day, as I would not be allowed anything to eat until after the coronation. Ti-Ameny and two assistants then bathed me in the most fragrant water I had ever experienced. Between the herbs and the delicious, spicy and floral scents, all I wanted to do was lay in the water the entire day, inhaling the intoxicating aromas.

I was then dressed in my Queen's clothing, an elegant fine linen gown, gold jewelry and a small gold crown, through which my hair was woven so that it nearly disappeared into my hairstyle. My nails were done in lush red coloring and my makeup artfully applied so that it was not overbearing. My room was a beehive of activity, the women servants, the priestesses, the artisans all talking, laughing, telling stories to one another. Every so often Ti-Ameny would call out for everyone to calm their bas, but her admonishment would last for only a few moments and once again the cackling would rise.

Finally in the minutes before Ra was again born from Neith's womb, all was ready. A line of Horus priests sounded their ram's horns and I was ushered onto the balcony of the palace to witness his life-giving presence and to thank him for his blessings. As the shadows created by Ra's light began to play over the mountains and valleys below us, I at first could not make out what it was that I observed. Soon Ra had risen enough to illuminate the valley and I noted with amazement what it was that I witnessed. It was a seething mass of my people such as I had never before seen. I had been so secluded during the purification process, I had no idea what it was that Amka, Tepemkau and their subordinates had prepared. Here before me were tens of thousands of Kemians, stretching from foothill to foothill and from mountain to Mother Nile, all eager to catch a glimpse of their Queen and to share in her blessing of them under Ra's golden light.

When I was done with the blessings, a great cheer went up from the crowd and the sound of it sent chills through my body. Whether chills of fear or exhilaration I was uncertain, but I had no time to think on it anyway. I was immediately taken out through the opposite side of the palace to begin the procession, for unless we adhered to Amka's rigid schedule, the spiritual significance of the ceremony would be compromised and only Amka and the Horus priests knew beforehand what that significance was.

No sooner had I exited the palace than another shock nearly overwhelmed me. Yes, Amka had described to me the next steps, but none could have prepared me for the sight of Herihor, dressed in his finest military clothing, standing at the head of what appeared to be an unending double line of soldiers, stretching from the palace stairs up to the Temple of Horus. Next to Herihor stood Panahasi, a general like Herihor but considerably older and next in line to become the Chief of the Army. Panahasi, a well-respected leader, had allowed age to win the war of his girth, so that as he stood squatly in the road he gave the appearance of a fierce hippopotamus. I almost smiled at the contrast he presented with the muscular Herihor.

At my appearance Herihor stood ready to give his order for his men to stand to attention, but no words came from his mouth. Instead he stared at me intently, his eyes moving over me as if he studied me for one of Amka's notorious tests. So long did he stare that Amka tipped his staff toward Panahasi and the old bull called out loudly to his men. They snapped to attention with their spears and shields, one pair after another, so that it took minutes for the line of soldiers to complete the maneuver far in the distance at the Temple's steps.

With the soldiers at attention, more horns were sounded and Herihor approached and bowed low before me, embarrassing me because he was my husband's finest warrior and one of his closest friends. Panahasi also bowed, but his girth prevented him from doing anything more than a slight dip of his head. As the two men rose, they each held one of my hands and escorted me to my gold-edged carry chair. I was lifted high by servants dressed in pure white and themselves ritually purified. With an order from Herihor, his men crossed spears and hooked their legs so as to control the throng of people pressing in on all sides.

With musicians surrounding us playing flutes and strings and drums, and dancers rattling their sistras before and behind us, we ever so slowly made our way up the main avenue of Inabu-hedj, a wide promenade that linked the palace with the Temples. Aside from people packed into the streets, observers were crushed together standing on the top of the white walls of the city. I heard later than more than a few had fallen and injured themselves, although none died. As the procession advanced, people shouted out praises and blessings and their wishes for my intercession to heal their sons and daughters, parents and friends. People threw flower petals of all colors before us, so that the ground was thick with them, rising even above the ankles of my carriers. As the petals were crushed their fragrances, all mixed together in the still air, soon became overwhelming.

When we finally reached the steps of the Temple of Horus, some two hours later, Tepemkau held up his staff and the crowd of people surrounding us hushed. The heat had risen and bordered on being uncomfortable and Ra's light was reflected from Tepemkau's bald head.

"Queen Mery-Neith," he called out as loudly as decorum allowed, "the Horus priesthood welcomes you to our holy temple, where the ka of Horus lives within his statues. He awaits your presence." With that, Tepemkau pointed toward the temple. A small statue of Horus stood atop the roof, his wings outstretched and his eyes peering down at us.

If it were at all possible, I would have turned around and run back to the palace at that moment, such is how the thought of Horus dwelling within the walls of the Temple affected me. At that moment I also wished that Ti-Ameny stood next to me to support me through what I knew lay ahead. But Amka and Tepemkau had decided that with Nubiti being the Head Priestess of the

Temple of Isis, it would be better to keep the Isis priestesses out of the ceremony entirely. I supported that decision since I had no inclination to see Nubiti until I felt grounded in my new position as Regent. I knew Ti-Ameny did not mind not participating for she had heard rumors about Shepsit's machinations and did not feel comfortable mixing her roles as my personal healer with that of an Isis priestess. And so she waited for me back at the palace and supervised all arrangements for the celebrations to follow.

Panahasi, our most senior military commander, and Herihor, his equal but in age, stepped forward and helped me down from the chair. They escorted me, one on each side, up the steps to join Tepemkau, with Amka right behind me. Tepemkau raised his hands and blessed me with the finger blessing of the Horus priests, his hands straight out, his fingers parted into a V shape. I bent my head to accept the blessing and with that we entered the temple itself, leaving Herihor and Panahasi outside.

Inside the temple it was far cooler than outside. Tepemkau called for water and I quenched my thirst with Mother Nile's sweet essence. As we walked down a dark corridor past each small statue of Horus we stopped for a prayer. When we had walked nearly around the entire building an immense wooden doorway stood before us, intricately carved from Lebanese cedar.

Tepemkau called for a sandal bearer to approach. The young boy trembled as he removed my sandals, one by one, and washed my feet, never looking at my face. Only then did Tepemkau call for his priests to open the vaulted doors and as they opened before me the pungent smells of incense filled my lungs. Yet the aromas were far different from those I had experienced at the Temple of Isis. Here the smells were more earthy, as if the priests were burning hay and soil fresh from Inundation.

Even with the doors wide open I could see nothing inside, for before us was a tall wall. There was a fire of some sort inside, for the walls flickered with an orange glow. I was immediately struck by fear, for no one that I knew save King Djer, King Wadjet, Amka and Tepemkau, and most certainly no woman, had ever entered the inner sanctum of Horus.

Amka and Tepemkau had also had their sandals removed and feet washed, for no one entered the inner sanctum without cleansing. The three of us took a few steps to our right and stood there as the immense doors swung shut.

"Queen Mery-Neith, we are about to enter the sanctuary of Horus," Tepemkau said softly. "Be not afraid, though Horus is a mighty god, for your heart is as light as a feather. But do not look directly into his eyes until you are instructed to do so."

I still trembled in fear and anticipation and despite the heat felt chilled. "It will be alright, Mery," Amka whispered in my ear as he squeezed my hand tight. I looked at him in the dim light and his face appeared worried. I gave him a slight smile and he leaned over and kissed my forehead. "It is time," he said.

I noted that the floor was sprinkled with newly raked sand, so that our feet left fresh footprints that indicated our presence. With Tepemkau in the lead and Amka by my side, we walked around the wall and stepped into the inner sanctuary. To this day I still shake in awe at my first sight of the mighty Horus for there, with his side facing me, he towered. Oh, Neith, did he tower! He stood in human form with his falcon head, his arms hanging powerfully at his sides. The way he was positioned, one foot forward of the other, made me feel he was about to turn to face us. I gasped.

Amka grabbed my upper arm and held me firmly until my sight adjusted. Horus was easily ten cubits high. His body was carved of black stone and his face was made of pure gold. Although I dared not look directly at his face, I knew with utter certainty that his ka resided within. Horus looked real enough so that I wanted to scream and run from the sanctuary. But I held my ground and breathed the sen-sen breaths, as I was taught, all the while thankful for Amka's support.

In front of Horus a brazier fire burned on a metal stand that was used for offerings. As the light from the flames flickered over his body, Horus appeared to move. I could not draw a deep breath, so in trepidation was I of this spectacle of his spiritual power.

Tepemkau turned his back to Horus and called me to him. "Queen Mery-Neith, you are born of royal blood, for your mother was the sister of Djer, King of all Kem. Your ka was joined with King Wadjet's and you carried his seed and birthed Zenty, his heir, the future King of Kem.

"We are here together under the watchful eye of Horus, the Eye of Truth, to determine if you are worthy to serve as King of Kem until Zenty comes of age. What do you say to mighty Horus? Will you look him in his eyes and tell him you are worthy, for he is ready to render judgment in this matter."

Never in my life had I been so frightened, not even as a child trapped in the bushes by that horrid rekhi laborer. Slowly my eyes lifted and swept upward and upward toward Horus' face. I remember every detail, even today, his chest so muscular, his face that of a powerful falcon. And then I looked into his eyes.

People will tell you how a person's eyes reveal much of his ba. I have heard priests say that they can even see a glimpse of a man's ka through his eyes. I would have to agree with these observations for I myself have experienced this in my dealings with my people. But that is only true for mere mortals.

What happened when I gazed into Horus' eyes that day in the inner sanctuary can never be explained and Amka later warned me against even trying to do so for fear of Horus' retribution. And I agree with that, although I believe the far greater danger lay in trivializing the moment. For later Amka told me that the experience lasted only a few moments, but of that I know differently. No, the time that I spent looking into Horus' eyes lasted a lifetime, for Horus also gazed through my eyes deep into my ka.

I vaguely remember Tepemkau standing in front of me as I whispered to Horus that I believed I was worthy to assume the kingship of Kem. I recall Tepemkau raising his arms and the fire behind me bursting forth with renewed vigor, brightening Horus' eyes as they penetrated me and mingled with my ka.

But to say that I was worthy of ruling Kem was the foolhardy statement of a young girl buoyed up by two very wise and devious men. Oh, I do not blame my dear Amka and brave Tepemkau for putting me up to this. I know now that what they did was right in their eyes and only the gods may judge whether it was right in theirs. But there is no doubt in my mind that at that very moment I was hardly worthy of governing our mighty nation. Much blood would be spilled and heartaches endured before I was truly worthy of serving the Two Lands.

And so, once Horus' all-knowing eyes penetrated me and after Amka awakened me gently from the trance the falcon god placed upon me, Mother Nile's sweet waters refreshed me again. We performed the ceremony of the Apis bull and after he was slain Tepemkau examined its still beating heart and found it strong, a good omen for my rule. In an adjoining room I washed myself of the blood from the bull and changed into clothes that had been prepared for me.

Back in Horus' sanctuary, Tepemkau greeted me. The entire sanctuary had been scrubbed clean of the blood of the Apis bull and fresh sand sprinkled upon the floor. "You entered this temple as Queen Mery-Neith," Tepemkau began. "You have been judged by Horus to be worthy of assuming the throne for your son until he comes of age. Under the Eye of Truth, Vizier Amka and I attest to Horus' judgment. From now on you will be known as Meryt-Neith for Meryt is the male form of your name. You will reign as Regent until King Zenty ascends to be King of the Two Lands."

Amka stepped forward and placed the gold

breastplate of the King upon my chest. Then Tepemkau handed me the crook and flail and crossed my hands into the proper position. With the two of them leading the way, we exited the sanctuary and walked to the rear of the Temple. Now Zenty, who was dressed in a headscarf woven with gold thread and a pure white linen kilt, joined us. Upon his feet were bejeweled sandals and around his little bicep was a gold armband with King Narmer's serekh. Chains of finely crafted gold hung from his neck. Amka carried Zenty until we reached the great doors.

"Mama!" Zenty shrieked as the massive doors swung open to reveal a restless crowd of two hundred thousand or more of my people spread across the valley floor. Zenty reached for me and my heart longed to hold him and together face this frightening scene. But Amka spoke reassuringly to him and soon Zenty was distracted by Amka's ornately carved staff.

I was surprised to see Ra nearly finished with his daily journey across the heavens. Long shadows from the surrounding mountains fell across the valley floor. Thus, by time the day had ended I had greeted Ra as Queen Mery-Neith and blessed his parting as King Meryt-Neith. In that manner, our plan had so far succeeded and none but simpletons, and certainly not my most vociferous opponents, would have lost the significance of the arc of my ascension.

SCROLL NINE

Nubiti

It was Shomu of the fourth year of Meryt-Neith's reign and it was the worst year yet of poor flooding and poorer still harvests. The oppressive heat of Shomu lay upon the land like a suffocating blanket. The only saving grace was that since Mother Nile had withheld her life-giving mud, the humidity was not as high as it otherwise would have been, but that was meager consolation, indeed. We were fast approaching Heriu-renpet, the five sacred days that preceded the New Year's celebrations of Wepet-renpet. Heriu-renpet is always a time of reflection and prayer, of terrible fear and desperate offerings, for who knows what the gods have planned for us in the New Year? One thing was certain; this year Heriu-renpet would be a time of extreme anxiety.

Like the three prior years, Wepet-renpet would not be one of celebration. Farmers were destitute. Children across the land would receive nothing more than a few pitiful toys pieced together from reeds by their grandfathers instead of fancy imported wood senet games bought from traders. Or they would receive verbal promises of more abundant celebrations once Mother Nile finally took pity on her people and gave us abundant floods.

Throughout the land, the rekhi suffered the most for they had the fewest resources from which to draw. Meryt-Neith's food granaries were ample at first to stave off widespread hunger, but those stores lasted for only two years. Last year was the first where malnourishment was everywhere. I could hardly walk to the temple without seeing poor rekhi squatting in alleyways, holding out their hands and silently staring at me with bulging, vacant eyes and even larger bulging stomachs. Cats were gaunt, for even mice were scarce since their food supply of grain was gone. Women flocked to the Temple seeking Isis' intervention, but without even a modest flood we were powerless to prevent undernourished women from dying in childbirth. Breasts no longer produced milk and children failed to thrive. Everywhere one looked people lay about conserving their strength during the hottest parts of Shomu, whispering about the curse that had settled upon the land.

The first Akhet after Meryt-Neith assumed the throne, no one thought much of the poor flooding. In fact, she was praised greatly by the governors for her foresight in building more granaries in each nome. But after the second poor harvest, when the grains had to be stringently rationed, people began to murmur that perhaps the gods were angry after all that a woman served as King, even if as Regent. After the third Akhet, in which Mother Nile barely flowed over her embankments, people complained bitterly and turned to drastic measures. Executions for stealing were commonplace. Bribery and corruption were everywhere.

It was after the third Akhet that mother and I did what we could to encourage the rumors about the gods being angry with Mery's regency. Yet I had to guard against encouraging these rumors too much, for although it was Mother Nile who brought us our life-sustaining soil, all knew that it was Isis who determined how fertile the soil was.

Due to the demands that women throughout the Two Lands made upon our priestesses- for prayers for healthy children, for food to feed their families- I traveled widely during these difficult times. I was often accompanied by a small contingent of King's troops, so that I could distribute food, herbs and medicines through our temples in an orderly manner. But these trips also gave me the chance to meet with supervisors in the civil service and gauge whether or not they were receptive to bribes. More often than not they were, and I would signal mother, who then would use her loyalists to seal the deal. In that way we were able to siphon off significant stores of grain to the Delta to use as incentives for those loyal to our cause.

Those excursions brought me to the Delta frequently, presenting me with opportunities to occasionally visit with my allies. Thus it transpired that I was in Dep during the sacred days of Heriu-renpet, drinking wine with Khnum on one of the boats in his fleet.

"Ah, how I look forward to these midnight sails with you, my lovely niece," Khnum said before he tipped back his cup, revealing the unkempt underside of his goatee. "Now that you live in Upper Kem, you bring such refinement to us miscreants," he added, laughing. The full moon reflected off his remaining front teeth. Gulls rose from the water as we sailed past and screeched their collective displeasure at us.

"And, so, where do you stand today with our plans?" I asked.

"Ever the businesswoman," Khnum responded, shaking his head, and I could not tell if he teased me or was serious. "Yes, yes, I know how little time we have."

The captain shouted an order to the boat nearest ours and in a flurry of activity all three ships came about, the reed bundles groaning against the sudden shift in load.

"In fact, we do well, my niece, very well, indeed. Many of the businessmen who had become cozy with the Royal Court in Inabu-hedj, are now seeing the light. Profits are down, contracts from the King or Queen or whatever she is today, are scarce. Every day we receive donations for our cause."

"They willingly part with their money? I find that hard to believe."

"Oh, I wish it were as noble as that. They do give willingly, not so much for the cause as... well, is anything simple nowadays? Ever since Unification, the rules have changed. No longer is governing a simple matter. Not that it ever was simple, but now there are layers upon layers, cloaks within cloaks, spies everywhere we turn.

"But, back to your question. The businessmen do give us money, but it arrives in waves, like the tides. One prominent businessman meets, shall I say... an untimely death due to his lack of cooperation with us and suddenly his associates see the light and come knocking on our doors, pleading their loyalty, their former allegiances to Inabu-hedj a misunderstanding on our parts, bless their light hearts." I had to smile at Khnum's manner of expression.

"How great is their support?" I asked.

"That's relative, my dear. After Narmer cleansed the Delta of our loyalists, we've slowly and painfully built our network of supporters. With the drought, disaffection grows and it's easier to recruit, but we are still not to where we need to be. Kem is a vast country. Our treasury has increased sufficiently so that we're able to undertake certain... hmmm, ventures, strategic ones that will bear much fruit in the years to come."

"Don't be so vague, Uncle. I've shared with you what's happening in the Royal Court. I need you to be as revealing to me."

"Of course!" Khnum replied as if I had insulted him. "I've saved this information for our face-to-face meetings, for I don't trust them to even my most reliable messengers." He sipped from his cup before continuing.

"I've sent a secret delegation to Kush to enlist one of the Ta-Sety kings to our service." I was so shocked at Khnum's words, I nearly choked on my wine and had to put down my cup to face Khnum directly.

"What? Has the drought made you mad? That was never in our plans."

Again Khnum smiled. "Even the best plans must take advantage of providence, Nubiti. And once the opportunity presented itself, we'd have been fools to pass it up."

"What's to be gained from creating alliances on our southern border? There's so much to do here. We can't afford the time or treasure to be distracted."

"An alliance with the Ta-Setys is no distraction," Khnum stated. "It may prove critical. Think of it, Nubiti. As pressures against the rulers in Inabu-hedj increase from here they will undoubtedly respond with force. They have a mighty, well-trained army. We keep only lightly armed men in each nome to keep the rekhi in line or to kick an abusive husband out of the house."

"And so we must train an army in secret. That's what I thought we were focusing on, and at the right moment send them in open rebellion."

"Nubiti, that'll never work. This has never been about armed conflict, not at this stage. Now it's about bribery and cabals. Open rebellion will happen only at the last moments of our victory, when the middle class and the rekhi have already convinced themselves that we'll win anyway. No, the gods have given us a new opportunity to aid our cause."

"Then explain it to me," I said, picking up on Khnum's enthusiasm.

"If Meryt-Neith sends the army here to sit on us we can still function. But if at some point, the powers in Inabu-hedj convince Meryt-Neith that we are to be crushed, there's nothing we can do to defend ourselves. Unless… unless we have a way to relieve that pressure."

It was then that I began to see the wisdom in Khnum's strategy.

"Were Meryt-Neith about to bring down the Army upon us, we'd call upon our alliance with the Ta-Setys to invade from the south," Khnum finished, using his hands for emphasis.

"An invasion? But… but no one has ever dared to invade the Two Lands. Skirmishes, yes. Raids, yes. The Ta-Tjehenus are hated for that, but the Upper Kemians tolerate it. But inviting an invasion from a foreign power would bring down the wrath of the gods."

At this Khnum let out a hearty laugh. "And who do you think encourages the Ta-Tjehenus to raid? We've done so for generations as a tool against the power of the Land of the Lotus. Have the gods punished us any more than the Upper Kemians who dominate and humiliate us?

"No, the Ta-Setys have a passion for gold rivaled only by our own. Those black muts worship the metal. For the rights to a few of our mines in the eastern desert, they would happily sacrifice every one of their firstborn sons. And my sources report they are fierce warriors."

I hung down my head, feeling like I sat naked before Isis as she peered into my heart, which now pounded in my chest. And yet…

"It's not as if we would call for such a distasteful action unless we were threatened, and even then only if we're truly desperate. But to have the sources of the Royal family's gold threatened by the Ta-Setys in the south would mean that any army troops sent against us in the north would have to be either diluted to deal with that other menace or moved there in its entirety if the Ta-Setys are the warriors we think they are."

"And if we do that? If we bring in the Ta-Setys, what then? Haven't we then surrendered some of our sacred land? Haven't we violated our most precious gift?" I was too shocked by the thought to sit still. I stood up and the boat rocked slightly.

"Sit back down, Nubiti. Your silhouette might tip

off any of the King's spies who are feeling particularly vigilant tonight. We're sailing close to shore." I quickly obeyed my uncle.

"In any event, I want you to attend an event tomorrow evening, so that you may see how eager our businessmen, even some of Amka's priests are to aid our cause."

I thought for a moment. "Tomorrow's impossible. There's an installation ceremony at the temple that'll take the entire night."

"For the life of me I can't understand what goes on in your temples that takes the entire night. From what I've heard, though, there is singing and dancing and… much more enjoyable pursuits." At that, I thought I saw my uncle wink at me.

"I could meet with you the next night," I offered, avoiding his baseless remark. "The priestesses will be retiring early due to the festivities."

"The next night it is, then," he said, finishing the wine in his cup. With that he waved his hand and the captain came about and headed back to shore.

Despite the long night spent initiating three new priestesses, I was eager to see what Khnum had planned for me. I had never had the opportunity to see his people in action and I thought it best to see how he operated, for if I learned one thing well from Shepsit it was to judge people by their actions, not their words.

Three hours after Ra had set in the sky, I heard the familiar knock under my window and scurried out. But instead of heading toward the shore, my escorts gave me a rekhi robe to dress in, the actual garment that smelled like it had never been washed. Its course linen irritated my skin as I slipped it over my own priestess robe. I used a kerchief to subdue the stench and put a scarf over my hair and face.

We walked the city's alleys, once passing a group of Army soldiers. When we got close my escorts feigned drunkenness and treated me as if I were a rekhi whore and the soldiers merely laughed and we passed without incident. But as soon as we turned a corner I quickly removed the men's hands and they immediately understood my intent. We hurried along in silence.

In a few more minutes we were at the edge of Dep, at a huge house owned by one of Khnum's cousins, Neben, a fisherman who it turned out owned the boats in which we held our surreptitious meetings. The house sat atop a small rise not far from the edge of Wadj-Wer. Although it was dark, I heard the waves gently breaking against the shore. A watch had been posted for our arrival, for as soon as we approached the door it opened and we were ushered in.

For some reason I had expected the interior to be dark and was surprised to find it well lit. Many men circulated throughout the room, giving the appearance of a celebration of some sort. I noted a few men clustered in one corner of the room, their sackcloth robes a dead giveaway. They were in whispered discussion with one of my other uncles, and I could only imagine how much gold was about to be passed from my uncle to these Horus priests. The rest of the guests stood around drinking beer and wine and eating figs and fruits and cheeses and stuffed fish. I started to take off my cloak, but the man to my right stayed my hand. Instead, he and his fellow escort each took me by an arm and pushed me through the crowd to a rear door. In a moment we were outside again and heading for the shore.

Ahead I could make out the silhouettes of a line of fishing boats bobbing up and down in the water. However, just before we reached the shore, we turned sharply left. In the dark I was confused, for we headed directly into the hill upon which Khnum's cousin's house stood. Only once we actually entered, did I see a dim candle and realize that this was the storage shed for Neben's fishing nets and equipment. There, before me, was Khnum.

"Greetings, dear niece," he said, for the first time not flashing me a smile upon our greeting. I peeled off my hood and nodded toward him. With that he dismissed my two escorts, who bowed at the waist to Khnum and me. They took up positions as watchmen outside.

"Tonight you'll witness something that not many Kemians have." At this he gave a hoarse laugh. "Prepare yourself for a powerful ceremony, daughter of Isis, led by none other than Bakht himself."

Once I heard that name, a chill ran through my body. I thought to ask questions of my uncle, but the rising sound of chanting voices stilled my tongue. Khnum took two steps to the side and revealed a thick wooden door. He motioned for me to follow him, opened the door and we both stepped through.

The room, dug into the side of the hill, was surprisingly large, lit by candles on stands mounted high upon the walls. The shape of the room was unusual. It was round. A group of perhaps twenty men dressed in dark robes stood in a circle around the room, chanting in a tone so low I knew that I would never be able to join in. The very air pulsed heavily with their sound, as it ebbed and flowed with some unseen energy force. The very candles seemed to flicker with life.

As soon as we entered, the circle opened to allow in Khnum, who gestured for me to stand behind him. It was then that I laid eyes on Bakht, standing opposite us. He was dressed in a black robe, the hood pulled up, his eyes closed as he chanted. He leaned on his staff and swayed slightly. In the center of the circle a fire burned in a deep pit and I noted that the room was already warm. Sweat began to appear above my lip.

The air in the room was thick with the smell of men, a pungent, musky odor that assaulted my senses and made it difficult to breathe, temporarily disorienting me. But I was quickly snapped back to reality when a drum began to beat slowly. Every few beats the tones of the chanting shifted slightly. I closed my eyes and I experienced something I had never before. The sounds and rhythms felt like I was being carried by a wave, propelled through the water by a powerful force, up and down, yet ever forward.

Now the chanting changed again and I heard a series of guttural sounds coming from Bakht. The sounds shifted yet again and he spoke words that were obviously some sort of prayer, but in a mysterious language unknown to me. The men around the circle chanted as he spoke, then stepped toward the fire. Now I recognized that Bakht prayed to Apep. In a flash, he threw off his robe, standing in the circle with nothing but a loincloth. He pointed his long, muscled arms toward the ground, summoning the serpent demon from the Underworld. Soon a black, curling smoke rose from the fire pit, creating such fervor in Bakht as I had never before seen in a man. His body was covered in a sheen of sweat.

I was so absorbed in the chanting and Bakht's prayer at first I didn't notice his tattoo, for his body was nothing but a tattoo, one enormous, frightening scene that sent chills racing through my body despite the heat in the room, such that I shook with fear. Bakht's body was Apep's, nothing less. Claws were tattooed on his toes and Apep's horrible scaly skin covered Bakht's entire body. Now Bakht writhed in a way that gave life to the snake god. But it was his face. Oh, mother Isis, protect me from visions of that face! For as he slithered back and forth, up and down, his face contorted into the most grotesque features imaginable and he belched forth words and spittle and guttural utterances that could only have originated in the foulest places of the Underworld.

Now the fire spewed dirty black smoke that quickly enveloped the room. The foul air circulated around and through us, and every place it touched my wet skin I felt invaded by the most evil presence I had ever known. I wanted to scrape that filth from my skin and run from the room and never stop until I drowned in Wadj-wer's currents. My breath came in short gasps, my eyes opened wide and in that moment I swear that I saw Apep enter the circle through the fire pit and his most vile ka slithered into Bakht's body through his opened, upturned mouth. Bakht's face was bathed in an eerie glow from the fire itself, illuminated from below, casting long, fearsome shadows on his features. I dare to say that not a man in that room believed that Bakht was anything other than the serpent god Apep.

Bakht slithered around the fire, contorting himself in a manner I'd have believed impossible for a mortal to achieve. This evil spirit before us hissed so hideously I wasn't the only one in that room to step back and shake with fear. Now Apep, for surely the serpent had possessed Bakht, stopped before one man. Apep opened his mouth wide and his tongue slipped out unnaturally long and flickered before the terrified man. I looked down and saw the poor man's robe become wet with his urine. The man shook uncontrollably and the men on either side of him had to support him under his arms. Back and forth Apep swayed, all the while his evil eyes fixated on the poor priest.

When Apep stood up the drumming stopped. The fire just as suddenly died down, yet a thick, dark haze still permeated the room. Every pair of eyes shifted between Apep and the unfortunate priest who stood shaking before him. Slowly, ever so slowly, Apep began to breathe more regularly and in the space of a hundred heartbeats all of us could see the priest Bakht's ka slowly take control of his body. His eyes were open now, but they were focused elsewhere, not on a place that existed in this world, but in another realm, the realm of muts and demons. Slowly Bakht returned and when he did, his eyes turned to the unlucky soul before him.

"Pakhneter," he began in a coarse whisper, addressing the man who was still held erect by his peers. "You have been a trusted Apep priest for more years than I can remember. You have served as a worthy captain and we have entrusted every secret of our sect to you. And yet..."

"I.. I did not intentionally do it," Pakhneter blurted out. "I... I mean it was intentional, but... but I was forced into doing so by my circumstances, my... my family's misfortunes." The man, who looked to be perhaps thirty years old, trembled uncontrollably.

"Fellow priests, what Pakh refers to is this; he has elected to become a highly paid spy, an informer, to the priests of that abomination, Meryt-Neith, that pretender king with a dildo between her legs for her manhood."

"And yes, we know, Pakh. We know all about your betrayals and what meager treasures you received for your deeds, tempting as they were to your weak ba." Now Bakht turned around the circle as he spoke and for the first time his eyes glimpsed mine. He stopped for just an instant and yet that moment was enough for me to feel his dark powers wash over me. To my own surprise I didn't recoil, but felt a new respect for this priest who possessed magic I hadn't even dreamed existed except in legend.

Continuing his movement, Bakht spoke clearly and forcefully. "Bring the traitor his just rewards," Bakht said to one of the men. The man returned quickly with a large clay bowl decorated with a serpent all along its edge and placed it before the fire pit which now glowed with charcoals. Pakhneter now shook so hard the men on either side had to struggle to hold him up.

"Pakhneter, you know the penalty we exact for traitors. You, yourself, have assisted me in this despicable chore in times past." Pakh doubled over and vomited at Bakht's feet.

"Yes, it's a bitter bile that you must now swallow," he said, his voice neither rising nor falling. "You will be executed and your parts scattered throughout the Delta so that you may never enter the realm of the Afterlife. We will feed your liver to Apep so that the memory of your betrayal will live into eternity. We will wipe out your sons so that no male heirs will survive you to whisper your name. And we will curse you and your heirs forever more." Throughout Bakht's litany Pakhneter whined and softly begged for his life.

"For your past service to our cause, we shall spare you the pain," Bakht said to Pakhneter. He reached into the bowl and took out a small pestle of some medicine, which he smeared onto a small section of Pakhneter's chest. Then Bakht's assistant brought him a lit pipe filled with a noxious smelling herb. Bakht offered it to Pakhneter, who shook his head. "It will make it easier," Bakht said softly. The two men on either side of the condemned man urged him to smoke it. He leaned forward and Bakht held the pipe as he inhaled. Within seconds Pakhneter's eyes glazed over, and he stood more firmly on his own.

Bakht turned and reached his hand out to his assistant. The priest withdrew an ornate ivory dagger from his belt and handed it to Bakht. "Goodbye, Pakhneter," Bakht said without emotion, "and may Apep devour your heart." With that he made a cut into Pakhneter's chest, reached his hand in and in one quick motion cut out the poor man's liver. Still, Pakhneter stood, staring vacantly ahead of him at Bakht, who held his liver high, blood dripping down his arms. I felt sickened. I knew if I did not look away I would fall to the floor, retching.

"This is the liver of a traitor, an abomination to Apep, whom we serve unquestioningly," I heard Bakht say. As he spoke, his hands red with blood, he cut thin strips from the liver. "Let all who worship Apep take a piece of the body of this traitor. Eat it so that you may forever recall his traitorous acts, so that we may forever curse the act that shames us all, and that we may forever know the fate that awaits those who defile the mighty Apep." Each man in the circle held out his hand as Bakht distributed a small piece of his grisly offering. When they were done, Pakhneter still stood, pale, blood pumping from his wound. He appeared dazed, looking confused as if trying to comprehend what was happening to him.

With a nod from Bakht, the two men who held Pakhneter bent him low to the ground, his head over the bowl. Now Bakht took hold of the man's hair and tilted his head back. I swear that I saw a look of peace and resignation on Pakhneter's face. With one swift motion, Bakht cut his head from ear to ear and his blood pulsed into the bowl. When most of it had emptied, Bakht's assistant made the final cuts that severed Pakhneter's head from his body. By now I stared, so shocked by this horrid display that my emotions left me entirely. I felt as if I witnessed this ghastly spectacle from afar.

How it happened I do not recall, but I soon found myself outside with Khnum, walking in the sand toward Wadj-wer, gulping its fresh air. I knew not how the ceremony had ended or if, in fact, it had. My mind was dazed. I followed my heart and it led me into the salty embrace of Wadj-Wer, where I sank to my knees in her sands and let her waves pour over me again and again. I splashed water over my face and rubbed until it stung, yet I knew then as I do now that I would never be able to wash away the dark, malevolent spirits that had soaked into every pore of my skin and had violated my ka.

In time I felt myself awaken from the horrors of what I had witnessed and looked up to find Khnum standing in the water next to me. "I wish to be alone for a few moments," I said firmly and without emotion.

"Of course," Khnum replied, and to his credit he walked away without further comment. Alone, I said silent prayers to Isis and thanked Wadj-Wer for cleansing me to the best of his ability. I tried to think of what had just transpired in the secret room, to draw some lesson from it, but my heart was still clouded and raw and my thoughts muddled. Instead, I stood and walked to Khnum.

"And your purpose for bringing me here tonight?" I asked as coldly as I could. In the moonlight I could see Khnum recoil.

"I… umm, it was… perhaps I should not have done so. Perhaps it was premature after all."

"Answer my question, Uncle."

For a full minute Khnum stood there, the waves lapping against his feet and said nothing. Finally, he turned toward the water and spoke as he peered out into the unyielding darkness.

"These aren't normal times we face, Nubiti. These are dark... dark and difficult times. We stand on a knife's edge, between our past and our future. We are only a few generations removed from King W'ash and his noble battle to save us from Narmer's grandiose plans for Unification. This," he said scooping up a handful of sand and closing it in his fist, "this was our land, our home, our destiny. If we do not act soon, we will lose our right to it forever. We will be buried in the mist of history and our grandchildren will have nothing... nothing." With that he threw the sand into the waters.

"I don't disagree with you, but you still haven't answered my question."

"Serious times require serious methods," Khnum shouted, turning toward me "What you saw was to help you understand that we'll stop at nothing to achieve our aims. Nothing! Lower Kem will be free once again to choose its destiny, no matter what it takes. And if you are true to your word, you will be the one to lead us!" He emphasized those final words by jamming the finger of his right hand into his left palm.

"I'll tell you this for sure, Nubiti. Those priests will well remember what took place tonight. Word will spread. If other traitors hide in our midst, this will bring them to the surface for no one here tonight will dare to be associated with them. And once Pakhneter's headless body is found and his sons with him, the businessmen and priests who support The Abomination who pollutes the very notion of King of Kem will tremble in their sandals. Those passionate enough to deal out terror will always dominate the weak and fearful."

"And what about the Army? If these terrorist acts continue, Meryt-Neith will send in her soldiers."

"Ha! To do what? Who will they battle, the rekhi shivering in their hovels? The businessmen or artisans who only seek to protect their own interests? The corrupt priests? Armies only know how to battle other armies. They are powerless to defend against an enemy who fights in the shadows, whose face is never revealed. They can't even imagine that the meek merchant they pass every day calls himself a priest of Apep when Ra's chariot sets in the sky. And if The Abomination chooses to have me and Bakht killed, so be it. We welcome dying as martyrs for Apep. There will be no dark place in Lower Kem that does not harbor one of our warriors. If they are killed, their children will take their place, even their wives and daughters. They will never conquer us for we will never surrender. Never!"

"Harsh methods are needed, Khnum, I agree. But we need to guard against overzealous passion. If we aren't careful we'll alienate those who we will eventually govern. At some point our own people must welcome us as heroes, not murderers."

"Yes, our methods are harsh and if you are to be our link to the future, then you must know exactly how serious we are and that we will stop at nothing to achieve our goal of a separate Lower Kem. That is why we felt it best to have you witness this event."

Together we stood, side by side, looking out into the living darkness of Wadj-wer as her waves broke rhythmically over our feet. Finally, I turned toward Khnum.

"Was it Bakht's idea to have me witness this event?" I asked, already knowing the answer.

"Yes, for he is the Master Priest of Apep. Only he could have allowed you to attend."

Suddenly my heart cleared. I nodded my head in understanding and a smile crossed my face. For only then did I comprehend what the message was in Bakht's invitation. Only then did I understand that in my attendance lay my entire future and that of the Land of the Papyrus.

SCROLL TEN

Meryt-Neith

"It is not the worst possible news, Mery," Amka said, pacing before me. "But these rebellions in the Delta have to stop or your rule will erode from within. They seem to be increasing in severity. Even the governors of the neighboring nomes are concerned. I suggest we send in Panahasi…"

"Ah, the barbarian to the rescue," I said, sarcastically.

"Yes, Panahasi the Barbarian," Amka responded matter-of-factly. "He is our oldest, most experienced general and he knows the Delta better than anyone in the army. He will deal with these rebellions quickly."

"And what of his critics who say he is too heavy handed? That he will slaughter one hundred innocents to get at one enemy?" I asked.

"Yes, he is aggressive in his pursuit, I agree, but his exploits have been wildly exaggerated. But we will keep him on a short leash. Narmer's genius in building our white-walled city adjoining the Delta becomes clearer with each passing generation. I will personally visit Panahasi regularly as your Vizier to be certain he is carrying out your orders against the rebels and not just pummeling the locals into submission."

"Make it so," I responded, not wanting to take more time when so many other pressing issues faced me. Amka immediately sat down at a table in the corner of the meeting room to write a parchment with orders for Panahasi. He applied both our seals and sent it off with a messenger priest.

"I must visit with Herneith this morning," I said to Amka. "She so enjoys when Zenty and I bring her morning meal. I noticed that she has been weaker these past few days. What is your opinion of her health?"

Amka immediately put down his scribe's pen and faced me, yet he did not immediately speak. "Mery, I offer no opinion when it comes to the disease that eats from within. She is very ill and seems to decline every ten-day. Ti-Ameny and I discuss her treatment every day, but there is no medicine for the mut that has invaded her body."

"Nothing?"

"Nothing that we yet know of. The Horus priests are always alert for new treatments as we travel to other lands or establish temples near our borders." He tapped his pen on the parchment a few times before continuing.

"I know how close you two are, Mery. Herneith has been like your mother and a good role model for you. And she and Zenty have a very special relationship. But you must prepare yourself for her passing to the next life. She has been a good woman in all her roles and a good Queen, too. She will have a life of abundance, free of pain and full of joy when she reunites with Djer."

"Your words are true, as usual, Amka. Yet I have no idea how you are able to act on them with so little emotion. Herneith's passing will grip my heart with grief." Before Amka could respond a tiny voice yelled into the room.

"Mother, are you done yet? I want to go visit with Mama Herneith!" I cast my glance toward Zenty and smiled. Abana had dressed him in his favorite kilt of fine white linen with gold thread borders. His hair hung in a single child braid to his right shoulder and was tied with a gold ribbon. Around his neck he wore a single gold chain with a Horus amulet that protected him and pronounced him future King.

I opened my arms and he ran across the room to me as fast as his five-year old feet allowed. I hugged him tightly, but as he did more frequently nowadays, he soon wanted to be released.

"And what about me?" Amka whined. "Am I unwashed? Am I undeserving of a hug?" With that Zenty threw himself off my lap and flung himself at Amka, who pretended to be knocked to the ground. Together, the two of them rolled back and forth in a tight embrace, Amka complaining loudly while Zenty giggled uncontrollably.

"You are growing up too fast, my dear boy," Amka said, looking stern. "You are becoming entirely too strong. The Horus priests must figure out a way to keep you little." With that, Zenty put out his arms and flexed his biceps. "Let me feel that," Amka said, reaching out to feel the muscles. "Great Horus, those are rocks, not muscles! What have you done? You... you... " Amka slapped his forehead in amazement.

"No, I just eat good stuff," Zenty said, still laughing. "And I get exercise making Abana chase me around. And when I grow up I will be a great warrior and hunt lions and hippos like Herihor."

And so they bantered until finally I stood and took Zenty to visit his grandmother. It was a melancholy visit, for Herneith had taken a turn for the worse and looked pale and lifeless, as if Thoth had already come to claim her ka.

"Why does Ma-Ma just lay there like that?" Zenty asked, pressing his head to my arm.

"She is ill, sweetie. Very ill."

"She looks sad. But how come she does not just wake up and talk to us like she usually does? That would make her feel better."

I kneeled down and put Zenty on my lap. He did not take his eyes off his beloved grandmother. "Yes, it surely would, Zenty. But she does not have the strength any more to do that."

"Then I will do it for her!" he stated and got up, took his grandmothers hand and shook it. "Wake up, Ma-Ma, wake up!" he commanded. But Herneith was too far gone to awaken. She slept on, not recognizing either of us.

"We should go now," Zenty suggested, turning from his grandmother. He wrapped his hands around my neck and together we rose and left the room. Back in his own room, Zenty crawled into my lap and allowed me to hug and snuggle him. He asked me to tell him stories about Herneith raising me, but he did not smile as he usually did. As I spoke I had the feeling that he still visited with his grandmother in his dreams and he soon fell asleep in my arms, something he had not done in almost a year. It was a bittersweet moment, indeed.

Late that night I visited Herneith alone, for I had a deep sense of foreboding. For the first part of my visit, Ti-Ameny came to check on Herneith, her face grim, her healing hands now useless. She avoided looking me in the eyes as she did what I thought was busy work, straightening Herneith's sheets and making her comfortable. After she left, I knelt next to Herneith, holding her hand and caressing it with my lips and cheek. I felt a movement in the bed and looked up to see Herneith staring at me. Her expression was serene, perhaps even joyful. I sat on the bed and, smiling, leaned down to hear her, for her lips moved.

"I go now, sweet Mery," she whispered in my ear and even then I strained to make out her words. "Djer beckons me from the Beyond. It is so, so beautiful there." Her eyes shone.

"Remember always these words, my dear daughter. There is much evil in the world. Yet love and kindness always endure. Be strong, be fair, and always, always leave room in your heart for love."

Herneith said those words and closed her eyes for the last time. She slept peacefully then and by morning her ka had left her body. If it were not for Zenty, I would have collapsed into a deep place of mourning, so much did I love my aunt, the only mother I knew. Zenty insisted on seeing his grandmother one last time. I told him she was dead, but that did not convince my headstrong son.

Amka, may his name be blessed, explained to Zenty that what he witnessed was the body without the ka present, which made perfect sense to Zenty. He touched the cool body only once, as if to convince himself of the difference. Strangely, he did not cry. He and Amka talked about the journey her ka was now making and what glories awaited his grandmother in the Afterworld. Zenty nodded quietly and seemed to take great consolation from Amka's explanations and turned to leave, holding tight to Amka's hand. Then, he spun around, ran to Herneith's body, dressed in her funerary shroud, her hands crossed upon her chest and hugged her one last time. He walked back to Amka, carrying himself with a regal bearing that later Amka commented upon, took his hand again and quietly left the room.

For me it was not so easy to let go of Herneith. I sat with her body for a long time, thinking of all that she had meant to me. She was a mother, but very different than was Abana, for Herneith did not bother with my care as far as the daily chores of life were concerned. Herneith was always there to teach me the values that the Royal family held most dear. She advised me on protocol. She read to me and discussed matters with me so as to teach me how to be a good companion. But above all she always instilled feelings of independence in me, whether for the good or bad.

Yet even my relationship with my sweet aunt was

not perfect, for my ba was of a more reflective type. I would often sit alone on the portico of my room and just watch the other girls in the Royal court as they walked through town with their mothers, or played games with their fathers. I would wonder about those relationships. Did they feel comfortable, like a well-used blanket? Did the children look forward to dinner around a table with their parents? Was there a secret, something, anything, that families shared, some magical connection that somehow made each member more whole? All I knew growing up was that I very often felt something was missing inside my ka.

With my heart still full of grief, barely a month later I heard the first murmurings of yet another challenge we faced within the Royal Court. It had not been a good day to begin with. The first order of business had been a meeting of the Council of Governors, now chaired by Amka, who had asked me to attend. The governors reported that the drought ravaged our people, both poor and wealthy alike. Crops wilted, the farmers had no goods to trade for staples, which meant the merchants were becoming destitute, leading to the artisans starving. The end result for the Royal Court was that tax revenues were not coming in and so the entire situation was a terrible cycle of despair, misery, illness and death.

Amka had sent emissaries as far away as Kush and Nubia to purchase grains and other foodstuffs, but the people of those lands, too, were suffering from Mother Nile's anger. Amka did report some success in obtaining grains from Babylon, since the gods of their twin rivers had been good to them and they were happy to receive the gold from our rapidly depleting treasury. Within a month we were to have modest grain deliveries to Inabu-hedj, to be parceled out to every nome.

In a perverse way, fish stores had actually increased due to the reduction in Mother Nile's depth. The governor of the southernmost nome reported that herds of antelope and water buffalo had migrated from

Nubia well into his nome in search of water and the local population was hunting them with great success. Amka arranged for a contingent of soldiers to travel to the borderlands to hunt the herds and to ship the salted and dried carcasses to the northern nomes to provide quality foods for our people. And so we all worked together to overcome these most difficult times. All, except for the nomes of the Delta.

No matter what the issue, the governors of these nomes protested that they lacked enough of this, or had too many problems themselves to help. This had caused the governors of Upper Kem to run short on patience with their brethren in the north and a rift soon developed which made it increasingly difficult for the Council to conduct its business.

So it was no surprise to Amka when one of the Governors in the Delta asked him when he thought Shepsit would be named Queen Mother. It was asked so casually Amka knew at once that he had been put up to it. He sidestepped the question, but raised it with me at our first meeting after the Council of Governors left.

"It has not even been one month since Herneith's death!" I protested. "What will that witch want next?"

"As if you do not already know the answer to that one," Amka replied, looking up from the notes of the Council meeting he committed to parchment before dictating them to his trusted scribes. "The governor's question was just a polite way of raising the issue. In another month the issue will become insistent and be cloaked in court intrigue. Shepsit is like a dog on a bone. The question remains what to do about it, before it gets to that point."

"And what do you recommend?"

"In truth I haven't given it much thought. I will discuss it with Tepemkau on his next visit here. But I will say that, like all affairs of state, it is complicated. My initial thought is to give her the title, for she thrives on pomp and privilege. The title of Queen Mother has little power to accompany it, but she would be at most ceremonies and as such would dip her fingers in everyone's stew."

"By all rights she has claims to the title," I offered. "To deny it to her would be perceived as another slight by our cousins to the north."

"True, especially now that Panahasi is beginning to have some success with the rebels in the Delta."

"And only against the rebels, correct?"

"Again, that is a mater of perception. I would say that it is mostly true, but in the Delta the people are interconnected in ways we do not completely understand. So killing a rebel means we have also killed someone's father, or perhaps an Apep priest, or a businessman's conduit to the grant of a trading right to the Lebanese. It is most unfortunate that we had to send in the army at all, but once they are in we must deal with the consequences. I have told Panahasi to complete our actions there and withdraw the regular army as soon as he can."

"Let's just make sure that we do not have to send them back anytime soon. As for Shepsit, I am inclined to grant her the right to the title and be done with it. Why let it fester? In fact, the sooner the better, so that we do it on our terms, not hers. I think it unwise for it to look as if we were forced into this."

"Ah, dear Mery, you begin to frighten me with your developing political skills. I would agree, but let's see what Tepemkau says. We cannot act on it anyway until a decent time after Herneith's funeral."

"Good. Let me know how it transpires." And with that, I went to bed that night feeling as if we had at least stayed in front of one problem.

As the day approached for Herneith's funeral, with the Royal Court in preparation, I awoke one morning with an unusual feeling, as if a bee buzzed inside me. Whether it was that I had without realizing it heard the movement of soldiers and my advisors as I slept or whether Horus had forewarned me, I dressed quickly all the while feeling a mounting dread. I refused anything for the morning meal except for my tea and when Amka came bursting into my quarters, I was hardly surprised. But when he addressed me by my royal title, I knew in an instant that something terrible was wrong.

"Meryt-Neith, Regent King of the Two Lands, I have come with dread news. We have been invaded!" Amka's eyes were open wide and he stood holding onto his staff, his fingers white, his body trembling.

"Invaded? But the Ta-Tjehenus have no army. They only raid us here and there. They are pests…"

"Meryt-Neith," Amka interrupted, calling me by my formal name once again, "we have been invaded from the south. It is the dark-skinned Ta-Setys who have poured over our border."

My breath went out of me and my heart beat fiercely in my chest. "But they… they have always been peaceful neighbors. They have never made war against us. Were they provoked?"

"No, I can say there was no provocation, none that the Horus priests to our south reported. And, yes, they have always been peaceful. In fact, Narmer's shaman, Meruka, was a dark-skinned Nubian, if you will recall your history lessons. But there is no doubt they have attacked. The governor's emissary himself arrived during the night to deliver the news, along with a Horus priest who I know well and who witnessed an attack personally. Our villagers flee before their assaults. The enemy is burning villages as they go. They are rounding up men and women and sending them back to their homeland, presumably as slaves. The entire southern region is in upheaval. We must respond immediately. Nekhen itself is in danger."

By the mid-day meal, using his Horus priests as messengers, Amka had assembled a group of advisors in the main meeting room. When I entered, they were gathered about in small groups, eating hurriedly and talking animatedly. In my presence they stopped what they were doing, bowed low and waited for my orders. I wore a simple gown with the King's gold and carnelian breastplate and a gold armband on my right bicep. With the intermittent reports from Amka throughout the morning, I had no time to put on makeup or to do my hair in a fancy manner, and so it hung straight down, with an ivory pin through the back. But the meetings with Amka were essential to prepare me for the most serious crisis of my rule and I knew that if there were ever a time for forceful action, now was that time.

The meeting room was the largest at the palace and therefore not the most secure, which surprised me at first. Then I saw that Amka had stationed guards around the perimeter to deter large ears and prying eyes.

"Amka, let's get started, for we have urgent business here today," I announced and climbed onto an elevated platform, upon which was the King's throne, the very same one used by every ruler since King Narmer. Once I sat everyone immediately took a seat in a circle around the room. There were eighteen people in attendance, including several ministers, the governor of the nome that included Inabu-hedj, and various military officers.

Everyone present had received a detailed briefing from Amka, so there was no need for preliminary items on the agenda. Within minutes all the assembled had agreed that our only option was military. I called upon the most senior military officer present, Keter, to discuss them in detail.

"My King, I cannot answer. With Panahasi in the Delta only Herihor knows which troops are..."

"I am here!" Herihor announced as he swept into the room. He immediately bowed low before me. "Forgive me, my master, I was in the field training a regiment. I came as soon as I was summoned."

"No doubt..." I said, "that you came directly from the field, that is," I said to the laughter of the men, for Herihor's legs were covered in sand and mud. There were streaks of mud on his face from where sweat had formed rivulets. And his left arm had a shallow cut on it that had blood caked all along its margin. He still wore his leather breastplate, which was well oiled from his sweat. All in all he presented a fearsome warrior's appearance.

"Please accept my apologies, my King," he said, bowing again and obviously embarrassed.

"No need to apologize, Herihor, for the training you provide our troops will surely be tested in the days to come."

Over the next thirty minutes, Herihor gave us a description of our troop strength and location down the minutest detail, including what might be needed in terms of supplies. He spoke forcefully, and it was quickly obvious to me how respected he was by every man in that room.

"And how soon can an army be assembled to deal with this incursion?" I asked.

Herihor thought for a few seconds. "In two days I will have scouting reports from our outpost in Nekhen. In eight days, ten at the most, I can have an army of five thousand men marching south from Inabu-hedj. By time the army gets to the southern nomes, it will number ten thousand or more."

"And who will you choose as leader?" Menenhet, the Minister of Trade with Lands to the East, asked Herihor.

"Herihor will lead the army himself," I answered, "for Panahasi is too far north and this is not the time for underlings, capable though they might be," I added, nodding to Keter and Herihor's other officers. The room was tense and quiet, waiting for a response from Herihor. For a moment, Herihor simply stood in front of his seat, saying nothing. Then, in an elegant movement, he bowed low.

"As you command, my King," he said. I was so pleased that Herihor had easily deferred to my command that I neglected to note a more serious threat to my rule, one that Amka later helped me to see when we later debriefed on the meeting. Menenhet had apparently sneered at me with resentment when I commanded

Herihor.

True to his word, on the eighth day I sat in review as Herihor marched his army south from Inabu-hedj. Tepemkau was absent to continue preparing Herneith's body for burial, so Amka conducted the blessings over the troops. Again crowds of people came to see the troops off and to shower them with flower petals and gifts of cakes and fruits, scarce though they were to our people. Those gestures made us all feel the pride we all shared in the Two Lands. Herihor himself was dressed in battle dress, which reinforced in many of our minds the gravity of the situation. Yet we all took comfort in Herihor's imposing presence.

That comfort turned out to be well deserved. Every few days a contingent of soldiers would arrive escorting a messenger from the southern battlegrounds. They would rest for a few days, until relieved by the next contingent of messengers, then return to Herihor's command. And with each group came reports of success after success in the war. Although we sustained casualties, they were far fewer than we had expected, for Herihor had proved himself as well suited to strategic planning as he was to battlefield tactics. It was immediately after one of these reports that I came to understand how it was that Herihor excelled in strategy.

"It is encouraging that Herihor is so decisive in battle," I commented to Amka as he dictated a letter to a scribe that was to go back with the messenger to Herihor.

"Yes, we are indeed fortunate that Herihor is as good a student as he is a general." That comment intrigued me.

"What do you mean?"

"What I mean is that Herihor learns his lessons well."

"You are talking in riddles again, my teacher," I said, frustrated.

"Does my King think she is the only student I have? Herihor has long been my student, too." This fact surprised me greatly.

"Herihor! Your student?"

"And why is that so surprising? Do you think I only teach the spoiled children of privilege? Herihor is a student of military history, and far less impertinent than you, I might add." I laughed at my teacher's prickliness.

"What is it you teach him?" I asked, curious. Amka seemed irritated.

"We discuss battles that previous Kings have fought, recorded by their Viziers and housed in the library in Nekhen. In that way Herihor has come to know what to expect from our warrior neighbors, for we find that without a similar historical record their methods of war do not change, while we are able to learn from the experiences of our forebears." This alone increased my respect for both Amka and Herihor and also for the many blessings that the gods had given to our people, such as the holy writing.

"In this latest report we learned that Herihor battled the Ta-Sety in a valley on the southern border. Yet the scrolls reveal that your own grandfather, Hor-Aha, son of Narmer, battled them similarly and lost more than four hundred men. Recalling that history, Herihor was not easily fooled into following them into the valley where they could be slaughtered by the Ta-Sety laying in ambush. I am writing this letter to congratulate Herihor for putting that lesson to good use."

In little more than a month, word came back from Herihor requesting permission to bring the army home, leaving a garrison in the south at the cataract of Mother Nile nearest to Kush. I immediately granted his request and within a ten-day the entire city was out to greet the triumphant army as they marched back into Inabu-hedj. The only thing missing were the celebrations that the army richly deserved. Yet Herneith was still not buried and any partying would need to wait until then.

On the eleventh day after Herihor's return, as Herneith's funeral was nearly upon us, a message arrived from Panahasi advising us of developments in the Delta. It was a disturbing message indeed, delivered by no less than Panahasi's most senior officer, Kemnebi, a fearsome warrior who was one of Wadjet's favorite officers and who served in his King's Guards.

"It does not go well for us, my master," Kemnebi began. "Every time we quell a secretive attack on one of our granaries or on the house of one of your loyal court scribes, another damned incident occurs nearby so that we rush from one uprising to another. Then, three or four ten-days ago, these cursed rebellions started appearing more frequently and all at once." Kemnebi spoke ever more excitedly.

"But now the character of these attacks has changed. The mut-possessed rebels will attack an army troop with no regard for their own lives. Most die from our spears before they get close, but they often will get in a knife thrust or their own spear strike and take down one or two of our men."

Herihor sat at the meeting, nervously tapping his foot, while Amka merely leaned on his staff and listened intently. "And what tactic does Panahasi use to discourage these attacks?" Herihor asked.

"They are nearly impossible to defend against, Herihor!" Kemnebi snapped. "We enter a village to investigate and we are attacked in an alleyway. Now... may Horus protect us... now matters have turned in an unexpected direction. Now we are sometimes attacked by women!"

"By women?" Herihor asked, sitting back forcefully in his seat.

"They walk by as if going to market and then, without warning, they will pull out a knife and kill a soldier. It... it is an... an abomination. It is against the natural order of the gods, but this is truly what we encounter. It is as if the Delta were possessed of demon spirits. My men tremble in fear at what goes on."

"And what of the Ta-Tjehenu?" Amka asked calmly.

"They have renewed their damned attacks and with a vengeance, as if they smell blood. They do not challenge our troops. They kill women and children. They attacked a temple of Bes, for Ra's sake! They murdered three priests, cut off their heads and mounted them atop the statue of Bes. My soldiers were sickened. They say..." Kemnebi's voice trailed off.

"They say what?" Herihor asked.

"Nothing. They say nothing. They are... dejected."

At this, blood rushed to Herihor's face and the veins in his neck stood out. "Do not lie to me, Kemnebi. Both Panhasi and I are your superiors. You will answer my question now, fully and truthfully. The men say what?"

To his men, Kemnebi is known as the Black Panther, a warrior best avoided in battle. Yet now he shriveled in his seat and looked more like Zenty's kitten than a prowling panther. "I... sir, please do not..."

"Answer me!" Herihor shouted, standing, his fists balled by his side.

"They speak of the curse that has settled upon the land, sir," Kemnebi whispered. "They whisper of the curse of a woman king. They speak of the mut spirit of... of Meryt-Neith roaming the land, of her male ka violating the ka of peaceful women who then kill us in the night." Kemnebi looked as if he would be sick.

Herihor paced away, took a deep breath and then returned. The room remained silent.

"I'm sorry," Herihor offered to Kemnebi. "You are among our best officers."

"It's alright, sir. I apologize."

"This is all of one fabric," Amka sighed. "Woven with deceptive care, but one fabric nonetheless." Herihor sat down hard in his chair.

"Kemnebi, has Panahasi called in Khnum to discuss the situation?" Amka asked.

"May I speak... I mean can I...?" Kemnebi asked, turning to Herihor.

Herihor glanced briefly at me and Amka. We both nodded.

"Speak candidly," he responded.

"I'm a damned soldier and no politician, sir. But Khnum is a damned liar. I've been present at least twice when General Panahasi threatened his mortal life. Khnum just sits there claiming his innocence. He's even made a request to the General to send more troops to protect the swamp dwellers from the rebels and Ta-Tjehenus. Yet we hear our own reports from our informers and they tell a very different story of his treachery. But every time we believe we have a witness, that person is killed in a grisly manner. We even found one of their own Apep priests, a man who was informing for us, with his liver cut out and his head left at the front door of our governor in Dep."

"What do you suspect?" I asked of Amka.

"Rebellions in the Delta, attacks by the Ta-Tjehenu, livers and heads cut off, war from the usually peaceful Ta-Setys. Now women warriors. It is the Delta leadership and the black arts of the cult of Apep at work, of this I am sure. King Scorpion, King Narmer's father, describes these tactics in a scroll written by Anhotek, and this was many years before Unification. But without proof we are powerless to act. We are a nation of rules and laws and Khnum and his scum know full well how to take advantage of that. They take our very strength as a people and make it into a weakness."

"And what are your thoughts on how to proceed?" I asked of Amka.

"Herihor, it would be good if you were to dismiss this good soldier from his duties for now, with our thanks. He looks like he needs a rest. But I would urge you to advise him to not speak to anyone else of our talk, not even Panahasi, at least not until we formulate a message to send back with him." At this, Kemnebi looked up at Amka.

"Did you understand the Vizier's words?" Herihor asked Kemnebi.

"Yes, sir."

"Then you're dismissed for now. Lodge in my quarters for the night. My valet will make you comfortable." With Kemnebi gone, Amka exhaled forcibly through pursed lips.

"What do you make of it?" I asked. "Khnum wants us to send even more troops? What kind of nonsense is that?"

"It is hardly nonsense, Meryt. They wish to draw us ever deeper into the quicksand. There are a few things I must do... information I must gather, facts I must check before we respond. That will take two ten-days or more. I suggest we wait until after Herneith's funeral and by then I hope to have the answers I seek. We must get to the bottom of this, and quickly."

In a little more than the first ten-day, we finally laid Herneith to rest in a tomb befitting the Queen Mother. Although Ti-Ameny pleaded her case to be allowed to travel to the Afterworld with her Queen, we persuaded her that in such tenuous times, the gods would agree that she was needed more here. Amka arranged it so that during the funerary procession and related ceremonies I would not have to interact with Shepsit. Nubiti, however, as Head Isis Priestess paid me a sympathy visit with two of her acolytes, but Amka planned for it to be squeezed in between two other official visits from foreign dignitaries, so other than a perfunctory hug we did not share any intimate time.

In another ten-day, Amka and I met to discuss the timing of Shepsit's appointment as the new Queen Mother. We both agreed to make the appointment by proclamation rather than a Royal celebration, defending our decision by citing the precarious situation in the Two Lands and the effects of the drought.

It was but another few days when Amka requested a meeting with me, Herihor and Tepemkau, who had stayed in Inabu-hedj after Herneith's funeral. When I arrived the three men were waiting, drinking beer and discussing something animatedly. They bowed as I entered. Both Amka and Tepemkau were unadorned, dressed in their plain linen priests' robes, while Herihor was dressed in a clean, crisply pressed kilt and sash, with the armband designating his military rank on his bicep. It was embossed with the figure of Sobek, the crocodile god. His dagger and scabbard hung from his belt.

"There are two items I wish to discuss with you," Amka started, looking at each of us in turn. "I hardly need to remind you that these are perilous times, so I plan to just move into the details, so we can act quickly. I've asked Tepemkau to begin."

"Here it is, then," Tepemkau began. "When Amka was first informed about poor Irisi's death many cycles ago, certain elements did not make sense to him. Yet he delayed investigating the matter further due to the many other distractions that arose since that time." He paused to gauge our reaction. Satisfied, he went on.

"With the recent crush of events, Amka asked me to send a group of Horus priests to locate her gravesite and dig up her remains."

"To what? That... that is a sacrilege!" I protested.

"Please, Meryt, hear him out," Amka said in his calmest voice. I sat back in my chair, fuming.

"You are quite right, master," Tepemkau said. "This is a terrible sacrilege, especially in the case of such a perfect being as Irisi, a gift from Isis herself in mortal form. She was loved by women and gods equally." Tepemkau coughed into his sleeve and continued.

"We convened a group of senior Horus priests at Amka's request and listened to his concerns and finally agreed with him that this must be done. We consulted the ancient texts for precedents and we removed her body ceremonially, with deep respect. I was present throughout." At this I took some comfort.

"Now, you know our priests are experts in preserving bodies, so we know what to expect in a preserved body such as Irisi's, even though she was only preserved by the dry desert sands. Our priests also include the finest shamans and medicine men in all the lands around us, so we understand how and in what manner various deaths occur."

"Please make your point, Tepemkau, for the thought of my sister's body being disturbed while her ka is in the next world is very upsetting to me."

"Yes, yes, of course. The reports given to Amka... and to you if I remember correctly, were that Irisi died from a viper bite on her calf, a horrible accident that occurred while she walked in the desert. And, in fact, such bites do happen from time to time. Her body was found by her sister priestesses, her face contorted in pain, which is also consistent with a viper bite, since it is a very painful death."

"Please!" I shouted at Tepemkau.

"I am sorry, but these are critical facts that bear on this case, Meryt-Neith. I will tell you that no bites were found on her calves at all."

"What are you saying?" Herihor asked, confused.

"There were viper bites, two of them, but they were on the back of her neck, right at the hairline."

"How could she have been bitten on the neck?" I asked. Tepemkau looked at Amka.

"He's saying she was murdered," Herihor said, turning to me. I gasped. "It's an old method, practiced by the Ta-Tjehenus to kill traitors or reviled enemies." My body shuddered at the thought of Irisi dying from the poison fangs of an evil mut viper.

"But... who... who would do such a thing?" I asked, confused. "Irisi was a god-mortal."

Now Amka stood and I could see immediately that he was in pain, probably from a lack of sleep and taking his infamous naps lying stiff as a corpse on the top of his writing table.

"We do not know for certain who did this evil act, but logic would suggest that the finger point to those who benefited most."

"Nubiti?" I asked in amazement. "No. I realize she has evil inclinations, but..." I quickly caught myself. Silence prevailed.

"Yes, the finger points to Shepsit and Nubiti, but it cannot be them alone. By being here they may be a threat to us through the information they are able to gather, but they are limited in what they can do. They are isolated and hold no real power within the Court. Tepemkau and I have also formulated a plan whereby they will be watched more closely by our network of spies and informers from this point forward.

"No, the real answer lies close to us. Putting together all that has happened in Kem over the past two years points to a far more dangerous cabal. I suspect that Khnum and his evil mut, Bakht, are at work here, for the worship of Apep can twist even the most benevolent spirit."

"Can anything be done? Should we arrest them and try them for treason?" I asked.

"If Amka is right, if all these rebellions in the Delta and the war in the south are coordinated from the Delta, then arresting Khnum and his evil cabal would make them martyrs and perhaps spark greater rebellion," Herihor suggested.

"Herihor is correct," Amka said, "especially since the Apep priesthood has a long history and a defined structure, much like the Horus priesthood. However, Herihor's words do point to a solution and one that I was remiss in not having recognized before this." Amka paced a few steps, then placed his hand on his back, trying to straighten himself.

"I am sorry. I am just a bit stiff." He stretched to his full height, which barely reached Herihor's shoulders. "Meryt-Neith, it is time to appoint a Chief of the Army. We have been without one since before Wadjet's death, too absorbed by the drought and the rebellions and the Ta-Sety invasion. We must have a coordinated plan and a military leader who can implement it. And it all must start with decisively quashing the rebellion in the Delta. If we can accomplish that, until Mother Nile again blesses us with fertile floods, all will be well. Our people will not provide fertile ground for Khnum and Bakht if they are well fed and happy. And when Mother Nile floods again we will use the increased treasury to build more granaries and roads and temples."

"Yes, yes, I had not thought about the need for a Chief of the Army, but you are right." I turned to Herihor. "And what is your opinion, Herihor?"

"I agree. I would serve Panahasi to my death. He trained me, as he has most of the senior Army officers. He is without equal. All the men respect him."

"Panahasi is the most senior officer in the army and thus in line to be Chief," Tepemkau agreed. "I have known him throughout his career. He served in Nekhen for years and improved the training of the soldiers. Wadjet respected him, too."

We sat silently for a long time and I weighed in my mind what Amka had said. It was true that we lacked a coordinated approach to our security. Beyond the drought and the internal instability, we would eventually need a strategy for providing security for our trade to distant lands. And with the recent war in the south, we needed to bolster our defenses in that part of the country.

"It is settled then, we must appoint a Chief of the Army without delay." I swallowed hard, for even I could not believe what it was I was about to command. "Amka, prepare to announce Herihor's appointment."

As I write these words, I swear that I noted a slight smile come to Amka's lips, or perhaps it was just a twinkle in his eyes. But the effect of my command was that not a word was spoken for a minute or two. We heard the yells of the servants and gardeners as they toiled below us. To my left I could hear Herihor finally take a breath.

"My master, please excuse me. I think you meant to say Panahasi." He made a slight laugh in his voice to sound unconcerned. "You used my name, but you meant to say Panahasi."

All eyes were intently focused on me. "No, I said what I meant to say. You, Herihor, are my choice to lead the army… my army," I emphasized.

"But…" Herihor started to say, before Tepemkau interrupted him.

"What Herihor means to say, Meryt-Neith, is that Panahasi is in line to become Chief. He is the most senior…"

"Yes, I know, you said that before, Tepemkau. But it is in Herihor that I have most confidence. He has won the war against the Ta-Setys, and without the loss of life we expected. He is now the officer who is responsible for training our troops. And, to be candid, the Delta is still a mess despite Panahasi's most valiant efforts."

I now turned to Herihor. "Times have changed, Herihor. We no longer fight a war for Unification. Now we fight a more insidious enemy, one who fights in the shadows, who does not engage on the battlefield. Old methods are no longer effective. I need a vigorous Chief, one who can adapt to changing conditions. It is not that I am displeased with Panahasi's loyalty, only his performance. It is you who I choose to lead my army, who I command to lead it."

Herihor, to his credit, just sat there, saying nothing. He did not presume to argue his case any further. It was then that Amka spoke.

"The King has spoken, Herihor, and in this case I must admit, that while it departs from our usual practice, I agree with Meryt-Neith's judgment. The King must handpick a new Chief, one he has confidence in, and one who is unapologetically loyal to him… or her. You are the King's choice. You must either accept or decline… now."

The quiet that followed was thick with anticipation. Herihor leaned forward in his chair and sunk his head between his massive shoulders. I could only imagine what went through his heart. I was not naïve enough to disregard the fact that he even weighed the unpleasant thought of being the first general ever to serve a woman king. That situation would certainly, repeatedly, test both his authority and his manhood as it reared its ugly head throughout his service. Finally, after minutes of silence, Herihor stood up, placed his right forearm across his chest, and bowed to one knee, his head bent.

"I accept your appointment, my master, even though I feel unworthy of such an honor. I will serve you faithfully and honorably and defend Kem from all enemies, whether internal or external and I will happily sacrifice my life in such service."

I smiled at this man who knelt before me. "Hopefully that will not be necessary, loyal servant of Horus, for we will need your service for many years to come. You serve me now in my role as Regent and so will need to swear to serve the one and only true King, Zenty, son of Wadjet, when he comes of age. Do you so swear, Herihor?"

"I do, master."

"Then rise and go about your duties, my loyal Chief. Discuss with Amka and Tepemkau what your needs are so that they may put them in place prior to the appointment.

"And one other matter. The discussions here must remain private, not to be shared with another under any circumstances, until I have a chance to speak personally with Panahasi. Are you in agreement?" They quickly gave their assent.

And so it was that I made my first real decision as King and one that I hoped I would not regret. In fact, despite my concerns over the repercussions of my decision, just to have decided rested comfortably in my ba. Later that day, after I had kissed Zenty goodnight and told him the story of creation for the hundredth time, Ti-Ameny came in to tell me that Amka was here to see me. It was a rare occasion for Amka to visit with me after Ra's disk set in the sky. As soon as Zenty fell asleep I went to the parlor to find Amka sitting in his meditative pose, his eyes closed, his back straight and his hands clasping his ornately carved staff.

"Thank you for meeting with me," he said without

opening his eyes. After pleasantries he got right to the point. "I have spent the rest of the day with Herihor and Tepemkau, planning. But I did not want to wait until tomorrow to tell you how very proud I am of what you did today. That took great courage and insight." Amka was not one to easily compliment, so I felt pleased and slept well that night.

In seven days, I was in Merimda, just a two-day sail downriver from Inabu-hedj, at a point where Mother Nile splits into many smaller rivers to form the Black Lands of the Delta. Amka had arranged our trip as a review of the troops, but in reality it was to have the meeting I dreaded with Panahasi. When I was a child Panahasi frightened me, for he was a large man with a big belly and a deep, booming voice. When he and my uncle began drinking, my aunt would scoop me up and carry me to a different area of the palace, for they had a reputation for getting rowdy and profane when drunk.

The meeting was a difficult one for both of us, for despite his gruffness Panahasi is a good man, loyal to Kem and a dutiful servant. I had requested that Amka leave us alone. We discussed his family, all of whom lived in a small village near Nekhen, before we turned to the rebellions and incursions in the Delta. Panahasi had aged in the last few years, so that his breath was labored and he groaned whenever he sat or stood. This only made me feel more secure in my choice. Yet I dared not disrespect Panahasi by delaying the inevitable any longer.

"Panahasi, you know we have been without a Chief of the Army since Wadjet's death and…"

"You need not go any further, Mery, for I would be honored to serve in whatever capacity you command. I am prepared to take over the reigns as Chief as soon as you issue the decree." He said this and struggled to stand before me at attention.

I was astonished. No matter how many times I had rehearsed this conversation in my heart, I was totally unprepared for his response. I wanted to talk, and I was conscious of my lips trying to move, but I was rendered speechless. My mind raced for a way out of this impasse.

"Dear Panahasi, please... please sit down," I said, pointing back to his chair. "I fear I have moved too quickly here. Let me...umm...let us back up a bit." I struggled for the right words.

"You have been a loyal, fearless soldier for your entire life. I know from reading the scrolls of your many valiant battles, of how you trained the troops, of how much you are respected by your men and the Horus priests." By now, Panahasi knew that something was wrong, for he stared at me with a quizzical expression.

"I have decided to do something bold and not in keeping with tradition and, therefore, a path fraught with risk. I have decided that we need to go in a new direction, Panahasi. I have decided to appoint Herihor as the new Chief of the Army." Poor Panahasi fell back in his chair as if I had hit him with a mace.

"Well, this... this is certainly not in keeping with tradition. I... I do not know what to say... I..."

"Panahasi, I will need your support in this matter. Herihor will also need your support. You are too old a soldier, too experienced, to simply be cast aside. I need you to show support for this choice and I will give you every opportunity to handle it in a way that accomplishes that."

Panahasi looked confused. "What do you mean by that?" he asked.

"Well, I was just thinking that if you would rather the scrolls reveal that I first offered the job to you, but you refused due to your desire to retire, I would make that so. I will also see that you are suitably rewarded."

"Ah, so that's the picture," Panahasi said and for the first time he stared at me with such a penetrating look I thought his anger would get the better of him. "So why didn't you say that you just wanted to kick me out, instead of shaming me as you've done?"

"That was not my intention, Panahasi."

Now he stood again and paced aggressively toward my elevated chair. "As for you, Mery..."

"Panahasi! You will call me Meryt," I said icily and he stopped in his tracks. Thus we stared at each other for several seconds. I tried not to breathe hard, but I was running out of air.

"Fine, Meryt-Neith, King Regent of the Two Lands," and he bowed slightly as he coldly said those words. "You were a spoiled brat child then and a bastard ruler now. I've been worried as to how I'd serve you as Chief of the Army, and now you've solved that problem. So, here it is. I resign. Have the almighty scrolls read whatever way you'd like, for I don't give a damn!"

"You will watch your tongue in the King's presence, whether Regent or not!" I said to him firmly, pointing a finger right at him. He breathed in such a labored way I feared for his life. Yet, whatever negative I might say about Panahasi, despite the many troubles he gave me in later years, he was still a soldier through and through. In seconds he regained his composure, stood up straight, saluted me with his forearm to his heart, turned around and stormed out of the tent.

I left Amka in Merimda to deal with Panahasi and sailed back to Inabu-hedj to be with Zenty. I tried to put the discussion with Panahasi behind me, but it kept me up a night and gave me much pause to think whether or not I had made the right decision after all.

In a ten-day, just after Amka returned, I had occasion to meet with Ti-Ameny regarding Zenty's care and also to answer Ti-Ameny's quizzing about my health, which she constantly worried about. When we had finished, Ti-Ameny just sat there, drumming her fingers on the table next to her. I finished eating my dates.

"Is there something else?" I asked.

"Yes, one more thing… a petty issue really, but one I thought you'd best know."

"Yes, go ahead."

"Well, it… perhaps it is improper to speak of this, Mery, but I have heard a rumor… well, two rumors actually, concerning General Herihor." Here she paused to gauge my reaction.

"Go ahead."

"Well, I am not asking whether or not it is true that he is to be the new Chief of the Army. It is just that I understand that Nubiti is highly upset about the possible appointment."

I thought for a moment as to how to respond to Ti-Ameny's information, but I immediately saw the complexity in the situation and decided to not discuss it further. "Thank you for sharing this with me, Ti. I know you do not like to spread rumors and I appreciate the way you have handled it."

Still, Ti-Ameny waited, sitting upright in her chair, her muscles tense. "There is more, isn't there?" The muscles below Ti-Ameny's left eye twitched.

"Yes, but this comes from my heart, not from the mouth of others."

"Speak your mind, Ti."

"You... you know that you and Zenty are my primary responsibilities. But I also get around the palace and I am an Isis priestess, too. I hear much of what goes on in the Royal Court, but I also hear from the common people, rekhi, artisans, traders. There are many questions in the minds of people, Mery, questions about your desire to demonstrate your male qualities. The people wonder who you are, what you are. They fear what your true desires are for kingship. And now, with the rumors of your appointment of Herihor, the way that breaks with our traditions, their worries are at a fever pitch."

"And you, Ti, do you worry, too?

Ti-Ameny looked down at her hands and then looked up directly at me. "Yes... yes, I do," she finally said, her voice choked with emotion. "I care not a flea's flick about Herihor, but I do worry about your ba. Women's' bas are different from men's, Mery. A little of a man's ba in us is good, but too much can be destructive. I look... we look at Shepsit and both of us see that, although neither of us has spoken openly about it. But, you are precious to me. I have known you your entire life. I have seen you grow from a carefree, pleasing child to a responsible, happy young wife and mother. I know every aspect of your body, even your monthly cycle. I helped deliver Zenty. But, I... I have also seen your ascension change you, Mery and that is what I fear. Your womanly ba has hardened."

So, Ti-Ameny had said it. She had expressed my deepest fears, the very ones that kept me awake at night, praying to Isis for guidance. That very night I could not sleep. In my heart I thought of all the problems that beset my lovely Kem, for which I was held accountable. I was supposed to be Zenty's Horus intermediary, but by now I was convinced that Horus' spirit did not flow in my blood. Famine gripped the Two Lands, my own sister had become my enemy and I had made a military decision that shocked me as much as my advisors. Worst of all, my own people questioned my authority. It did not help at all that my monthly bleeding was due and I felt myself bloated and ready to explode.

I got up from my bed and walked onto the balcony that overlooked Mother Nile. She flowed silently below me. I could see three of my King's Guards patrolling the royal compound, swords at the ready. At that moment I was overcome by despair. I leaned over the cool mud brick balcony wall.

"Herneith, my dearest mother, Djer my dear father, Wadjet my loving husband, why do you not look after me? Why do you not rally the gods in my behalf, for surely your hearts are light and you now sit by Horus' throne. I beg you, send mighty Horus to deliver his people from harm. Implore Mother Nile to release her waters, for we have surely suffered enough."

Perhaps it was the time I spent praying to my closest relatives, but I felt their comforting presence more strongly than I had ever before. Their kas surrounded me, infusing mine with feelings of family and love. And so it was that I was able for the first time since becoming Regent to let down my guard.

I sank to my knees on the portico, weeping, my

chest heaving with the burdens that I had too long carried without relief. It was then that the words of my loved ones came to me as echoes in my heart. There was my sweet Wadjet, telling me that he feared not that I was incapable of politics, but that I might become too effective at it and with that be changed forever. How true were his words. For months I had been troubled looking in the mirror and had, in fact, avoided it whenever I could, for the woman who stared back at me was a stranger to my heart.

I thought of Herneith on her deathbed, of her advice to remain open to loving, that love and kindness always endure. And so as my crying subsided, I thought of the love in my heart. I felt the love of those in my family who had journeyed to the Afterworld and I thought of Zenty, my precious, precious Zenty. And again Herneith's words resounded, always leave room in your heart for love. Then, from her all-seeing throne in the Afterlife, she whispered a name to me. Herihor.

SCROLL ELEVEN

Nubiti

I hate Nekhen. I don't mean dislike, for that would be too soft a word for the disgust I feel for this filthy place forsaken by the gods. Of course those self-righteous pigs that call themselves Horus priests and who consider themselves gods in mortal flesh, they surely have not forsaken this place. They swarm around Nekhen like flies, their necks stuck high in the air, as if just because it was Narmer's birthplace by fortune, it is therefore the portal through which the gods visit the Two Lands. I spit on such arrogance!

Yet I find myself forced to visit here regularly, for our very finest Temple of Isis is located in Nekhen, on the opposite end of the village as the original Temple of Horus. Since my first visit to Nekhen, when I was given a tour of the Temple of Horus there, I was astounded by how its legendary importance far exceeded its size, for it was small, especially in comparison with the Horus temple in Inabu-hedj.

Being in Nekhen does have its advantages, though, for it affords me the opportunity to be in the heart of the Land of the Lotus and its power structure. It has allowed me to meet with some of those who are disenchanted with the state of affairs in Kem and even more so, with its usurper Regent King.

Ah, if Mery only knew. Discontent is the foul fragrance that draws civil servants to the dung heap of corruption. The south, even more than the swampy Delta, was hurt terribly by the drought. Aside from the villages that border Mother Nile, the South is an unending vista of burning sand and barren rock and even more sand. I knew from the start that this visit would be a gift, for although it had been planned for nearly six of Ra's silver disk cycles, only recently did I learn that Meryt-Neith would also be here on an urgent mission.

It had been a long day of meeting with my sisters, planning for the annual Festival of Isis and hearing of their appeals for more food and for expansion of our buildings to accommodate girls cast aside by their families during times of famine and waiting to be acolytes. Yet I managed to get through the day knowing that in the evening hours, when most of the King's spies would be asleep, I would meet again with my group of informers to receive the latest news of our southern alliances and of, of course, revealing gossip about Mery and her court.

The Ta-Setys were still lurking about in the far southern border, having feasted their eyes on the gold that lay in our desert mines. Despite their losses, they were eager to attack again, but wanted greater assurances that they would not be repelled. Such negotiations I left in the hands of Khnum's proxies, for I did not want my hand tainted by such affairs.

It was in unraveling the inner workings of Mery's court that I was most interested anyway, for if our plans were to continue forward I might be inheriting that court soon, within the next few years at the latest. To that extent, one of my sister priestesses and my closest informer, Nyla, whom I had personally trained, arrived at midnight.

"Well, sister, it's taken you long enough." I said when she appeared at the back entrance of the temple, her hood covering her head.

"Excuse me, mother. I had to wait until the other sisters were asleep," she said, taking off her hood and kissing me on both cheeks. I smelled enticing rose water fragrance on her neck.

"Well, what have you for me?"

"Much... much. Our Regent has been in Nekhen for several days and already there is much talk." She hesitated and I realized that I had not offered her any refreshment. I pointed her to the food stores and she poured us each a glass of cheap Nekhen wine, no doubt the foulest in all the lands.

"Meryt-Neith is quite agitated," Nyla began. "We are not sure of all the reasons she has come to Nekhen, but we do know that she wishes to confer with Tepemkau and his most senior priests, ones who are also seers. She wanted to make a show of solidarity with the nobles and businessmen in Upper Kem and to talk to those who suffered at the hands of the Ta-Sety."

"How long will she be in Nekhen?"

"I'm not sure, but likely a silver disk cycle, maybe longer. They have laid in large amounts of stores for her contingent." This was cause for concern to me, because I didn't want to be away from Mery's court in Inabu-hedj for too long a period while she herself was in the south. When Mery traveled, members of her court were more willing to meet with me. Besides, our network of spies and allies was still weak in the south and my information limited.

"What else?"

"Now the interesting part. Meryt-Neith has taken Herihor into her confidence." My heart immediately skipped a beat and I was glad for the dark, for I was certain I flushed.

"Confidence?" I asked, trying to sound unemotional.

"One of our spies is a soldier in the King's Guard. He reports that she walks with him in the desert. They are seen discussing matters, sometimes animatedly."

"Discussing what?"

"Little is known, Chief Priestess. We have eyes on them, but not always ears. However, it appears from Herihor's use of sticks and clay soldiers that he describes or instructs her in… in battle strategies."

"Battle strategies? You say battle strategies?" Nyla nodded. "For the life of me that woman desires a penis hanging between her legs. She truly is an abomination. Do the soldiers not see that?"

"Some do, but most are blinded by their loyalty to Herihor."

"Battle discussions, walks…" I mumbled as I paced back and forth. "Is there anything else, Nyla?"

"Yes, mistress, one more item. One of Meryt-Neith's handmaidens overheard a conversation between her and Ti-Ameny, a long conversation. She was outside the royal tent, sewing a tear in one of Meryt-Neith's gowns. The handmaiden was so embarrassed by hearing them talking, she wanted to flee, but was more afraid of being found out, so she stayed and caught nearly the entire thing." Nyla looked at me, her eyes wide.

"Well, what did she find out, or are you holding out for a better price for the information?"

"Oh, no, mistress. You know I'd never do…"

"Nyla, I'm joking, but get to the point."

"Oh, yes, of course. Here it is then. The Regent was asking Ti-Ameny for her advice regarding Herihor."

"Advice? What kind of advice?"

"Of the romantic sort."

"What? That can't be. He's… Herihor's nothing but a common soldier, albeit a General. He is dirt beneath her feet." I was seething at this point and I immediately tried to get my emotions back under control, but my head throbbed with this latest news.

"And did this informer give details?"

"Oh, yes, mistress. The Regent asked Ti-Ameny what she thought and Ti-Ameny was speechless for a long while. She advised Meryt-Neith not to consider such a foolish notion and to get it out of her head. She suggested the Regent send Herihor off to the Delta to deal with the insurgency there, so that she would not be tempted. That was her advice, mistress."

"Thanks to Ra that someone put some sense in her head."

"But... but mistress, I thought you... I mean we... I thought we were against the Regent."

I quickly recovered. "Yes, yes, of course we are, of course. All we want is to bring back the Land of the Papyrus to its former glory. It's just that this is such a surprise, so unpleasant a business." I walked to her and hugged her to me. She hugged me back and her small breasts felt good against mine.

"Dear Nyla, I'm so sorry that you have to witness this... this seedy side of royal business. But until that usurper is unseated, I'm afraid that you'll have to be exposed to this filth."

"I understand, mother, and I do so willingly for you and for Isis and for Kem." She placed her head on my shoulder. Her warmth and the smell of her body had an unsettling effect on me. I kissed her gently on her neck and she slowly looked up at me, her eyes half open, her full lips just a finger's width from mine.

Over the next ten-day I heard many reports, from Nyla and others, describing Meryt-Neith's meetings with Herihor, who was in Nekhen and the surrounding nomes to fortify Upper Kem's southern defenses and to command his officers to make their training more rigorous. Although none of the reports said anything improper was going on between the two, we encouraged Meryt-Neith's handmaiden to spend more time sewing clothes outside the tent. In one case she overheard another conversation between Ti-Ameny and Meryt-

Neith, in which Ti-Ameny admonished Mery for sharing her fears with Herihor, since Meryt-Neith was the chosen of Horus and Herihor's commander.

I had to leave Nekhen and return to Inabu-hedj to be present at another initiation ceremony for new acolytes. I didn't relish leaving the Royal Court in Nekhen and so planned to perform my duties and then sail back upstream to Nekhen on some pretense. But on the day after my return, mother arrived unannounced to visit me in my quarters at the temple.

"Mother, how pleasant to see you so soon after my return," I said as sarcastically as I could. With my now strong connections with Khnum and Bakht, and the vast network they controlled, I'd come to the realization that mother was increasingly a burden to our planning. Admittedly she had a knack for the fine details of relationships but lacked the ability to see the larger picture. Her constant nagging had become quite irritating.

"I had to come quickly, for you have become more slippery than a river frog. You stay for a day or two and never seem to have time for your mother."

"I'm very busy, mother. Aside from my priestess duties, I also have a husband and a household."

"Husband, ha!" she spit out. "He sees even less of you than I do."

"True enough, but he hardly notices. He's too busy stuffing his face with honeyed barley cakes and thick beer. He's a hippopotamus, or haven't you noticed?"

"He's unhappy."

"Well, that makes it unanimous. I make both my mother and husband unhappy. So, other than your failure of a daughter, how are you doing mother?'

Mother sighed loudly and went to the table to pour a cup of water. She sat in one of the simple wood and cane chairs that were placed about my room. "Please, Nubiti, let's not argue. You're not a failure. You're smart and quick and ambitious. It's just that… well, I thought we were a team."

I suddenly felt very weary. I knew that I would have to spend the time boosting my mother's ill feelings, but the thought of it tired me.

"Of course we're a team," I said, knowing full well that mother often had valuable advice to offer, as well as juicy bits of gossip that no one else was able to obtain. She had carefully cultivated a network of informers from the first day Djer moved her into the Royal Palace. "It's just that I'm a tied up with my priestess duties and events move so quickly. There are times when I say to myself that I must tell you of this or that development, yet by time I'm back in Inabu-hedj, those developments have already changed.

Mother drank from her cup and said nothing for a while. "And so how is our strategy unfolding?" she finally asked.

"I had no idea when we first formulated it that it'd be so involved and take me on such a winding journey."

"Yet from all outward appearances you seem to be in control and, I dare say, even enjoying it." This latter comment gave me pause for thought, for I often felt beleaguered by the intricate details of our plot, by the need to keep a certain matter secret from one informer, and another tidbit secret from a different informer, by the need to miss sleep in order to hold meetings with critical elements of our cabal.

"Yes, yes I think you're right, mother. I feel burdened by the obligations we've taken on, but also energized by our vision." I also poured some water for myself and added some to mother's cup.

"But, to answer your question, the plans appear to progress, but more slowly than I'd like. Have you heard anything about Mery's activities while in Nekhen?"

Mother gave me a wry smile and put down her cup. "How did I know that your first request to me for information would be that? I assume you are referring to the fact that she is copulating with your virile soldier."

"He's not my virile soldier!" I yelled at my mother. "I was just asking for information about…"

"We agreed not to put on airs with each other," mother interjected. She had long ago stopped screaming at me and instead had resorted to using a firm voice without emotion, which infuriated me even more.

"You're right," I said, closing my eyes and breathing in to balance my ba. "You've confirmed that they're lovers?"

"No," mother replied. "I know nothing of their romantic exploits, other than the fact that Herihor's her confidante. However, that's not unusual. Wadjet's best friend was General Panahasi. Mery obviously is not a warrior and may want Herihor near her for assurance, to gain confidence in his command of the army." I felt my anger rise even at this information, although I had known it for days. I decided to change the subject.

"I've arranged a meeting with Khnum again, this time in Turakh, to..."

"Why Turakh?" mother asked.

"There's a little temple there that commands a view of Mother Nile. It sits almost halfway between Inabu-hedj and the Delta."

"Yes, I know the temple. Djer insisted our entourage stop there when we made our way to Inabu-hedj the first time. But it's still in Upper Kem and too near Inabu-hedj. Amka's spies are all over that area. It's on an important trading route up and down Mother Nile and also to Lebanon. Do be careful, dear. Don't allow hatred or desire to affect your judgment."

"I'll be careful, but if you are referring to Herihor, this has nothing to do with him," I said. "Khnum suggested the meeting. It's the only time we can meet and he has valuable information for me... for us. Besides, I have to be in the Delta anyway, since we're building several temples there."

Mother's face lit into a broad smile. "Smart, very smart, my dear. There is nothing like building contracts to create ties that bind," and at that we both laughed.

In six days Khnum's men picked me up after midnight as I waited in Turakh, camped next to the temple of Isis that was under construction. As had become customary, Nyla provided cover for me. Khnum's men rowed us across Mother Nile and after we had landed they hiked with me until we were just a few cubits from the temple. I suspected Bakht had consulted his charts and picked this night when Ra's silver disk was but a sliver for the meeting. The temple was surprisingly small, a mere outpost at the top of the bluff.

"Welcome, Queen Nubiti," a voice called out from inside. "Enter quickly so that your silhouette is not visible to prying eyes." I entered, but could make out nothing. "If you'll hold out your hand I'll escort you to a seat. It'll take a while for your eyes to adjust."

Although I could not see well, once I sat I could feel the walls close around me. Tiny arches were cut in each of the four walls. I soon made out the shape of an altar and an unlit brazier in the center of the room.

"Do you know the history of this temple?" Khnum's voice whispered. I listened for other breathing to determine if Bakht was present. When I did not hear anything, I relaxed.

"No. Please enlighten me, Uncle."

"Well, it was built during Scorpion's reign, perhaps before, but not long before."

"Narmer's father."

"Yes, Narmer's father. But it has a unique history for us. As long as our stories go back, the people of the Delta have used this as an outpost. There was even a minor festival that was held here every year by our people. And so, when Scorpion or his father began to imagine conquering Lower Kem, they captured this bluff and built a symbolic temple here.

"As you can see it is fairly useless, tiny as it is. In fact, other than the initial blessing of the site, I know of only one other time that a Horus priest ever graced this place."

"When was that?" I asked, intrigued by Khnum's tale.

"It was during Narmer's time, when Anhotek, his

Vizier, met secretly with an informer who revealed to him a plot by Mersyankh."

"Ah, Narmer's second wife. One of our relatives, correct? Your penchant for irony shines nearly bright enough to light this Horus-forsaken temple," I said, laughing.

"I thought you'd appreciate that," my Uncle responded and from his voice I could hear him smiling. "I received your messages."

"And I yours."

"Good, then you are probably wondering what manner of information would bring me to call a meeting at this time."

"Indeed."

"It is this. Panahasi has joined us!"

"Panahasi! General Panahasi? That... whew, that's wonderful news!"

"Better than wonderful. It's an unintended consequence of that harlot Regent usurping the throne, for a soldier such as Panahasi would never have violated his oath unless he truly believed that Meryt-Neith is an abomination and threatens the good of Kem."

"This... this is... enormous," I mused, standing, then quickly sitting again when I lost my balance.

"This is the magic that Apep creates, as Bakht is quick to point out. This is the break that will turn the tide in our favor."

"I hope so. My spies tell me that Mery may send Herihor to the Delta to deal with the rebellions."

"Hope is what Herihor will have to hang onto, for Panahasi was his teacher and mentor. Panahasi is a great general who, I might add, still counts many soldiers under Herihor's command as secretly loyal to him. They would come over to our side in an instant when Panahasi so commands them."

Whether it was the irony of history or the excitement in Khnum's voice, I soon felt a wave of intense emotion sweep through my ka. For an instant I clearly saw myself with the crown of the Queen of the

Two Lands upon my head and before me a vanquished Mery, bowed low, still grieving the loss of her new love.

SCROLL TWELVE

Meryt-Neith

"They live on Abu Island, in the middle of Mother Nile, far south of Nekhen," Tepemkau said, pointing his hand behind him as he faced me.

"And why have I not been told about them before?" I asked, irritated.

"There are many things we have not told you," Amka chimed in. "And many more things that we have not been told by the gods. I had planned to take you there as part of your education as Regent. But we've had a few crises to deal with up to now, so it has not been a priority."

"I wasn't even aware there was an Abu Island. Why is it named so unusually?"

"There are a number of large boulders that stick out of the river at that point, right after the cataract, and they resemble elephants, so the name Abu. The Ta-Setys believe that they were living elephants long ago and that they were turned to stone by the gods. They believe they will come to life when Mother Nile sends a disastrous flood and they will reduce the flood by sucking up the water with their trunks and spraying it far into the desert."

"Pray to Horus that they come alive soon for we sorely need that flood," I said sardonically. Amka and Tepemkau nodded in agreement.

"So what you are telling me is that there is a colony of black Horus priests on Abu Island?"

"Yes. They are descendents of a Ta-Sety man named Meruka and his closest relatives."

"A Ta-Sety named Meruka?"

"That was his Horus name, given to him when he was made a Horus priest by Anhotek," Tepemkau offered.

I was exasperated to a high degree. "So, you are telling me that Anhotek, Narmer's Vizier and shaman, made this Ta-Sety, this Meruka, a Horus priest?"

"Yes, we are. Let me fill in the story," Amka finally said.

"Well, thank you," I said opening my arms. "Please, any time you feel I am worthy to know about the history of the lands I rule."

Amka cleared his throat, a sure sign that I had pushed the sarcasm too far. "Anhotek received his early training traveling far and wide, from Lebanon to Ta-Sety, thus his unequaled knowledge of medicine and magic. While in Ta-Sety as a young man he lived with an old shaman, a medicine man who was highly respected by his people.

"Now when Narmer was a young boy, Anhotek traveled with him throughout Upper Kem and into Kush and Ta-Sety, mostly to avoid the ill feelings between Narmer and his father, Scorpion, and his step-mother, Mersyankh. This is all well documented in the scrolls that Anhotek meticulously kept, so that future generations might benefit from his knowledge.

"At any event, while he and Narmer were in Ta-Sety, they stayed with the same shaman that Anhotek had known. That is when Narmer took ill with the holy shaking sickness and nearly died."

"Yes, I vaguely remember that from your teachings," I interrupted.

"Well, it was actually Meruka who helped Narmer and from then on he and Anhotek were inseparable. Narmer, your great-grandfather, always considered Meruka his ka brother. When Anhotek passed on to the Afterlife, Narmer named Meruka his chief shaman. In old age, Meruka retired to Abu Island, so he could be closer to his native land and entertain visits from his family, but he maintained his first loyalty to Kem. There he established a temple to Horus and recruited his people, trained them and to this day they carry on the holy work."

"Very interesting. I do wish I had known of them before this." I took a sip of my beer. "And you feel they can help?"

"We do. I have sent messengers back and forth raising this issue with their leader, a priest named Nekau. He has agreed to serve as an intermediary with the Ta-Setys. He knows which tribe invaded our lands and he is eager to be of service. He has been waiting to be summoned."

"And, so what makes them so different from the black priests that we already have here in Nekhen?" I asked, curious.

"They are different, for sure. Anhotek has written about this is his scrolls. Perhaps, while you are here in Nekhen, you will study the scrolls," Amka offered.

"I'd love to do that, dear teacher, and we shall start tomorrow. But for now, what decision do you need from me?"

"Shall we send for Nekau?" Tepemkau asked.

"Yes, of course. Send for him. Immediately, go, make it so," I said, waving my hands at them.

It wasn't until late morning that I recalled how much I disliked being in Nekhen during Shomu, with its oppressive heat. It baked us like an oven, not even a breeze blowing to cool one's skin, except in the depths of the night. Normally this would be an active time of year when our farmers were busy gathering crops. But this year even the soil was baked hard into bricks that burned their feet.

Over the objections of Tepemkau, I commanded him to take me along the streets of Nekhen and into the fields to see for myself the plight of my people. The sights I saw plagued me terribly. The ancient streets of Nekhen are narrower than those of Inabu-hedj. There were places were I had to climb down from my carry chair in order to pass between houses. Each rekhi house was build of simple mud-daub taken from Mother Nile's shores, baked to a light brown by Ra's light, with splotches of darker brown here and there where recent repairs had been made. The wall of one house was joined to its neighbor's, so that the streets and alleyways were nothing but winding walls, punctuated by doorways and side entrances for goat pens.

People came out from their houses and stopped whatever work they did in the fields to catch a glimpse of their exalted King and to prostrate themselves before me. But in the midst of such grinding poverty, I hardly felt exalted.

The people were emaciated, their eyes set deep into their sockets, ribs protruding from overly thin bodies. Pitifully thin goats and chickens scavenged for whatever they could find. Refuse accumulated in the alleys and the stench of it as it decomposed in the hot sun was overpowering and I had to discreetly cover my nose with a piece of my perfumed gown to keep from gagging.

Yet wherever I went, the people ran into their houses to find something of value, a trinket or flower, to give to their King. They cried and shouted, asking for me to intervene as the chosen of Horus to end their plight. One extended family, in particular, drew my attention. They lived in an alley off the main street, but from my chair I caught a glimpse of them as we passed. I instructed my carriers to put me down and with my

King's Guard leading the way, I approached. I could hardly breathe from the overwhelming stench, for there was a dead cat that no one had bothered to remove and a sick goat that had voided its runny bowels into the alley. The heat was oppressive, too.

The family lay about, listless, taking advantage of the meager shade. An elderly grandmother, her skin dark and wrinkled, held her tiny granddaughter in her lap. Both of them were deplorably skinny, their eyes distant and vacant. The grandfather lay on a blanket next to the house, his fingers twisted and his spine bent from a lifetime of working in the fields. The mother tended another child, a boy of perhaps eight years. She dished out a scant piece of cheese placed upon a crumb of old bread. She wore the black shawl of widowhood. Yet when I approached they tried to bend low to the ground.

"No, please, humble servants of Ra, do not bow low, for it is I who am indebted to you," I said, tears now flooding my eyes. They stared at me uncomprehending. Slowly they stumbled to their feet, still unsure of whom it was who addressed them. I knew it was futile to explain. My guards looked at me questioningly.

I reached behind me and unclasped my breastplate, not my ceremonial gold one, but a bejeweled one of far greater value for it contained silver, imported from far away lands.

"Here," I said, reaching out, "take it." The mother looked toward the grandmother, who looked toward me, her mouth agape, revealing her toothless cavity. Still, no one moved.

"Take this. Sell it in the market. It will fetch a good price. Feed your family. Find some shelter. Help others. Come, take it, mother," I repeated, thrusting the breastplate out to her.

Finally, the mother reached out hesitantly. Bowing slightly she reached out with her hand. As I handed it to her, I watched her dirty, chapped hands wrap around the carefully polished jewels. She stood and gazed at the deep blue lapis-lazuli and orange carnelians jewels, all set artfully in silver brackets. They must have appeared to her as if they were of another world and she probably wondered if she had, indeed, entered the Afterlife. She looked from her mother, back to me and then again to the treasure in her hand, the worth of which far surpassed the lifetime earnings of her entire family and friends and neighbors. Ever so slowly she closed her hand around the jewels and pressed them to her own breast. She shook her head and raised her eyebrows as if asking for permission. I shook mine back and tried a wan smile. Then she dropped to the ground and crawled to me to kiss my hand, but my guards prevented her from touching me.

Back on the main roadway we also heard shouts of another kind that day, ones that caused some of my King's Guard to break rank and drag away a protesting husband or father. The experience I had that day was surely not pleasant, but I swore from that moment on, whether in good times or bad, I would never again lose my connection to my people, and each week I stayed in Nekhen, I again went out to distribute what limited aid I could directly to my people. I also forbade any parties or special events in the Royal Court, other than holidays for the gods, for the thought of living in such abundance as my people starved had become anathema to me.

Thank Horus, Zenty was with me in Nekhen, for he provided what little pleasant relief I had from my endless meetings and hours each day taken up by judging land disputes and property settlements in divorce cases of the nobility and merchants, cases that the senior Horus priests were unable to resolve.

Now six years old, Zenty was required to study every day with Amka, as had his father before him. But with Amka's busy schedule, Zenty's lessons were often entrusted to Amka's able assistant, a rising Horus priest named Semni. On this day, however, when I went to check on Zenty's lessons, I found Amka hard at work.

"But how did it all start... before the gods and

before men came along?" Zenty asked.

"Oh, my, what an inquisitive mind you have, my dear boy. Perhaps if you study your picture letters harder, I might tell you the Creation story, the real Creation story, not the one your mother tells you. But until you give me your promise to learn at least ten characters this ten-day, I'm afraid I will not be able to tell you this amazing story."

Zenty tried to think of a way out of his predicament, but he relented. "Alright, I give you my promise, but they cannot all be hard picture words, Amka."

"Oh, so now you have become a great negotiator, eh?" So they bantered back and forth in their loving way and soon Zenty was sitting knees-to-knees with Amka, completely absorbed in the Creation story, all the while asking questions of the old man, to which Amka would respond with a tease or even a downright insult, followed by a laugh. I thought to myself how easily Zenty was learning this male banter and then it dawned on me that perhaps this was one of the ways that men acquired their thick skin when it came to withstanding the trials of relationships.

"Well, what did you think of it? Amka asked of Zenty when he was finished with the story.

"It was interesting," Zenty replied thoughtfully and I instantly marveled at how much he sounded like Amka. "But I will have to think more on it, for I do not think I yet understand about the egg of creation."

"Good, we can discuss it more tomorrow. For now, I notice that Semni is preparing your history lesson." Semni had unrolled a scroll and placed weights in each corner to hold it open.

"Please, Amka, it is too hot to study any more today. I would rather go swimming," Zenty pleaded, sneaking a peak towards me to see if I would intercede on his behalf. Instead I looked down.

"You are quite right," Amka said with a smile. "And that is why Semni has prepared only a short history lesson for you about your great-great grandfather, King Narmer. As soon as it is over and you answer a few questions correctly, you two will go for a swim, right Semni?" Semni nodded.

Zenty dragged himself over to me and laid his sweaty head on my shoulder. I grabbed a fan from the table next to me and slowly moved it over him. He sighed.

"I am so proud of you," I whispered into his ear. "You are so smart, even Amka has a hard time keeping up with you."

Zenty turned his head to face me and stood on his tiptoes to whisper back to me. "Yes, but it is hard work, mama. And I have to always be careful not to ask old Amka too many questions. He's not as patient as Semni." I reached down and hugged Zenty and suppressed my laughter so as not to upset Amka, but when I looked up I saw that my old teacher had heard Zenty and he smiled broadly. With that Zenty reluctantly trudged off.

"And when, dear teacher, will you instruct me on Narmer's scrolls, and Anhotek's, too?" I asked as soon as Zenty left.

Amka looked up at me and struggled to stand. He walked to the food table and gulped down water. I noted that he hardly ate anything during the day, but always drank of Mother Nile's bounty, which he considered an elixir. "We should begin immediately. It was always my intention to prepare Zenty to become King. Your ascension came so quickly, with so many crises, I had not prioritized your education. Now, it is time." Amka leaned against the table and thought.

"I will assign Semni to Zenty's lessons while we are here in Nekhen and we will use that time to study together. I have copies of all of Anhotek's important scrolls back in the library at Inabu-hedj. While in Nekhen, we will focus on Narmer's scrolls and any we have not completed I will assign the temple scribes to copy so we may take them with us." And so began one of the most important experiences in my entire rule, and one that had implications for my personal life as well.

The very next day Ti-Ameny woke me early and told me that Amka had instructed her to tell me to take a ritual bath and for Ti-Ameny to shave my head and genitals, for as Regent and chosen of Horus I was to enter the holy of holies, the Temple of Horus in Nekhen.

Once I entered the temple, Tepemkau and Amka took me into Horus' chamber and conducted a prayer service to spiritually cleanse me. Tepemkau left to attend to other chores while Amka escorted me to the adjoining library. There, much like in Inabu-hedj, was a large room, larger even than the temple itself, where clay jars were stacked on their sides, one atop each other, from floor to ceiling. Large tables were distributed around the room. As soon as we entered, two young priests bowed low to me and quickly scurried out of the room.

Amka swept his hand to indicate one entire wall. "Here then it is," he said, his voice surprisingly choked with emotion. "The sacred scrolls of King Narmer, may his name be blessed for all eternity, and those of Anhotek, his most loyal Vizier, scribe and shaman… and a Horus priest, too, of course," he added, bowing slightly.

"Here, too, you will find Meruka's scrolls, for he became an adept at the picture words, too. I will get you started, Meryt, and I will show you the order of the scrolls, starting when Anhotek became Vizier to Narmer's father, Scorpion, who was basically illiterate.

"Anhotek kept meticulous records, until Narmer came of age. Then we have dual scrolls, Anhotek's and Narmer's, who was known as Meny as a child. It is interesting to compare the two records of the same events, I might add."

"You say you will get me started. Are there not lessons you wish to teach? I mean certain learnings?" I could not imagine Amka passing up any teaching opportunity, for if there was ever one born to such a craft, it was the man who stood before me.

"Mery, I just spent a sleepless night meditating over this issue, and early this morning I asked Tepemkau for his opinion. We agree that this must be a private matter, an opportunity, while we await Nekau's arrival, for you to connect with your lineage." Amka sat down, looking tired.

"There is so much to say... so much. But I believe Narmer's and Anhotek's words will do a much better job. The gods gave us a blessed land, but they also placed mut spirits on it for balance and to help us to understand just how blessed we are. Never forget, Meryt, that the Two Lands were in great peril during Scorpion's rule. Our people lived on a knife's edge and could have been reduced to petty warring tribes. But difficult times sometimes produce great leaders. Anhotek, Narmer and Meruka were such leaders. They lived by a vision, a vision that sustained them, nourished them, and that ultimately guides us today."

"What vision is that?" I asked, my curiosity peaked. Amka stood up, bowed and made ready to leave, picking up his staff.

"A great leader can only be gifted a vision by the gods," he said solemnly. "Prepare to meet one who walked the Two Lands not long ago. You shall see whether or not King Narmer chooses to share his vision with you."

For the next ten-day, Amka made certain that I was not interrupted from the time Ra rose in the heavens, and I appeared in the library, to the time Ra's chariot set, at which time I spent a little time with Zenty. I hardly slept during this period and I ate only the bread, cheese and beer of the priests. Even Ti-Ameny kept her distance, to be sure due to Amka's instruction, for I know she fretted about my eating and lack of sleep. And although Amka and I later discussed the fact that he suspected what was happening to me, the truth is that no man or woman who walks our land can ever know, ever truly understand, what transpired over the course of that ten-day and half of the next.

It started simply enough, just a story, albeit miraculous, of Narmer's birth as described by Anhotek, who delivered him. For Narmer was truly born under Horus' outspread wings, a day of clouds such as is rarely seen in Kem. Anhotek's scrolls told of Narmer's shaking illness and how hard he tried to find a cure, even journeying to distant lands for medicines that eventually controlled it but did not cure it. He told of the fears and disdain of Narmer's father, Scorpion, for his son and of the rivalry between Narmer and his stepmother, Mersyankh, who was from the Delta. And, of course, it was here that I felt my first heart connection with my great-grandfather, but hardly the last.

When I read of his love for the desert, it forced me to reexamine my own views, for although we are born in its midst, we are also taught that those barren lands are filled with evil mut spirits, like vipers and scorpions, waterless territory to be avoided unless absolutely necessary. So I pledged to myself that from this point on I would become more acquainted with the territory that made up at least ninety percent of Upper Kem.

It was on the eighth day that I awoke earlier than usual. Ra had still not risen and all in the Royal compound were asleep. I quickly bathed, brushed my teeth and hair and left to walk alone to the temple, wrapped in my shawl so that I would not be recognized.

In the library I was surprised to find two papyrus scrolls already set upon the table, each opened to a particular section. On top of them was a note, from Amka: My heart tells me you are now ready for this.

With trepidation I began to read Anhotek's description of Narmer's first vision experience, visited upon him by none other than Horus himself. I had to remind myself that this account was written by a shaman priest who had experienced miracles and wonders beyond imagining as he traveled throughout Kem and nearly all the known lands beyond.

Anhotek nursed Narmer through that long night of visioning, fearing many times that Narmer would not survive the night, so violent were his shakes. That Horus believed that such a young boy could handle the responsibilities of such a weighty vision convinced Anhotek that night of Narmer's greatness. As Narmer lost his reasoning and lapsed into one shaking fit after another, Anhotek knew without a doubt that the boy was chosen to bring Unification to the Two Lands.

It was night when I began reading Narmer's own accounts of his visions, compiled by Anhotek into one scroll called The Visions Scroll. I had not eaten all day. The food left by the priests that morning went untouched. I had even forgotten to go back to the court to put Zenty to bed. Yet I knew in my heart that Amka was right, that the past eight days were spent preparing me for what lay unfurled before me.

I lit candles all around the table, which had the effect of walling me off from the outside. The light nighttime breezes began and by the flickering of candlelight, I began my journey, Narmer's journey, the journey of the Two Lands. The picture words took on a life of their own as shadows and light played across their surface.

In one moment Narmer felt normal and in the next he lay unaware on the ground shaking violently. He was transported then to what he called the Other World, a world with no mortal bounds. He saw the great light and in the magic of his descriptive words I, too, saw it. It is my belief that I did read Narmer's words that night, but I could no more swear to that than I could swear I was the true mortal representative of Horus. Instead I felt it, I experienced it and it was more real than anything I had experienced before.

I flew. That was the first thing I remembered. My finger pointed to the text, but I flew from my earthly body and ascended effortlessly to the light, and the light warmed me and infused my ka, it became my ka. I had no body, not even wings, yet I saw through the eyes of

Horus. And what I was shown was a magic I had never dared imagine.

I shared Narmer's vision. I flew through the sky, back and forth over Mother Nile as she wound her way from the lush mountains of Kush, painted in shades of green such as I had never before known. Down, down, I flew to our southern desert border. I sailed upon the winds, high above her watery body as she turned and twisted from village to village, from Nekhen to Inabu-hedj. Then Mother Nile fanned out into five tributaries and I saw the marshes of Lower Kem as never before, connected by Mother Nile's unbroken, life-giving string.

I do not say that I saw all of Narmer's vision, but I will swear upon Horus that I grasped its miraculous essence and it is this, simple in its message, elegant in its beauty. Mother Nile gives us life. She sustains us, she nourishes us, she blesses and punishes us. But throughout her journey she is one, unified, whole. Mother Nile does not differentiate the Land of the Lotus from the Land of the Papyrus, Kush from Kem, man from beast. She nourishes us all. She is one. We are one. And that is the gift the gods gave Narmer. We are one. One people, one culture, one nation. Only through Unification could ma'at thrive. Only united as one people could we ever live in balance with our plants and animals and achieve the greatness that was our destiny.

Narmer's scroll tells of the thriving nation he witnessed in his Other World, of the monuments he saw built of everlasting stone, not feeble mud bricks. He described great white cities shimmering in Ra's light and immense temples worthy of the gods themselves. Until that night, sitting in the library of the Temple of Horus in Nekhen, I did not comprehend my role in that vision. I felt like a weak link in a chain of leaders needed to achieve Narmer's vision. I vowed that very night to repair that link and to hand to my son the unbroken strength of Narmer's vision, a strong Kem, one people governed by one ruler.

With Ra's rebirth, I walked the few cubits to the

sanctuary of Horus. Tepemkau was already in the vestibule, preparing for morning prayers. When he saw me he smiled, stepped aside and waved me into the Inner Sanctuary.

It is hard to describe now how I felt, turning the corner and seeing Horus' presence there, for the statue of Horus in the temple of Nekhen is the oldest and holiest in all Kem. Yet I did not waver or feel fear. I looked into Horus penetrating eyes and I knew at once that he saw me and understood. I knelt before him, fell to the floor and prayed. Tears fell freely, but they were tears of gratitude. I thanked Horus for the honor of King Narmer's visit, for his ka was surely borne on Horus' wings.

For the next two days I slept, on and off. Amka said that I tossed and turned in a feverish pitch, murmuring, my limbs twitching. Of course he and I knew that I was possessed with Narmer's ka, and every day since, when I make my offerings, I thank my great-grandfather for visiting with me and clarifying my purpose.

On the fifteenth day after beginning my studies, I awoke refreshed, knowing that while many scrolls remained, I had extracted from them enough to begin the difficult work ahead. Amka would copy the rest and bring them with us back to Inabu-hedj. That very day I called in Herihor without discussing my intent with Amka.

"Herihor, what do you make of the desert?" I asked.

"Hmmm, interesting question, master. In what sense do you mean that?"

"Do you find it interesting or frightening? Is it mysterious or understandable to you?"

"It is all those things, and more. The desert is our friend and our enemy. It is beautiful and terrifying. A sandstorm is impressive from afar, but I have lost men to them when they descend upon us directly. A viper is a terrifying creature, but its skin is beautiful to behold."

"Herihor, I wish for you to take me into the desert, where your troops are camped."

"But, master, that would not be wise. It..." And later Herihor would tell me that although he was surprised at my request, he knew at once that it could not be denied, that something in my ba had changed since our last visit.

In a few days Amka had run through all his objections to no avail. Herihor made arrangements for a suitable encampment in the eastern desert, for that was his admitted favorite, since its mountains and rocky soil were more diverse and interesting. When I first laid eyes on my desert tent, it was as if my heart was finally comfortable in my chest and I recalled reading of Narmer's own deep love for this land.

The large tent stood in a narrow ravine between two mountains, one with brown rocks and the other with vibrant blue. A contingent of King's Guards blocked the entrance to the ravine affording me protection, yet they were far enough away for me to be able to conduct business without prying ears and eyes. Herihor had thoughtfully placed the tents of my retinue outside the ravine.

For the next ten-day, Herihor and I met twice a day, once in the morning before the desert's heat and once after the evening meal when the desert was still warm but not oppressively hot. We settled into a comfortable routine. The morning session was devoted to instruction in the desert's mountains, wadis, sands and rocks, as well as the living things that hid so well in every available crevice and even buried in the sand. We discussed the mut scorpions we saw, but also the graceful ibex standing so precariously upon just a sliver of rock. We climbed a mountain and watched dik-diks scurrying across the desert floor, pursued by a lioness and watched one morning as a falcon circled above us, piercing the air with its shrill cries.

On the second day of our outings, we came upon a strange pattern of ripples progressing up a small sand dune. When I asked Herihor what these were, he laughed.

"Let's see," he said. "But do be careful. Stay behind me and keep your distance." We climbed the dune slowly and at the top Herihor pointed. Slithering down the other side was the most hideous viper imaginable, its head almost a perfect triangle and its body easily the length of Herihor's. I instinctively grabbed Herihor's arm with both my hands and trembled.

"Let's go!" I cried out.

"We'll go if you insist, but I assure you that viper will not be a threat to us. It is more afraid of us then we are of it."

"By the love of Isis that is an ugly animal!" I ventured. "And so evil looking."

"My master, I do not agree," he said, turning half towards me yet keeping a watchful eye on the beast. "It's certainly not ugly to a female viper, nor is it evil, except when a man is about to step on it. They bury themselves in the sand like this," he said eagerly, making motions with his hand and lowering his head to his shoulders. "They wait for a small desert mouse or perhaps a scorpion or a dung beetle, then strike. If a man accidentally steps on it, the poor mut hardly knows what it's doing, it merely strikes in self-defense. Ask Amka, for he knows more about these creatures, but I find no malice in the way they behave."

I marveled at Herihor's view of the viper and looked up at him. Suddenly, I realized I was squeezing his arm and let go quickly, embarrassed.

"Besides," he said, continuing as if nothing had happened, "the viper plays an important role in King Narmer's history."

"How... how do you know about Narmer's history?" I asked, curiously.

Herihor turned to me and Ra's rays cast the scar on his cheek in deep shadow, making it appear more pronounced. "For years I have studied his scrolls, as well as Anhotek's, and every scroll written by Narmer's top generals. Amka has instructed me. From time to time

Tepemkau, too."

I was shocked at this revelation. "Dear Horus, I cannot believe that! I have done little else but study them for the past two ten-days."

"Yes, we've all noticed your absence."

And so began the most extraordinary series of conversations I ever had with another person. Every day we would compare notes on the scrolls and what we learned from them. For Herihor, the scrolls provided wise counsel on the historical aspects of war and leadership, combined with Anhotek's and Meruka's careful observations about treatments for battlefield injuries and meticulous descriptions of the various animals and plants of Kem.

For me, the experience of sharing my newfound enthusiasm with Herihor is difficult to describe. For the first time I found someone, other than Amka, who could engage with me on a topic, question me, challenge my positions and freely offer his own.

On those days when Abana brought Zenty to me for a visit, he and Herihor had a marvelous time together. Herihor had one of his men fashion a dagger and sword made of wood for Zenty and from then on the two of them battled each other constantly. Zenty would lie in wait, hiding, until Herihor came into view and then he would pounce from behind a rock and chase poor Herihor around and around the tent and up and down dunes, giggling until he hiccupped uncontrollably. Then they would both fall down laughing and Zenty would jump on top of him. So much for the saying that little boys grow up to be men. I think the opposite more true. It takes but a spark, a new toy or the loud expulsion of foul vapors from a friend's rear end, to see the instant transformation from man back to boy.

But thankfully, Zenty still dwelled in his mother's house. I cherished those evenings in the desert before Ra set, when Zenty and I would walk, hand in hand, across the dunes, watched over by the King's Guards. Once, Amka arrived for two days to discuss some urgent Court matters. He joined us, with Zenty walking between us, holding each of our hands. It pleased me greatly to have Zenty know Amka, but it also saddened me to know that the day would come when Zenty and I would no longer have Amka in this world. Who would take his place? Who would be there to answer the detailed questions for which only Amka had the wisdom and experience to know the answers?

And I still marveled at how this little boy, this bundle of joy, emanated from Djet's and my ka and came forth so perfectly formed from my own body. Our kas were entwined for all eternity. How could this tiny person grow to become the King of the Two Lands? As he ran up the side of a tall dune and then rolled down, again and again, I realized how awesome was our responsibility. I shuddered with the enormity of the task before us.

It was after a three-day visit by Zenty that Herihor and I went for our evening walk and discussion.

"You do seem in an excellent mood tonight," Herihor commented.

"Yes, it is Zenty's visit. He's so inquisitive, I sometimes find it hard to even keep up with his many questions. I feel like I am in the midst of a sandstorm!"

Herihor laughed. "Yes, he's becoming more independent. I think that Amka's way of teaching allows him to think more deeply of things, to... to try to make sense of all the amazing things the gods have put in our world."

Certainly, Herihor was right. "Yet it worries me greatly that we have only ten or twelve years before he is old enough to rule the Two Lands. How will we ever teach him all he needs to know?" At that we walked in silence for a long way before Herihor spoke.

"Narmer's vision, that is it," Herihor said.

"Meaning?"

"We each have a role to play in his education. But the most important thing he will need is King Narmer's vision. If he blesses him with his vision, then all else is but details."

"Blesses or curses him with it," I thought aloud.

"Hmmm, that's an interesting thought. I see what you mean. But assuming he does gain the vision, it will give him the direction he needs to lead. It will add force and rightness to his decisions. He will be a great leader of a great nation."

"Yes, if…" I sighed. "If, if, if."

By now Ra's light had faded and we had ambled back to the entrance to the ravine. Two of Herihor's guards saluted us. We rounded the mountain's base and my tent glowed with the candles that my servants had lit for me. Ra had set over the mountain, but his last light faintly lit the sky. It had been the perfect day, with few demands on me other than my loves. My loves. The thought hit me just as we approached the entrance to my tent.

If I were possessed by mut demons of the desert I could have excused my behavior, but I was not. I turned to Herihor and as I looked into his eyes my body burned with desire for the first time since Wadjet's death. I felt an ache inside me to kiss him, to have him take my body and to feel him inside me. I slowly put my hand up to his face to gently touch his scar.

Herihor reached out to hold me and then, in an instant, it was over. He withdrew his arms, my hand still reaching for him, and turned away from me.

"Oh, Horus! I… I cannot do this," he said, his voice anguished. He turned back and came close to me. "Mery, there is nothing more that I would want than to hold you in my arms. I have dreamed of this moment, " he said, reaching out, once again, before dropping his arms. "But Wadjet was… he was my closest friend. I cannot name the times we fought together, drank together, even… yes, even whored together before he wedded you." Herihor's brow was furrowed and he hung his head as if in shame.

"I understand, my dearest Herihor," I whispered.

"Mery, I held his hand as he drew his last breath. I

yet pray every day for his happiness in the Afterlife."

A strange feeling came over me in that moment. It was as if Isis stood next to me and opened our wounded hearts to each other to be healed, for did I not feel the very same way about my beloved Wadjet? And yet I also experienced the unadulterated joy, even if only for a few moments, of once again being a woman, and only a woman. Being with Herihor I did not have to play the roles of Queen or King or Regent, roles that sucked energy from my ka and twisted my ba into personalities I hardly recognized as the true me. And so we left it.

The next day I was scheduled to leave for Nekhen to make appearances for the Sed Festival. Amka appeared at my tent to escort me the very next morning and we left without Herihor seeing me off. I assumed he was to meet my boat on the other side of Mother Nile, but he did not show up there either. I found out later that day from Amka that he was called away during the night to attend to a military matter, but I was not concerned by his absence, for Isis had revealed to me what lay in his heart.

In normal years the Sed Festival was one of the happiest festivals in Upper Kem. It had been practiced for generations before even King Narmer. It was the annual celebration of the King's renewal, for our people wisely believe that both the gods and the King lose some of their power during the course of ruling the Two Lands. Each year during Sed we renew our power.

On Ra's appearance the next morning, we set out from Mother Nile's shore, as surely a symbol of rebirth as ever there was. Yet this year she flowed past a much wider and higher embankment than usual. A throng of dignitaries, merchants, artists and scribes cheered for me when I arrived, although I thought less heartily and with far less passion than they might have. The Apis Bull was waiting for me, restrained in a halter by four large Horus priests.

"We begin immediately," Amka said, "before the heat of the day." He leaned closer to me. "And remember, it would appear unseemly to run. You are a mother now as well as King."

The bull was pulling at his restraints and from his mouth hung long strings of drool. Every so often he would shake his head and the drool would fly in all directions, to the amusement of the crowd. I received many of the dignitaries as we waited to start the festival.

"Ah, here comes Zenty," Amka remarked.

"Zenty? What is he doing here?" I asked, surprised.

"He will be along with you, carried by servants on a platform."

"Why... why have you not told me of this before?"

"It is nothing, Mery, just a formality. We will discuss this later if that is alright with you, for the festival route is lined with revelers who have waited through the night." And so we began the processional designed to prove the King's strength by pitting it against the King's Apis bull incarnation. Throughout the route people cheered and shouted, yet I saw them on tiptoes and hiking children onto their shoulders and pointing to Zenty's platform, too. Then I realized the purpose of Zenty's company.

"That was no formality!" I shouted at Amka the next day during our daily meeting. "You did that to... to..."

"I did it because the nobles were clamoring to see the future King," Amka answered. "You really should work at not being so childish about your objections," he added condescendingly.

"Do not talk to me that way, Amka!" I responded angrily. "I know the real reasons. They still do not trust me. Despite our laws some still do not believe a woman is equal to a man, as if having some ridiculous protuberance hanging between ones legs makes one better able to govern. Or that breasts make one less able to rule."

"It's not..."

"And don't you forget that every one of you... you and the one-eyed muts you carry around between your legs, has suckled at a woman's breast. Your attitude infuriates me!" I stormed off to stand at the palace's overlook. Below me Mother Nile flowed tranquilly. In a few minutes Amka joined me.

"Mery, you know Tepemkau and I supported your ascension. We..."

"Yes, I know," I said in a more conciliatory tone. "I'm sorry I lashed out against you, dear teacher. I know I rule as Zenty's Regent, but I also know that to rule the Two Lands is less exalted than those outside these walls imagine. I beg your indulgence for what I am about to say, but either man or woman can be King, it makes no difference, for it is the Horus priests who hold the real power anyway."

"Mery, I..."

"No, no, don't bother to explain that away, dear friend. I have given much thought to it and it is probably as it should be. People's bas differ and one king's wishes might reverse ten kings before him, so the Horus priests must vigilantly and consistently defend ma'at. I see the stability they bring to our land. I have come to see how the festivals, the prayers, the sacrifices, the holy scrolls, how you tie them all up into a neat knot that protects us from the chaos that might otherwise result." To his credit, Amka just bowed his head and remained silent. Nothing further was said about it.

As was our tradition, I spent the following days in seclusion, participating in ritual cleansings and meditations. When that was over I entertained petitions from many of our elite regarding access to trade routes, exclusive rights to sell certain types of goods, even payments to the Royal treasury in exchange for favorable placement of tombs in the Royal necropolis. By the end of the ten-day I was weary and wished to escape from the non-stop procession of people and favors.

I had heard that Herihor was still on his so-called military mission, whatever that was. I realized that I missed the quietude of the desert and so I instructed Ti-Ameny to prepare us for another stay. My tent still stood in its spot and for the next three days I walked the paths that Herihor had shown me, sometimes with Ti-Ameny and at other times alone.

On the third afternoon I hiked alone part way up the blue mountain in order to meditate and surprisingly found a cave with a huge entrance. The cave was shallow, no more than five or six cubits deep, but at least fifty cubits high. Its ceiling held a small assortment of bats and I noted evidence of the cave having been previously used. The charred remnants of a small fire lay in front of a boulder in the middle of the cave. The entrance overlooked the valley and the surrounding mountains. Far below me I saw my tent and my servants going in and out with food and clothing.

I spread out my meditation blanket and sat on the boulder, crossed my legs and began to meditate as Amka had taught me to do. It was only then that I heard for the first time the true silence of the desert. There were no people talking at me, no leaves rustling on trees, no water flowing beneath my feet, no wind blowing through palace rooms. Silence. Utter, complete, the perfect silence of Nun.

I closed my eyes and breathed, conscious of my breath in a way I had never before experienced. I could feel every part of my breath entering, circulating in my lungs, and leaving through my mouth and nostrils. I could feel Horus' strength and spirit moving within me. It was spiritual. It was sensual. I felt rejuvenated, reborn.

"I see you have found my spot," he whispered, yet his presence did not startle me. "May I join you?" I shook my head and he sat next to me, our knees touching. For the next few minutes- or was it hours?- we meditated together, sharing our breath, our kas intermingling. When I opened my eyes, Ra's dim light was fading quickly.

"I come here when I need solace, when the burdens of leading men to die in battle weighs heavily on my shoulders," Herihor said softly.

"Is it you who lit the fire?" I asked.

"No. The desert wanderers introduced me to this spot. They seek refuge here from time to time."

We sat in silence watching Ra's orb sink further until the mountains across from us were black silhouettes. When I turned to Herihor, his body was half-turned and he looked at me with an expression of longing. For the second time I reached out to him, but this time he did not resist. I looked deeply into his eyes in the fading light. We kissed then, tenderly.

"Master, this… do you really… do you want to do this?" he pleaded, leaning back from me.

"I am hardly your master, Herihor, for exactly the opposite is true. There is nothing I would rather do than please you." I took his hand and drew him to me.

Oh, how Isis entered my ba that night! Before that night Wadjet had been my only intimate companion and I had always considered him a good lover, kind and gentle. That I was blessed with two wonderful lovers in my life I only came to learn later was rare, indeed.

Never before had I been kissed so passionately, our lips and tongues thirstily exploring each other. More than once Herihor pulled away to be sure that I was comfortable with what we did and in each instance my reaction left no doubt as to my intent.

Herihor lifted me off the boulder. We spread out my blanket and kneeled face to face. I took the straps of my gown off my shoulders and let it drop. Herihor's eyes opened wide as he took in my body. He quickly stood and removed his dagger belt and kilt. Standing before me he left nothing to my imagination as to his desires.

He dropped back down to his knees and in that position we embraced each other. The feel of his skin against mine, the press of his chest against my breasts, my nipples exquisitely sensitive, was so erotic I shuddered.

"Is something wrong?" Herihor asked in alarm.

"No, no, nothing at all. I have waited so long for

this moment," I whispered.

Herihor wrapped me in his massive arms and kissed me deeply, moving his hands over my back and buttocks. His cock was so engorged I had to grab it to keep it from poking by stomach. He gasped with pleasure and gently moved his hand between my thighs.

I was so slippery, his finger slid in immediately. Yet he did not persist and instead gently caressed my pleasure spot, until I begged him to enter me. He grabbed me around my waist and, still kneeling, picked me up and slipped inside me as I wrapped my legs around him. Thus we rocked back and forth, kissing passionately, both of us moaning with pleasure.

I cannot recall how many times Herihor brought me to the heights of pleasure as we rolled on the blanket that night. We both dripped with sweat and yet could not get enough of each other. Finally, Herihor, arched his back and shot his seed into me again and again, before collapsing onto his back.

That is how Herihor and I became lovers, that night and the following night and the nights after that for the more than two ten-days that I stayed in the desert. They were wondrous days and nights, filled with passionate discourse about desert life, visions and leadership, yet even more passionate lovemaking in my tent or under the lights of the gods.

Finally, Amka sent a message that it was time to return, for Nekau was due to arrive within the next ten-day. I was reluctant to leave, yet I recognized my responsibilities. I knew that to mortar Narmer's vision would require great efforts over the next several years and Nekau might prove critical to their success. Still, shortly after I returned to Nekhen I fell ill. Amka, who every year dreaded Shomu for the illnesses the hot, sticky weather bred, blamed my illness on returning to the crowded and stale air of Nekhen. He gave me herbs to quell the nausea and sniffling.

On the fifth day after my return to the palace in Nekhen, just after the mid-day meal, Amka appeared.

"And how is my patient?" he asked.

"Between you and Ti-Ameny and your foul potions, I can hardly eat or sleep. But, yes, my symptoms are better."

"Good, because Nekau's entourage arrived last night," he said, a pleasant expression on his face. "He is refreshed and waiting for your audience."

"And what has put your usually dour face into such a pleasant countenance?" I asked, teasing him.

"You will see," he replied. "Shall I ask him in?"

"Yes, of course," I answered.

"Good, we will meet in the Great Hall," which I found amusing, since everything in Nekhen was built on a far smaller scale than in Inabu-hedj.

When I arrived at the hall, I ascended to the throne chair and sat. Amka was there, as was Herihor, several high-ranking priests and six of my King's Guards, all dressed in their formal leather, spears at the ready, waiting to honor the visitors. Amka waved to Semni, who left the hall. When he returned, a delegation that included Tepemkau followed him.

When my eyes fell on Nekau, I gasped. Never had I seen a man of such gigantic proportions, nor of such intense blackness that at first I could only make out his eyes. He easily stood at least two heads taller than Herihor, the next tallest in the room. I heard the creak of Herihor's leather as he tensed.

Nekau was younger than I had imagined and he was dressed in leopard skins, with a necklace made of lion and hippopotamus teeth. He wore a gold band around his left bicep and I noticed at once that it carried Narmer's serekh of the catfish and chisel, such a rarity that the only other one I had ever seen was in the Temple of Horus in Nekhen. His sandals were woven with gold thread and around his ankles he wore gold jewelry and feathers.

When he approached my elevated chair I still had to look up to him. He stopped before me and bowed low and stayed that way.

"You... you may arise," I said tentatively, my throat suddenly dry. As he did so he had a huge smile on his face. That smile triggered a vague recollection and in the moment of silence that followed, I recognized that I was reliving Narmer's first meeting with Meruka, Nekau's great-grandfather, just as Narmer had described it in his scrolls. That our bloodlines were connected so far in the distant past made me shiver.

Nekau's eyes were set deep and when he looked at me they gave him the impression of being very intense.

"Welcome, Nekau," I said, holding open my arms in tribute. "I appreciate the long journey you have made to offer me counsel."

Nekau bowed his head and when he straightened he again stared deeply into my eyes, such that I felt uncomfortable. To my side I again heard the rustle of Herihor's leather breastplate.

"May I approach my master?" Nekau strangely asked. I glanced at Amka for a clue as to the protocols of these dark people, but Amka just shrugged his shoulders.

Without waiting for an answer, Nekau took two steps forward, reached out his long arms and grabbed my shoulders. Herihor's reaction was immediate. In a flash he held a dagger to Nekau's throat and in another instant all six of the King's Guards had a spear pointed at Nekau's ribs.

Frightened though I was, I shook my head at Herihor. Nekau shut his eyes tight and began to sway slightly and a deep guttural, animal-like moan came from his throat. Herihor looked frantic. I saw Nekau open his eyes and then they rolled back in his head and the next thing I know I lay on the floor, my face being slapped gently by Amka while Semni held my head. I vaguely heard a commotion in the hall and then I passed out again.

I learned later that night that as I passed out Herihor rushed Nekau and arrested him. That he did not kill him outright amazed me, for I heard he was incensed at Nekau's audacity to lay hands on me. Amka, too, was

surprised by the behavior and sent Tepemkau to speak
with him. Nekau, for his part, surrendered meekly,
appearing dazed and confused by the entire sequence of
events, according to those who witnessed his actions.

The next morning I still felt sick, but improved
from the night before. When I got up from bed I had
none of the dizziness. I had hardly finished bathing and
dressing when Amka appeared with Tepemkau.

"We have spoken with Nekau and we believe the
entire thing was a misunderstanding," Tepemkau began.
"While Nekau is a Horus priest, that colony also carries
on traditions of its parent land. Apparently his touching
you was to be part of a blessing that somehow went
awry."

"He wishes to apologize and see if he can repair
any damage that may have been done," Amka said. "I
suggest we meet again immediately."

"I am not sure," I said. "You two did not prepare
me adequately for that meeting. His... stature... I was
surprised."

"You are quite right," Amka answered. "We were
not prepared either. Yet I continue to believe that Nekau
and his people can play an important role in keeping the
southern border secure. We should give the relationship
another chance."

I agreed to a meeting that afternoon and this one
went smoothly, with no incidents. We drank beer
together, broke bread, and spent hours in discussion
learning about our different cultures. Nekau told one
story after another about his great-grandfather, for their
tradition is an oral one, not written down like we do in
Kem. Herihor, once he relaxed, was eager for every
tidbit Nekau could provide about Narmer and Meruka.

One interesting incident occurred at the end of the
meeting, or I should say an incident occurred that caused
the end of the meeting. After we had met for more than
three hours, Zenty came running into the room, having
seen Herihor enter the meeting earlier. Zenty was
dressed in the leather chest armor that Herihor had

ordered made for him. He barged into the meeting, his wood sword drawn.

"It is time to end this meeting, for it has gone on too long already," he declared, to the laughs of everyone attending.

Then Zenty saw the dark Nekau, seated opposite me, and his eyes widened. His sword hand dropped as he surveyed the dark face and deep-set eyes. Now smiling, Nekau stood to bow to the future King, but when Zenty saw the priest stretch out to his full height, he dropped his sword and ran screaming from the room. I excused myself to tend to Zenty, who Abana now held tightly, while the rest of those in the room laughed uncontrollably.

Later that day I received word from Tepemkau that Nekau wished a private audience with me. Herihor objected strongly, but after that day's earlier session I felt safe. Herihor, however, would not relent and privately defended his position not as that of a lover but as Chief of the Army and Overseer of the King's Guards. We compromised and Herihor stationed himself and a contingent of King's Guards immediately outside the meeting room, but outside hearing range. Fortunately, the palace was built so that the central meeting room was skirted in plantings that deadened sound, a direct result of Anhotek's planning generations before.

To this day I look back on that meeting with a mixture of, even now I am not sure of what. Nekau was most pleasant, truly a joy to be with, modest, yet with a wry sense of humor that was partly his unique ba and partly due to the differences in our people that governed our talk and customs. His laugh was deep and hearty and lit up his eyes. And while the meeting did not last long, it changed my life forever. All I can do now is pray to Isis and Horus for forgiveness, which I do every day.

"I wish for you to know that I am here to serve, like my great-grandfather before me," he said matter-of-factly. "Since Meruka walked from the Two Lands into the Afterlife, our priesthood has waited patiently to be called upon to serve once again, for it is written that that is our destiny."

Later that night, as I lay awake or else paced back and forth throughout my quarters in distress, I thought back to Nekau's words, trying to comprehend by what powerful magic he was able to divine what he said next to me. By dawn it was clear to me that Nekau was not only a respected priest, but an even more powerful shaman, like his great-grandfather before him.

"When I laid my hands upon you," he continued, "a great vision began to appear to me, but it was soon overshadowed by another vision. Horus himself threw me off you."

"What... was it that you saw?" I asked, the hairs on my neck rising like a plucked goose.

"You are with child," he said without emotion, "and Herihor is the father."

SCROLL THIRTEEN

Nubiti

"Do not take too much, for the line between reality and dreams, between life and death is a fine one," he said. As he leaned forward to hand me the parchment filled with a powder, his tattooed arm slipped out of the sleeve of his black robe and it gave the appearance of the serpent Apep slithering out of the Underworld.

"I'll stay with you throughout," he added.

"How long will the journey take?"

"Perhaps a few hours. Perhaps a few days. Perhaps forever. It's unpredictable and that's why I have strongly warned you against this method."

"It's the only way," I said.

"Sometimes it is," Bakht whispered, nodding his head. "Sometimes it is."

I opened the parchment and saw the dark powder, laced with small black bits that were not fully crushed. It smelled earthy, musty. Bakht handed me a cup of tea.

"How much do I take?"

"Here, let me add it for you." He took the

parchment from me and used an ivory scoop that he withdrew from his shaman's bag to put a small measure into the tea, which he stirred carefully.

Unscented candles burned in the corners of my quarters, unscented so as not to interfere with the magic contained in the powder. Kainefuru and Nyla stood with their arms interlaced, trembling behind Bakht, as much from his presence as from what was to transpire. All furniture had been removed and Bakht and I sat cross-legged on a stack of blankets set in the midst of the floor. Pillows were scattered about. Bakht had chosen my quarters for the ceremony, because he said it was necessary for me to be in familiar surroundings. That is why he insisted that Nyla and Kainefuru attend to me. As he explained it, their familiar faces might serve as an anchor to the real world if my ka needed to be restrained from venturing to worlds beyond, worlds that might hold mortal danger.

At Bakht's insistence, I wore nothing but a loincloth to avoid becoming entangled in my clothing if I were to roll about. In one corner a small harp stood, in case Bakht called for soothing music to calm my ka.

"Close your eyes and breath deeply for a minute or two," Bakht said softly, in his gravely voice. "As you do so, think of what it is you wish to attain from the experience. The clearer you are now, the easier the transition as you enter the vision state."

I breathed in and out, with each breath thinking of my purpose, my desire for clarity in my mission, for a vision of Kem under my rule, for signs from the gods that would illuminate our path, for we surely did not have the history and resources of the Horus priesthood to light our way. Suddenly, thoughts of Sekhemkasedj came to me and I shook my head to dispel his bulbous image. But as soon as I did so, Herihor loomed large in my heart and then his sculpted body over me and just as quickly, him atop Mery, as my spies reported to me they had done many times. Bile rose in my throat.

"You are troubled," Bakht cautioned. "I can see it

in your eyes and your tense muscles. Relax, or there is the real danger that this magical powder will turn rancid in your body and sour the experience."

I opened my eyes, shook my arms and bent my neck to and fro. I again breathed deeply, trying as hard as I could to focus on my breaths, as I so readily reminded my acolytes to do when they practiced their meditations. When I felt I had regained control, I reached out my hand to Bakht. In it he placed the cup.

"Drink it steadily, all at once, although it will not taste pleasant," he cautioned.

I did so and felt the gritty liquid warm my throat and stomach, followed by a slight burning and metallic sensation on the back of my throat. "And now what?" I asked.

"We wait. It may take some time to work. You might try to lay down or else meditate until you begin to feel the e-f-f-e-e-e-e-c-t-t-t-t...." Bakht's voice deepened to a slow, echoing rumble and his words trailed off into the corners of the room and now I could see them streaming from his mouth, although I believe my eyes were closed. I tried desperately to catch them and to place them back in his mouth so that they would emerge more slowly and I could better understand what he said. I felt hands on my wrists restraining me, and a deep rumbling sound emanating from a cavernous, black void. I turned, my eyes open or closed, I could not be sure, and saw Nyla's face, dear sweet, lovely Nyla. I felt an urge to suckle her breast, to feel her hard nipple on my tongue. I tried to reach out my hand, but instead I fell backward slowly, ever so slowly, drifting, as does a leaf. I was later told I slept, but my ka did not sleep. My body remained in that room, but my ka drifted above and I saw Bakht and Nyla and Kainefuru all huddled around my body, and I laughed at their concern, for I saw how insignificant my mortal body was.

I floated, I flew, I soared up and down. Below me was Dep, but it was not Dep, not the Dep I knew. A hill lay below me and at its top was the walled city of Dep and strewn about the field were the rotting corpses of men killed in battle. And then it occurred to me that I witnessed the effects of Narmer's battle for Unification, when our noble King W'ash lost more than twenty thousand valiant Delta warriors. Arms and legs and headless torsos lay scattered about like crumbs and vultures feasted until they could eat no more and all the while the faces of the dead called out to me, but nothing but picture words came from their mouths and I could not hear their words.

I swooped lower and suddenly the severed arms of King Narmer's warriors reached up and clutched at me and I fought them and I pushed and kicked, trying to fly away, but I could not do so, and then there was Nyla's face again, just inches from my own and oh, how I wanted her, to kiss and hold her, how I wanted to taste her, to eat her and make her part of me. But instead the rumbling sound grew louder and it shook me to my core and I hated it. I screamed at it, I flailed at it, but still it penetrated me and finally I tore off my ears to remove its frightening presence.

Silence. Again my ka drifted, gently, peacefully, for how long I do not know, but time itself stood still. With no ears I heard no sounds, not Mother Nile's waters gently swishing through the papyrus reeds, not a breeze rustling leaves, no sounds of donkeys braying. Nothing. And in that nothingness I knew with all my heart that this was a message from the gods, although hard though I tried I could not discern it. I struggled, but all my ka wanted to do was melt into the fog of nothingness that swirled about me.

I floated, alone and aware of my loneliness. A gray haze surrounded me and I shivered with cold and fear. Slowly the gray became darker and darker and yet the fear was gone. I was at peace. I commanded my ka to stay, to rest, to absorb every bit of the utter blackness. I was home.

A being surrounded me. A presence. A thing without words. It massaged my skin, it caressed me. I

256

drew sustenance from it. I floated on my back and when I turned to see what was below me, it was Dep again, but the corpses were gone. Dep stood strong once again and Ra's rays shined brightly upon its walls. Calm breezes blew in from Wadj-wer and I could smell the salt in the air. I felt whole, I felt happy.

Below me, on the same hill, stood a woman and from the distance I felt her loneliness. She knelt in prayer, trembling, her arms outstretched, pleading, pleading, but I could not hear her words. Again I swooped down and too late saw that it was Mery who pleaded, but to whom I still could not tell. Was it to me or to her beloved Horus? Suddenly she withdrew a dagger from her robe and sliced me with it and I fell on the ground. And behind her I could hear Herihor laughing and urging her on.

I thought she had sliced me in the abdomen, but instead I felt a sharp pain in my head like none I had ever experienced before. The pain was intense and I held my hands to it and rolled on the ground screaming.

"Do not fear, Nubiti, for I shall remove your head and you will feel pain no more!" I think Mery called out, for the rumbling sound had come again and shook the ground beneath us and it was hard to be sure of any sound but that. She advanced toward me with her dagger, a look of pure hatred on her face. I pulled at her gown and she fell and I jumped up, frantic, for I had no weapon. I quickly glanced about and found a rock and when I turned to face her it was no longer Mery I faced, but a man dressed in battle gear. His back was toward me and I thought it to be Herihor, for his body was rippled with muscle and he grasped his sword in his hand with such force his forearm bulged. But when he turned to face me, his breastplate insignia was not that of Sobek the crocodile god, but instead bore the serekh of the catfish and chisel. I knew at once that I faced Narmer himself!

I circled to Narmer's left, to avoid his striking hand, for his reputation as a fearsome warrior was legendary. I heard a shrill cry above me and looked up to see a falcon soaring above us. I knew I was in danger for Narmer, too, looked skyward, smiled and bowed to his beloved god. I felt the ground below me shake and something whispered into the hole that had been my ear and told me not to fear.

"Horus has reigned far too long," it said, its voice a drawn out growl with no words, but profound meaning. "It is time for Apep to reign supreme." And from below the ground that separated Narmer from me, a serpent slithered up from behind a rock. At first Narmer laughed and he turned backwards and there were Mery and Herihor laughing, too. But the serpent grew taller and taller and its shiny black head expanded and became monstrous, swaying back and forth and spewing thick venom from its fangs. Soon Apep blocked out Ra's rays and Narmer and Mery and Herihor were cast in deep shadow and they shook in fear.

Now a piercing cry came from the sky again and Apep looked up. The falcon had become huge and it spread its wings and there could be no doubt that it was Horus in his falcon form. He dived at Apep and struck him in the head. Black blood oozed from the wound and an agonizing cry escaped its mouth.

But before Horus could rise again for another strike, Apep grabbed him and threw him to the ground. Feathers flew in all directions as Apep prepared to strike him with his venomous teeth. I instantly felt a pang of regret, for Horus the mighty was about to be vanquished and the battle between good and evil would finally end.

I watched Apep hesitate and I wanted to help, to take a sword and finish the job, but I was defenseless. Only Narmer and Mery and Herihor carried weapons. I screamed and ran about frantically searching for a weapon. I ran and I ran and then I awoke.

"Mistress, mistress, wake up, please wake up!" Nyla called to me as she shook my face. Kainefuru held down my shoulders.

"Water," I whispered and Nyla quickly tilted my

head up and helped me to drink cup after cup. My mouth had never tasted so foul. My head throbbed in pain and my ears felt like a Horus priest had disciplined me by twisting them. My assistants helped me to pee and then I fell back on the blankets and slept fitfully, but without dreams that I could recall. When I awoke, Bakht knelt beside me and I could see that it was still dark outside.

"Whew! That was quite something," I said, still groggy. "I… my head aches. What time is it?" I asked.

"Maybe four hours to Ra's rise."

"So, I journeyed for… what?… four hours?" Nyla walked over and knelt beside me.

"It was yesterday you began your journey, my mistress. You have been away for more than a day."

I was struck dumb by this news. "A day?" I struggled to sit up, but my head ached and my muscles felt as if I had run for miles.

"You would do better to rest right now and have some food and drink," Bakht said. "You battled terrible demons throughout your journey."

I managed to sit up and drink the water that Nyla gave me. She offered me a bowl of dates and dried fruits.

"I must go back," I said to Bakht, as I pushed away the bowl of fruits.

"Oh, no, my mistress!" Kainefuru shouted from across the room. "Please, you mustn't. I could not stand it." She began whimpering and Nyla went to comfort her.

"Why?" Bakht asked.

"My work isn't finished. Yes I battled demons, great demons, but the battle's not over. I didn't see my vision. I came close, but it evaded me."

"Well, I'm sorry to hear that, but it is of no matter," Bakht said. "You cannot take more of this magic powder. It's too strong. It could kill you." He began to put away his medicines and potions. "And if not you, those girls will die of fright," he said, trying to make light of the situation.

But I was not to be so easily denied. I knew in my heart that the battles held a message and that if I were to get past them, whether with evasion or cunning, I would triumph. Beyond the battles lay the vision of the future Kem, whether united or divided. I had to know. I was willing to risk all to find out.

Once more Bakht tried to dissuade me. "I have witnessed shamans, respected shamans, die from a second dose. If you die, all our plans, our entire strategy, goes up in smoke. We will have wasted twenty years of efforts. You mustn't do this, Nubiti. I will have no part in it."

"We don't have the advantage of a Horus priesthood casually reading the omens," I began.

"Ah, that is nothing. Our priests read the omens, too."

"And have you provided me with an answer, with a vision of how this all plays out?"

"The omens are mixed. They always are, for there are too many paths one can walk. You know that. At each junction we make a choice. Eventually the destination becomes clearer."

"No, I must know the destination... now. That will make my choices easier. I want answers from the gods themselves, some glimpse of our future, a direction to which we can march. Khnum has given me the authority to command your actions, Bakht. I command you to give me another measure of your foul powder!"

Bakht leaned back, his hands on his knees, his brow furrowed. For their parts, Nyla and Kainefuru stood together, shaking their heads. Kainefuru whined something unintelligible.

"'I'll do as you command, princess, but before these two priestesses as my witness, I advise you against it. I'll pray to Apep that he protect you in your journey and I suggest you two," he said, turning to my assistants, "do the same to your Isis." At this point Kainefuru began to cry.

"But I do it under one condition and that is that

these two leave your quarters. They can serve as guards. Their negative emotions will contaminate your ability to see or to comprehend your vision."

I agreed with Bakht, for I was already distracted by their emotions. I sent them from the room, asking them to be ready to help Bakht if called upon.

"But you are not to enter unless I call you," Bakht added sternly. "No matter what you may hear." He stared at them until they nodded their assent.

The pair rushed from the room. Bakht asked me to tell him everything I had seen in my journey thus far. I explained every encounter, but also the satisfaction I felt floating in utter silence.

"These are important omens," he pronounced. "The gods appear to be preparing you for some great battle and Apep's appearance is a very positive sign. And the silence, Nubiti, that is a profound omen, although I did wonder at the time when you pulled so viciously at your ears. We had to hold you down. I believe the gods are trying to send you an important message."

"And what would that be?" I asked, gently touching my ears, for they still throbbed in pain.

"There are times when you gather information, when you plan and strategize and ask others for their counsel. But finally you must listen to your inner voice, when you must shut out all distraction and retreat to that quiet place inside and make your decision." I nodded with the wisdom of Bakht's interpretation.

And so, Bakht made me eat some food and drink a special potion that he said would fortify me for the most hazardous journey I would ever take. Once I was done, he mixed the powder into a tea and I drank it.

This time the effect was immediate. I do not even recall putting down the cup. In an instant my head was hit with a pain that felt like the crushing blow from a mace head. I gasped and fell backward, screaming.

I knew instantly that this journey was to be far different. I felt fear grip me like the jaws of a crocodile and not let go. I looked about me to see what there was to fear, but I could not move. I was in a confined space, a place with no air and no light. It stank of the mud of the Delta marshes. It was musty and rank and worms and maggots crawled throughout and I lay in their midst and I felt them crawling over my body. I tossed and turned to get them off me, but my hands would not function. I screamed and screamed, begging for help, but instead into my open mouth a snake flicked its foul tongue.

And then the rumbling again and the ground beneath me shook and a demon whispered into my ear and said not to fear for there was magic here beyond my comprehension and that with it I could overcome all obstacles. And then it entered me. At first I shrank back in horror, but the reverberations infused my ka and I surrendered to its power. Now the darkness dissipated into a gray mist and I could make out the form of Apep above me, thrusting into me, filling me. I tore at his flesh, urging him on, begging for him to enter me harder and harder.

All thoughts left my heart and the sole sensation I had was confined to my private parts and all I could feel was Apep's monstrous organ filling me. I came to the heights of pleasure again and again and again, so that I knew nothing else, so that there existed nothing else. I screamed in ecstasy, but I could not hear myself.

How long this lasted I do not know, but it seemed to go on and on. I floated between vague sensations that something powerful was happening to me and the intense reality of my pleasure until finally I felt Apep tense and become still harder. And then he shot his seed and I felt every contraction, every spurt. He came and came until his seed filled me and only then did I know; only then did I understand.

At first his seed stayed within my womb. But soon the demons it contained spread throughout my ka, shimmering like gods in the night sky. And I knew now that the magic they contained had become part of my ka. The power of Apep was mine for all eternity and none could ever take that from me.

For a long time after I floated, light as a feather, as the power within me grew and multiplied. I rested in the black abyss and the rumbling would come and go and each time I felt ever calmer, stronger, wiser. And then, far above me I saw a faint light and a calling and I went toward the light. But my arms still would not move, so I slithered through the soil, turning and twisting until, with a final push, I was birthed from the ground and into Ra's blinding light.

Up and up I soared until below me I saw Mother Nile in all her majestic glory, a long, unbroken ribbon of green winding through the Land of the Lotus, a land of unending light brown sand and barren rocks in shades of blue, green and red. Finally, her magnificence split into five different rivers and she became the lush, green Delta, as different from Upper Kem as Babylon was from Ta-Sety. That was the unmistakable message from the gods, laid before me through Apep's magic. Mother Nile herself changed her ba as she transformed herself to create the Black Lands of the Papyrus. The truth was finally revealed to me. We were Two Lands, two different people, now and ever to be.

And there, where the Two Lands met, stood two armies poised for battle. I knew they awaited something. I looked about for the answer and I thought that the silence had something to do with it, but I could not be sure. Frustrated, I closed my ears and meditated. Only then could I feel the offspring of Apep's seed inside me. The gods had shown me that the answer lay within.

I opened my eyes and below me the Delta warriors began to disappear, sucked down into the marshy soil. Herihor's troops marched forward, but wherever they turned they could not find their opponents. Then, suddenly, our warriors began sprouting from the ground, spit up by Apep. They emerged behind the Upper Kemian soldiers, around them and mixed in with them. In Upper Kem the sandy soil itself began to shift and crumble. I turned southward. Angry mobs poured into the alleys to protest Mery's rule. The very walls of Inabu-hedj shook and the Temple of Horus began to topple. I smiled, for the gods had finally shown me Truth. And then I felt a searing pain in my head and my journey abruptly ended.

SCROLL FOURTEEN

Meryt-Neith

"Why haven't you told him?" Ti-Ameny asked. "He has a right to know. He was the baby's father."

"It was my fault. I was not careful enough, as you taught me to be. And since he was not to blame, I saw no need to involve him or make him feel badly. Besides, there was no other alternative, since we could not marry anyway." I was beginning to feel irritated at Ti-Ameny's persistence in this matter, for what was done was done.

"Alright, I will not argue with your choice in not carrying this baby's ka, even though it may have serious implications for ma'at, but…"

"Serious implications?" I asked, not entirely sure of what Ti-Ameny meant. She stared hard at me.

"Did you not think what mighty happen if, Horus forbid, Zenty does not live to adulthood? Why do you look at me like that? It happens. And what about the baby's ka, which now wanders in the Nun?" At that I suddenly felt a horrible chill run through my body.

"Of course I considered those things, Ti! Do you

not realize I agonized over these matters? We preserved my entire flow after I the herbs took effect. They will be buried and prayers offered so the baby's ka will travel to the Afterlife, where he will grow. I will yet raise him, you will see!"

Ti could not help but notice how distraught I was. "I am sorry, Mery. I... it's just that I'm angry that you did not ask me to help you. I am your personal healer. Amka and me, not that... that..."

"That what, Ti? His name is Nekau, not the insulting terms you have used for him since he has arrived."

The veins in Ti's neck and temples throbbed. "He is monstrous, that black mut, and he is strange. His methods of healing are primitive... very different than ours."

"Different, perhaps, but I have seen his magic work. He knew the instant he saw me that I was with child and he immediately divined that Herihor was the father."

"That is not magic, Mery, that is..."

"Neither you nor Amka divined it, and you two live with me and have known me since birth." Ti-Ameny stood still, trying to respond, but the words did not come. After a moment, she breathed in and seemed to calm herself.

"How did he do it? Did it hurt?" she finally asked.

"He gave me an herb for three days and he said some prayers and then I had my monthly flow and some cramps. That is all."

"I'm sure he prayed to his heathen gods," Ti-Ameny said, disgusted.

"Ti, he is a Horus priest... a respected Horus priest and leader of his colony on Abu Island. The prayers sounded just like the ones that Tepemkau or Amka would use."

"Pregnancy is the province of Isis, not Horus!" she shouted at me. I recoiled at her anger.

"Ti, I understand that you are angry with me, but

do not address me in that fashion. Do I make myself clear?"

Tears welled in her eyes. "In any case, it is done," I added. We stood for a moment in silence.

"I do feel I owe you an explanation," I ventured. "I was...it was... insensitive of me to not include you in my decision, and in fact Nekau asked me if I had a personal healer I would prefer. But at that time I was terribly distracted by my predicament. I had just seen his magic power and I decided it would be good for our relations with his people if I gave him the honor of treating me." I could see Ti-Ameny softening.

"I will confide in you, Ti, something I have told no one else. Our plan is to use Nekau as an intermediary to negotiate with the Ta-Setys. Amka and Tepemkau believe it is our best option, short of war. In any event, he will be gone from the Royal Court."

Whether or not that helped Ti-Ameny's feelings I could not tell at that time, but she appeared to accept my explanation and we hugged before she left. The very next day, Amka called a meeting with Nekau so that we could settle the matter of his negotiating with the Ta-Sety tribes that still plagued us. Amka had spent hours each day talking with Nekau and his delegation, as well as private hours exchanging information with him about medicines and treatments for illnesses. I had not seen Amka so happy as when they worked together with mortar and pestle, mixing potions, talking about plants and animals and vigorously discussing the fine points of the illnesses they faced. Amka would dictate to a scribe a description of the animal or plant, along with the potion, and the scribe would quickly write down the passage.

Recruiting Nekau into our cause was a foregone conclusion by time we met. He was eager to serve in any way he could and seemed genuinely honored to be asked. Our meeting was brief and as he stood to bow, Zenty ran into the room, Abana close behind.

Abana looked terrible. She hobbled rather than walked and her face looked haggard and drawn. I made a note to talk to her about retiring, but I would need to structure it with Zenty in such a way that Zenty would see her replacement as a step toward manhood. Perhaps Semni or another of Amka's trusted students would take over day-to-day responsibility.

The day, like nearly all days during Shomu, was uncomfortably hot and somewhat humid. As soon as Zenty came to my side, he coughed, a mild nagging cough. I hugged him and he leaned his head into my breast.

"How long has Zenty had that cough?" Amka asked.

"Maybe two days," I responded, looking to Abana, who nodded.

"We should give him an herbal," Amka offered. He always worried about the illnesses of Shomu, for they spread quickly and the still air always seemed to worsen them. Many of the rekhi became gravely ill during Shomu and died.

Then Amka, to my surprise for I had never before seen him do this, turned respectfully to Nekau and inquired as to how Nekau treated coughs.

"I use an herb mixture from Ta-Sety. Coughs are more severe in the jungle area where Meruka and my ancestors are from. The herbs to treat coughs and colds are more powerful. We base them on two roots that grow in the jungle."

"Can we try it with Zenty?" Amka asked, shocking me.

"Of course. With your permission," Nekau said, bowing to me. Having just had the argument I did with Ti-Ameny, I hesitated, wanting with all my heart to insist that Ti treat Zenty. But with Amka making the offer to Nekau I felt it would be a sign of disrespect, or at the very least it might reflect a lack of confidence in Amka's judgment and Nekau's medical skills. I deferred.

Nekau motioned to his assistant, who brought his case to him, a case such as I had never before seen. It was made of a strange wood called ebony and it had streaks of black in it as dark as Nekau's skin. In a few moments, Nekau and his assistant prepared a thick syrupy mixture, which he administered to Zenty. By now Zenty had gotten used to Nekau's immense size and, as long as he was at my side, stared at him at every opportunity. Still it was a shock to him when Nekau's hand approached him, for his hand was as large as Zenty's head. And so, with as simple an act as my not acting, and thereby allowing Nekau to minister to Zenty, I created a problem that would all too soon come to haunt me.

In discussions over the next two ten-days, Amka, Tepemkau, Herihor and Amka's Council of Advisors prepared Nekau for his role. Toward the end of Shomu, Nekau and his fellow priests departed for Ta-Sety, with a small contingent of army soldiers for protection. They also carried with them many gifts to pass out as signs of respect.

With Nekau gone, the Royal Court returned to normal, or as normally as it could function while we stayed in ancient Nekhen. Periodically my cousins and other nobles would request permission to return to Inabu-hedj, which I usually granted, for life in Nekhen with only four thousand inhabitants was far less attractive compared with the White-Walled city which was at least six times as populated. There were always parties to attend, festivals and celebrations. Inabu-hedj, being at an intersection of various trade routes, was also better able to weather the drought and poor harvests that plagued the smaller towns in the south.

In less than a ten-day, at our regularly scheduled Council meeting, Amka brought a disturbing piece of news to our attention. In Gebtiu, a village a day's journey from Nekhen, a group of citizens had angrily attacked two of my tax collectors, beaten them, and driven them from town.

"Has this happened before?" I asked, shaken by the news.

"Never in the south," Amka replied. "It happens

every so often in the Delta whether during drought or times of plenty." The ministers and governors nodded their heads.

"In our defense," said Thotmi, the Governor of the nome that included Gebtiu, "the situation among the rekhi is most difficult. They are hungry. They feel as if they have nothing left to tax. Yet... I beg your forgiveness, master, but the tax collectors still come. Even the businessmen are angry."

"They may be angry, Thotmi," Tepemkau said, "but taxes are the obligation of every citizen to the King. It is part of ma'at. The King's treasury pays for..."

"I know what the taxes pay for, Tepemkau, but... it's just that the people do not feel they are getting much in return," Thotmi said, turning to me. "We have no grain. My family was recently threatened in the marketplace and had to flee."

Amka stood up. "Wait a moment, Thotmi. You have been sent regular allotments of grain, just like the other nomes. I just approved a shipment to you perhaps six ten-days ago. It was not much, but it was something."

Thotmi looked puzzled. "Amka, I swear we haven't received any grain recently, nothing. Our granaries are bare. No one bakes bread. Even the supervisor of the King's estate complains to me regularly." Thotmi looked from person to person in the room, as if they might provide him with answers.

Amka tapped his staff on the floor, thinking. "We will get to the bottom of this, I promise."

"But in the meantime," I said, addressing the Council, "we must act quickly to stop this rebellion. We cannot have the people think they control the tax process."

"I agree," Amka responded. "There is dissatisfaction throughout the Two Lands. We do not want these rebellions to spread. We will discuss it, Master, after the Council meeting."

With the meeting soon over, Amka asked Herihor and Tepemkau to remain. "This is not good," Amka began. "It smacks of the Delta power structure fomenting unease beyond the usual nomes. The pattern is too familiar. I did not wish to mention this in Council, but we are already hearing reports of agitators in Nubt, Tjeni and Inerty."

"It's unlikely that the southern rekhi would act in open revolt," Herihor added.

"In any case, it will fall upon your troops to restore order and allow the tax collectors to do their duty," Amka said. We discussed the need for haste and Herihor promised to send one of his best captains with fifty soldiers to accompany the tax collectors within the next few days.

In five more days, I was in the midst of my morning bath when I heard a commotion outside. My handmaiden left to see what it was about and she returned with a towel. "Master, Amka begs an audience in the private meeting room. He said it was urgent."

I quickly made ready and hurried to the meeting room. Amka was in a heated discussion with Herihor, who sat in a chair, his head hanging low. Amka spoke in a loud voice and drove his staff onto the floor for emphasis. When Herihor spotted me he rose and Amka immediately turned around to face me.

"Sit, Meryt. I fear we have bad news."

"Well, there is a first time for everything." Amka ignored my sarcasm.

"Herihor, you might as well start. You know the details."

"My men sailed to Gebtiu. From their very arrival, people were hostile. Mostly it was just insults heaped upon the collectors. There was some shoving. But on the third day, an unruly mob waited near the temple. They demanded that my captain hear their grievances. He's a soldier, Meryt, not a politician. He did not handle it well. They refused his command to disperse, someone began throwing rocks and he ordered his men to charge."

My back stiffened. "How many?" I asked coldly. Herihor hesitated.

"Three were killed, including a child. Several more were injured."

I turned away, distraught. Had it really come to this, my own people in open rebellion against my rule? Had I really ordered my army to kill my own people? My heart pained thinking of how seriously ma'at was endangered, that all the tedious prayers and careful work of the priests might be in vain and chaos would engulf us. My heart raced.

"Make ready, Amka. We go to Gebtiu today!" Amka appeared shocked but said nothing.

"It isn't safe, Meryt," Herihor protested. But the pain in my heart would not abide his words. I turned to him as I stood.

"Then make it safe!" I said sternly and left.

Herihor dispatched a division of soldiers in advance of our leaving. During the entire day that we sailed down Mother Nile, Amka and I discussed how we might handle the crisis we faced. I agreed that the best strategy was for Amka to conduct a thorough assessment of the grain and food needs of Gebtiu and remedy it quickly. He sent a message to Tepemkau requesting several specially trained priest scribes known to Amka who would help him with his accounting.

As soon as we arrived in Gebtiu I met with Thotmi, who apologized profusely for the mob incident, which he blamed on agitators from the Delta. I urged Thotmi to call a meeting in two days with all the businessmen, landowners, and artisans. I also required that he gather up several of the most vocal rekhi protestors and have them attend the meeting, too.

I believe the meeting served to calm the people. I urged my ministers to listen to the complaints and in the end all who attended understood both the need for calm and the consequences of extreme actions. Thotmi was helpful in calming the situation. As a gesture of compassion and to support Thotmi's difficult rule, I had him award the widows and the mother of the child who died at the hands of my soldiers lifelong pensions. This went a long way toward easing tensions.

But the strains resurfaced the very next day. Some rekhi accused their neighbors who attended the meeting of having betrayed their cause. People threw rocks at officials from rooftops and some even threw clay pots of wet hippopotamus dung. All the while, Amka and his fellow priests steadfastly pursued their inquiries.

On the sixth day after our arrival in Gebtiu, Amka sent me a parchment from the local temple where he and his fellow priests met throughout the day. The temple was more than an hour's walk from our campground, which Herihor had thoughtfully placed in the shade of the desert mountains.

Master, please excuse the necessity of this letter. I would deliver its news in person, but I feel it is best for me to stay here and complete our work, as you shall see.

We have concluded our assessment of the situation in Gebtiu regarding their food needs during this difficult period. We would like to announce it to the entire community as a show of the King's power and justice. We have also uncovered what we believe is official corruption. With your permission, we will schedule this meeting for mid-morning tomorrow. I urgently request that you attend.

Faithfully,

Amka's official stamp was affixed to the scroll. I thought it odd that Amka would require my attendance, but I knew not to question his judgment.

The next day, I rode my carry chair to the temple, where Amka had assembled the meeting. To my surprise, every person in the village must have been waiting outside. They gave me a courteous but cool reception. In the temple, chairs had been commandeered from throughout the village to accommodate the wealthy guests and political leaders.

Amka stood up and the buzzing in the room quieted. Holding tight to his staff, Amka paced before me, addressing the crowd. With each sentence he uttered, a voice in the back whispered its essence to the crowds outside.

"People of Gebtiu, you better than anyone know the sacrifices Kem has had to endure during the drought. King Meryt-Neith, may her name be blessed forever, in her infinite wisdom as Horus' representative and as her son's Regent, wishes to help." Amka waited for his words to be relayed to the crowd outside. As he did, we heard someone distinctly call out: "Dung!"

I was mortified, yet I maintained my erect posture, my crook and flail resting in my arms. I saw Herihor nod to one of his captains, who immediately left the hall.

"As you all know, we have been here in Gebtiu to determine how much grain you require to carry you through this terrible drought. And yet..." Here Amka began again to pace before me, his head down as if lost in thought.

"And yet, the more we studied the problem, the more curious it became."

"To the point, dear priest!" Someone shouted from the rear.

"We need food, not words!" someone else shouted.

Amka held up his hands. "We are a nation of laws and traditions," he admonished his audience. "We can stand here and shout at one another or you can listen to how the King applies the laws fairly and equally without regard to rank or privilege. Which shall it be?" The audience immediately quieted as Amka's glare surveyed the crowd.

"Now, as we determined how much grain Gebtiu needs today, we could not reconcile this with how much grain you have received in the past year. For if our records are correct, your granaries should still be one-third full. Yet, by the records of our capable administrator, Thotmi, they are empty. In fact, his records appear to be accurate, for we have checked carefully and the granaries are indeed bare." Thotmi was seated in the front dignitary section. His girth was substantial and his abdomen poured over his waistband. He sat perched on the edge of his seat looking as if he might fall off.

Amka now motioned to one of the priests from Nekhen. The elderly priest stepped forward with an assistant who carried with him several scrolls. Amka instructed the assistant to unroll the first one. It was filled with columns of numbers.

"Here then are Thotmi's disbursements of grains to the people of Gebtiu," Amka said loudly for all to hear. "Very well done, Thotmi. Very precise figures as well as dates." Thotmi turned around as his fellow dignitaries nodded their approval.

"Further, if you take our most capable Governor's figures and reconcile them with the status of the granaries today, they match perfectly!" People around the room murmured their approval and some even called out to congratulate Thotmi, who smiled and held up his arms in acknowledgement.

"So, when will we receive more grain?" one of the dignitaries shouted out.

Amka smiled down at the crowd. "Soon, my fellow Kemians, very soon. And much of it, too!" To that there were expressions of gratitude from around the room. "In fact," Amka continued, "at the King's insistence we have already sent a messenger to Inabu-hedj instructing the Treasurer to make the purchases immediately." Now the room erupted in applause and cheers that extended to the crowd outside. When the crowd quieted, Amka held up his staff.

"But, the odd thing is that while your Governor's records match his disbursements, two other matters are troubling." Amka now paced before the dignitaries. "Ammon, please explain."

The elderly priest stepped forward and unfurled another scroll. "These are the grain shipments that we sent to Gebtiu since the second year of drought. Each shipment was noted as it left Inabu-hedj. You see, here are the amounts and here are the dates each was sent." Ammon pointed to columns meticulously entered by the Royal scribes. At this point I glanced at Thotmi and noted him perspiring profusely. He mopped his brow with a scarf he kept tucked in his kilt.

"The figures we have do not match the amounts received in Gebtiu," Ammon said, his voice so soft I had to strain to hear. "Every shipment from Inabu-hedj," he said, motioning to his assistant to come forward with the scrolls from Thotmi's office, "results in only a quarter or half of the shipment being received here."

"Curious, is it not Thotmi?" Amka asked. The room was hushed, for they now suspected where Amka was headed. All eyes were riveted on Amka or Thotmi.

"The soldiers, umm... the soldiers who... who delivered it... how shall I say this?... perhaps they helped themselves to some of it... for their families, no doubt," Thotmi offered. He tried to mask his nervousness by smiling and waving his hands, but his smile was crooked and his hands shook.

"Of course. That is what we thought must have happened, Thotmi, because we would never doubt your integrity. Yet, and here is where things become even stranger, Herihor here has questioned his men and they have sworn an oath that they did not steal even one deben from the shipments. Besides, the army escorts and the scribes who manage the orders check each other to prevent such occurrences."

"So, you know nothing of these discrepancies, Thotmi?" Amka asked.

"No, I... I know nothing about them. I had my supervisor record them as they arrived. Perhaps he's the one who has..."

"Well, fortunately he is here today, Thotmi. Unfortunately, we have questioned him thoroughly," Amka said, turning to Herihor, who nodded to one of his officers. Two soldiers brought in the supervisor.

"He lies!" Thotmi suddenly stood and shouted, his finger pointed at the poor man. "The man is an ignorant idiot. I took pity on him and hired him to do a job that was above his abilities. He... he's the one who stole the grain!" Thotmi turned in desperation to his civil servants seated directly behind him as if to seek their support.

"Perhaps it is you who is the idiot," Amka countered, "for this ignorant civil servant's wife has never trusted you and made him keep careful records of what you commanded him to do. And yet there is even more, Thotmi, something so vile that I hesitate to mention this before the King you were sworn to serve, for your acts have dishonored Horus himself."

"Stop this!" I commanded, standing and turning to Amka. "State the charges and your evidence and be done with this insult to my rule and my son's. I will not wait another minute for justice to be done!" I was enraged by Thotmi's deception. Every face turned to witness my reaction.

Amka took a deep breath and turned toward me. He reached into the band of his kilt and withdrew a small parchment. "King Meryt-Neith, favored of Horus, at your command and in your name the Horus priests have investigated the matter of grain shipments to Gebtiu. We have examined the records of all transactions and have interviewed witnesses. We accuse Thotmi, Governor of Herui Nome, of dishonoring his title, of theft of Royal stores, of corruption, and of affliction and even murder by allowing his own people to starve. We also have absolute proof that Thotmi sold the grain to middlemen who, in turn, sold it to rebel factions in the Delta."

The audience was shocked. Men talked with their neighbors and it slowly dawned on them to what extent Thotmi himself was responsible for their considerable misery.

"Traitor!" several called out.

"How could you betray us?"

Thotmi's kilt was soaked through and his body shook. "I... it was not as if I had a choice. I swear, I... I was forced to do this..." he said, wheezing.

And so it was that on that day I ordered my first execution. Yet I did not shrink from that duty, for what Thotmi did was against everything Kem stood for. I had trusted him and he lied to his King and to Horus himself. His criminal actions were responsible for the death and illness of many of his brothers and sisters. He violated ma'at by his traitorous deeds. By the end of that day Thotmi's wife was a widow and his three children orphans. All those involved in this corruption plot were immediately put to death and their parts scattered in the desert for the jackals, with no hope for an Afterlife. I left Gebtiu sadder, but much, much wiser.

The people, no matter what their rank, believed that justice had prevailed and that as King I had done all in my power to restore ma'at. The rekhi bowed low to the ground as our entourage made its way to our ships to sail back to Nekhen. News of these events spread far and wide in Kem and did much to ease discontent, at least for a while.

Oddly, the events in Gebtiu did little to ease my discontent, for my decisions that day had created many orphans. This knowledge plagued me greatly. Did I, more than anyone else, not know the effect of growing up an orphan? As a mere child, did I not feel the melancholy of my ka after a day spent witnessing the affections of mothers and fathers and their children in the Royal Court? At those times I remember the sadness in my ba lasting for days.

"Ever it is this way," Amka cautioned me many times during the early years of my rule. "A ruler must decide matters of life and death. Even deciding not to decide may result in the deaths of many." I remember once Amka pacing back and forth, tapping his staff as he did so.

"Yet that is the only way to maintain ma'at," he said, turning on his heels to face me. "You do see that, do you not?"

Yes, I saw that, how could I not? Yet the terrible sadness of that inescapable truth weighed heavily on me. For what was ma'at, anyway? In the case of Thotmi we had preserved ma'at by bringing the divine justice of the King to the people of the Two Lands. But what of ma'at for Thotmi's wife and little children? If Thotmi's wife did not remarry, an unlikely prospect at best, they were condemned to a life of begging in the stinking alleyways. Yes, the children still had their mother, but little comfort would that be when their bellies ached from lack of food. I felt the burden of guilt descend upon me like a shroud.

After Thotmi's trial, I was resolute to at least maintain ma'at consistently and fairly and so I asked Amka to instruct me further on the legal scrolls. As the days passed I understood more of what each case brought before me represented in the larger scheme of ma'at. Amka and I would often argue over fine points in our laws and I found him smiling as he engaged in these debates. In some cases, he even agreed with my position and we issued decrees that corrected contradictions that had arisen.

Periodically we would receive a message from Nekau's delegation advising us of their progress. Nekau had contacted several Ta-Sety tribes and received assurances from them of their peaceful intentions. He spent a few days in his ancestral village and was told to continue deeper into Ta-Sety to find the villages of the tribes that had invaded Kem. Since that message we had not heard from the delegation.

As for Herihor, it was difficult for us to get together now that I was back in Nekhen, while he trained his troops in the desert. But he freed himself from his work every so often and late at night was able to sneak into my room so that we could enjoy a few hours of pleasure in each other's company. Therefore I was surprised one night to be awakened by Amka. He escorted me to a small meeting room. There Herihor waited for us.

"We have received word of Nekau," Herihor started, "and it's not good. He's been taken prisoner by a Ta-Sety tribe."

"His party was besieged," Amka continued. "One of Herihor's soldiers was wounded in the skirmish and managed to get away and deliver a message to a Horus temple, and it was relayed here."

"How many were killed? Is Nekau alive?" I asked, my heart beating rapidly.

"We have no way to know for sure on either question, my Master," Herihor said, the expression on his face radiating his concern. "Nekau was alive after the attack, that we know. My soldier said the Ta-Sety's were in awe of his size and recognized from his leopard skins that he was a powerful shaman. Whether that will spare his life I don't know."

"Was it the same tribe that invaded us?" I asked.

"Nor do we know the answer to that," Amka answered. "From what I know of the Ta-Setys, the invasion was the result of several tribes banding together, for their numbers were too large for any one Ta-Sety tribe.

"What I do not like," Amka continued as he paced before me, "is the timing of this. I believe that word got out of Nekau's mission and this is an attempt to undermine us. He was apparently successful making peace with several tribes and that must have frightened Khnum and his conspirators. They obviously do not want their alliances with the Ta-Setys endangered."

"They count on them for the southern tactic of their strategy," Herihor ventured. "But for them to attack our peace delegation worries me. It may mean they are close to a major action."

"Exactly," Amka said, tapping his staff on the floor for emphasis.

"Explain how you know this," I said.

"Gold is a powerful motivator, Meryt," Amka began. "If the Ta-Setys had ample time, they would let Nekau strike a rewarding peace deal with them and then go back to Khnum with a sweeter offer to undo it. However, that takes time, a great deal of time."

"So what prompts their rush to action?" I asked.

Amka hesitated, a sure sign he was thinking of a tactful way to express himself. "I could say it is the continuing drought," he said deliberately, "and that is surely part of it. Or the fact that many are set against your rule. But those are issues best left to time and to pressure steadily applied by our adversaries, for they certainly have plans, do they not? No, I think the real reason for the sudden rush is you and Herihor."

I stole a glance at Herihor, but at that moment could not read his face in the candlelight. "What? You think this old man does not know love when he sees it, that he is too old to know of late night trysts in desert tents and palace bedrooms? Oh, Horus, how blind is love!" Amka said, laughing.

For my part I must admit to feeling relieved that Amka knew, although I should have suspected that he would find out sooner rather than later.

"I'm sorry I didn't confide in you sooner," I offered. "It… it took us both by surprise."

"The only surprise is that it took you two so long to consummate your love," Amka said, laughing again, and I took that as his way of approving. "However, this does create a complication… lots of complications."

"Go on," I said.

"I am not the only one to know of your affair. Nubiti also knows. She has always had an eye for Herihor… and Wadjet, too, for that matter, may his name be blessed. This is more than mere sisterly rivalry."

What Amka said hurt me to the core. "But I never harbored ill will against her," I protested.

"Yes, but it was not she who was betrothed to Wadjet or who was allowed to follow her heart and plead for the affection of Herihor. No, Meryt, the priests… and the priestesses… know that there is nothing more terrifying in the Two Lands than a woman whose love is denied. You ask what the rush is? I will tell you. It is Nubiti's rage over you and Herihor."

I was too stunned to even speak and the silence hung heavy over the room. "I have received vague reports of Nubiti's dealings with Khnum's shaman, Bakht," Amka continued. "He is a powerful shaman, Meryt, and dark as Ra is light. They are mixing an evil brew, my dear, they and Shepsit and their kin, and I feel their pincers closing in on us from all sides. We must act, and quickly and decisively."

I nodded in agreement, although my heart felt pained. "What do you two suggest?"

"The army is ready, Meryt," Herihor said, dropping the pretense of title in Amka's presence, but still using my male name. "They are trained to a high degree. I have also been meaning to bring a plan to you for recruiting more men to the army. With times so bad, people are desperate for work of any kind. If the treasury can support it, I would recommend we do so. The army is spread thin with our need to quell rebellions in the north and battle the Ta-Setys in the south and also the Ta-Tjehenus to our west."

Amka paced. "Herihor's plan has merit. Putting people to work will have a ripple effect. Craftsmen will need to make their weapons and leather workers will make their armor and sandals and so on. I will speak to the Minister of the Treasury and see if he feels we can take this on. It may not cost us as much as it would appear, since many would work for bread, cheese and beer alone. Eventually Mother Nile will flow full again and our treasury will be replenished.

"But for the present, I say we dispatch Herihor's army southward immediately, for we need a show of force against the Ta-Setys or they will not fear our might or our resolve."

"And we must rescue Nekau, too," I added. "How soon can you be ready to leave?" I asked of Herihor.

"I have kept the army at the ready. Three days at most."

"Good. Amka, make it so. I must make ready," I said as I stood to leave.

"Make ready?" Herihor asked, turning around sharply to face me.

"Yes. Amka will stay here to take care of the affairs of Kem and supervise Zenty's care. I will take only Ti-Ameny and a few attendants with me." Herihor's jaw dropped.

"Surely you… are joking," he said tentatively.

"Surely I do not," I answered testily.

"Mery, this… this is nonsense. We go into battle. Do you understand what horrors war involves? We march double time. We'll be on food rations and water restriction. Soldiers act crudely. This is no place for a woman."

"Herihor, I speak now as your King, not as your lover," I began self-consciously, for I had never spoken openly about our relationship. "As Chosen of Horus I feel I must accompany you in battle, although I promise I will never interfere in your military business." My breath now came in gasps, so much did I hate having to talk to Herihor like that.

"She makes a good point," Amka said, tapping his staff lightly. "Think of it, Herihor. With your military skills and your knowledge of the history in the scrolls you will no doubt easily subdue the Ta-Setys, as you did before, of that I feel certain. With Meryt-Neith returning triumphant, it will help her to govern more effectively. There are few things more effective than war to distract people from their miseries at home. And through your actions, she will have proven her Horus energy." At once I could see Amka's reasoning, but also his appeal to Herihor's male vanity. I smiled inside for I still had much to learn from my old mentor.

And much to learn from my son, too, for if there is anything at all that would help a women understand her limitations, it is raising a boy to be a man. If ever a living thing in this world differed from a woman, it is the ba of a boy. It is only through the determined efforts of their mothers and caregivers that boys ever mature into men who wash, brush their teeth or sleep in anything other than their filthy clothes atop a dung heap! There, I have said it and recorded it on the holy scrolls, for I swear the following happened.

Zenty had just come home from a walk with Semni, the purpose of which was to learn from the animals and plants surrounding us. Amka had instructed

Semni to teach Zenty how the gods created life in the most unexpected places. And so the two of them walked along Mother Nile and explored... dung. Dung!

When Zenty burst into the palace and told me this I was less than amused, but Zenty was obviously excited by what he found. He kept thrusting in my face a filthy dung beetle whose life the gods ordained involved rolling little pieces of dung into balls and scooting them around the desert floor for no apparent reason, or at least for no reason that I dared consider.

Yet even with six hairy legs designed to roll dung into balls, that disgusting beetle was far cleaner than was Zenty, who stank, having spent the day up to his knees in Mother Nile's mud, breaking open crocodile and hippopotamus dung cakes. Oh, Isis, did he smell!

So with beetle in hand, he kept coming toward me, only wanting to sit on my lap and show me this creature that Semni had explained was perfectly made by the gods for this job and no other. And I held out my hands and backed away until we had gone around in a complete circle.

Thankfully, by the time Abana showed up, he was sitting in the corner of the room, completely absorbed in torturing the poor animal, which I had actually begun to pity.

"Oh, by the gods, look at you!" Abana wailed and she mercifully persuaded him to bathe. He agreed, but only if he could take his now five-legged beetle with him.

"And why is that so funny?" Amka asked me later that day when I had told him what happened.

"I did not say it was funny funny. I said... or I meant to say that it is funny... more like odd, how boys are... how... how they like dirt or... or torturing animals and the like." Amka just stood and stared at me.

"And you do not think it is... odd, or crude, at the very least?" I asked, incredulous, when he remained silent.

"And how, may I ask, do you think the Horus priests learned all about the animals and plants that inhabit our lands and so have made valuable medicines?" Amka finally asked. "Do you think they just asked each creature and waited for it to answer? Hmm?" I could see that I had angered my old vizier. He stood silently again, I suppose hoping that I would absorb his point.

"Do you think your beloved Herihor plans his battle strategy to avoid marching through elephant or hippo dung?" he continued. In fact, I was now beginning to think that it was I who had indeed stepped into such a pile.

"Mery, I will tell you this and I pray you listen well. Women raise girls to be women and none could argue that it should be any other way. But when women raise boys to be men, our entire land will be in mortal danger. Ma'at will be destroyed more surely than if the gods themselves were to wreak vengeance upon us. We each have our place in ma'at. If men were to become more like women, they would cease to hold their women's respect or affection."

I thought long and hard about Amka's comments, painful as it was to contemplate, for I still too easily exhibited the weakness of only considering my narrow perspective. Yet, there was no denying Amka's wisdom and that in this matter he was surely correct. I felt blessed to have such a one in my life, a vizier who always spoke truth to me as he saw it and who considered not himself, but the Two Lands and all our gods before he spoke.

And so in three days, and with newfound humility, I sailed south from Nekhen with my army, some six thousand strong in countless ships. Amka had the head arms-maker in the King's workshops create a set of armor for me, including a fearsome-looking helmet that I wore it on the day we left. People lined the path from the city to the wharves and bowed low to the ground as I passed, sitting on my carry-chair, one hand holding my sword the other the flail. Only one did not bow to me that day and that was Ti-Ameny, who thought my accompanying this campaign outrageous. Although I suspected that Ti-Ameny might be resistant, I wanted her along for her undisputed healing skills if they were needed to assist the Horus priest shamans. I also knew that whores accompanied the troops wherever they went to serve their male desires and I felt that having a woman healer and her assistants along would be a worthy use of my resources.

Each day of the journey I became more impressed with the conduct of the army and the ordeals the soldiers had to endure, for Herihor drove them hard and long and even then they rested only for the evening meal before he had his captains drill the men in the finer points of using the sword, mace, dagger and shield in battle. I saluted the men who fought bravely and even suggested to Herihor that he make a contest of it every ten-day, so that I could reward the men who bravely fought in my name. I was pleased that this proved to be a popular diversion and the soldiers drank and laughed heartily at the mock battles. Even Herihor fought demonstration rounds with his captains and the men roared whenever an opponent managed to ground him. But I could also see that they reserved the highest respect for the leader who sailed, marched and fought with them side-by-side, not demanding of them anything he would not do himself.

For many days we sailed and rowed upstream. Groups of villagers came to the shores to witness the spectacle of hundreds of ships carrying soldiers and supplies. Children, mostly naked and covered in mud, jumped up and down, waving at the soldiers. As word passed that the King accompanied the army, people lined the shores and bowed low as we sailed past. Finally, after rowing and portaging past the cataracts, and picking up five of Nekau's fellow priests from Abu Island, we reached the border of Kush and began the desert march to the land of the Ta-Setys. The desert sands were hot as burning coals and the dust kicked up by the marching soldiers was suffocating. Thanks be to Horus, the desert soon gave way to savannah, to the cheers of the soldiers. Their joy did not last long, however, for even on the first night the insects began their merciless attacks on man and beast.

Thankfully, Nekau's priests were prepared for the deluge and in large pots they simmered an awful smelling mixture of herbs that we rubbed on our skin. It repelled the bugs, but tainted everything we touched and ate with a foul smell.

In three days march, an advance party of our soldiers and one of Nekau's priests came back to camp with news. They met up with a tribe that had befriended Nekau's delegation. The friendly Ta-Setys knew that Nekau had been captured, but would not help due to their fear of the warring tribes further south. At the request of the Abu Island priest, the tribe sent word to Nekau's ancestral village of his plight and of our army's advance.

Herihor now faced a dilemma, whether to send a rescue party in the direction of Nekau's captors, or instead find a suitable open plain upon which we could fight the hostile Ta-Setys. For two days I listened to Herihor and his officers debate the merits of each tactic.

Two of Nekau's priests had made several trips during their lives to their ancestral village and were intimately acquainted with the terrain we found ourselves in. They suggested a southwesterly route that would detour us only slightly, but had several advantages for a marching army because, due to the drought, it would take us through a dry river valley that would be easier on the feet of man and donkey. Once at the end of the valley, which the priests estimated would take us three or four days to traverse, we could send a smaller force to rescue Nekau while the main army continued southward.

Moving an army is no small feat, I learned. There are the soldiers, of course, but there are also their weapons and replacement weapons. Every ten soldiers required a valet to service those weapons and provide replacements during battle. But I was most surprised by what it took to feed and water six thousand warriors.

Behind the army marched another army, of men and beasts of burden. Everything had to be transported, food, water, cooking utensils, medical supplies. Then there were the cooks and the medical priests and all their supplies. And, of course, there were the caravans of whores.

Managing this horde was even more difficult than managing a city, for a city counts to its credit an equal number of men and women. Herihor was correct. Men, in great numbers and without the calming influence of women, are quite disgusting. They whip out their privates wherever it suits them and unleash a stinking stream of pee that would splash on other men to great peels of laughter. They would fight on the slightest provocation and Herihor's officers were hard pressed to keep order. And even the best of friends talked to one another by trading insults and profanities I had never before imagined. Yet I kept Amka's wise words in my heart and learned to appreciate their courage and sacrifice for their King and land.

So long as we stayed on or near Mother Nile, food and transportation were easily managed. But I learned that once an army marches across land, especially desert, every detail must be meticulously considered. The men were already on strict food rations. They were allowed one piece of cheese and a slice of rekhi bread for their morning meal. They would not eat again until evening camp, where they would have a hot meal twice every ten-days, but usually only another wedge of cheese and their own small loaf of bread with a dollop of honey. Once camp was made the cooks began preparing loaves of bread for the next day.

But it was water that I learned proved the most difficult of all for an army. All my life I had lived within the abundance of Mother Nile and never considered that if you do not know the location of natural water sources, then water must either be carried or stored at places where it can be easily accessed. Perhaps nothing else Herihor did convinced me more of our need for far flung army outposts than the need for water, for one of the most important reasons for outposts is to always have fresh water available for soldiers in case of war. This fact was brought home to me when we were but a day's march from the dry valley we were to cross.

Herihor had sent an expedition of soldiers ahead of us with enough gold to enlist the help of a local, peaceful tribe. For two days they hauled water from a nearby spring to the valley's mouth. They had filled three hundred clay urns with water and left one of the Abu Island priests, one who spoke the local languages, and a small contingent of soldiers to guard it. However, when we arrived at the site, Herihor was shocked to find his soldiers dead and the priest seriously wounded. Every urn had been smashed. The priest's injury was curious, in that the attackers had brutally cut off his right hand, but left him to live.

Once the priest's injury had been treated, I attended Herihor's interview with him. I did not at first realize the seriousness of our predicament, until I saw how earnest Herihor was. As soon as the priest relayed the exact location of the spring, Herihor himself accompanied his soldiers on a run across the grassland to the spring. As I later learned he already expected, the spring was fouled by the priest's putrid hand that had been thrown in. For good measure the attackers had defecated in the watering hole.

Herihor and his officers faced a major decision, whether to advance or stay put until another water source was found. I listened to the debate amongst them but, as promised, I kept away from Herihor's military role. After all his officers had weighed in, Herihor thought for but a moment.

"We push on," he said, looking each officer in the eye, "and we do it now."

"Now, as in tonight?" one of the junior officers asked.

"Yes, tonight. It will be cooler and the men's need for water will be less. Each of you will inform your men of our predicament. Tell them we're on strict water rations and so no bread, only cheese and dried fish. We will travel by night until mid-morning, when we will rest during the hottest part of the day. Let them know we expect it to take us three days to get through the valley, at which point we are told there will be ample water sources."

"What about wild animals?" the same officer inquired.

"The Abu Island priests are experts," Herihor assured him. "Still, we'll march with arms at the ready. Have guards protect the supply caravans, and to discourage stragglers, for that's where lions and hyenas are most apt to attack."

"And the enemy?" Akori, captain of the King's Guard, asked.

"Be vigilant, but from what I know this was a raiding party. I don't believe they would attack us directly. And if the Abu Island priests are correct, they won't attack at night, for they fear strong magic in the darkness."

And so, that very day, with Ra's disk descending rapidly, we entered the valley. Herihor had his men arranged four abreast. A scouting party moved ahead of the formation, watching for vipers, scorpions and other demons of the night. Knowing the dangers they faced, the soldiers were unusually silent.

As we began Ra painted the sky the most brilliant colors of red I had ever seen. The dry grasses that waved all around us were cast in a shimmering gold and as we trampled a path the smells they released were intoxicating. In the distance we could see herds of antelope, much larger than the tiny dik-diks we hunted in Kem. At first the hills that defined the margin of the river valley were far apart, but as night fell and we continued our march, they drew nearer and taller. The soldiers said nothing, but I noticed from the rear that they turned their heads more frequently and held their weapons tightly.

By mid morning the men were exhausted. Herihor had them pitch camp amidst a long, winding rocky outcropping and I could imagine water coursing through it during the Ta-Sety rainy season that Amka had described to me. The soldiers took advantage of the respite and other than those who were on watch, they slept soundly, finding whatever meager shade they could. I noted that Herihor did not insist that they practice their skills that day.

Late that afternoon, we took off and Ra again treated us to a magnificent display, which the Horus priests told me was a good omen. By now water was scarce, but I heard no reports of the soldiers complaining, for the rumor was that Herihor refused to take even a sip of water until the captains reported to him that every man had his share for the day. Like the others, I insisted that I adhere to the ration, despite Ti-Ameny's objection that it was inadvisable for a woman's health, let alone the King's.

We marched through a much rockier terrain now and the ranks of four abreast was abandoned which, in turn, slowed our progress. Marching around the boulders and rocks took more energy and without water the men appeared to suffer for it. But we also made progress and on the second morning, under Ra's heat, we rested knowing that we were almost through the valley.

Before we headed out on the third afternoon, Herihor summoned his scouts and asked them to find out with certainty how much longer the march would take. Stripped down, and carrying double the ration of water, the men took off at a brisk pace.

On this afternoon the soldiers struggled. The night was dark and our pace was cut in half. The faces of the men were vacant, their lips chapped and crusty with salt. Some took their ration of water immediately to give themselves strength, and then sneered when their companions took their share later in the night. Instead of marching sharply, the men staggered.

Still, we pushed on. As Ra's disk began to rise over the rim of the hills on that third morning, a strange thing happened. We all noted a strong smell of smoke. Within the hour, the men at the front of the marching column spotted the scouts in the distance. As Ra rose over the hills, we were confronted with the most fearful sight any of us had ever witnessed.

The scouts were running for their lives toward us. Raging fire snapped at their heels, sending huge billowing clouds of smoke into the air. The savannah itself was aflame. But the most incredible sight of all was that beside the men ran lions and antelope and water buffalo and other strange and exotic animals none of us had ever seen, all focused on but one thing, escape.

The soldiers panicked, broke rank and began to run to safety up the steep hills. Herihor shouted to his captains.

"Form into your units!" he screamed. "The fire will rage through here quickly. Do not battle the beasts! Make way and allow them to run through." The captains began barking orders and running to gather their troops.

"Meti, move your unit to the rear! Help the attendants and the women to safety up into the foothills. Keep a tight reign on our pack donkeys." With that Herihor turned sharply.

"King's Guards, follow me!" and he ran toward me and formed his men around me and Ti-Ameny. "Move them there," he said, frantically pointing to a swath of boulders midway toward the hills that towered over us. "Pull out all the grasses for fifty cubits around and assume a defensive perimeter. Move fast!"

In minutes, the smoke engulfed us, a choking, acrid fog mixed with the smell of burning animal flesh and the dung of panicked animals. All around us the donkeys brayed in fear. Then we heard a deafening sound and out of the smoke came a thunderous heard of animals, bleating, roaring, screeching, voiding their bowels, all to be free of their fiery tormentor. Their cries were so pitiful I covered my ears. And in a moment, in what seemed at the time like a lifetime, it was over. The animals passed through the narrow valley and continued on their way.

Now came the fire itself. By now the other units had also pulled any sign of grasses from their roots and tossed them far away from their positions. Others in the units battled whatever blazes erupted nearby by stomping on them and smothering them with their capes. The smoke, however, rose from the valley floor to our positions and we all sank to the ground to breathe whatever pure air we could. Soldiers from my Guard rushed over to cover Ti-Ameny and me with their capes.

Soon, the fire also passed, driven hard by the wind that barreled through the valley. With the smoke all around us abating, soldiers stood up, coughing and rubbing their eyes, to survey the damage. Herihor came running over to make sure we were safe. And then a great cry arose from Akori.

"Battle positions!" he screamed. "We're being attacked!"

From atop the hills on both sides of us poured wave after wave of Ta-Sety warriors, as black as the night through which we had just marched. They ran down the hills, screaming loud war cries that made my blood curdle with their ferocity. Amidst the smoke we could only catch glimpses of them as they approached us, wielding their spears and knives. Some wore leopard skin kilts and others wore simple cloth kilts, but every one had his face painted in frightening designs. Emerging out of the dense smoke they presented a fearsome appearance.

In an instant, Herihor sized up his opponent and called his men to battle formation. "Scorpion defense! Scorpion defense!" he screamed, "Around the King!" Without thinking or hesitating, the men ran around in a manner that made little sense to me. Suddenly, just as the Ta-Setys were upon us, I discerned a pattern and Ti-Ameny and I found ourselves in the midst of a tight formation of King's Guards, one hundred strong, surrounded by a larger wedge of soldiers in rows of four or five, spears pointed outward, with Herihor at the point of the wedge. Wherever he commanded, the point of the wedge would rotate in that direction. Surrounding the wedge was a huge circle of soldiers, some four thousand strong, wielding spears, swords, maces and daggers.

In that second, all time stood still. The Ta-Setys struck with the full might of their advance warriors. Where one attacked our line, the chances were even that he would be struck down or else deliver a fatal blow to one of our own men. Where they attacked in groups of four or five at one location, our soldiers were trained to allow a few in to be dispensed with by the spears of the wedge formation. In this initial assault the wedge held tight.

The din of the battle was horrendous. Men summoned their courage with war screams, but in the blink of the gods' eyes those screams turned to mournful cries of anguish. Before me men were gored, blood spurted everywhere and the putrid smells of bellies cut open and human feces were overpowering. I gagged and noticed Ti-Ameny on the ground, bent over and retching next to one of soldiers who had fallen. His bloody head was nearly severed and through the smoke and haze his eyes stared up at Ti-Ameny as if begging for help.

Yet the enemies' numbers had shrunk and soon we all heard the sound of a ram's horn blowing loudly again and again. The Ta-Setys fell back. Our soldiers quickly put the finishing blows to those Ta-Sety left behind, before collapsing to their knees in exhaustion. They looked dehydrated and Ahori called back to the supply lines to bring up whatever water could be found.

From all around me came the moans of fallen warriors crying out for help, for someone to put them out of their misery, for water, or for Horus to unite them with their wives and children in the Afterworld.

I noticed that Herihor was slightly wounded.

Blood dribbled from a cut on his left forearm, but he refused medical attention from the priests who now circulated among the wounded, imploring them instead to treat his fellow soldiers. Now he looked over the battlefield and made a decision.

"Every man still standing, to the rocks!" he shouted, pointing to a clump of boulders and rocks in the center of the valley. His voice cracked from yelling battlefield commands and from a lack of water. "Cordon defense around the King! Hippo unit on the perimeter! Wati, you are now in charge of the unit. Go! Now!"

With that, Herihor stormed over to me, took me by the arm and without a word dragged me to the center of the rock formation. Ti-Ameny struggled to keep up. As I passed a fallen Kemian soldier I bent down to retrieve his dagger from his hand.

"I will not go down without a fight!" I said. Herihor looked at me, but said nothing.

In minutes, the army units again surrounded me, with my King's Guard, relatively untouched, circling me. But on the battlefield we just abandoned it was a different story. More than a thousand of our soldiers lay dead or mortally wounded and a lesser number of Ta-Sety's.

Suddenly, from the hills above came another series of blasts from the ram's horn. We all turned our heads to the hills before and behind us. What confronted us lay heavy on our hearts. For there, massed atop the hills, were at least five thousand Ta-Sety warriors. They rushed downhill again and at one point it looked like an anthill that had been disturbed, so steadily did the enemy flow down to kill us.

The outer defense consisted of five rows of soldiers. The outermost cordon held their spears pointed out and as the first wave of Ta-Setys hit us it was carnage. Once one of our soldiers gored an opponent, another behind him assumed his position and did the same to another enemy warrior. Attendants ran from place to place replacing broken spears and swords.

Soon, our soldiers began to run out of weapons

and it was in those areas of momentary weakness that the Ta-Setys attacked with abandon. Wielding spears and daggers, they pierced our outer perimeter and were soon furiously attacking both the wedge and the perimeter from the inside.

Our swordsmen inside the cordon began to counter-attack and for a while it seemed to us they might prevail, but the Ta-Sety numbers were simply too great. Finally, Herihor could stand it no longer.

"Stay and protect the King until your dying breath," he commanded Akori. "I will return after I patch up the holes in our defense." He leaped off the rock he used to survey the battle and in a moment was in the thick of the battle, his sword in his right hand, his dagger in the left. Every step he took meant a Ta-Sety succumbed to his sword for he was fearless, even reckless in his resolve. As he fought, he brought a contingent of swordsmen with him, until the major holes were, indeed, reinforced.

Now the outer cordon fought as one unit and the Ta-Sety could not penetrate. The battle continued this way for an eternity. As each Kemian soldier fell, another took his place, but soon the men were standing on the bodies of their fellow soldiers to take a position. But, for now the line held and many more Ta-Sety bodies were added to the perimeter than Kemian.

Herihor ran back and forth, checking in with Akori and the King's Guard, then mustering his troops to fight to the end. Once again, the Kings Guard, which had yet to fight, froze for a second when they heard that dreaded ram's horn blare an insistent message. Now, from both hills, a line of Ta-Sety warriors came down the hill, but these did not scream and yell. These were the elite warriors, kept in reserve. They brazenly danced coming down, uttering a deep whomp-whomp-whomp sound as they went, accompanied by the ominous sound of drums coming from atop the hills. For a moment, the clanging of swords and the dull thud of mace heads meeting bone subsided and to the day I go to the

Afterlife I will remember the chilling sounds of those fearsome warriors.

As the Ta-Sety closed in on our cordon, we made out their faces, which were hideously scarred. Large welts laid out in patterns were also on their arms and torsos and backs. They made no secret of their intent, laughing and daring our weary soldiers to do battle with them. They intended to charge our perimeter at opposite ends of our circle.

And charge they did. They had only crude weapons, a small leather shield, a short sword and a dagger. But our poor soldiers in the perimeter never had a chance. The Kings Guard, now with Herihor back, watched in horror as these elite Ta-Sety warriors brushed aside the spears, danced swiftly around and slashed our men. They thrust their swords in front of them and with equally deadly accuracy behind them.

Herihor knew that when they pierced through the line the other Ta-Sety warriors would pour in behind them. Our only hope was to keep the line from collapsing.

"Akori, take the Catfish guards, split them in two and fortify those lines. Swords and daggers only. I stay with the King. May Horus strengthen you. Hurry!"

Without answering, Akori rallied half the Guard and they swept down from our rocky fortress into the fray. Without a word, Herihor pushed Ti-Ameny and me back to the reformed center.

"Chisel Guards, spread out... give each other a better purchase to fight!" he reminded his men. "If the King is harmed, let it be because none of us is left alive! We fight for Narmer and Horus, for King Meryt-Neith and Kem!" They responded with cheers and drawn swords, eager to finally prove their mettle.

The perimeter to our right suddenly broke and now dozens of Ta-Sety challenged the inner core. It took only thirty minutes more for them to break the inner core and now and again a lone Ta-Sety would make a run for the King's Guard, which dispatched the man with ease. But soon the challenges came faster. Ahori fought below us to reinforce the gaps in our defense, but there were too many Ta-Setys. Finally, a group of three Ta-Setys broke through the inner core and rushed the Kings Guard. The lead warrior was one of their elite and as he delivered the mortal blows, in each case he laughed.

Infuriated, Herihor jumped to the boulder directly in front of the warrior. When his opponent saw the gold band on his arm, he smiled broadly and decisively slashed at Herihor with his blade. The swiftness of his stroke magnified its threat. Herihor spun around as he deflected the blow, but the sword caught his leather breastplate and slashed it, drawing blood underneath.

I screamed and for just a fraction of a moment both the Ta-Sety and Herihor glanced toward me. Then a sign of recognition appeared on the Ta-Sety's face as he glanced from me to Herihor and I would swear that he actually bowed slightly to me, with a wide smile. He thrust at Herihor with renewed vigor and soon Herihor was stepping backward to avoid the swift and deadly blows.

The Ta-Sety soon tired and one plunge of his dagger left him off balance just enough for Herihor to land a solid thrust with his dagger. It entered between the man's ribs, a lightening quick blow that knocked him to the ground. As he turned to get back up, Herihor finished him off with his sword.

But as they battled, other Ta-Setys had come between the King's Guard and Herihor's position. He began to fight his way back to us, but I could see he was tiring. Blood seeped over his breastplate and ran down his tunic, already splattered with Ta-Sety blood and flesh.

Now another black warrior challenged him and as they battled Herihor clambered over the rocks until he was not more than two cubits in front of me. Another enemy approached from his right and if he saw him, as he later reported to me he did, he was powerless to act for he was precariously balanced on a rock as he delivered a mortal blow to the Ta-Sety before him. Herihor fell forward as he thrust and he toppled onto the enemy's chest. Just then the Ta-Sety on his right saw his opportunity. He leaped onto the rock before me and as he lifted his sword high to strike my beloved, I lunged, my knife at the ready. The blade easily sunk between the man's ribs and I could hear the breath whoosh out of him. He turned in disbelief and in that instant Herihor thrust his dagger into the man's neck and he immediately fell to the ground.

Herihor rushed to me and hugged me with his free hand before he pushed me behind the boulder. I will never forget the look he gave me in that moment, a mixture of thanks and wonder and all I could think of at that moment was to say a prayer of thanks to Horus for giving me the courage I did not know I possessed to serve my beloved.

Herihor climbed back atop the boulder and what he saw sank his heart, for the scene of carnage and mayhem below shocked even him. Bodies, contrasts in black and brown, lay next to one another, atop one another, intermingled in the final death throes of battle. Blood and entrails covered the surface of every rock. Disembodied limbs littered the ground. And still the Ta-Setys came. At that moment, Herihor later reported, he understood that all was lost and he accepted his warrior fate. Although he never told me this himself, I know that he pondered how to deal with my death, for he knew even at that terrible moment, that he would kill me himself and spend eternity with Apep, rather than let me fall at the hands of a foreigner.

Herihor looked skyward and what he saw he could not comprehend at first. For although the valley floor was filled with Ta-Sety and Kemian soldiers, still thousands more Ta-Sety warriors suddenly massed on the crests of the hills. Their leader held his arm high and then dropped it and two thousand warriors descended the hills, screeching in a tongue he had never before heard. I immediately stood up to see what was happening.

Suddenly, the Ta-Setys in the valley stopped for a moment to look up and it was only then that Herihor realized whom it was who stood atop the hill and commanded these men.

"By the might of Horus," he exclaimed. "It is Nekau!"

No one who stood on that valley floor that day could mistake Nekau's ancestral brothers, for they towered over our Ta-Sety enemies and our soldiers alike. Nekau himself ran down the hill to help his countrymen, and wherever he wielded a sword, his opponent either ran or perished. In an hour it was over and when Nekau fought his way to the King's Guard, it was Herihor who greeted him. They both dropped their swords, fell to their knees and embraced.

From that day forward, the Horus priests named the battlefield The Valley of Horus' Glory and placed it on the map of Kem's expeditions. Nearly three thousand of our men fought to their deaths that day or else died in the following days of putrid infections. Five hundred men lost a hand or arm or other limb and survived due to the magic of our priest shamans. But for the fifteen hundred Kemian soldiers who marched out of that valley five days later the name the priests gave it mattered not. To them it was forever known as Nekau's Valley.

To the debasing horrors of war I have nothing to add, other than I felt I made the correct decision in accompanying my troops. The experience changed me in profound ways and for the rest of my days it gave me pause whenever I had to put my troops in harm's way. But also for the rest of my days our Ta-Sety neighbors did not trouble us again. That same day the Ta-Setys buried more than five thousand men and surrendered one thousand as slaves to the alliance of tribes that Nekau had brought with him.

Of the five thousand Ta-Setys killed in battle, I was responsible for the death of one. As Horus is my witness, I did it only to protect my beloved and I would do it again whether for Herihor or Zenty. Yet the look on that Ta-Sety warrior's face as I plunged in my knife will plague me to my own passing, for it was not the look of a hated enemy, but that of a brother, sent on his final journey by my own hand.

Nekau told me later that the Ta-Sety I killed was a great warrior, made immortal by his valiant battle with Herihor and the King of Kem. Herihor assured me that the poor man's people would forever whisper his name. And Amka assured me that his bravery would secure him a place in the Afterworld.

Yet I could not help myself from wondering if a child waited anxiously at home for their father who would never reappear in this world; if a mother would never again gaze upon her son's grateful face; if a woman would never again feel her lover's breath upon her neck. Eight thousands fathers, sons and lovers dead in a day. For what? For what?

With the help of the Abu Island priests we were able to determine that the Ta-Setys were bribed with the lure of gold and land and that none other than Khnum was behind this plot. The Horus priests officially recorded these confessions before the witnesses were tried and executed.

Nekau also told us that his capturing party included at least a few individuals from the Delta and that he overheard them talking about a spy in our midst. With that information confined to just Nekau, Herihor and myself, we set back to Nekhen and Inabu-hedj determined to ferret out that traitor and his informants.

Word reached Amka in Nekhen and he met us at the temple at Abu Island. From there until we were welcomed back to Nekhen we discussed strategy for how to deal with Khnum and his fellow Delta conspirators. By the time our ships arrived in Nekhen, Herihor, Nekau, Amka and I had outlined our plans. My insides ached with the thought of what I must do next.

But those plans would wait, for Amka had arranged a celebration for me and our army such as had not been seen since the time of King Narmer. For we had won a major battle against foreign invaders and the now much enhanced rumors had circulated that I had saved the life of the Chief of the Army and had engaged in hand-to-hand combat with dozens of Ta-Setys. I was hailed as a hero and no one but those closest to me would ever again address me as anything but Meryt-Neith.

On my final day in Nekhen, Amka and Tepemkau arranged a special ceremony to celebrate the victory and to reward the soldiers who fought so bravely for the Two Lands. There was a parade down the main streets, leading to the Temple of Horus and the King's treasury made beer available for free for everyone who attended. Amka had commissioned a special tablet that commemorated the victory, showing me in my male form vanquishing the Ta-Setys. I made sure that Herihor was suitably publicly rewarded.

Herihor and I had planned to make a presentation to the widows of our fallen warriors who were from the area in and around Nekhen. We had just given them a gold pendant and the promise of a lifelong pension of bread and cheese from the King's estates, when I noticed a commotion going on to the right of me. A black priest was animatedly whispering in Amka's ear. He, in turn, whispered into Tepemkau's ear.

As soon as our presentation was over, Amka had one of his priests blow the ram's horn in three long blasts. Everyone in the crowd shushed each other and when the crowd was quiet, Amka stepped to the front of the stage.

"King Meryt-Neith, people of Kem, we have just received a very important piece of news. Horus is justly pleased by our King's victory. He has persuaded the gods to act on our behalf. The star of Sopdet has appeared in the sky in the south. The priests of Abu Island report that Mother Nile is sending us a huge flood!"

SCROLL FIFTEEN

Nubiti

"And what's your point?" I asked Odji, one of the so-called generals in Khnum's rag-tag army. The man stank of cheap barley beer. Bakht sat to my left, Khnum to my right. Around the table were another of Khnum's generals and two of Bakht's most senior priests.

"My point is that recruiting men is still a challenge, especially in the years since Khnum has gone underground," he answered, obviously annoyed with me for questioning him.

"You're flinging dung again, Odji!" I responded. "It's been eight years since Khnum went into hiding and you've still not figured out a way to add to our numbers?" I felt frustrated with these incompetents.

"In his defense, Nubiti, we're having greater success with the poorest of the rekhi, for whom the benefits of Meryt-Neith's public works projects hasn't reached," Khnum objected. "It's slow going. We're as frustrated as you."

"No. No you're not!" I shot back. "Passion for our cause is diminishing among our own people. Our farmers are being bought off by her damned granary storage projects. Our engineers and skilled laborers are corrupted by her plague of temple and road building. And our businessmen are won over by her import and export contracts. Our politicians would rather go to one of her damned Council of Nomes meetings than make love to their mistresses! Damn Mother Nile! Just when we were having our greatest successes, she rewards the usurper with more than ample floods and abundance everywhere!"

They sat in silence, staring at their feet. The room we met in was the same secret one that I witnessed the sacrifice of the Apep priest so many years before. How naïve I realized I was then, thinking that in a few years we would achieve our aims. Men plan and the gods laugh. How true.

"Is there one damned good thing to report?" I asked.

"The assassinations of royal loyalists goes well enough," Khnum answered. "None of the old Delta families would consider accepting a royal appointment. Meryt-Neith has been forced to appoint Upper Kemians and that does help us in the long run."

"And the Ta-Tjehenus?" I asked of Bakht.

"They're ready at our command," he answered without pause. "We have begun training with them in the far western desert, away from the eyes and ears of Amka's spies."

"Training for what?" I asked.

"Up to now we've relied on them for raids to keep the army off guard. But we do not fully understand their methods of fighting. We felt... I felt that we needed better coordination in preparation for the time we might need to coordinate attacks."

I smiled at Bakht's foresight. "Well done," I ventured. "As for the attacks, is it time? What do you each say?"

For the rest of the morning we debated the issue of whether to accelerate our plans to separate from Upper Kem. I was surprised at the unanimity of our group.

"So, we agree we can't wait any longer. Bakht, how long before our men can coordinate with the Ta-Tjehenus and advance on Inabu-hedj?"

"On Inabu-hedj?" Odji asked. His eyes opened wide. "I... I never thought that was in our plans... I..."

"Inabu-hedj was built on our land. Let us not forget that," Bakht reminded the group. "Narmer intentionally did this to rub his victory in our faces. We will reclaim it as our own and remake it. Let the Upper Kemians go back to Nekhen." Bakht spit on the ground before him.

"We'll be ready in a month or two, perhaps a bit more. But we'll need you to work your magic from the inside, so to speak," Bakht said, smiling at me.

"I plan to meet with one of my most valuable spies just as soon as I get back to Inabu-hedj," I said, thinking about my next move. "I promise each of you here today that I'll do my part. When you march on Inabu-hedj you'll find a weakened Royal family and a city unable to resist your forces." I looked into each of their faces. "But this I promise you. There will be consequences if each of you does not do your part. The time is now!"

After clarifying a few more details, I adjourned the meeting. Once everyone else left, I turned to Bakht.

"We must get rid of Odji. He is…"

"I've already arranged for a rather unfortunate accident to happen to the old man. Pity." I shook my head in amazement and Bakht smiled.

"How's Khnum holding up?"

"Being in hiding does not agree with him. He likes the trappings of power."

"That's the way it should be. It'll keep him motivated." At this Bakht laughed.

"Did you bring what I requested?" I asked.

"Of course." He withdrew from his robe two packets of burlap, tied tightly with hemp string. "You remember what I told you about how to use this?" he asked before handing them to me.

"Yes. Slowly and consistently." Bakht nodded his head. I immediately put the packets in my robe.

"And the boy?" I asked, looking directly into his dark eyes. He smiled broadly.

"Doing well. The priests train him daily. He already displays certain… shall we say… aptitudes."

"And you're sure he'll be ready?"

"He'll be ready." And with that Bakht reached out and took me in his arms.

In eight days I was back in Inabu-hedj and had already spent two days meeting with the head Isis priestesses from each of our nomes. The abundance Mother Nile brought us was not all bad, for it brought to the Isis cult gold and goods from both the Royal Treasury and the people themselves. Woman give to the temples far more of their possessions than their husbands ever know about. And with these resources we issued contracts to build a few temples, buy goods from merchants, and hire scribes to write our legal documents. In this way we gained power and influence right under the noses of the Royal Court.

Despite my heavy schedule of meetings, I added one more that day or, more accurately, that night. It was well after Ra's half silver disk rose that I heard a familiar knock on my door at the Temple, for I dared not meet with this spy in the house I shared with Sekhemkasedj. I made sure there were no candles still lit in my room. I knew that Nyla would have arranged that no other priestesses would be nearby.

I opened the door and my most important informer slid in gracefully. She wore a dark robe and her flowing hood concealed her face.

"I'm glad you could make it tonight," I started.

"It's best we get this done quickly," she said nervously. "Eyes and ears are on alert everywhere in the Court these days."

"Yes, quickly then." I stepped away from her, but kept my voice to a whisper. "We are planning to act."

"With my respects, Mother, you have been planning to act for many years now." I quickly subdued my anger at her petulance. I was her superior in rank as Head Isis priestess, but she was older and had known me nearly all of my life.

"You're right, but there have been many obstacles in our way. Now's the time and we act sooner rather than later."

"How soon?" she asked impatiently.

"That will depend on you," I answered. She stood quietly for several seconds.

"In that case you should plan to act tomorrow!" Her anger was so near the surface I wanted to smile.

"Good. I don't need to remind you that the very cult of Isis is in mortal danger. If we don't act soon we risk becoming a lesser cult and think what that would mean."

"And you believe that is what brings me into this cabal?" she said, every word measured. I searched her face for a clue to her mood, but it was cast in dark shadow.

"I suspect it plays a part at least."

"I do not care a flea's worth on an elephant for the plight of your precious temples," she said with disdain. "I am an Isis priestess and that is between she and me and I need no temple to verify what is in my heart."

I was taken aback by the vehemence of her words, but there was business to transact and so long as her motivation to aide our cause was high, I saw no need to pursue this line of discussion further.

"What we're asking you to do is this," I said, explaining in detail to her what must be done. Finally I handed her the two bags of herbs that Bakht had given me.

"Be careful with these. Just a pinch at a time, mixed in food. It is slow acting and will take many weeks to reach full potency."

"I know, I have healed others from various poisons," she responded, looking down at the bags.

"Not these. They're an exotic variety not known to us in Kem. I urge you to be careful, but if you're caught…"

"If I am caught I would never reveal your involvement, even under torture. We have learned how to deal with that eventuality, haven't we?" With that she placed the packets inside her robe and made to leave.

"Wait. Before you go I have something to tell

you," I said. She hesitated, then turned to face me.

"Did you know... no, that is silly, no one here knows. I'm telling you now that I have a son."

"You? When? I..."

"No one knew at the time, except for my two able assistants and some Apep priests in the Delta. I used an extended tour of temples in the Delta to hide my pregnancy. He is now eight years old."

"So, why are you telling me this?"

"We're placing a great deal of trust in you. Our plans, our very lives depend on you succeeding. I wanted you to know that we've got a succession plan in place. His father will serve as Regent for our son, and I as queen, until he comes of age. He's being groomed right now for that eventuality. I wanted you to know how serious our plans are."

She rocked back and forth, contemplating my words. "I realize that for a long time you have wanted to know what brings me into your cabal," she finally said. "I have never pried into your alliances, into the other members of your group, for I have no interest in politics. I know I am but a Senet game piece and you will use me until I am of no use anymore... no, please, do not interrupt, let me go on.

"I appreciate your trusting my purpose and you have not pried into my motivation. So here it is, now, laid bare. I have loved Mery since she was but a child. I have taught her and healed her, as well as Zenty. And so, when she cast me aside in favor of that... that monstrous black mut spirit, that arrogant shaman priest Nekau... well, I soon pledged my revenge."

"I understand, Ti-Ameny, for..."

"No, my Isis mother, I doubt you do. I do not mean any disrespect, but I truly doubt that you do." I had to smile inside for if there is anyone in the Two Lands who understands better about being cast aside in favor of another, I have never met her.

"However, this I will tell you," she continued. "Your vision is obviously far broader, far more important than is mine. My single focus is to see Meryt-Neith be shamed and suffer as have I. That in itself will be my reward." She said nothing more that night, opened the door, peered out and then disappeared into the night. I knew then with more assurance than I had ever had that our plan would succeed.

I have thought many times since of that conversation with Ti-Ameny and the lessons it taught me about people and their motivations. I have learned not to judge, not to persuade, but to just use, unquestioning, whatever people bring to me in a way that mutually benefits us both. We are each of us full of contradictions and hypocrisy. We can justify anything to ourselves and in our self-righteousness feel morally superior. Yet here is the biggest learning of all. Forget lofty justifications. Forget appeals to reason, or duty, or higher purpose. The greatest motivators in all of Kem, in any land, are love and hate and it makes not a whit of difference in what order. They are one and the same.

And so, on the very next day, Ti-Ameny began to administer the deadly poison to Meryt-Neith. It's funny, really, what the gods have wrought. A mere plant or two, one perhaps standing tall and colorful in a grassy meadow, another thorny and tenaciously rooted in a mountain crevice, can produce such a venomous brew. Just half a pinch Bakht told me. Just half a pinch each day. That is all it took.

In several ten-days the first signs appeared. Ti-Ameny reported that Mery looked fatigued, with dark shadows under her eyes. It was all the work she did, Nekau and Amka said, the many meetings, the architectural plans to approve, the laws she and Amka enacted. This went on for many ten-days until she sat as judge in a land dispute between a nobleman and a rekhi couple. Just a few minutes into the dispute, she began to scream at both parties and left the room holding her head.

In the weeks following that, she complained of severe headaches and would nap for much of the

afternoon. Her appetite decreased and even Zenty was
forced to take a leave from his military training to spend
time with his mother. In time, her body took on a
ghastly, yellowish pale.

One evening I had arranged a party for
Sekhemkasedj and his fellow Royal agricultural estate
supervisors, as well as the various suppliers that regularly
bribed him to gain lucrative contracts. The Minister of
the Royal Agricultural Estates attended, as well as the
Governors of each nome immediately surrounding
Inabu-hedj. It was an eclectic mix of cultured and
common individuals. With the return of Mother Nile's
floods, business had been good for Sekhem and our
house had been enlarged and the furnishings all replaced
with fine handmade pieces. Pottery from some of
Nekhen's finest artists adorned every cubby. The food
was endless and the wine imported by caravan from
Babylon. In all we entertained more than one hundred
and fifty guests that night. Many were so drunk they
spent the night passed out on the floor or on our
downstairs couches.

I had worked hard to make the night succeed
because it afforded me an opportunity to advance our
plans. Throughout the night I, as well as my allies, spoke
with key people about Mery's declining health.

"And to what do you attribute Meryt-Neith's poor
health?" the Minister of Relations with Foreigners asked
me as a crowd gathered around us. "I mean as her
relative you must suspect what is at work. You two are
so close."

"Oh, I wish that were still true," I said, tittering
and playing to the crowd. "Poor Mery is so busy since
she ascended to the throne, she's hardly had time to
breathe, let alone gossip with one so unimportant as
me." The crowd was eating this up.

"We correspond about matters of the Temples
from time to time, but as for sisterly time together, she
hasn't had a moment to herself in a very long time, what
with making war, listening to disputes… well, you know.

All those male activities I think are terribly difficult for a woman." The women in the group shook their heads in agreement.

"I've heard… well, I don't believe this for a moment, but recently someone who'll remain nameless, but is in a position to know," I said, winking my eye, "told me that she is plagued by having to send troops against her own people."

"Yes, yes, it destroys ma'at!" one of my allies in the crowd assented. "Perhaps the gods punish her for such effrontery."

"Oh, no, don't say such a thing!" I responded loudly enough to draw more into the crowd. "We priestesses pray for Mery every day. I mean, yes, Isis has spoken in dreams to my sister priestesses about some of Mery's acts appearing to be heresy, but she is also a forgiving goddess. Oh, now you've upset me. Please excuse me. I go this instant to offer prayers for poor Mery's redemption." I heard later that the guests talked of nothing else the rest of the evening and in the weeks that followed, as Mery's pain increased and her health declined still further, the entire Royal Court whispered of her punishment from the gods.

"The gods seem to favor our plans," mother said to me one day when I visited her. It had been a while since I saw her and her age had finally caught up with her. She was stooped from the bent bones of old age and her face was as wrinkled as a prune. She wore a wig to hide her baldness.

"What've you heard?"

"I know that The Abomination is failing. My informer tells me she looks like death and that Amka and his Horus shamans work day and night to find a cure. But they won't, eh daughter?" she said, giggling.

"No, I don't suppose they will. And all the while our other plans solidify. I'm most pleased." I had a pang in my heart with the realization that it was entirely possible that the woman who had put all of this in motion might not live to see our good fortune return.

So it came as a great surprise when I was awakened one night by Nyla, who had rushed from the temple to my house to get me.

"It's bad, Mother," she whispered to me. "Come quickly." I threw on my robe and together we hurried through the quiet streets of the city where only the cats were about hunting their nightly meals of mice and the occasional rat.

"Alright, what is it?" I asked as soon as we entered my quarters. Instead of answering directly, she turned me around to peer out the window that overlooked the palace. What I saw made my heart sink, for deep in its center the light of many candles burned bright.

"He's exposed Ti-Ameny!" Nyla said.

"Who?" I asked, my heart racing, although I already suspected the answer.

"The black mut... Nekau. He somehow found out that Meryt... I mean, Mery, has been poisoned. I... I don't know how he found out. But I am told they are questioning her now."

I paced around the room, weighing our options, yet I did not feel panic, for I knew that Ti-Ameny would never reveal who conspired with her, even under torture. Ti-Ameny was already dead, if not tonight then in a day or two. Instead, I weighed in my heart how her being caught might affect our plans.

"Nyla, find out all you can. I need every bit of information you can gather. I'll call in my informers, too. We meet again, here, after morning prayers." As soon as Nyla left I wrote a cryptic set of prayers and instructions to the Head Priestess in Dep, who would know to deliver it to Bakht and Khnum, and called in my trusted Kainefuru. She left within the hour for Dep.

In a ten-day, allowing time so as not to arouse suspicion, for now Amka's spies followed me openly, I left to make my rounds of the Delta temples. On the second night after my arrival, I met secretly with Khnum and Bakht.

"How bad is it?" Khnum asked anxiously. "How

did they find out?"

"It was Amka, no doubt," Bakht said.

"No, it was Nekau. Eventually he suspected a poison for in Ta-Sety they have similar ones to the one that you gave me. He blames himself for not recognizing it earlier. Then he laid a trap for Ti-Ameny and caught her in the act of administering it. He grabbed Ti-Ameny by the throat and held her in the air until she confessed."

"What is to become of her?" Bakht asked.

"We don't know. The palace is keeping a very tight lid on this."

"The fact that she has not already been executed speaks loudly of The Abomination's weaknesses," Bakht suggested. "The two were close, so she will have a difficult time bringing herself to issue the order to execute Ti-Ameny."

"And Meryt?" Khnum asked purposely, knowing that I refused to refer to her by her masculine name.

"She's still gravely ill, but Nekau's ministering to her, but they must have ten Horus physicians at her bedside. That black mut took the poison himself, in small doses, to experience the symptoms and understand how he can best treat her. She's recovered slightly, but she's not her former self. The poison affected her liver... just as you said it would," I noted, turning to Bakht. He bowed slightly.

Khnum stood and began to pace. "So, we must strike now!" he said, punching his fist into his other palm.

"That's unwise," I said. "Herihor and Amka are in control now. They're taking a hard line. Herihor's mobilized the army. They're strong and well trained, thanks to the inflated treasury. We wouldn't stand a chance."

"We can't stay here and do nothing. It's our last chance!" Khnum yelled. "We must act now!"

I stood up and paced opposite Khnum. "I'm not suggesting that we do nothing," I said. "I'm suggesting a different strategy, though. Think of it as the tactic that will lead to our final act. I don't understand why we haven't thought of this before."

Khnum immediately sat down, his eyes riveted on me. Bakht actually smiled. "Here, then, is my idea. We kidnap and kill Zenty."

It was as if I had sucked all the air out of the dank room. Khnum actually gasped. Bakht remained silent, his eyes now nothing but slits, so that he gave the appearance of a serpent ready to strike.

"You're joking, right?" Khnum finally said.

"Does she look like she is joking?" Bakht responded, never taking his eyes off me.

"This is madness," Khnum protested, jumping back up. "We can't just kidnap and kill the future King."

"Why not?" I asked as calmly as I could. "Either way, once we take power he'd have to be eliminated anyway. Why not now?"

"Well, for one thing we do not have the soldiers to do it. For another…"

"But, suppose we were able to do it," Bakht interjected. "I agree with you, my master, that on the surface it appears to be a crazy idea. However, if we could do it now, then think what it would mean.

"By my calculations, The Abomination is too weak, her liver too destroyed, to ever function as she did before. She wavers even now in the decision to execute Ti-Ameny. And the scandal with Ti-Ameny proves to those who sit on the fence deciding whether or not to support us that there's significant opposition to her rule. Now, if the future King is suddenly eliminated, people will be desperate… they'll clamor for someone powerful to take over the reigns and restore ma'at. Unification is still new enough so that people will accept our contention that the Two Lands should remain separate but equal."

Despite Bakht's eloquence, in another three days Khnum was still not convinced that Ra was ready to shine light on a new era for Kem, at least not using the methods that Bakht and I advocated. And so, we agreed to meet one last time before my duties called me back to Inabu-hedj.

"Tell us again what your objection is to eliminating the boy," Bakht said to Khnum.

"First, you make it sound like we will be snatching a child. Zenty is fifteen and already a well-trained soldier at Herihor's and Akori's hands. Second, he is assigned to an army unit. Do you suggest we walk in and ask his commander to kindly hand him over to us so we may send him on his way to the Afterlife?" Even I laughed at Khnum's humor, but I was already wondering about his usefulness to us after we assumed the throne. "And even if we were to kidnap him, he might be worth more to us alive than dead, at least for a while."

Upon Khnum's last point I thought to myself that there might be merit to that notion, for Mery, Amka and Tepemkau certainly realized that the hopes for the continuation of their dynasty rested entirely with Zenty. They would therefore attach much value on his life and we could exact concessions and considerable treasure and, more importantly, needed time to grow our troop strength. Once the people of the Delta found out what had happened, they would undoubtedly flock to our side.

"You know, Khnum, I have been pondering how to win you to our side for the past few days," Bakht said." And I thought I had come up with a solution, yet something was missing. But with your suggestion to keep Zenty alive, it only adds strength to the solution I propose." By now our eyes were on Bakht and he relished the moment.

"We forget that we have the most capable ally imaginable. I have kept close contact with General Panahasi since The Abomination forced him out. He has not lost any of his hatred for that whore. In fact, her falsely claimed role in the victory over the Ta-Setys only inflamed his anger.

"He still has loyalists in the army and he need only give his word and they will flock to his command. He can easily find out where Zenty is stationed, the troop strength and any details he needs to mount an expedition. With a relatively small force of our men, well trained by him, of course, I am certain he could do this."

And so, with the agreement of Khnum we set upon a path that had no return. In one month I was back in Inabu-hedj, in the midst of prayers, when rams horns began blaring from the palace. By the end of the day it was confirmed. Twenty-six soldiers in Zenty's unit were dead and the fruit of The Abomination was in our hands and would never bear seed.

SCROLL SIXTEEN

Meryt-Neith

Oh, Horus, how cruel you can be! Isis, my Isis, where are you now? Neith, my namesake, my huntress and protector. Have you all abandoned me? What will be next? Will Ra deem us unworthy and not rise in the sky? Why is this all happening?

There are times during the day, every day, when I cannot even stand up, when the pain in my abdomen is so great it feels like fire will burst from my body. Most days I can tolerate only one meal and then my stomach hurts for hours afterward. And the pounding headache never leaves me, although it has decreased in severity since Nekau has taken over my care.

I wake in the morning to his wide black face smiling at me and forcing me to drink cup after cup of water, until I am sure I will float away down the palace walls and join Mother Nile in her journey to Wadj-Wer. He prepares potions that he requires me to drink three and four times a day. And while I complain that he devises new and devious ways to torture me, I am grateful that come evening he forces everyone from my meeting rooms and makes me retire to my bed early so that sleep can continue to heal my body.

The potion he gives me at night quickly sends me off to the world of dreams, but I have not told him that it lasts only so long. In the hours between when I awake and Ra's appearance, that is when the nightmares of my present life confront me. Yet I would rather face them in those quiet hours than be in a constant haze from the medicines that Nekau and Amka concoct.

One of my recurring nightmares comes when I think of the gift we sent to Nubiti as she prepared for her evening offerings to Isis. For days, even ten-days we debated Ti-Ameny's fate. To this day I could not say which is worse, my bodily torments from the poison or Ti's betrayal, for if ever I loved a woman with all my heart and ka it was Ti-Ameny. It was she who taught me the mysteries of men, who attended me during Zenty's birth and who was my personal healer. Herneith, I am certain, now suffers in the Afterlife over Ti-Ameny's disloyalty.

Once the betrayal was discovered, Herihor, Amka and Nekau tried to persuade me to allow her to be tortured, for how else would we obtain the information as to who was behind this grievous act? When a goat suddenly disappears under Mother Nile's swirling waters, do you wonder what has taken it? I asked them. It was now clear beyond any doubt who our enemies were and torturing Ti-Ameny would accomplish nothing except plague me for eternity.

The next issue was not whether to execute Ti, but how. Coming right after my poisoning was discovered, my heart was too muddled to sort through the complex arguments. I attended the meetings and in the end my closest advisors decided the matter for me. The deed was done and a wood box sent to Nubiti at the Temple of Isis. In the box was Ti-Ameny's headless body and on her arm the gold Isis priestess armband she always wore with pride.

I understand the priestesses spent the night preparing her body as best they could and placed her in a rekhi grave dug at the outskirts of the temple's burial ground, for without her entire body she could not answer Anubis' questions and would not be granted the privilege of an Afterlife. We sent her head by armed escort to Dep, where it was impaled on a pole directly in front of Narmer's statue, his penetrating stare looking down at Ti-Ameny with contempt.

Amka's argument was that the beheading would show our enemies that we were serious and that I, as King Regent, was not to be taken lightly. Herihor believed it would serve as a lesson to others who were considering aligning themselves against the Royal family. I hope it accomplished its purpose, for Ti-Ameny surely accomplished hers. Her betrayal damaged my body, but its real effect festered deep within my ka. I no longer knew who I could trust.

In two ten-days I called a meeting with Amka and Tepemkau, since Tepemkau was already in Inabu-hedj to train a new group of priests as scribes. They arrived just after I awoke from an afternoon nap.

"How are you feeling today, my dearest Meryt?" Amka asked.

"Better, thanks to yours and Nekau's ministrations. Not well, but better."

"The poison took long to act and it will take even longer to cleanse from your system," Tepemkau ventured. "You must be patient."

"And I would be more patient if my trusted advisors did not bring me so many problems." Amka thought me serious. "I am only teasing you, teacher." He bowed slightly and I could see that age and the many problems he carried on his shoulders continued to take a toll on him. His right hand shook as it gripped his staff.

"In any event, I have called you here to discuss a critical issue with you and that is Nubiti. It weighs greatly on my mind. We must finally resolve it."

"Resolve it? Meaning what?" Tepemkau asked.

"I need to know what the law allows me to do with her."

Tepemkau and Amka looked at each other curiously. "My dear," Amka said slowly, "you are the law. You are the King and may do whatever you feel is in the best interests of ma'at and Kem."

"What I may do and what is right might be different. What I am asking is for you to research the holy scrolls. You have always told me, dear teacher, that our history still lives, that it can teach us many lessons. I want to know what Narmer, blessed be his name, and his father and grandfather before him did in similar situations, if there were any such situations."

"Ah, the precedents," Tepemkau offered.

"Yes, the precedents." And so Tepemkau left in a few days for Nekhen, where the complete collection of original scrolls was housed. He took with him Amka's best scribes and legal scholars.

During this period of my recovery, I keenly felt the absence of Zenty. Ever since his birth he lit up the room for me as well as Ra ever could. I wrote to him every other day, but his responses were sporadic and brief. As Herihor explained it, he had placed Zenty with one of his toughest and most experienced field commanders and had sent his unit to the Eastern desert along Wat-Hor, the Way of Horus, our most important trade route to Babylon. Zenty would have little time available to sleep, let alone write for the unit commander was sure to be tough on the future King.

But I was still plagued by my decision to let Zenty go, for I had seen with my own eyes the awfulness of war. I had smelled the stench of the battlefield and still wake to the dreadful screams of dying soldiers. I still live with the nightmare of seeing that enemy warrior's tortured face as I plunged a knife between his ribs. In the end Amka and Herihor presented a powerful argument that the future leader of Kem needed to prove himself worthy in Horus' eyes. Military service was crucial for his rule, although serving on the Wat-Hor, they assured me, meant that his worst enemies might be vipers and scorpions. I relented.

Nor was my writing to Zenty easy for me. I would start dictating a letter to a scribe and soon my thoughts would wander to a simpler time when Zenty and I lay sprawled on the floor of his nursery playing a game with his carved wooden soldiers as we waited for his father to return. When I taught him Senet as a child, his cat, Bastet, ruined our first game when she stepped onto the game board and he did not know whether to laugh or cry and just sat alternating between the two, his tiny stomach heaving in and out. In moments like that I could still smell his baby unguents on his scalp or feel his soft child's side-braid brushing against my chest. Even though he now served in the army, my breasts would sometimes ache with the memory of his suckling.

I remember once, he had just turned 13, and he wandered into my quarters after a morning of reading one of Anhotek's scrolls and debating its merits with Amka. Zenty still dwelled on the border between childhood and manhood and on this afternoon, tired and hngry, he sat next to me and gently placed his head on my shoulders. How sweet was that moment; how unexpected and therefore even more memorable.

Moments later Amka was announced and as he entered my room, Zenty winked at me, although I knew not why.

"You know, mother, today Amka had me read one of Anhotek's most important scrolls, or so he says." Amka immediately stood erect, his hands on his staff.

"Really?" I said playing along. "Well if Amka said it was important, I imagine it was."

"Except in this case I do think he was testing to see if I could tell the difference between an Anhotek scroll and a forgery."

"A forgery?" Amka asked in amazement. "What are you talking about, Zenty?"

"You know, a scroll written by a lesser being, like a Horus priest, for instance."

"Need I remind you that Anhotek was a Horus

priest?" Amka replied, but I could see that Zenty had already gotten his goat.

"Oh, of course, of course," Zenty said. "What I meant to say was that this scroll that you had me read was... how can I say this? It was not of the caliber of Anhotek's usual thought. It was... hmmm... ordinary. Yes, quite ordinary, that's it."

"Ordinary, you say?" Amka responded, and I would hardly be accused of exaggerating much when I say steam was about to rise out of poor Amka's head. "Ordinary! The greatest Horus priest who ever walked the Two Lands, the most brilliant vizier..."

At that Zenty began to laugh heartily, and Amka, knowing full well he had been played, made as if he chased Zenty around the room, about to beat him with his staff. "If I catch you, you..."

Just dictating this recollection, images from Zenty's childhood played in my heart, and when I came back to the present moment, there were my scribes waiting for my next words.

The only pleasure I could indulge in during my recovery was sleeping with Herihor, although in my state such pleasures did not extend very well to matters sexual. I would sleep restlessly after taking Nekau's sleep potion, until Herihor slipped between my sheets later in the evening. Then I would sleep deeply and peacefully in his arms until I awoke before Ra's appearance. To his credit, and my eternal gratitude, Herihor's sole concern was my recovery, even though sexual enjoyment was infrequent, indeed.

One day, after Herihor finished his morning meal, he advised me that his sources in the Delta reported less rebellious activity. Although I was still plagued by our decision to send Ti-Ameny's head to the rebels, I had to agree with Herihor that it probably served its purpose.

Toward the end of the next ten-day Tepemkau returned, with a boatload of scribes and scholars in tow. After a night's rest, he requested a meeting with me. Amka, Herihor and Nekau joined us.

"We have completed our study, Meryt, and we have determined various restrictions on your actions, but also some solutions. Amka and I discussed this in detail last night. If you have any questions about our interpretations of the texts, you need only ask. In the next room I have assembled the scribes and we can retrieve the precise text..."

"I feel most certain I will not need to do that. I trust both your knowledge and wisdom, Chief Priest," I responded and I believe that Tepemkau was truly disappointed, for his preparation was thorough and I think he would have been pleased to demonstrate that to us.

"I'll summarize, then." And here he unrolled a papyrus and spread it out on the table, carefully placing gold weights at each corner to hold it down.

"While there are many texts from before Narmer's time that hint at troubled relationships within the Royal families, there is nothing specific until we get to King Narmer himself, may he rest in eternal glory. Part of this was due to Anhotek, who not only kept meticulous records himself, but also trained the young King to do the same.

"King Narmer's mother died during his birth and his father, King Scorpion, remarried a woman from the Delta named Mersyankh."

"Yes, I remember her name from Amka's teachings."

"Surely you do. Scorpion hoped that by marrying the woman he would appease the tribes of Lower Kem. In any event, Mersyankh and Scorpion had a son, who Mersyankh tried to position to succeed Scorpion. It created a terrible rivalry between King Narmer and his father until Scorpion's early death in battle. From then on King Narmer and Mersyankh were locked in an almost daily struggle."

"From our reading," Amka continued, "we know that Mersyankh formed alliances with her Delta kin, much as Nubiti appears to have done. Narmer was attacked by swordsmen trying to kill him at least once and at one point Mersyankh did something so terrible, King Narmer was within his rights to have her executed."

"Well, did he?" I asked.

"No he didn't," the booming voice of Nekau chimed in. "And that's where my people come in. King Narmer exiled Mersyankh to Abu Island, where she tried to continue her mischief by bribing one of our priests and sending messages back to the Delta. Until her dying day Mersyankh held out hope that her son would inherit the throne."

"I was not aware of the connection to Abu Island and your people," I said to Nekau. He simply bowed his head, but said nothing more.

"The long and short of the story is that we Upper Kemians are not the only ones who have created legends from our history," Amka suggested. "The Lower Kemians see Mersyankh in an altogether different light, as a heroine, and they curse King Narmer, as you well know. The victors get to write the history, but the vanquished carry their legends like burrs in their robes."

I nodded once again at Amka's deep wisdom. "So, how does your reading limit my options?" I asked Tepemkau.

"It tells us that despite the fact that King Narmer would have been right to execute Mersyankh, the gods stayed his hand. Once Scorpion married Mersyankh, she was part of the Royal family. To kill her would have thrown ma'at to the wind. It might have brought down the wrath of the gods. Horus might have forsaken the throne.

"But, since King Narmer did not kill her we - that is Amka and Nekau and me - we believe you are constrained from executing Nubiti, although by her possible involvement in your poisoning she deserves nothing less. And her plotting with Khnum and Bakht would make her responsible for the death of thousands of our soldiers in the Ta-Sety war."

"So what are my options?" I asked the group in frustration.

"Isolate her. Strip her of her duties as the Isis Mother, which would restrict her travel. Send her away. Nekau has assured me that the priests on Abu Island would gladly step forward once again." Nekau nodded to Tepemkau.

I was already feeling fatigued from the meeting. "I will think on this for a day or two. Tepemkau, do your duties allow you to stay for a few days until I decide?"

"Your needs are my first concern, my Master." Tepemkau said, as he bowed.

On the second day, after speaking individually to Amka, Herihor, Nekau and Tepemkau, I made a decision and called my advisors together for a meeting. I included the Council of Ministers so that they could witness the resolve of the King. They had gathered in our largest meeting room and when I entered and stepped onto my platform, they all bowed low as I sat.

It was important for Tepemkau to set the stage and he did so methodically by retracing the steps he took in his research. Just as he approached the end of his talk, I noticed one of Amka's assistants enter the room, take him aside and whisper in his ear. For the first time in my life, I saw Amka react in shock. He blanched. He began to shake and his assistant took him by the arm and together they left the room. Five minutes later, I caught a glimpse of the assistant waving to attract Herihor's attention. Herihor, too, hurriedly left the room.

Now it was my turn to speak to the group. As I stood to address them, Herihor strode back into the room. "Excuse me, my King." He turned to the group. "Ministers, advisors, the meeting must be postponed to a later time. Something has come up which will require the King's urgent attention." The men looked at each other quizzically and then turned to the corridors outside to pick up a clue as to what had prompted this. They buzzed amongst themselves.

Herihor came to the platform, bowed, and then

took a step up. "Quickly, follow me," and I could tell from his voice that this was an extraordinary moment. I left with Herihor placing himself between me and the assembly, so as to avoid them taking me aside to plead for their usual favors.

Herihor escorted me to my private chambers, which I thought unusual. There waited Amka and Tepemkau. Just after I entered, Nekau walked in.

"She is neither in the palace nor the temple. She left no word," he said to the others.

"What is going on here?" I asked, turning from one man to the other.

"Sit down, Meryt, for this is terrible news we must impart," Amka said, his eye twitching. My heart stopped for a moment as I sat. "We have received a ransom note."

"A ransom note?" I asked. My mind raced thinking of who could be so important as to warrant a ransom. The very instant before Amka responded, my heart sank, for it suddenly hit me who it might be.

"No!" I screamed. "It cannot be him, it cannot be!" Herihor rushed to my side and despite the lapse in decorum, he held me tight.

"Why does Horus test me so?" I pleaded, tears streaming down my face. "Tell me, why?" But even the mightiest Horus priests in the Two Lands could not give me an answer.

"Zenty is alive, Meryt. We must be thankful to Horus for that. They have kidnapped him, but he is alive," Nekau offered.

"How can you be certain?" I cried, and all I could think of was Ti-Ameny's head impaled on a spear in Dep. Now the image of my son's head so displayed came into my vision and I screamed and cried into Herihor's chest.

It is said by the priests that nothing happens without a reason. As mortals we try to discern what those reasons might be, but in our pitifully limited states, we often cannot. And so it was in that moment. Amka and Nekau later said my statements were foolish, but thanks be to Horus that Herihor at least understood me. For I truly believe that my poisoning served me well that day. It weakened my heart so that I could no longer bear the pain of Zenty's abduction and I simply fell into a deep, but troubled sleep.

I dreamed then of Zenty being held in a dark and damp cavern by demons and serpents that slithered around him, flicking their hideous red and black tongues and threatening to strike. I could feel his fear. I screamed warnings to him, but I was powerless to do anything but watch him struggle to free himself. I tossed in anguish.

Then Horus swooped down and lifted me upon his back and I rode atop his wings. Together we flew until night became day and then Horus pulled back his wings and down we glided, the wind whipping our faces. I could make out the narrow ribbon of green that wound its way through the red and brown sands of our Two Lands and my heart filled with joy at the sight of Mother Nile. We followed her through towns now well stocked with grains, with verdant farms, with livestock grazing along her banks and my people peacefully working, trading, making love. New temples honoring our many gods shone like tiny stars. My heart felt light.

Suddenly Mother Nile branched out to form the Five Rivers of the Delta and the blackness of its rich soil stood in stark contrast to the barren deserts of Upper Kem. Rekhi toiled in the fields, temples stood on the banks of the rivers and granaries bulged with abundant foods. But then the black mud began to swirl and to suck in the people. In their confusion they did not understand what was happening to them. The granaries began tumbling into the muck and the temples crumbled into the thick mess.

The dark muck became a poisonous slurry and everyone who touched it contorted in pain. Buildings disappeared in the blink of an eye. The black ooze slid swiftly toward Dep and when it met Wadj-Wer it swirled around and around, sucking in everything in its path.

Then, in a massive wave, it turned on itself and ran backward along Mother Nile's path wreaking utter destruction.

I awoke with Nekau and Amka around me shouting instructions. My abdomen seared in pain and I found myself vomiting onto my robe. Nekau gave me a potion to settle my stomach, as my handmaidens cleaned me and brought me a change of clothes. Herihor stood nearby, waiting his turn to hold me.

"I had a vision," I said when the wave of nausea passed, yet still holding my hands to my mid-section. "That poisonous brew in the Delta now boils over and threatens to destroy us all. I have been too distracted to resolve it completely… until now. For the future of Kem we must destroy both the pot and the cooks who stoke its fire." I looked around and each man shook his head somberly in agreement.

"We will act and with such force as they will remember for generations," I added.

"What do you suggest we do about Zenty?" Tepemkau asked.

"We will develop a plan. My heart pains me to think of Zenty in their filthy hands, but Horus will protect him. Things in the Delta are tenuous, but Horus also showed me a bright future for Kem. But it is time to act."

Over the next few days, the palace was abuzz with meetings. Amka called in his informers and squeezed them for information, as did all of his advisors and fellow priests. Herihor's men managed to extract from the messenger who delivered to us the news about Zenty's kidnapping information as to who had relayed the message to him. Bit, by bit, they traced back the elaborate chain of messengers until the last one was found dead before they even arrived. But by then, the chain of command was already clear.

"Khnum is truly desperate," Herihor advised me, "for he makes no attempt to hide his maneuvers this time. I fear a major move on their parts."

"And Nubiti?" I asked of the group. "Has there been any word of her?"

"Nothing," Amka answered. "She is being hidden well. She is probably with Khnum. We have not pursued this further so as not to force their hands with Zenty. At the very least she has isolated herself, although I would rather she be under our watchful eyes on Abu Island."

"Any word from Zenty?" I asked. I had slept fitfully every night since his kidnapping, waking shortly after going to bed, my heart full of anxiety.

"Nothing specific, other than a message sent through a Horus priest in Dep to us. They wish to negotiate."

"Negotiate? Are they mad?" I asked, incredulously. Amka looked from Herihor to Nekau. "The King of Kem negotiates with no mortal!"

"Wait. It is not such a crazy idea," Amka answered. He breathed in sen-sen breaths to calm himself and center his ka. "Herihor, Nekau and I have discussed this and we have a proposal to offer."

"Go ahead," I said, leaning forward in my chair.

"Let us negotiate."

"But…"

"Allow me to finish, Meryt. Negotiations are like having the best-placed spy in your opponent's camp. We will negotiate. We will take our time. We will extract information regarding their numbers, their leaders, their locations, their plans."

"To what end?" I asked. "What if they kill Zenty? I would not be able to continue living!"

"While Amka and Tepemkau handle the negotiations, Nekau and I will train a special group of our very best soldiers," Herihor said. "An elite core trained just for this occasion, to rescue Zenty. With the information Amka gets from the negotiators, we'll surprise his captors and bring him home alive."

Thus began one of the most trying periods of my life. The first thing we demanded before even beginning negotiations was proof that Zenty was alive. After keeping us waiting for an entire ten-day, proof arrived at the palace in the form of Zenty's gold ring and a brief note in his writing, along with a warning that unless we showed them corresponding good faith, the finger that wore that ring would soon follow. That night I dispatched a convoy with abundant gifts of gold and silver and choice jewels.

Knowing full well that Khnum used this time to build his forces and to mortar his alliances with the Ta-Tjehenu, Herihor immediately chose a complement of soldiers to train. Some were handpicked from my King's Guard, but others were soldiers loyal to Herihor who had distinguished themselves in hand-to-hand combat in battles against the Ta-Sety and Ta-Tjehenu.

Herihor used an ancient, abandoned village in Upper Kem to train his troops, for he felt certain that we would eventually find Zenty held in a deep cellar in the midst of an innocent-looking farming village. Every day and night he conducted drills for his men to handle different situations they might encounter.

As we negotiated, selected members of our Council of Advisors also used their own informers to exact information concerning Zenty's whereabouts. When three ten-days passed without definitive word from Zenty's captors, Herihor felt certain Zenty was not being held by a large contingent of troops, for their very presence in one location would have been leaked by now. Yet he had no idea about the conditions of Zenty's imprisonment. What anxiety I had now began to appear as panic. I spent nights anxiously wandering the corridors of the palace, often with Herihor by my side.

"I do not understand why this is happening," I confided in Herihor one night as we stood on the portico. I had a shawl over my shoulders to protect me from the cool evening breezes.

"You are King, my dearest. All manner of things, good and bad, come to the King."

"I did not ask to be King," I replied bitterly.

"None of us are chosen for leadership. Most often

it's thrust upon us. We have certain talents and the rest is a matter of whatever play the gods wish us to perform." I looked at Herihor's battle-scarred face, chest and arms. Daily he made decisions of life and death. I felt foolish questioning his observations.

"It is... I often wonder what it would be like to have lived the life of Aunt Herneith," I ventured, looking up. The lights of the gods shone brightly in the sky. Ra's silver crescent shimmered in Mother Nile's reflection.

"All I ever wanted was to be a loving, supportive wife and mother. I would have settled happily for a life of presiding over festivals. I would have willingly traveled to lands close and distant as an emissary for the King." Herihor came up behind me and enveloped me in his arms. How I loved to be held by them!

"Instead I am besieged by flatterers seeking favors, by governors fighting for morsels of the treasury, by priests who argue with each other over the arcane interpretations of our laws. We send men to their deaths. Half of the women in some of our towns still die in childbirth." I turned around to face my beloved.

"Herihor, it is sometimes too much for a mortal to bear!"

For a long time Herihor just held me close to him, my face pressed against his muscled chest. He smelled strongly of a salve that Amka had dispensed for a sprained shoulder.

"You know, Mery, the gods truly do not place upon our shoulders burdens we can't bear. Horus has brought Wadjet to his side in the Afterlife for reasons we can't comprehend. I believe Horus and Wadjet together have chosen you to rule for Zenty. But it takes many mortals to represent one god's power here in the Two Lands. All I can say is that I will always be at your side, as will Amka, Tepemkau, Nekau... people you can trust... truly trust."

Herihor's words opened my heart and fanned the embers of our dying lovemaking. We made love slowly that night, perfumed lamps softly lighting my bedroom. We even talked and laughed at times during our coupling. At one point Herihor withdrew from me, turned me over and gently massaged my back with scented flax oil, as I drifted off to a deep sleep. But it was not long before he raised my rear end and entered me from behind. It felt good to have Herihor's manhood in me once again and after he shot his seed we slept the deep sleep of lovers, the pains in my chest temporarily relieved.

When I awoke the next morning, I started the morning meal with Herihor, but he soon had to leave to attend to army business. I sat alone on the portico, just staring at Mother Nile as I often did and my heart felt touched by sadness. This surprised me for I had just had such a wonderful connection with Herihor. I thought of Zenty's plight and although my heart ached, I knew it was not his predicament that just now affected my heart.

I thought of Herihor's words to me last night and his assurances that I could always trust him, Amka, Nekau and Tepemkau. Yet I already knew that. I thought of the many times in my life that I had relied on Amka's wisdom, Tepemkau's spirit, Nekau's strength and, above all, Herihor's loving support. Yet there was something missing, something that had deeply affected my ka.

I thought of others upon whom I had relied over the years and I suddenly understood from where my sadness sprang. For the first time in my life I had no woman with whom I could share life's experiences, or in whom I could confide my insecurities or deepest secrets. It was as if a part of my heart was now walled off, for how can a man understand the workings of a woman's heart? Could a man ever feel the tug of our monthly cycle or the fullness of a breast ready to suckle? What man could experience the depths of tenderness that a woman does or allow himself to feel the desperate despair of another's afflictions?

Herneith now sat with Horus and Wadjet. Ti-

Ameny's ka wandered in the dark, cold mists of Nun. Nubiti was a pariah, an evil mut who had pierced me to my core. I shuddered with the realization that I was close to no other woman with whom I could laugh or cry, listen and share. Gone were the conversations about our men and children, the gossip about our friends and relatives. I felt my tears run down my cheeks and a profound sense of loneliness descend into my ba. Thus I spent the rest of the morning, postponing my morning bath until my resolve returned and I began to feel my mood improve.

The tightening cordon around Lower Kem eventually did produce information. One bit came to my attention after four ten-days of negotiations, when Amka called one of his regular meetings to update me.

"We know Zenty was not taken out of Lower Kem," he said once we had begun. "One of our traders to the western lands passed a large bribe we had given him to the Ta-Tjehenu tribes. They swear they had no part in his abduction. They only recently heard of it, although they smack their lips in anticipation. There are also no reports of even small bands of rebels stationed anywhere within the eyes and ears of our Horus temples."

"So what new have we learned?" I asked, desperate for any information that would bring back my son.

"There is something to report, but I caution you it is just rumor at this point."

"Rumor important enough to bring to my attention," I said.

"Yes. It is worrisome." Amka paused and I knew that he feared telling me. "Do you recall many years ago, toward the end of the great drought, Nubiti unexpectedly took a long tour of the temples of Isis. She claimed to be doing an assessment of the need for new temples should Mother Nile bring good floods."

"I vaguely recall that, yes," I said. "She was gone for what... half the year?"

"There is a rumor that we heard from an Apep priest, unsubstantiated, that Nubiti was with child and gave birth while she was away."

"Oh, Horus, that… that is…I cannot believe that is true!" I said, shocked to my core. "To not know that Nubiti had a child…"

"A son," Amka interrupted. The import of that one fact hit me harder than a physical blow. I gasped. I noted that even Herihor blanched.

"I need not tell you what that means," Amka said.

"If anything were to happen to Zenty, Nubiti's son would be in line for the throne," Herihor said, shaking his head in disbelief. "If this proves true, it adds a motive to recent events, doesn't it?" We sat there quietly, each of us absorbing what this disclosure might mean for us and for the Two Lands.

"How old would he be?" I asked.

"Nine or ten by our estimates," Amka responded. "Old enough to be immersed in training for whatever role they have visioned for him."

"Why haven't we known of this before?" I asked.

"If what we hear is true, then the Apep priesthood must have a central role in his rearing," Amka said. "They are a highly secret sect. It is almost impossible to penetrate them. I have told you this before, Meryt. The Horus priesthood basks in Ra's light, while the Apep priesthood hides in the dark recesses of the Underworld."

That afternoon I paid a visit to the Temple of Isis, for due to Nubiti's role it had been years since I had last prayed there. My King's Guard escorts waited outside while I entered the enclosure where the acting Head Priestess, a loyalist from Upper Kem, greeted me warmly. We talked for a brief time and then she left me in the inner chamber. There the statue of Isis stood, full with her loving ka.

I bowed low before my heavenly sister and knelt in front of the brazier. The glowing embers cast a warm glow on Isis' face. I watched her eyes flicker for a moment, before I closed my eyes.

"Dear Isis," I prayed, "Please let me feel your sweet softness in my ka, for I fear my heart is becoming hard from the scars of leadership and ill fortune. Did I so wrong my sister, Nubiti, your servant? If so, please illuminate my heart so that I may correct my errors." I sat waiting, but nothing came, not a glimmer of recognition, not a tingle of warmth in my heart.

From the Temple of Isis I asked to be taken to the Temple of Horus, where Amka greeted me on the steps. As weak as I felt, I noted that Amka had even more difficulty climbing the stairs. He leaned heavily on his staff and his breathing was labored.

I had asked Amka to prepare an herbal for me to better relax in Horus' presence, for my desire was to thank him for carrying me aloft in my dreams and for revealing to me the threats and hopes for Kem. Before entering the inner sanctum, Amka sat with me for perhaps thirty minutes and we discussed Horus' relation with our dynasty as I drank the tea he had prepared.

When I emptied my cup, I felt a lightness in my heart such as I had not experienced for many years. My aches disappeared and I felt a deep sense that my heart had enlarged greatly within my chest. As we entered the inner sanctum, Amka kissed me on the cheek and wished me well.

I remember gazing up at Horus as I entered the room. The fire burned brightly and cast such shadows on him it seemed as if he moved to greet me. I immediately humbled myself and lay prostrate before his penetrating, all-knowing falcon eyes.

As I came back up to sitting I felt the immensity of Horus' power in his gaze. I sat cross-legged, relaxed by Amka's herbs and in only a moment I felt sucked into Horus' ka. I looked out through his eyes at my form sitting meditatively before him.

We did not soar into the heavens then. In fact we never left the temple. But for the first time I experienced Horus from within his own body. It was an encounter with power that I would never have imagined.

Gone were my insecurities, the self-doubts, the questioning of my own judgment. Instead I experienced the feeling of pure and just power surging within. It was not a haughty or even a giddy sense of unchecked power, but rather a fullness of purpose legitimized by Horus' divine authority. I basked in a glow that radiated from within. When I left the temple Amka himself noted a profound change in my ba.

And so, I acted. By then Herihor and Tepemkau had traced the messages and messengers to their source. It came as a surprise to them, for the source was a rekhi neighborhood in the busy town of Dep itself. But instead of soldiers standing guard, they disguised themselves as ordinary citizens and posted watches from surrounding houses.

This news came to me in an odd way. Herihor mentioned to me that he had recruited some able women as soldiers in his elite rescue unit, a practice unknown to our army. I later found out that the only way our forces could gain access to the neighborhood was to infiltrate it with innocent-looking women, posing as roving merchants selling reed baskets and trinkets. Once they determined the likely house where Zenty was being held, we were ready to strike.

Our negotiations with Khnum's representatives had reached a critical stage. We had agreed in principle to grant Lower Kem greater autonomy, a transparent attempt on their parts to force a wedge into Unification. We also agreed in principle to transfer a certain amount of gold and silver into their treasury. In the midst of Proyet, with barley and flax just beginning to emerge from the ground, a force of soldiers sailed from Inabu-hedj, the boats supposedly laden with the treasure. They were to meet up with a similar delegation of rebels near the shallows of Merimda. Unknown to the rebels, our surreptitious forces, led by Herihor himself, had already infiltrated the area around Dep. The women members of the unit had been in place for a ten-day prior to their arrival.

On the day before the transfer of treasure was to take place, my negotiators had arranged a meeting with their counterparts. On a large barge in the middle of Mother Nile, our people gave a good will gift to each of the opposing negotiators. To much drinking and merriment the Delta schemers toasted our good sense in agreeing to their demands. They also hinted at the fact that there were a few other demands that they had unintentionally neglected to bring up. We would be required to meet all of them in order for them to release Zenty. They agreed to bring them to the table in another day or two.

That very night we struck. Over the course of the preceding week, the women had determined precisely the house in which Zenty was being held. Under the cover of night, dressed in revealing robes, they paraded in pairs as whores in the neighborhood. Their supposed customers received a whole lot less sex than they bargained for and soon the lookouts were eliminated.

Herihor had already replaced the guards normally stationed on the parapets of the walls with his own warriors that night, for it was well known that the regular army guards were bribed. On a pre-arranged signal the women approached the house.

Immediately shouting erupted and men emerged from the house to shoo the women away. Our women soldiers had been trained to argue and cause confusion and soon nearly twenty rebels, dressed as poor rekhi, were outside yelling and beating the women. It was at that moment that Herihor attacked.

From the houses nearby Herihor and his men rushed into the narrow street. The rebels were shocked to see themselves surrounded by armed warriors. They tried to rush back into the house, but Akori and his King's Guards cut them off. The women quickly slid their daggers into their nearest opponent. In seconds the fight on the street was over and every last rebel lay dead or mortally wounded on the ground.

Akori and a contingent of his guards burst into the

house where a dozen armed rebels stood ready to fight. When they saw Akori's resolve, several surrendered and others dashed out the back door. Due to the restricted space, Herihor's unit could not enter.

In a back room, the captain of the rebels held Zenty in front of him as a shield, a dagger poised across his neck. Zenty's hands were bound behind him. "I'll kill him. I swear to Apep I will!" the captain shouted. "Back off!"

Herihor entered the house and held up his hand. "Stay your weapons!" he called out. To a man they held their daggers to their sides. "You heard the man, back off!" Slowly they retreated out of the room, yet stood hidden on either side of the door, weapons ready.

Zenty stood nearly half a cubit shorter than his captor and half his weight, too. Yet Herihor later reported that Zenty did not appear the least bit frightened, only alert. His eyes were riveted on Herihor, trying to read in the face of his instructor any clue as to what he should do. Herihor's face was expressionless.

The rebel leader was agitated and his eyes shifted constantly to gauge his position. Finally, Herihor spoke.

"I am Herihor, Chief of the King Meryt-Neith's Army. I know you're wondering what to do, what your options are, perhaps even what's the right thing to do. I won't insult you with lies, for we are both warriors and you... you must be a fervent believer in your cause if you're a leader of these rebels." The man's eyes were opened wide and he breathed hard. Herihor waited for his words to register on the agitated captain.

"We both know you hold the future of the Two Lands in your hands," he said without emotion. "From your position you know what the right thing to do is. Kill the boy and be done with it." The man tightened his grip on the dagger and a small stripe of blood appeared on Zenty's neck.

"But hear me well, sir, whose name I do not yet know. Either way you're a dead man and we both know that. The question is whether you'll doom your wife and children to a grisly death or not. If you kill that boy," he said without emotion, pointing casually at Zenty with his dagger, "I will personally, and happily, gut your children one by one as your wife watches and leave them in the desert for the vipers and jackals to dine on. Then I'll do the same to her before I cut her into pieces and scatter her parts." Herihor watched the man swallow hard.

"I'll have your entire extended family present to watch them die and then I will kill every one of them, too." Here he paused. "Do you understand me?" The man remained paralyzed. "With no heirs your name will be stricken from the Book of Life."

Shouts could be heard outside the house and the rebel knew that his leaders had sent reinforcements. He sweated profusely and nervously tightened and loosened his grip on the dagger as he tried to weigh his options. His legs shook in fear.

Then Herihor looked at Zenty directly for the first time and shifted his eyes slightly to his right. Herihor turned his head and yelled out to his men: "To the street!" And in that instant Zenty spun to his right and pinned the man's forearm in the crease of his neck. At the same instant Herihor also spun around and threw his dagger at the rebel's exposed neck. In a burst of blood the man collapsed immediately.

Herihor rushed forward, pulled the blade from the dead man's neck, cut the cords that bound Zenty and gave him his dagger. "Well done!" he said. By now the entire King's Guard was in the room. "Surround our future King. Every man's life to his service!" Herihor called out.

In the street ram's horns sounded. More and more of our soldiers filled the street and the winding alleyways that fed it. Herihor had foreseen the possibility of a larger battle and had assembled his men under cover of night in the drainage ditches that surrounded the city. Now they poured into the walled city just as Khnum's ragtag rebel army charged their position.

It was immediately obvious that the rebels were well

trained in hand-to-hand combat. Herihor's regular soldiers wielded heavy swords and long spears, both of which proved useless in the restricted environment and the poor lighting of a night with only a sliver of Ra's silver disk in the sky. The enemy quickly threw heavy objects from nearby houses into the path of our advancing soldiers, blocking their paths and causing mayhem and confusion. As the army's unit discipline broke down, the rebels attacked from side alleys or leapt upon them from the second story of the mud-brick houses.

As soon as Herihor and Zenty stepped outside they found their entire elite unit besieged by rebels. The unit fought with daggers and small shields that were strapped to their forearms, but the rebels fought fervently. They did not appear to have a leader and Herihor seized the moment.

"Itafe!" he shouted to the leader of the army unit. "Turn your men around and clear us a path to the gates!"

As Herihor's unit began to adjust, Herihor and Akori picked three men to help them hold off the rebels massing behind them. The fighting was so close, men resorted to punching or throwing their enemy into a headlock while a comrade delivered the mortal blow. In that moment, Herihor thought to himself that they had seriously miscalculated the strength of the rebel forces and he silently cursed himself for not bringing with him more specially trained troops. As he ran to the rear, a rebel suddenly appeared in the window above and leaped out at Herihor.

Zenty was not involved directly in the fighting, surrounded as he was by the King's Guard. Instead he keenly observed the battle around him and noticed a rebel furtively watching from the upper floor of the house across the street. Then he saw Herihor take off, his gold armband plainly visible on his bicep as it reflected the meager light from Ra's silver disk. As he later told it to me, it was as if Horus traced for him the intersection of the two fighters.

And so Zenty bolted through the double line of King's Guard soldiers and reached Herihor just as the rebel jumped. He greeted the man with the blade of his dagger in the abdomen and both fell to the ground behind Herihor. The rebel struggled to get to his feet, but one of the King's Guards in pursuit of Zenty quickly finished him off. For a moment Zenty stood in place staring at his first kill in battle.

"Quickly," Herihor shouted in his ear. "Retrieve your knife and follow me!" With Herihor and Akori beside him and the King's Guard behind and in front, Zenty fought with them as a unit. Though slightly wounded, as were Herihor and Akori, he continued to fight until they made their way through the gates of Dep and the advantage of an open field.

But Horus had devised yet another test for Zenty, one far more difficult than a pack of rebels. No sooner had they burst through the gates of Dep, leaving rebel casualties heavy behind them, than they were surprised to find their own regular army troops in battle. In the dark of night it was impossible to make out who was fighting whom, but from the high-pitched war cries of the attackers there was no doubt in Herihor's mind that they faced Ta-Tjehenus.

"They attack on two fronts!" Nekau yelled toward Herihor. Due to his immense size and black color Herihor had positioned him outside with the regular army. "The Ta-Tjehenu come from the north," he said pointing. "Another group attacks from the east, but I have no idea who they are."

In the distance the sounds of men fighting, screams of bravado and agony, could be heard all around. Herihor ran back towards the gates to command a better view.

"Akori, take the King's Guard, all of them except for these here, and protect the western flank. Remember the lessons on fighting the Ta-Tjehenu. Create two attack wedges and drive through their ranks. As soon as they are attacked from the rear they will run. Go!"

Throughout, Herihor made certain Zenty was beside him. "Can you hold out?" Herihor asked, taking Zenty's left arm and examining the superficial cut. Zenty nodded. Herihor swiftly grabbed the tunic of one of the King's Guards, ripped off a strip, and wrapped Zenty's arm.

"Brothers," he shouted, looking into the eyes of each of the dozen men who now faced him, "you are each known to me for I've trained you and we've fought bravely in battle together. I'm entrusting you with the future King of the Two Lands." He grabbed Zenty by the arm and pushed him into their midst.

"Nebtawi, take him quickly to the shore of Wadj-Wer just over the hill," he said pointing behind the captain.

"I am a soldier!" Zenty protested. "I will stay and fight."

"Exactly. You are a soldier under my command and not yet King. You will obey my orders!

"Sneak along the walls, Nebtawi. The darkness will give you cover. Our garrison from Ahnpet awaits us in their boats. Put Zenty on a boat and tell Sebhi to send him off, well protected. Tell Sebhi to have the rest of his men come to our aid on the double, but to come in through the marshes from the east, behind those enemy troops. Understood?" Nebtawi nodded. "Go! Now!" Herihor urged and Nebtawi turned immediately and, pushing Zenty before him, made for the wall.

Herihor now ran back down the hill where Nekau came to his side. "Itafe, the King's Guard defends the western flank. We must find out who it is we battle to the east. Have your men retreat to the high position along the eastern wall. We already have troops on the wall. Quickly now."

Itafe shouted commands and as his troops vacated the battlefield, Herihor could make out the outlines of rebels scurrying here and there, picking up weapons and shouting to one another. Herihor's initial thought was one of disgust, yet another example of undisciplined rebels looting the bodies of those who sacrificed their lives. But the men soon re-assembled themselves in units. Messengers ran back and forth from the units into the far darkness. Then the enemy units spread out and began to move forward. Suddenly, as if Ra had lit the sky, it all made sense to Herihor.

"It is Panahasi we face!" he whispered to Itafe and Nekau.

"With respect, Herihor, that's impossible. He would never..." Itafe objected.

"I know him. He's about to use the battering ram maneuver," Herihor said as he observed the enemy's movements. "Quick, Itafe, grab your finest unit and charge his center! You must be fast and strike without mercy. Our only hope is for you to punch through that line and once you do, circle southwest and come up behind the battering ram unit."

"But... I don't see a battering ram unit."

"Don't question me! Panahasi trained me well in its use. He'll call them to charge in minutes and by then it will be too late. Charge! Now!"

Under direct command, Itafe called out for his personal battle unit to rally to his side. As the enemy slowly advanced, he quickly explained to them what they must do. Without waiting for their reaction, he charged down the hill directly at Panahasi's center unit. Itafe's men had to run over fallen soldiers and amidst great cries they engaged the enemy soldiers before they had completed preparations for their own charge. By now Herihor could see how well Panahasi had trained those deserters for battle against their own brethren. His anger against such a traitorous act grew.

Herihor sent a messenger to check on Akori's position and then took command of half of the remaining soldiers and rallied them to his side.

"Men, if ever there was a time of danger for the Two Lands, it is now. King Narmer's Battle of Unification was fought on these very hills where we now stand. If we emerge victorious then all future generations will whisper your names.

"Below us the traitorous General Panahasi faces us with other deserters from the army." Immediately the men looked confused and whispered to each other. "He's pledged to break the bonds of Unification and let loose a plague of chaos and mut spirits roaming the land against our children and grandchildren.

"We go now to fight this menace. I pledge personally that Panahasi will not see Ra's gold disk this morning. Are you with me?" A great cry went up from the men and they shook their swords and beat their spears into the ground in assent.

"Keep your eyes on alert, men. The first to see movement of troops in that direction will get a year's provisions for his family." In a few moments two soldiers called out.

"We charge directly at that movement," Herihor called out. "Itafe's troops will soon come to aid us from the east, as will the garrison from Ahnpet. Once we punch through their lines, we'll split up. Half will go east and circle around Panahasi's remaining traitors and half of you will go west and come up behind the Ta-Tjehenus. Show no mercy, men, for we battle for the survival of Kem!" With that Herihor took off down the hill.

The battle was fierce, for although Panahasi's troops were small in number, he had personally trained them. Having seen the bloody battle in Ta-Sety with my own eyes, I could not even imagine how difficult it was fighting in darkness.

Herihor's initial charge was rebuffed and for nearly an hour the two sides battled to no advantage. But Herihor's charge did accomplish one immediate goal and that was to keep the battering ram tactic from succeeding. Without the full effect of Panahasi's main units battering the center, his entire strategy began to crumple.

As the faint outlines of Ra's light began to appear in the east, the Ahnpet unit appeared quietly out of the marshes like spirits from beyond. They mobilized at the fringes of the marsh and then charged Panahasi's eastern flank. It did not take long for Panahasi's warriors to be crushed in the pincers of the Ahnpet soldiers and Itafe's troops. With that flank destroyed, our soldiers pushed toward the center.

Ra's first rays now peeked out over the marshes. Herihor, although exhausted, caught a glimpse of a reed platform erected next to the drainage ditches that ran around Dep. And there, standing on it surrounded by his captains, was Panahasi. Herihor's blood boiled at the sight.

The battle to the east and south had shifted to our advantage, but the King's Guard fought mightily against the Ta-Tjehenus on the western flank. Even from this far away, Herihor could plainly hear the piercing war cries of the Ta-Tjehenus as they periodically charged our positions. Herihor was conflicted on what to do.

To his right he saw the huge bulk of Nekau, surrounded by three of Panahasi's troops. Herihor could see the fear in the enemies' eyes. He ran toward Nekau and cut down his closest opponent. Nekau quickly finished the other two.

"Take the army and move behind the Ta-Tjehenu position," he shouted. "I'm going for Panahasi." Nekau did not budge. "Now!" Herihor shouted.

"I will not leave your side, no matter how loudly you shout," he said simply. "Command someone else to lead the soldiers." Herihor was not used to being disobeyed, but he instantly knew better than to pursue a lost argument. He quickly scanned the battlefield and saw Itafe not more than a hundred cubits away.

"Come then," he called out to Nekau. In the light of Ra's early morning rays, Nekau's body glistened in sweat and blood. Particles of his opponents' flesh stuck to his arm and bare chest. He presented an altogether fearsome sight.

In seconds they reached Itafe, whose sword hung loosely in his bloodied hand. "Brother, if you can summon the strength to rally your troops one more time we can end this battle. Can you do so?" Herihor asked of his army leader.

"The men will do as you command, Herihor."

"Good," Herihor answered, giving him a half-smile. "Take our remaining soldiers and make a wide path along the drainage ditches," he said, pointing below him and to his right with his sword. "Cross at the most convenient point and circle around the Ta-Tjehenus and strike them from behind. Be quick and this battle will be over and by Horus' name I swear I'll see to it that this is the last time Kemians sacrifice their lives upon these cursed fields."

As soon as Itafe and his men left, Herihor and Nekau took off for Panahasi's position. To his credit, Panahasi did not vacate it to save his own life, but stayed to direct his remaining troops. As they ran down the hill, Herihor watched messengers running back and forth toward the western flank. Before they were even half way to the platform, one of Panahasi's captains pointed toward them and even from this distance Herihor could see a smile cross Panahasi's face.

Herihor slowed his charge so as to regain his wind and he saw Panahasi turn and wave behind him. Herihor quickly realized that in his fatigue he had miscalculated Panahasi, for from behind Panahasi came a battalion of reserve troops. They rushed out from either side of the platform and formed a wide pincer around Herihor and Nekau.

"Ah, the petulant student has come to teach the teacher, eh Herihor?" Panahasi shouted. "Except the teacher still has a few lessons left to teach his ambitious upstart. Your whore King will no longer have you to poke her!" He then looked from Herihor to Nekau.

"Kill the black mut, whoever he be, but capture Herihor for I've yet another lesson, a painful one for him to learn before he dies."

Slowly the enemy advanced, swords out, testing Herihor's and Nekau's reaction. Both of them remained calm, their backs to one another. Their forearms, with their small shields across their chests, stood at the ready. Step by step the enemy cautiously advanced. Herihor saw the faces of men he knew and had trained with in the file and a profound disgust arose in him that it had come to this, the turning of brother against brother.

Suddenly Herihor shouted out: "Now!" and both he and Nekau spun around, swords held high and cut down the first two men they faced, then parried with sword strikes and cut down two more. It all happened so fast the enemy was taken off guard and retreated a few steps in fear.

"Well done!" Panahasi yelled. "Damned well done! A valuable lesson for my loyal soldiers, but still… Now you men understand why you cannot engage these warriors one at a time. Charge them!"

With loud war cries the enemy charged Herihor and Nekau. The fighting intensified as each enemy soldier sought to close in on their position. In this fighting both Herihor and Nekau excelled, deflecting daggers and swords with their shields and parrying with sword thrusts.

Not a minute into the engagement, Herihor broke his sword over the scalp of an enemy soldier. As he reached for his dagger, an enemy sword sliced his forearm below the elbow so that his arm hung limp at his side. Blood spurted from the wound. Herihor quickly retrieved his dagger with his left hand, but he knew that the fight was soon to be over.

Then, from behind the enemy came a series of shouts and commands and now the traitorous soldiers turned to fend off a plague that had descended upon them. There, emerging from the marshes and drainage ditch were the King's Guard unit that Herihor had sent away with Zenty. As his eyesight faded before him and he sank to the ground, Herihor saw another vision. It was Horus who had arrived to save them, Horus in his half-human form, flying into battle with his talons extended and his face was that of Zenty.

SCROLL SEVENTEEN

Nubiti

I read it again, and compared it to my key, to be sure I had deciphered the code correctly. The news wasn't all bad for a change. Menetnashte was safe and thoughtfully asked how I was bearing the strain. Khnum was increasingly morose and drinking heavily, but still functioning. And Bakht, well what could I say about Bakht? He never seemed to worry about anything but his devotion to Apep and therefore preserving the priesthood forever. In his opinion the sect was doing well and had actually grown in response to our humiliating loss upon the fields of Dep a year ago. He made no inquiry about how I fared.

It's been a difficult year for me, secluded as I am on Abu Island, which was long ago forsaken by the gods. The island is nothing but a big, tall rock squatting in the middle of Mother Nile. Abu is an apt name, for it looks like a huge elephant, or more accurately a mother elephant and her offspring, for there are many large boulders scattered around the island, protruding from the waters of the cataract.

The people on this flea of an island who are not priests live by farming the rich soil in tiny plots. The women and girls, barely dressed in filthy, torn clothes, hoist buckets of water up the steep rocky slopes and pour it into small irrigation ditches that crisscross their fields. All day long they do this tiring work. Mostly, though, the families sustain themselves by fishing. Each morning the men and boys climb into their little reed boats and shove off from shore. Those who cannot afford a boat cast their nets from shore. I admit that I enjoy watching them from time to time. Once I saw a man snare a catfish longer than he was tall. It took three of his friends to help him haul it in and it must have fed many families for weeks.

It is the housing that I find so abysmal and backward, for the people here still build in the old fashioned way of mud daub construction. They haul buckets of mud up from the shore. Then they take bundles of reeds and stack them upright on the ground and weave reeds through the bundles so that they are all interconnected. Then they simply take handfuls of mud and daub it on the reed latticework, starting from the ground and working their way up. They leave it for three days for Ra to dry it and then they move in. Of course such primitive methods means they can only build walls as high as a man is tall and they refuse to consider using mud brick construction.

Like the priests here, all the people who live on Abu are as black as the Delta mud. All, that is, except for me. I'm certain that Mery and her ilk would say that I should be thankful to them that I am still alive, but following the defeat in Dep I did not truly care either way whether I lived or died. It was Bakht who convinced me of the need to preserve our hopes and dreams. Together we concocted a lie that Mery believed... or wanted to believe.

At the end of the battle, with Panahasi dead at Nekau's hand, it was obvious that we had lost. Bakht put me in one of his secret caves, tore my clothes, rubbed me with mud and fastened the door. He told one of his spies to feign drunkenness and to casually inform a Horus priest that I was alive and imprisoned by Khnum's forces. When Herihor's forces later rescued me, I showed great humility and appropriate gratitude. Before Mery's court I pleaded a convincing argument, much to Amka's frustration, for that old jackal didn't believe a word of my story. Still, I knew from the outset that Mery would not have me executed, for she foolishly still harbored feelings of sisterly love that she should have long ago abandoned.

Before Mery I admitted my guilt in conspiring to create dissension in Lower Kem, for we only wanted to be equal to Upper Kem in stature and influence, I explained. I strongly denied having anything to do with her poisoning and Zenty's kidnapping. In fact, I maintained that it was when I protested such heinous acts that the plotters imprisoned me. As a result of my imprisonment, I had no idea where Khnum or Bakht or any of the other conspirators hid. I told Mery that I personally believed they were dead.

As far my son, Amka did a thorough job of questioning me on that matter, for of course he saw Menetnashte as a threat. Bakht and I decided that I should tell the truth. After all, he was taken from me by Bakht and raised by his Apep priests. I didn't even know where he was and had only seen him a few times in his entire life, I told Amka. I cried convincingly as I told this part of my defense and when I was done I noted Mery trying to hide the tears that ran down her cheeks.

In the end she exiled me within the Two Lands, but so far from the Delta it might as well be in Babylon. I'm free to wander about this pitiful island, for there is no easy way to escape. Even if I were to escape, those black charlatans would find me before I ventured far. And make no mistake, they are charlatans. They claim to be faithful to Horus, but I've heard them at night drumming and dancing to whatever ancient mut gods they still worship.

In two days short of a ten-day, as I prepared my possessions for my exile, to my utter surprise I was summoned to Mery's meeting room. When I entered the empty room, Amka motioned me to a seat at the side, where my mother sat stiffly in the chair next to mine. I noted that as a sign of disrespect he had us arrive earlier than any of the other guests. Soon Tepemkau, Herihor, Nekau and various ministers and governors filled the room and sat around a large table.

When everyone was seated, Mery entered and all bowed low to her. I tried to avoid bowing, but I could see that all eyes sneaked glances my way and I had no choice but to do so. Mother, who had become too frail to get up, cringed as I made a show of bowing as low to the ground as possible.

Amka tapped the ground with his staff and called the group to order. Mery immediately took control of the meeting.

"Gentlemen," she said, intentionally excluding me and Shepsit, which I thought a fitting touch. "We have sustained days and days of debate on the matters before us. I have made a decision." Amka handed her a papyrus scroll.

"Beginning tomorrow, at Herihor's urging, I am sending Zenty to lead an army of fifteen thousand men to the Delta." The room immediately came abuzz with chatter.

"But, Meryt-Neith, is this a wise move?" Ahmate, the Minister of Agriculture, called out. "After their humiliation at Dep," he continued, looking uneasily at me and Shepsit, "do we really need to rub their faces in the mud?"

Amka stood. "Allow the King to finish her proclamation."

Mery nodded to Amka and at that moment Ra's rays peeked through the slats in the roof and shined directly on her face and I saw the toll that governing had taken on this woman so ill-suited to the duties of leadership. Her face had begun to show wrinkles and she sat stooped over and looked frail. Her hair had thinned and she had to squint to read the proclamation. I dared not smile, but inwardly I recognized how her poisoning contributed to her ill health and deteriorating looks. I thought with satisfaction how that must have affected Herihor's desires.

"I hear your objection, Ahmate, dutiful servant of Kem, but we must end this resistance once and for all. The Delta was defeated. Any humiliation is of their own making. Our Two Lands must eventually learn to live as one people. So, Zenty is instructed to sweep up all pockets of resistance and crush them, and I do mean crush and I do mean all." At this Mery looked directly at me.

"He is also commanded to chase all Ta-Tjehenus from our border and establish well-stocked garrisons there, as well as deep in the western desert to protect us from future attacks. And finally, he is instructed to eliminate the Apep sect, for to all other sects in our lands it is considered an abomination."

At that I could not help but utter a quick laugh. All eyes turned toward me, but I sat there staring straight before me. "Have you something you wish to say?" Mery coldly asked, turning directly to face me.

"No," I said, stingingly refusing to address her by name or male title, for at this point I saw no need for pretense. I didn't even look in her direction. I noticed Amka's face twitching, restraining himself from getting to his feet and ordering me to stop my insolence at penalty of death.

However, to her credit Mery still managed one final surprise on that day. As the servants carried my belongings from Sekhem's and my house to the boat, I received a parchment, delivered to me by one of Amka's legal assistants. He insisted that I open it before him, read it and confirm I understood its contents. I was to indicate that by stamping my ring on a wet clay tablet he carried.

The document was brief. In it Mery had granted Sekhemkasedj a divorce and had awarded him all our possessions. It took considerable effort to not reveal my emotions at that moment, for I did not wish the priest to give additional satisfaction to that pretender to the throne. But the truth is that once he left I cried for the first time in many years. Sekhem was such a pitiful creature, I felt humiliated that he sued me for divorce. Yet I also humbly accepted my fate. In the days that followed I swore to revenge that humiliation.

That evening I spent time with mother discussing our respective futures, but I saw at once that the fire was gone from mother's belly. She had aged to the point where her passions were subordinated to a good night's sleep and a satisfying bowel movement. But the old woman had one last trick to perform. She provided me with the name of a fisherman's family on Abu Island who would agree to ferry messages back and forth to loyal spies who would eventually deliver them to Bakht, a process that I found took two ten-days or even an entire cycle of Ra's silver disk to complete for each message and response.

Over the next five days that black mut Nekau never said a word to me as we sailed and rowed upstream. Occasionally I would notice him staring at me with contempt, which I found amusing, since it was his people who were the foreigners in Kem, not mine. Yet it was the people of the Delta who suffered at the hands of the arrogant pigs of the Red Land.

Three boats filled with soldiers and eight boats filled with provisions for the garrison there followed us on our journey upstream, for Abu Island now figured to be a major garrison for future wars.

Once we arrived at Abu Island, I found it highly amusing that on my first night I found a note hidden in my bed. Someone had taken a great chance in doing so and I never did find out whom it was. The note was from Bakht, written in the secret code we had agreed to use back in Dep.

Being alone on Abu Island gave me much opportunity to think and rethink all that had happened over the past ten years and to dispel with any illusions as to what successes we might have had. If anything, my time on Abu Island taught me patience; patience and irreverence, for since my experiences in the Delta with Bakht I no longer believed that Isis or Horus or any other god of the Above would support the downtrodden and come to our rescue. Indeed I came to agree with Bakht that Apep was the only meaningful deity to counteract the deities of the Above. And so with prayers sent to me by Bakht I prayed to Apep every day when the others were asleep, satisfying prayers that touched my deeper self.

One thing I learned from Bakht's messages was that for all these years I had a distorted view of Apep. It was as if I looked at a beautiful garden through thick faience glass. Bakht pointed out that we cannot stand with our feet squarely in the Two Lands and try to understand Apep's workings. To truly comprehend his divine nature one had to dwell in the Underworld, to understand the darkest parts of the human heart, to envision a land where power did not rain down from above, but emanated from below.

By living within the Royal family, my expectations were of order and structure, the essential ingredients that mortared ma'at. The worship of Apep is no less demanding or righteous. It simply acknowledges our shadow selves and so appeals to our most common elements, our deepest, darkest natures, where order and structure are not as important as the basest passions.

It was a good thing that my involvement with Apep came so quickly in my confinement, for my patience was promptly tested. One afternoon, just three months into my stay, as I walked along the shoreline, marveling at Mother Nile rushing through the rocks, I noted Nekau and another priest walking in my direction, deep in conversation. We were nearly upon each other when he noticed me.

"Nubiti!" he exclaimed, as if I had jumped out from behind a rock to attack him. I simply stood there, staring up at his huge face and big eyes. He wore only a pleated linen kilt and his massive body still looked more like a warrior's than a priest's.

"M'shai, this is Nubiti..."

The young priest simply bowed slightly, but said not a word.

"Go on ahead, M'shai, we will continue the discussion later," Nekau said. The young priest nodded and hurried along the rocky path toward the temple.

"Are you being treated well?" Nekau began.

"Am I being treated well you ask? Treated well... hmmm, let me think. Yes, of course. I love the quaint mud daub box I live in, filled with vermin. Oh, and the delicious foods that never vary from one day to the next, let's not forget that. And my favorite treat of all, priests who pass me every day yet say not a word to me."

Nekau looked down at me and a funny thought crossed my mind. My head came only up to his chest and for a moment I imagined stepping right up to him and biting his nipple. "Exile is not meant to be desirable, Nubiti. It is only by the grace of Meryt-Neith that you are alive."

"Can you at least give me news of what is happening in Kem?" I asked, avoiding the issue of Mery's misplaced devotion.

"Yes, but you will probably hear little more than your fishermen already tell you."

"You obviously don't talk to them much yourself, Nekau, for they're one ignorant bunch. They know of fish and making babies and not much more." Nekau actually smiled at that.

"It is news of the Delta that you wish to hear, no doubt," he started. "It is not good news from your perspective, perhaps, but from ours it strengthens ma'at and once again unifies the Two Lands."

"Go on, for I'd rather know than not know."

Nekau looked out over the water. Fishermen in

two boats called out to each other as they maneuvered a large net between the reed craft. "Alright, then. Zenty excels at his military duties. He has destroyed the Ta-Tjehenu appetite for alliances with the Delta leaders and has pursued them far across the western desert.

"The resistance in the Delta has been severely reduced. As more people see the resolve of the future King, they allow themselves to believe in a united future, one anchored in ma'at. They now serve as informers, allowing us to find and eliminate resistance leaders."

"And Khnum?"

"Neither he nor Bakht have been found, so we presume as you said that they are dead. In either case they wield no power."

"Yes, you're probably right," I said, playing the part.

Nekau looked down and kicked a stone with his foot. "There is another matter, Nubiti. I was planning to visit with you soon to tell you. Shepsit is dying."

"She didn't look well when I saw her last. Will I be allowed to visit her?"

"No. She will be buried with honor when the time comes. Her mastaba is being prepared as we speak."

"So you... do you expect it to be soon?"

"A messenger will arrive any day, I expect. I visited with her perhaps ten or twelve days ago. All is being done to make her comfortable. I will inform you when she has begun her journey."

Nekau kept his word and it was only a few days later that he informed me that mother had journeyed to the Afterworld. By all rights I should have been prepared to handle her death easily, I was still a priestess of Isis, after all. But instead I found myself thrown into a dark period that lasted for days and days. I could not help but dwell on thoughts of mother and how, when the story was fully told, she had persevered in our struggle. As much as I had spent my life thinking differently, I was truly my mother's daughter. In the end, I had even become my mother.

It was during my grieving, when I had time to explore the deepest parts of my ka, that a plan began to develop within me. For days it simmered slowly and finally, when I felt the ingredients were right, I sat down on a night when Ra's silver disk was full and wrote to Bakht.

My dear Bakht,

With much time to think I've come to make the following observations. If there is any one thing that doomed our cause up to now, it was the fact that we lacked enough treasure with which we could mortar alliances with outside forces to make up for our inferior military. Now, with that little runt and his sickly mother wielding their power over our people, it will be even more difficult for us to exercise a military option.

I urge you to consider using this time for us to secretly amass the treasury we'll need to wage a full-scale war in future years. Let's use this time both to rebuild and to teach lessons to those who prematurely grieve the death of our rebellion.

I'll send you more details in future messages, but in a nutshell here it is. Create a small, but trusted force of priest assassins. With utmost secrecy, make a few grisly examples of the most egregious collaborators. Then, using the fear you have created, extort payments from other collaborators. Make our businessmen pay a small tax for their own security, especially those who bow to the powers in Inabu-hedj in order to curry favor with them and so win lucrative trading rights. I leave it to you to keep the dream of an independent Lower Kem alive for Menetnashte.

The second part of the strategy is to make sure that certain key businessmen and former Delta loyalists know that Menetnashte is alive, strong and being groomed for leadership but of course, only do so with our allies. And it might also be beneficial for them to remember that I have willingly martyred myself for the cause.

I know you will figure out a way to implement this

strategy. Let Menetnashte know that I think of him every day.

    Faithfully,
    Nubiti

I waited patiently for Bakht's response. I had settled into my own routine on Abu, but there were no others with whom I could hold a decent conversation. Looking back over the past ten years, I was also aware of how much my focus on my goals kept me busy throughout the day so that at night I always seemed to regret that the day had been so short. Now I had nothing but time. So, I had several months before I asked Bakht to send me a potion that would allow me to enter Apep's heart and better understand his divine nature.

I used the time waiting for Bakht's response to enter deeply into a series of meditative states. Twice each ten-day, for I feared doing so more frequently, I did as Bakht instructed and set a fire in the small brazier in my tiny room. I put a pinch of the herbs into the glowing coals and inhaled the vapors as I covered my head with a cloth. It only took a few minutes before I began to feel the effects and I was soon transported to Apep's world.

When I first began these meditations I was frightened, for I vividly recalled my initial encounter with the Underworld under Bakht's supervision. But whether it was that these herbs were different or weaker, the experiences I had were both milder and more satisfying. I was able to relax. I even allowed Apep to enter my heart, where he would reveal things to me.

On one such encounter, as the winds outside blew down the valley of Mother Nile, I had a strong vision. In it Menetnashte stood tall, towering over Zenty. Menetnashte carried Narmer's mace and stood ready to hit Zenty with it. But his hand was stayed by Mery's presence, flying and flitting around the room in a mut form. I watched frustrated, wanting to help, but unable myself to move. The walls of the room began to rattle and shake and cracks suddenly zigzagged through them.

People screamed all around us. As the walls began to fall I knew, I truly understood what was about to happen. Then I awoke. I walked all over the island that night, trying to remember what it was that I saw as the walls fell, but I could not.

Finally, as I walked among the fishermen many days after that vision, my contact nodded at me and I knew that a message awaited me. I wanted to run to retrieve it from our hiding place, but I waited and that evening, as the priests were in prayer to Horus, I took a stroll and came back with a folded parchment in my undergarment. By the light of a candle I opened it.

Nubiti,

I heard of your mother's passing into the next world and hope that the time on Abu Island will be one of healing for you in this moment. Before getting to your recent suggestions, here is some news.

Zenty continues to plague us. My guess is that he feels he must prove himself worthy to be King to Herihor, his mother and the Horus priests. He is relentless, leading many of the skirmishes and searches himself. We have had to change our location constantly, in some cases staying in one hiding place for only a day or two before moving again. Khnum does not bear this well and he is nearly always drunk.

I rely increasingly on only a very small group for fear that Zenty buys the loyalty of our leaders. How else to explain late night raids on secret places? Yet we have a secret society within our secret society, so we are often able to expose these traitors and exact revenge. Yet Zenty's attacks on Apep's priests seems to be backfiring and we have more volunteer recruits than ever before, men and boys who are willing to sacrifice their lives for the Black Land.

There is one thing about Zenty that works in our favor. He is reckless and makes enemies easily. In his youth he rushes to judgment and often does not take time to weigh options before acting. If this keeps up we can count on additional allies as the years go by.

You should be very proud of Menetnashte, who has become an able warrior, adept at various forms of fighting. He is also sharp and challenges even our most senior priests over discussions on matters from the Creation Egg to arguments about the Afterlife. He shows promise as a magician and shaman, too.

In fact, I do like your idea of how we can raise treasure and will begin to plan with Menetnashte how we can best implement it.

In Apep's holy name,
Bakht

Reading Bakht's message, I was suddenly gripped with the realization that perhaps we had erred by launching our strike when we did. Perhaps if we had waited until Mery's illness forced a change of rulership we could have created enough turmoil to win the day. But as Bakht periodically reminded us, we mortals plan only to provide the gods with a good laugh.

These thoughts, combined with my mother's passing, kept me in a dark mood for days. Then, shortly after I woke one morning, I noticed in the waters below me much activity. Several of the boats the priests used to ferry their goods were being readied for some other purpose. I noted priests carrying goods from the temple grounds to the boats throughout the day.

After I dressed and drank my tea, I wandered down to the water, where a contingent of eight or ten priests had assembled. They were checking off items in their kits and making sure they had whatever supplies they needed on the boat. As I approached they turned their backs to me in what was a typical response for they are forbidden to talk to me.

In minutes I saw Nekau's towering figure at the temple gate. He was calling out orders to other priests. For the first time I noticed that a woman ran after him and he turned and embraced her. They kissed for a moment and then two children ran to Nekau and he picked them both up and turned around and around with them in his arms, smiling broadly all the while. When he saw me below he stopped abruptly and put them down. With a quick goodbye he wound his way down to the shore.

"This is not a good time to talk," he said sternly in his deep voice. "If you have a problem it will have to wait until my return."

"Problem?" I replied. "I've never approached you with a problem, have I? I accept my fate without complaint."

Nekau took a deep breath. He handed his bag to his assistant and motioned me to follow him. In a few paces he stopped to face me.

"I am sorry I allowed my worries to get the better of me. I do not condone your past actions or your beliefs, but it does not excuse my being rude." I nodded and he continued.

"I will tell you this, for you will undoubtedly find out from your own sources," he said and I am certain my look of surprise betrayed me, "but Meryt-Neith is gravely ill. Amka has become too feeble to be of much assistance, so I go to treat them both. May Horus guide my hands and heart."

As I watched Nekau turn and walk to his waiting boat, elements of my recent vision came back to me and I nodded in understanding. The breezes over Mother Nile picked up and I breathed them in. They held scents of wildflowers, of rebirth, of hope. For the first time in a long time I felt a strong urge to make love again. I wanted to once again feel Apep's passion flowing through Bakht, filling me.

SCROLL EIGHTEEN

Meryt-Neith

"It is not me you should be thanking," Nekau said impatiently as he put his potions and herbs back into his bag. His assistant waited by his side. "It is Horus himself."

"I do not disagree with that," I said. "But it was your able hands that ministered to me, not Horus' talons!" I joked. How happy I was to live to see this day, a day I thought would never come.

"You weren't so thankful when I forced you to drink the medicines that would help drain the poisons out of your body." I shook my head in disgust remembering how awful those medicines tasted and the constant diarrhea and stomach pains they gave me.

"But please hurry, Master. The priestesses from the Temple of Isis wait outside for you. They have been here since before Ra rose. I must be quick and change and then help Amka." With that he hurried away.

As soon as he left, my servants rushed in, beset upon by none other than Abana. As old as she was, she took her new job as Head Mistress seriously and her penchant for organization served her very well. She marched into the room and barked orders here and there.

Djeserit made me sit still as she applied my makeup, every so often handing me a polished silver mirror so I could check the results. "Perhaps not so much kohl around my eyes," I said at one point.

The finest dressmaker in all Kem created the gown I was to wear and he had done his best to hide the bulge in my midsection caused by my swollen liver. The gown was gathered under my breasts and tied with gold ribbons. Pleats draped from the seams to further distract one's eyes from my belly.

My thinning hair was braided with gold chains and pulled up and held with a gold and jeweled tiara. Upon my upper chest was an intricate gold plate that took three months of work to create in our Royal goldsmithing workshop. Gold threads were interwoven throughout the reeds in my sandals and orange carnelians and jade jewels were affixed at various points to the leather thongs. But most striking were my nails and toenails, each one meticulously painted by Djeserit in intricate designs.

Once I was dressed, Abana announced Herihor's presence and she immediately shooed all my servants from the tiny room, for the entire palace in Nekhen was but a fraction of the size of the palace in Inabu-hedj. If the expression on my face reflected my shock at Herihor's commanding presence, it was far overshadowed by his own. As soon as he saw me his jaw dropped open.

"As Horus is my witness, I see Isis before me!" he exclaimed, smiling. He walked slowly to me, looking me up and down, taking in every detail. "Mery, I have never seen you so beautiful. You... you are perfect." He put his arms lightly on my shoulders as if he were afraid to upset anything I wore and he leaned down and kissed me gently on my lips.

"And you... you look like a god yourself, although I

would be challenged to say which one," I joked. Herihor wore a new uniform, complete with new leather. Although he wore no other jewelry, his gold armband with its ornately carved Sobek crocodile had been polished and smoothed so that it glittered with his every movement. Despite our advancing years, Herihor still gave forth a commanding presence. At that moment I felt my love for him most deeply.

"Have you seen the crowds?" Herihor asked.

"I was cautioned by Nekau to stay away from the balcony for fear of exciting the people."

"He is right, for all they talk of in the streets is catching a glimpse of you or that... that pest in the next quarters."

"That is my son you speak of," I protested.

"Yes and, Horus help us, the soon-to-be King. I care not a whit that he's the son of Horus, he still deserves a stout scolding now and then."

"And what has he done now?"

"He doesn't listen. He is impetuous, arrogant and foolhardy. I sometimes..."

"Your love for him shines through," I said smiling. "And his for you."

"Accchh! I should've stayed a lowly soldier in your service and never risen to these lofty ranks." He paced before me, obviously nervous.

"We have waited for this moment for sixteen years now, my beloved. It is time, is it not?" Herihor stopped his pacing and turned to me.

"It is. He's a man who has proven himself in battle. He's commanded our army and accomplished our goals in the Delta. He still has much to learn to govern wisely, but his time has come to make his own mistakes. We will each of us butt heads with him until he learns patience and earns a measure of wisdom.

"In any event, we can wait no longer. I'm to escort you to the Temple of Isis to begin the day."

"I am ready," I said, straightening my dress. "It is odd to think that by time Ra sets in the sky I shall no longer be the King. Only a mother."

"And the Queen Mother, sure to be a more difficult job than it appears with that... that arrogant ass sitting on the throne!"

With my entourage formed behind me, Herihor walked ahead into the early morning light. I was not prepared for the sight that confronted me. We had exited at the rear of the palace structure, which was high above Mother Nile. For as far as the eye could see, boats were moored in the river and a tethered boat occupied every cubit of shoreline. Tens of thousands of people stood in packed crowds waiting for the ceremonies to start. Small braziers burned in the morning mist, sending up a delicious mix of smoke and the smells of breads baking and foods simmering in garlic and flax oil.

"They've been gathering for days," Herihor whispered. "The caravan routes are jammed. Wait until you see the crowds near the Temple of Horus."

As soon as I walked out into the light, the throngs cheered wildly for me and then, like ripples in a lake, they began to bow. My heart rejoiced at the love and respect my people showed me, for together we had braved the darkest storms and now we basked in Ra's bright rays. We had each learned important lessons about rule and the place of women in the Two Lands, and I was exceedingly proud at that moment of the role I had played in each.

My carry chair began its journey to the Temple of Isis. All along the route people, mostly women, ran toward my entourage and threw flower petals at my carriage. It was shortly after Proyet and the newly emergent crops painted the fields and low hills in many shades of green and white. Even the air smelled sweet with hope and renewal.

The Head Priestess met me at the modest temple and together we spent an hour worshipping at the feet of Isis. I tried to contain my enthusiasm at being able to pray to her for the first time in sixteen years as a simple mother. I prayed fervently for Zenty to weave the Two

Lands together in peace and prosperity. I prayed for him to find a steadfast love who would bear an heir to the throne, soon enough so that I would live to see him with my mortal eyes. I prayed for Isis to speak in my behalf to Wadjet and to seek his blessings and his forgiveness, for I knew in my heart that my illness hastened the day when Wadjet and I would be reunited. When I was done I ordered my servants to come forward with baskets containing hundreds of loaves of bread, as well as wheels of cheese and barrels of beer and fine wine. The priestesses thanked me profusely.

On the way back to the palace, I was anxious to see Zenty, for he had been in seclusion in Nekhen for the past two cycles of Ra's silver disk. Under Tepemkau's guidance his entire body had been shaved clean and after seven days of purification he had been circumcised. Once he had recovered, he again went through a series of purification rituals before taking the ben-ben seed just yesterday. Throughout his purification and until today, no one but Amka and Tepemkau had laid eyes on him for he was in a state of deep meditation with his brother Horus.

And so I was suitably shocked when I first laid eyes on Zenty, for indeed he had transformed into a different person. He was no longer a boy, but a man. Tepemkau escorted me into Zenty's chambers to review the final arrangements for his ascension ceremony. There he sat upon the throne chair that I had so long occupied. He was shaved entirely bald and his makeup was cleanly and sparingly applied, mostly a liner of kohl around his eyes and a light touch of green malachite on his lids. As slight as was his build, his chest and arms were firm. He radiated power, an aura of confidence that seemed tempered by some new wisdom, some meaningful insight. I looked to his side at Amka and noted the old man nod his head as if in agreement.

Without arising, Zenty extended his hand to me, his fingers resplendent with the most exquisite jewelry in the land. Upon his chest lay the gold plate of the King. I grabbed his hand, my heart so full of joy I felt it would burst. Tears streamed from my eyes. For a moment I hesitated, wondering whether it was the proper protocol now for me to bow.

"If you dare bow to me my first act as King will be to lop off your head!" Zenty joked, and we all had a good laugh.

"This all feels very strange, Mother," he said, whispering so that Amka and Tepemkau would not hear. "I am supposed to feel like Horus' brother, but instead I feel like... like some pompous... oh, I don't know what to think right now!"

"If there is one piece of advice I can give you it is to try to stay aloof from all the excitement until after you have had time in Horus' presence in the Temple today. Once you are done with the rituals, you will feel differently, I promise." He smiled at me and nodded. I was the only one in all of Kem who understood how the next few hours would penetrate his Ka and bind him forever to his brother, Horus.

In the mid-morning I was summoned to Zenty's chambers, where a series of loud and long blows on rams horns sounded outside the palace. At first the crowds cheered at the start of the ceremony and then we could hear the murmur of people silencing one another as they waited anxiously for their first glimpse of their future King.

Now that I was not the focal point of the ceremony, the magnitude of what was about to transpire fell upon my shoulders as a heavy weight. Here, in this very hall, King Narmer had waited to begin his ascension day, as had Hor-Aha and Djer and Wadjet and even me, as Regent. It was an unbroken line and Zenty was to be the next link in the mighty chain of Kem's divine rule.

Had it really been sixteen years since my ascension? I tried to recall that innocent, naïve wife who inherited the mightiest throne in all the lands. I could not. She had disappeared into the haze of my past. I had traded her for the immense glories and the weighty responsibilities of the throne. I had seen the best and the worst of mortals and those experiences had changed me forever. Chills ran through my body.

With Herihor and the King's Guard in the lead, Zenty walked to the palace stairs. A massive cheer erupted from the crowds, a noise so loud it felt like a storm wind blowing across the land. I noticed Herihor scan the route to the temple, which was lined with army troops. The commander of the procession saluted Herihor, assuring him that all was readied.

A long procession of soldiers preceded Zenty's platform and we in his retinue followed. People pressed toward us, deluging us with flower petals in red and pink and white. They handed the King's Guard escorts holy papyrus, tiny scrolls for which they had paid scribes dearly, and asked the soldiers to give them to Zenty so that he would intercede with the gods in their prayers for fertility or cures from illness or success in business. It took us more than an hour before we reached the Temple.

Lining the temple grounds were the wealthy and powerful from every part of Kem. Every Governor of a nome was present, as well as dignitaries from all surrounding lands, even from many Ta-Sety tribes. The Ta-Tjehenus, of course, were absent, for their humiliation at the hands of the new King was still fresh in their history.

Zenty stepped from his chair, holding the crook and flail across his chest. He wore a simple headdress of purple cloth that draped over his shoulders. The Temple of Horus in Nekhen was the holy place from which all legitimate power emanated and there, lining the stairs, were its glorious priests. Tepemkau stood at the top of the line. Together, Amka and Zenty and I walked up the stairs toward him. Amka held his staff in one shaking hand and rested his other on my forearm.

Tepemkau raised his hands high in the air and parted his fingers in the way of the Horus priests. As soon as the huge crowd hushed, he called out loudly.

"Whom do you bring with you, Amka, great Horus priest and Vizier to the Royal family?"

"I bring Prince Zenty, son of King Regent Meryt-Neith and King Wadjet, son of King Djer, son of King Hor-Aha, son of King Narmer, may his name be blessed forever into eternity. Prince Zenty comes to claim the throne of the Land of the Lotus and the Land of the Papyrus," Amka called out, pointing his staff toward Zenty.

"Because your hearts are light, King Regent Meryt-Neith and Vizier Amka, you may accompany Prince Zenty to the innermost sanctuary, so that Horus alone may judge whether he is the rightful heir to the throne."

As we entered the temple, our sandal bearers removed our sandals and washed our feet. We followed Tepemkau through the dimly lit corridors as his assistants waved incense in the air and chanted prayers. Finally we reached the inner sanctuary.

Candles lighted the sanctuary and sand had been carefully sprinkled on the floor to ensure that only the pure would enter. Horus stood in the middle of the room, his gold falcon head sitting atop his human form. His dark eyes penetrated the kas of all who entered and I could see Zenty stiffen and gooseflesh rise along his arms.

On the brazier in front of Horus burned a fire. Next to the brazier was a large stone altar upon which Tepemkau had set several tools.

"Horus, I bring before you Prince Zenty, the heir of your servants, King Wadjet and King Regent Meryt-Neith. The Prince brings you a holy sacrifice, that you may judge his fitness to become King."

Amidst a great deal of noise, Nekau suddenly appeared, leading the temple's Apis bull, an enormous beast that towered above me. I assume it had been given a special potion to keep it manageable, for its eyes looked peaceful, as if it knew its fate and was content. Its black hide was beautifully groomed and it had been brushed with flax oil to make it shine.

"Horus, guardian of Nekhen and all the Kings of Kem! Behold Prince Zenty in his holy bull incarnation. As he leaves this world, we shall examine his heart. If it is deemed worthy, he shall be reborn as our new King!"

Nekau took Zenty's own battle sword that had been propped up next to the altar and slid it from its sheath. He handed it to Zenty and for a moment closed his eyes and held his hands over Zenty's head in loving blessing. Then Zenty stepped forward and in two swift strokes beheaded the beast. With a resounding thud the mighty beast fell to the ground, blood spurting and covering the floor. Nekau quickly took an intricately carved ceremonial ivory knife from the altar and sliced open the bull's chest, reached in his arms up to his shoulder and cut out the heart. With the massive organ still pumping, he placed it in Tepemkau's hands.

Together, Amka and Tepemkau observed the heart carefully, watching it beat, squeezing it, sniffing it and finally taking a drop of blood on their fingertip and tasting it. The two looked at each other and nodded. They showed it to Nekau, who also examined it and nodded.

"It is a strong heart," Tepemkau said confidently, as he placed it into the gold basin that Anhotek held out to him. "It is perfect."

"Behold, Horus, Prince Zenty is dead!" Tepemkau called out, pointing to the fallen bull. "His heart is strong. His heart is pure. His heart is perfect. His heart is light. May our new King reign until he is aged beyond number. May he serve you proudly and bring credit to our people."

Zenty then kneeled before Horus. "Behold, Horus!" Tepemkau called out. "Here before you kneels the new King of Upper Kem, Land of the Lotus, and Lower Kem, Land of the Papyrus. We dedicate his name to you for all eternity, for he shall bring credit to you and his people. Behold King Den!"

Even I did not know what Zenty's Horus name would be, for it was our custom not to reveal the King's

Horus name in advance to prevent others from casting an evil eye on it. Only Amka and Tepemkau knew. Now I understood. Horus Who Strikes was an apt name for the man who had settled the Delta uprisings and who would need to continue to instill fear in the hearts of his enemies for many years to come. It was also fitting for the King to have a strong name, following my association with Neith, a nurturing, protector goddess.

Tepemkau moved close to Den and leaned down so that his mouth covered Den's nostrils. Seven times he softly breathed out the name Den and seven times Den breathed it in, so that his ba was filled with his new manifestation. That is how it happened. That is how Prince Zenty was reborn as King Den.

With me out of the room, two assistants came in and bathed my son and dressed him in the finest linens. As was our custom, he gave all the jewelry he wore to the priests to support the work of Horus' temple. They then dressed him in even finer jewelry made for his ascension.

They invited me back in. Amka came forward. "King Den, place the crook and flail across your chest as an oath to Horus." As Den did so, Amka placed the double crown, White and Red on his head, symbolizing Unification of the Two Lands. At that moment I wondered what Den was thinking. But Den's eyes were closed and I saw that he breathed in the sen-sen breaths and it made me very proud that he seized the essence of the moment.

Tepemkau left to announce Zenty's rebirth as Den to the crowds gathered behind the temple. Amka, Nekau and I accompanied Den outside and as soon as he saw the crowds he gasped. "Oh, Horus!" Before us were at least half a million people, according to Herihor.

Now Tepemkau called out: "Praise your King! Praise King Den!"

The crowds below the temple stretched for more than a mile to the base of the mountains and filled the entire valley. Tents were scattered everywhere, their colorful family banners waving in the light breeze that blew down Mother Nile's waters. Den's bearers lifted him high in his chair and turned him around so that everyone could catch a glimpse of their new King. Den played his part, a countenance of pure calm and confidence upon his face, sitting erect, the crook and flail braced across his chest. Cheers erupted and turned into a deafening roar. People danced with joy. Women screamed their piercing ululations. Musicians banged their drums and shook their sistras. The regency had passed peacefully to Wadjet's son and heir and a respected warrior in addition. Ma'at was again strong in the land and the people rightfully rejoiced.

For the next ten-day, Nekhen and Inabu-hedj hosted one party after another as nobles from many lands brought gifts and promises of peace and trade and laid them at Den's feet. I was required to be present for these meetings, for I knew many of these guests and it was proper decorum to introduce Den to them. But the pace of Den's meetings was that of a virile young man and with my illness I simply could not keep up, although I tried, for at times I felt that Den did not truly comprehend the importance of these meetings.

"I noticed you were not well today," Den said to me one afternoon after we had been back in Inabu-hedj for four ten-days. He had come to my quarters, where I had just awoke from a short nap.

"I'm surprised that you noticed anything beyond yourself at all," I responded, a bit more strongly than I had intended. For a moment Den was silent.

"Oh, oh! Here comes the nagging mother again," Den said, laughing.

"The nagging mother?" I said, now infuriated. I stood to pour some water, trying to use the time to calm myself. "Again, you say, as if I nag all the time."

"Well, it does seem as if you do so regularly."

"Has it not occurred to you that I have to nag you because you will not allow anything of value to pass through that thick, stubborn head of yours? Nothing else seems to work, not my advice, not Herihor's, not

Amka's."

"I do follow Herihor's advice…"

"Yes, in army matters you do. But what you do not understand, what you will not allow yourself to understand is that being King is more than making war. You cannot rule by the power you command alone."

"It has worked pretty well in the Delta, has it not?" he replied acidly.

"Oh, I suppose your barb is aimed at my inability to put down the rebellion. Well, let me tell you something," I said, now standing directly before him, "when you were still a baby I made war with the Ta-Setys and they have been peaceful ever since."

"Yes, I do know that," Den replied, chastised. "Herihor has told me the stories of your exploits many times. I… I did not mean to… well you know."

"No, I do not know," I said angrily. "I love you, Zenty, but you still too often show the flawed characteristics of irresponsible youth rather than the mature judgment of a leader."

"Perhaps you forget that I did lead the army in the Delta," he retorted in a haughty manner.

"Yes you did and for that you are to be commended, in fact you have been praised highly for that. But the army is an extension of power, it is not all there is to governing. Zenty, you have an entire people living in the Two Lands. There are rekhi and nobles, priests and foreigners, artisans and fishermen. Some foreigners wish us ill, and for that your military knowledge at the hands of Herihor is most useful. But most foreigners simply want to trade with us. That is what makes a nation prosper and will make your people happy."

"Isn't that what I'm doing, signing trade agreements with all these dignitaries?"

"No, that is what we are doing… meaning me and Amka and your ministers. What you are doing is drinking and partying until you are drunk. You do not understand that this is not a game, it is life and death for Kem!"

This was but the first of many such conversations that Den and I had over the course of the next six cycles of Ra's silver disk, each one as seemingly frustrating as the last. Den was reluctant to give up his army ways, in this case days of intense meetings and ceremonies followed by equally intense nights of drinking and partying. It made me angry that none of the young men who surrounded him appeared to lead him to more responsible behaviors.

But I was wrong, at least about one of those men, as I learned one day when we thankfully closed upon the first anniversary of Den's rule. Den had just adjourned a meeting of the Council of Nomes, a body that I supposedly still led, but had been trying to maneuver so that Den gave it more leadership. That he hated meetings was obvious even before he ascended to the throne, but his rude manner during these meetings kept everyone on edge. After an hour of debate one of the governors could be assured of being disrespected by Den in some manner.

The issue at hand was relatively trivial, or could have been had Den handled it well. As was often the case, the matter involved apportioning resources between the farthest southern and northern nomes, both of which had been growing due to the increased trade with foreign lands. Because of his kidnapping and military experiences in the Delta losing men in battles with the rebels, Den had little patience for their demands and was about to rule that the resources be apportioned unfairly in favor of the south. I called for an adjournment for fear of the meeting descending into a shouting match.

My intent was to take a nap, freshen myself and then confront Den with specifics from the meeting so that he might view it dispassionately and thus learn lessons in governance. As I arrived back to his quarters, I saw that he was in heated conversation with Herihor. I decided to wait and sat down to the side of the entrance to his quarters.

"The reason is because no one else will tell you what

you must hear!" I heard Herihor yell.

"I am not deaf, Herihor," came Den's response.

"Good, for I sometimes wonder if your advisors are talking into the wind. Listen then and listen well, young man, for this will be my last attempt at advice to you. Mark my words, for if you do not change, and soon, the next conversation we will have will be for me to announce my retirement." I held my breath in shock.

"You are threatening the King…"

"And you are flinging dung, you impudent ass! For to be respected as King you must first act as one. You look at this as a… a game for your benefit alone. Everything is about what pleases you, not what helps your people."

"My people, as you call them, seem quite content," he said angrily.

"Content? Sure. As long as Mother Nile flows and fortunes are made then, yes, there are no visible problems. But the lean times will come as surely as Ra rises in the sky each day. Famine follows feast and then where will your adoring people be, the ones that kiss your ass because you have favors to dispense?" Den was silent for a moment.

"And your behavior frankly is an embarrassment. Does all life consist of drinking and whoring with your friends? Have you learned such models from me or your mother or from Nekau?

"Look at me for a moment, Zenty. Look at me! Your mother's more of a man than you are! She may not know how to wield a sword, but she understands, she… she bears her many responsibilities. You have the luxury of reigning in abundance because of the evil she has fought throughout her life, even in her own court, even against her own mortal body. I placed you on the battlefield to harden you for rule, but it has only given you the excuse to act arrogant and selfish and…"

"Please, no more," Den protested weakly. "I would rather be skewered on the point of a sword." His voice sounded as if it would break. For a long moment both men were silent. I heard Herihor sit hard into a chair.

"I... I'm not sure how to get out of this predicament I am in, Herihor. You are right. I... I need your advice."

"Advice that you will listen to and act upon?"

"I will listen to you as a father, for you are the only one I have known, and Amka my grandfather." My heart wanted to burst upon hearing those words. Tears flooded my eyes.

I heard the creaking of chairs, the sound of sand grinding under sandals and then the slapping of backs and my heart felt so full of love I wanted nothing more than to rush in and join their hug.

"It is settled, then," Den said. "We will meet each day for the morning meal and you will serve me humility with my bread and cheese. Agreed?"

Herihor laughed. "Agreed. When do we start?"

"Tomorrow, of course. But there is one thing I would like you to think about beforehand."

"Good. What is it?"

"My mother. I am concerned about her health." I swallowed hard hearing those words. I knew I should leave but I felt mortared to my spot.

"Yes, we all are. You, me, Amka, Nekau."

"Do you think she worsens?" Herihor waited before answering.

"We all worsen, Zenty. We are mortals, we age."

"You well know what I'm asking. I will also speak to Amka and Nekau about this."

"I speak with them almost daily," Herihor responded quickly. "They, too, are concerned. If not for Nekau she would be watching us right now from the next world." Herihor's voice was pained.

"I know how much you love her. I want to do something to help her, but I know not what that is."

"She's an obstinate one, isn't she?" Herihor said and they both laughed. "But if you're serious about helping, and I can see you are for we both love her dearly, I can suggest two courses of action that would ease her burdens."

"Name them."

"First, listen better to her counsel. She may not be the warrior you are, but she's adept at governing... very adept. She understands people. She listens well. Her ministers love her... well, anyway, most do. She has had to learn these skills, for as a woman she had much to prove." Again there was a long period of silence.

"I promise I'll try harder," Zenty said, sincerely. After a moment's pause he asked, "What else?"

"You've been on the throne for a year, but you haven't started a mastaba complex for her. That is a son's duty."

"Yes, yes, yes, Amka has mentioned that to me several times. I have been remiss. I will attend to it. Amka already has an architect in mind."

"Good, see to it soon. But there's one thing I will beg of you now, as your loyal servant. I want to settle it before the press of grief sways your decision."

"Go ahead, Herihor. I can think of nothing I would not grant you."

"If your mother leaves this world before me, then I wish to accompany her on her journey, for I... I could not walk the Two Lands without her."

The silence hung heavy in the air. I felt a weight bearing down on my chest and the pain in my liver served to remind me yet again of my mortality. My heart pained me with thoughts of my beloved Herihor drinking the holy poison, but then I saw visions of us living a life of peace and health and abundance in the Afterlife, together for eternity at Horus' side. Then an image of my dear Wadjet entered my heart and I felt a deep pang of regret.

Just then I heard a commotion in the hallway and the voices of Amka and Nekau arguing over some medical matter. I used the opportunity to slip out of the antechamber through a side passage.

True to his intent, Den did spend the next year of his rule listening more to his advisors. He learned from Amka to develop an agenda for every meeting and to hold his ministers and Vizier responsible for following up on his initiatives. He learned from me, albeit slowly, how to gauge the measure of a man's ba so as to know which ones were dependable and which not, which ones could be trusted and which lied through their false smiles. He learned from Herihor to select friends who would give him truthful opinions and help him stay on a path that would enforce rightful actions and thus strengthen ma'at.

But, it did not come easily. The decisions he made regarding the Delta continued to plague him, for it has always been true that leaders are blind to their own weaknesses. Requests from the governors of the Delta nomes were frequently delayed, often mishandled and nearly always reduced in scope. While none of the governors would complain to Den's face, they grumbled loudly behind his back, according to my informers.

Perhaps this would not have mattered, if it were not for a meeting that Amka called nearly two-and-a-half years after Den's ascension. As soon as Den and I, Herihor and Nekau, Amka and Tepemkau assembled, Amka began the meeting.

"It has come to our attention that Khnum and Bakht are yet alive." The news came as a shock to all of us and for a moment hung heavy in the air, for we had heard no rumors to that effect. I glanced at Herihor whose furrowed brow showed his concern.

"How have you come to this knowledge?" Den asked. I looked at Den to see if he was serious. "Sorry, your network of spies, I'm sure," Den said.

Herihor was about to speak up, but the aging Amka leaned forward, holding his staff to steady his shaking hands. "Master Den, whether you call them spies or informers or whatever else, the priesthood uses them judiciously to serve you. We check their information before it is ever brought to your attention. Without spies, a King cannot rule."

"Hmmmn. I suppose that's true, but I don't like having to use them. I look at my servants and wonder which ones spy against me. It feels dirty to me."

LESTER PICKER

"Think of spies as you would a battlefield scout," Herihor said. "Their role is to gather information."

"Yes, but a battlefield scout seems somehow purer. It is all done under Ra's light. Each side knows how scouts are employed and the limit of their usefulness. Spies in the court masquerade as your friends and then stab you in the back. Isn't that true, Amka?"

"No, that is not quite true, Master, for they can be a tool or a weapon, depending on how they are used. In each case their information can prevent a tragedy or cement a victory." At this Den was quiet.

"And Nubiti?" I asked, already suspecting the answer.

"Yes, well that is how we have come to find out about Khnum and Bakht," Tepemkau responded. "They correspond. Apparently they have corresponded since her exile."

"Nothing like timely spy information," Den wryly remarked as he reached for a cluster of grapes. Herihor held up his hand to Den. "What?" Den asked as if he did not already know that his sarcasm was an insult to Amka. The look Herihor shot towards Den left no doubt as to his meaning.

"I will not bother you with the details of how we found out or how they managed to secretly correspond, but suffice it to say that we now have inserted a spy into their chain of transporting the messages. The messages are written in a very deep code. Our priests are working now on deciphering it."

"And this message chain continues?" Den asked surprised. "You haven't destroyed its operations?"

"No," Tepemkau answered, "it is better to know what your enemy does than to be left to wonder."

"If we can trace the chain from beginning to end, then we can finally eliminate them," Den suggested, his face animated. "Then we will be done with this damned rebellion once and for all."

Amka looked at Tepemkau. "That might not be the wisest path to take," Amka said slowly. Den looked frustrated.

"How can that not be the best path to take? You have done a commendable job planting the spies. Now we can find those two bastards and we can kill them with few casualties on our side. It seems to me like the best course to take."

Amka breathed in deeply and I worried about the labor I heard in his lungs. "Master Den, you've been patient listening to us. But, allow me to explain something to you. Khnum and Bakht are worth far more to us alive than dead, especially once we are able to decode their messages, which we will undoubtedly do very soon. Then we will know where they are and what they plot.

"But dead, they become martyrs. Well hidden though it is from our eyes, righteous beliefs in an independent Delta still form an undercurrent there. The Apep priesthood will never be completely destroyed, only driven underground. They will keep the hope of an independent Delta alive, for by so doing they maintain influence and gain adherents. Yet change does happen, albeit slowly. A subjugated people eventually learns that it is better to assimilate than to continually live in misery."

Den nodded his head as if to absorb what his advisors told him. "And so, what would you suggest we do?"

"Loosen the reigns on Lower Kem," Amka responded calmly.

"Loosen the reigns you say? Interesting..." Den drummed his fingers and looked from Amka to Tepemkau. "Now I wonder just how would that look?" Herihor's and Den's eyes met fleetingly.

"First we suggest you start by granting the Delta governors more of the projects they request," Amka began cautiously.

"In fact, you might consider funding projects they have not yet even requested," Tepemkau added. "We have such a list," he said, not noticing the expression on Den's face.

"Of course!" Den said loudly. "Brilliant! Herihor, instruct the army in the Delta to lay down their swords. They should immediately replace their mace heads with backscratchers. Oh, and issue a ration of fine linen to each soldier, so on a moment's notice they may wipe the asses of our Delta cousins." By now Den's face was red with rage. No one spoke a word.

Amka tapped his fingers on his carved staff, his forehead pressed to its well-worn surface. "You know, Den, we priests have a saying," he said so softly I had to strain to hear him. "Your throne may be exalted above all others, but it is good to remind yourself that you sit on it with your ass." Den did not know what to do with Amka's remark.

"Meaning?" Den finally burst out, angrily.

"Meaning that you might consider confining your warrior mentality to the battlefield, where matters are simpler and nuance is discouraged. Ruling a nation demands far higher skills, greater than any one man... or woman," he said, tipping his staff toward me, "can master."

"I know that those priestly sayings can infuriate," I quickly added, seeing Den's angry expression, "but in those words are contained deep wisdom. Look Zenty," I continued, using his child name to soften his anger, "I have been wounded as deeply as anyone by the scheming of our Delta cousins. Yet I came to realize that if we continue to rule as if it is Upper Kem pitted against Lower Kem we will win most skirmishes but in the end lose the battle of Unification. That is Horus' promise, given to King Narmer as a sacred vision. Two lands, one people. That will be the ultimate victory and we have a sacred duty to achieve it."

For several moments all sat quietly, absorbing the significance of my words. Amka nodded his head, his eyes gently closed and my heart was filled with love for my elderly, but wise teacher.

"She's right," Herihor said before Den could respond. "I think we should listen to Meryt-Neith... and the priests. It's time to heal the wounds of the past if we're to move forward as a nation."

Coming from Herihor the words carried great import for Den. And so it was that Den slowly began to consider a vision of a truly united Kem, where both lands were equal in the eyes of Horus. In this he required much help and I had many conversations with my son, explaining to him my vision experiences with Horus. To my continuing surprise, he never reported having been visited by Horus or Narmer. I was not certain whether Horus and Narmer never actually visited with him or whether he was reluctant to share those visits with me, preferring to discuss them with Amka and Tepemkau instead.

During one conversation we had about the Council of Nomes, Amka hobbled in. Our poor Vizier now suffered greatly from the disease of the joints and he depended heavily on his staff to support his bowed and crooked body. Nekau walked beside him, his hand under Amka's elbow, ready to catch him if he stumbled, which happened with increasing frequency in recent months.

Den and I had spent many an hour discussing Amka's replacement, but none seemed to have the experience and wisdom possessed by Amka. None, that is, but Nekau.

"Ah, what have we here?" Den called out good-naturedly to them. "Dear Amka, isn't it tiring supporting that big, black priest as you do?"

"Yes, yes it is," Amka replied weakly as Nekau helped him to his favorite chair. "I tell him to get his own staff, but he insists that mine can support us both." We laughed heartily at Amka's humor.

"So, what is on the agenda for today?" Den asked.

"We come with a suggestion," Amka said. "We think it is time to release Nubiti from exile."

My heart skipped a beat hearing my sister's name. The ache it brought surprised me and I knew at that moment that I still suffered the pain of betrayal. Oh, Isis, how I wished for our younger days, when I innocently believed that she had my best interests in her heart. Many times since her betrayal I wondered whether that was ever true or merely an illusion.

"What... what prompts this suggestion?" Den asked. I admired him for not reacting angrily.

"Much has changed since you have embraced Unification," Amka said softly. His breathing came with difficulty. "The Delta governors have increased their power due to the projects you have commissioned for them. The Lower Kemians are a happier people now. We know what Nubiti and Bakht discuss in their notes and we know the weaknesses of the Apep priesthood and their rebel army, if you can still call it such. There is no reason to keep Nubiti exiled, for it serves no other purpose at this point except to make her into a legend that keeps the flame of the rebellion burning."

"Better to keep your enemies close at hand," Den said.

"You sound more like Amka every day," Nekau replied, but he said it without emotion. I watched Den look at each of them in turn.

"And so, this is a unanimous recommendation of my advisors?" Den asked. Nekau studiously examined the design of the mud brick floor.

"Not exactly," Amka responded. "Nekau here does not agree."

"Tell me why not," Den said, looking directly at Nekau. Only then did Nekau stand straight.

"She is a curse and a troublemaker. Evil is in her bones. It is best to step wide around sleeping lions. There is still mischief left in that woman."

"And what of Menetnashte?" I asked. "What would you do about him?"

"That is part of the problem," Amka said. "We know little of him. None of us has laid eyes upon him. We suspect he is a trained Apep priest from the messages that Bakht sends. According to our laws he would have a claim to the throne if something were to happen to you, Zenty, Horus forbid, before you have an heir of your own. Menetnashte is still young and we wish to see what type of threat he poses. Again, it is better to have that entire cabal exposed to Ra's light than for their poison to simmer in a dark cave."

We discussed our options over weak beer, cheese and fruits. Finally, Den turned to me. "Mother, I leave the choice to you for I know how Nubiti's betrayal wounded you. What would you have me do?"

It is hard to describe how I felt at that moment, both for the blessing of having such a strong and compassionate son, and also for the pain of having to again deal with my sister. I thought of the many times I ran giggling in the garden with her, carefree and full of life and hope. I thought of our many talks as I prepared for my role as a woman. As my confidante I believed her to be my ka-mate, for there was nothing I would not share with her. But our intimacy allowed her treachery to penetrate me to my core. It was a wound from which I had never recovered. I missed her face, but I also knew that I could never look upon it again without the sharp sting of grief.

"Release her," I said.

As he adjusted to healing a divided land, Den conferred regularly with Amka, Tepemkau and the royal architect, Nomti on the many building projects that years of abundance enabled. Often the tall and pitifully thin Nomti would arrive trailed by his assistants with tightly wound scrolls under their arms. Hours later they would leave with the scrolls disheveled and even torn and at times I heard poor Nomti grumbling as he left. After months of these meetings, Den called me into his quarters.

"I have a wonderful surprise for you, mother," he exclaimed as soon as I entered.

"I have had enough surprises to last me a lifetime," I replied. "The best surprise is to simply be summoned to your quarters for a talk."

"Well, this surprise is for the next lifetime," he said smiling and standing up to hug me. On the table I noted a large scroll. In a moment Tepemkau walked in, with Nomti right behind him.

"Show it to her," Den instructed. Nomti reached over with his long, skinny arms and unrolled a large papyrus scroll that was on the table. He placed gold paperweights on each corner and stood back, smiling proudly. The scroll showed a huge temple surrounded by a hundred or more tiny buildings.

"Well, what do you think?" Den asked excitedly.

"It... it is extraordinary," I said, looking at him. "It is a grand temple, but to which god?"

"You!" he exclaimed, beaming. "It's your funerary complex!"

"You must have been quite proud," Herihor said to me when I recounted to him the meeting with Den and Nomti. "I can tell you he's been quite absorbed with it for a long time."

"I am proud. It is like nothing I have seen before."

"You seem worried," Herihor suggested, coming closer and taking me in his arms.

"It does worry me. Not even Narmer's mastaba is so grand, nor Wadjet's. It is beautiful and it overlooks the Gates to the Afterworld. When they took me to the site I had gooseflesh all over. I... I do not feel worthy of such tribute."

"Aahh, there it is. You feel unworthy again. Den loves you. The entire leadership of Kem holds you in high regard, Mery. You have forged remarkable achievements for the Two Lands."

I turned away from Herihor and suddenly felt swamped by confusion in my ba, for Herihor had hit upon an essential burden in my life. Often did I not feel worthy, even when I sat upon the most important throne in all the lands. And the questions came back, yet again. Would my ba have been so different had I a mother and father to raise me? Would I have felt worthy of tribute, worthy of accolades for a job well done, worthy of Herihor's love?

It is true that none could have been kinder than sweet

Herneith, yet each time I saw her with Wadjet I felt in my heart the difference between a mother's love and that of an aunt. Even watching a parent scold a child in the streets of Inabu-hedj made me keenly aware of my hidden secret, my profound loneliness.

"Looking back my achievemnts hardly seem remarkable," I said. "I had you and Amka at my side. I only did what had to be done."

"And what had to be done wasn't easy," Herihor said, coming to stand in front of me. "What you did took courage and daring. You battled the Ta-Sety and saved my life and we have had twenty years of peace with them. You've built granaries throughout the lands. You've given the nomes a say in governing. And you've quieted the rebellions in the Delta."

"It was you who quieted the rebellions."

"At your command. Why do you deny all you have done to strengthen the Two Lands? Even our trade has increased beyond measure."

"Oh, I think it would be hard to explain to you, my love."

"Try," he said, "please." I could see the sincerity in his eyes. I took Herihor's hand and walked to the portico.

"Although I walk in the world of men, I am still a woman in my heart. Am I a success because I rule a mighty nation? And so what if people bow low to me because I command the mightiest army? Yes, to you these are successes, for you see them through a man's eyes.

"Yet to me they matter little, except...except perhaps for how they have contributed to ma'at for Kem. Do you know what would have been a success in my eyes, my dear Herihor? To have been able to marry you after Wadjet passed on to the next life. To have been your loving wife for all eternity. To suckle a baby we made together and raise her, along with Zenty."

Over the years the portico had become my favorite view in all the land, for it overlooked Mother Nile as she flowed around a point. Directly below the portico were our gardens, lovingly tended by my servants. Trees, imported from lands near and far, bloomed. Flowers of every description grew in colorful abundance and birds flitted here and there, their cheerful sounds filling the air. To the right and left were the verdant fields of our agricultural estates.

"But, to answer your earlier question, you are right, my dear, it is not the grandeur of the mastaba and the temple that Den builds in my honor that troubles me. I..." My throat choked with emotion and I felt my eyes fill with tears.

Herihor came closer and held my arms in his hands. The years had taken their toll on my love. He had endured new battle wounds and the scar across his cheek had hardened so that the skin around it appeared dark and stretched. Yet to me he looked as handsome as the day I first laid eyes on him.

"Mery, what is it?" he whispered as he peered deeply into my eyes, and in that moment I was certain he already knew.

"I worry that my mastaba will not be finished in time," I said, holding my abdomen. "I... I am dying."

SCROLL NINETEEN

Nubiti

"You do miss it, though, Nubiti. I can see it in your eyes." Our fishing boat sailed upon Mother Nile, our trusted captain tacking to and fro, trimming the sails just right, every so often his crew pretending to cast a net so as to avert suspicion. Before us lay the gleaming white walls of Inabu-hedj.

"I don't deny it. Had the gods supported our plans we'd be sitting behind those walls. It's an impressive sight, after all." I sighed. A scarf covered my face, even though we sat on a side bench in the stern, under a protective cover.

"Thanks for accompanying me," I said to Bakht, whose face was similarly covered by a scarf. Night was about to fall, which would provide us with relief from the searing heat and an opportunity to shed our disguises.

"It's not a problem. I know how much you have wanted to return. And it gives us a chance to talk." I did not want to reveal the pain in my heart, knowing that behind those walls lay a life I had left behind.

"Fill me in on the state of our treasury," I said.

"The security plans go well," he started.

"I love the way you phrase it."

"Well, extortion would not sound quite so nice now, would it?" he said smiling. Black stains showed between his teeth from chewing the drugs that gave him his visions. Yet his eyes still held an undeniable attraction to me.

"In any event, the Delta merchants do pay up, quietly of course. They fear their balls being served up for dinner." He laughed hard at his own remark.

"We also get continuing contributions from the old families, the ones who see themselves benefiting if… when we eventually advance our position. It costs them little to play both ends of the rope. With the recent favorable changes in Den's court toward us, they are getting an increasing slice of foreign trade rights, so their payments to us are little more than a nuisance tax."

"So, all in all we're doing well?" I asked.

"Very well. We have storehouses of gold, silver and precious jewels hidden throughout the Delta."

"It does us no good underground," I ventured.

"Agreed, but we continually draw from it to pay our spies and to exact favors from certain sympathizers in the court. It also pays for our small group of rebels who train now in camps in Ta-Tjehenu."

The evening breezes began to pick up and I dropped my scarf to breathe in the fresh scents coming off the land. "I had hoped that since my return we would have advanced our cause more substantially."

"My dear, I know you are disappointed, we are all disappointed, but we're lucky to be alive, and we are growing… slowly, but noticeably. We must face the fact that our cause is no longer what it was. It will take years, perhaps until Menetnashte's son or grandsons are grown, before we are again in a position to challenge the court. Den and his advisors keep us around only because it suits their plans to grind the Delta under their sandals."

The knowledge that Bakht was correct made the bile rise in my throat. In exile I had replayed the choices I had made many, many times, always second-guessing myself, wondering why the gods favored Mery over me. In the end I knew that I would rather have made my own choices as I did and suffer their effects than be a Senet piece in the hands of the Horus priesthood, to be played as they saw fit.

"What have you heard of life inside the court?" Bakht asked. "Rumors abound."

"I'm told that Mery worsens day by day. She's in great pain. Since Herihor retired from the Army, he does nothing but play nursemaid to her, mopping her brow, holding her hand as she sleeps, even wiping up her messes. Disgusting!"

"How the mighty have fallen," Bakht mused. "He was once a force to be feared."

"He still is, according to my sources, only now he advises his mousy protégé."

"Speaking of the protégé, have you heard that the black priest has sent word to the Delta families that he is looking for a Second Wife for Den?"

"Second Wife? He has not even married his first."

"No, but apparently he's close. Amka is too old and feeble to take an active role in the selection, so he has farmed it out to Tepemkau and Nekau, and the black one is more efficient, I suppose. In any case, you should know that Den has marriage on his mind... which is surprising."

"Surprising? How so?"

"There are rumors."

"Stop being vague with me, Bakht," I demanded. "Spill all or be quiet." Bakht smiled broadly at me.

"I do so like your expressions when you get angry with me. With you I enjoy spilling all," he said, winking, as if I would not get his sexual reference without the added emphasis. "There are those who believe that, unlike his mother, our little Den should have been given a female title when he ascended."

"No! Could that be true?"

"Well, there are rumors... men leaving his quarters with Ra's silver disk waning. It seems that his preferences have left his need for women behind, so to speak." Bakht smiled at his wittiness.

"So, the plot thickens." I said, pondering the possibilities. "This makes the Second Wife a far more important choice than I would've predicted."

"Yes, I thought you would like to be involved in the choice. The Delta nobles are ready to take direction from us."

"We need a strong woman, but not one who appears such on the surface," I mused. "We must assume that Tepemkau and his minions will intentionally pick a weak First Wife so she will not appear to be more the man than her husband. If we offer up a similarly appearing Second Wife, but train her well, she could be just the tool we need." The more I thought of this unexpected gift from the gods, the more excited I became.

"You play us like game pieces!" I shouted to the sky, shaking my arms at the heavens, "only your board is far larger. You must laugh at our folly."

"And that is when Apep is most powerful," Bakht reminded me, smiling wryly. "He bides his time awaiting the right moment to emerge." One look at Bakht's groin alerted me to the fact that it was not Apep that was emerging. Yet the thought appealed to me, for it was typically long periods between when I could feel Bakht's power inside me. Night could not fall quickly enough for either of us.

As Ra set below the hills and lit the scattered clouds with an orange glow, we anchored off the point of land below the palace walls. Bakht commanded the captain and crew to transfer to one of the other boats that accompanied us and as soon as they did we slid from our bench to the blanketed deck.

Although it had been more than a year since Bakht and I coupled, we took our time, for I imagine we each realized it might be even longer to our next opportunity.

My skin was exquisitely sensitive to his touch as he ran his fingers up and down my body. I felt an ache deep inside me and I wanted nothing more than for him to penetrate me. Yet we didn't rush the moment.

Bakht pulled apart my robe and cupped a breast in his hand. I shuddered as he squeezed my nipple until it stiffened between his fingers. He leaned down and placed it in his mouth, sucking and pulling it gently with his teeth. My breath came in gasps now as he alternated between each breast.

"As Neith is my witness, I so enjoy these," Bakht said, looking up at me and smiling. I did not ask him to stop to explain whether the Neith he referred to was the protector goddess of the Delta or the Queen. For a moment I imagined Mery on her balcony, looking over Mother Nile, unsuspecting what went on right below her. I felt myself moisten.

I rolled over and grabbed Bakht's already hard organ and ran my fingers along its length. At my touch he groaned and tensed its muscle so that I felt its life force pulse in my grip. I squeezed back as I knew he liked. He lifted his face and kissed my lips and in a moment our tongues met and then there was no more waiting.

Bakht pulled me on top of him and I slid his erect penis into my wetness. "Oh, Isis!" I gasped and Bakht immediately began to thrust deeper into me, filling me completely as I rode him to the heights of my pleasure. I could feel my inner walls spasm again and again and I collapsed in his arms. In just a few moments I felt his thrusting begin once more and once again I flew to Isis' lair.

Finally, Bakht could take it no longer and he rolled me over and finished me from behind, as he liked to do. As he groaned in delight, I heard the sailors on one of our other boats laughing.

With Ra's silver disk high in the sky, we sat side-by-side nibbling on bread, cheese and grapes and talking and reminiscing. Bakht's seed dripped from inside me, and it pleased me. Then, just as quickly, I thought of my present diminished circumstance and in a quiet space in our conversation I felt momentarily saddened by what might have been.

Bakht was accompanied from the Delta by envoys of several prominent families, ones who traced their lineage back to King W'ash, who nearly defeated Narmer during the War of Unification. The next ten-days were filled with activity, as I met furtively with these representatives. It wasn't easy to arrange these meetings since Den had his spies and soldiers follow me everywhere. But the Apep priesthood still maintained safe houses and caves where secret meetings could be held in comfort during the long hours of night.

One of the joys in being back in the Delta was the chance to get to know Menetnashte better. We had been estranged for so long, it was as if we were strangers. Our brief messages were not enough to mortar a strong bond, but the Apep priests had done well by him. He was a strong and stocky young man, possessed of Bakht's dark and deep-set eyes and the intelligence of us both. He carried himself in a regal manner, his back straight, his shoulders square. Just by looking at him one would assume that he could handle himself in a fight, yet that only hinted at his real physical prowess.

Soon after I returned to the Delta, Bakht arranged for an exhibition of Menetnashte's martial skills. As an Isis priestess I had many times been called upon to bless the soldiers before their warrior games or to minister to their bruises afterwards. So I was well versed in what constituted a good set of warrior skills. Even so, I was taken aback by Menetnashte's performance. He carefully weighed his opponent, circling, his keen eyes taking in every tendency of his enemy. He would wait until they struck, parrying their blows or nimbly dodging them despite his size. But when he attacked, he did so with a vengeance. He was an irresistible force and more often than not it only took one volley from his mace or one parry with his sword to quickly dispense with his rival.

So it was that I was out one night in a secret meeting when Bakht barged into the meeting, grabbed my arm and took off with me. As we ran he explained that the King's Guard had arrived at my house to summon me. We had become complacent in our belief that Den's troops would never summon me from a sleep. Yet here we were, rushing back to my house in Dep, as my handmaidens stalled the soldiers.

Rushing in through the back door, I quickly changed into my nightgown and came toward the front of the building where the Captain waited.

"You are perspired," the Captain had the audacity to say. I maintained my calm.

"It's warm and I had a nightmare about soldiers barging into my home," I said with as much bearing as I could. The Captain did not know how to respond. He cleared his throat.

"The Queen Mother summons you," he said, drawing himself up.

"Mery? At this hour?" I asked. "Couldn't she wait until morning?"

I noted the other soldiers looking uncomfortably at their Captain. "Gather your belongings. We leave in ten minutes for Inabu-hedj," he said. "We will make double time, so prepare accordingly."

Within the hour I was aboard one of the King's skiffs, part of a flotilla being rowed by specially trained oarsmen in the King's employ. As Ra's chariot rose in the sky I was surprised by how swiftly the shore ran past us. Each team of oarsmen rowed for perhaps an hour and another crew would quickly assume their seats and continue. They alternated thus throughout the day and the next night. By the end of the second day we tied the boats up to the docks below the white walls of the city.

A fresh troop of King's Guards surrounded me at the dock and walked me up the stairs to the palace. There a somber, and much older, Tepemkau met me. He looked me up and down and with only a nod turned and walked toward Mery's quarters with me following.

Mery's bedroom was large. Candles burned throughout the room, with clay shields in front of them to block their light from Mery's sensitive eyes. They threw their flickering light across the white walls. Handmaidens scurried about quietly, bringing fresh baskets of fruit and flowers, replenishing the water pitchers and taking out the bed sheets that had just been changed.

Nekau stood at Mery's bedside, the candlelight reflecting off his dark body, accenting his still muscular form. His eyes were bloodshot and swollen bags hung below them. Sitting on the bed was Herihor. There was rage in his eyes as he looked at me. So intense was his stare, so full of venom, I was forced to look away from him. But what I saw in the very next instant was far, far worse.

Lying on the bed was a ghost, a mut spirit from the world beyond. I must have gasped, for Nekau snapped his head around to chastise me with his look. I stared at the figure in the bed, trying to make sense of what it was I saw. Even I, after all these years, after all my hatred, could not control the tears that flowed from my eyes.

It was Mery, or what was left of her. She was so thin it seemed as if her blanket covered only a few thin reeds. Her cheeks were hollow and the bones of her mouth and jaw jutted out from her emaciated, yellowed face. Her breath came so infrequently that at first I thought she had already passed from this world. I saw a twitch in her hand and Herihor leaned his ear down to her mouth. He nodded.

"We will clear the room for a few minutes," he called out to the maidservants who immediately left. It was then that I saw a motion in the corner. It was Amka himself, as if raised from the dead. He slowly shuffled directly toward me, hunched over his staff.

"Why she has requested you by her side is one of Horus' great mysteries," he whispered. He leaned back as far as his contorted back would allow so that he could look into my eyes. "Such chances for redemption do not happen often." He continued to stare at me, his eyes shifting just a fraction right and left, scouring me to see what might be my reaction. Despite my tears I stared brazenly back. He shook his head and shuffled away, Nekau's large hand under his elbow.

It was only Herihor and me left with Mery. He stood slowly, bent down and whispered something to her and walked toward me, his hand on the handle of the knife that was sheathed on his belt. "I would that Horus grant my wish to slit your throat, you evil mut," he whispered through gnashed teeth. "But he whispers now in the ear of that beautiful woman there and they have exacted a promise to stay my hand. I'll be at the door. One wrong word to her, one evil gesture... just one and I'll gladly appear before Anubis with a heavy heart and your blood on my hands."

I had never before experienced such a venomous attack and my throat felt dry as sand. He walked away before I could reply and there we were, alone again, Mery and me, for the first time in so many, many years. Were we truly sisters just yesterday? Was it not just a ten-day ago when I chased her through Djer's gardens?

I stood at the foot of her bed listening to her breath come in soft rattles. Her eyes fluttered behind her wrinkled lids. Suddenly, they sprung open.

"Nubiti, is it you?" she said so softly at first I thought it my imagination. Her voice sounded rough as she struggled to speak.

I walked around the bed to sit on a chair by her side. "Yes, it is," I answered.

"Take my hand," she whispered. I was so shocked I could not react for a moment. As I finally reached for her, I noticed a movement by the door and saw Herihor ready to pounce. But Nekau's swift hand stayed him.

Her hand was so slight I feared that even the gentlest of touches would break it like a desiccated jackal bone. Even in the heat of Shomu her hand felt cold. She closed her eyes and I watched as they moved behind her lids, first slowly from side to side, then in all directions. At once I felt a buzzing in my heart and my breath came in short gasps. My eyelids became heavy and I could not resist closing them. I heard a strong breeze blowing in my ears and I shook in my chair. My inner eyes looked over a high precipice in the deep desert, the winds buffeting my body. There were buildings below and people, many people. But when I dared to look down to make sense of what was laid out before me I felt dizzy and disoriented.

I quickly opened my eyes and there was Mery, staring at me, her lips straining to smile. "I have missed you, sister," she said.

I did not know what to say for this strange scene was entirely unexpected and had been sprung on me without warning. I wanted to say something, but words would not form around my jumbled thoughts. Images of our childhoods swirled in my heart and then as quickly the fateful discussions that led to my approving her poisoning. There was no doubt that her wasted condition was my work. I thought of Ti-Ameny then and I wished she had been able to complete her work before being discovered. Then I would not be confronting this unfortunate situation, but who knows what paths the gods would have had me follow? I knew that I should feel remorse, but my heart only felt empty.

"It is alright," she went on. "I have seen it. All is forgiven." Then she simply closed her eyes. I sat by her side still holding her tiny hand. In a moment Nekau came in, took a look at Mery and called to Herihor and Amka. A messenger was sent to get Den, who I heard running down the hall. By then I had been ushered out. One of the captains of the King's Guard escorted me to the rear entrance of the palace, where a phalanx of his troops awaited to bring me back to Dep.

There are many things about that event, from being summoned in Dep to sailing back after my visit with Mery that I have long ago forgotten. But among my most vivid memories of the event was this. As I crossed the threshold from the palace to the outside I was confronted by a seething, silent mass of humanity. Below us stood tens of thousands of loyal Kemians, men and women, rekhi and noblemen alike, looking up at the palace for word of their Queen. They stood, hardly a sound rising to us, except for the whispers of their prayers. Incense burned in braziers scattered throughout the periphery of the walled palace and long lines snaked through the streets and alleyways to offer their meager sacrifices.

"They love her dearly," the captain said, daring to speak to me. Then we were off.

On the third day after I returned, as Ra rose above the horizon, I was awakened by a long, mournful blast of a ram's horn that came from the Temple of Horus. I instantly knew what it announced. I bathed and dressed quickly and waited for the messenger. He arrived within the hour to tell me of Mery's passing.

'I have seen it,' she had said to me that day upon her deathbed. What was it she saw? Did she stand upon that same precipice as did I? Did the winds that blew by my ear whisper some secret of the gods to her? Did she see remorse in my ka, for if she did her gaze surely penetrated deeper than my own?

I often wonder why she felt it so important to bring me to her side, after so many years and so much heartache between us. Was she only aware of the pain I caused her, or did she finally understand that she was also the cause of my own life's suffering? To be so close to the throne, to fall from grace and to be banished, these cruel twists and turns hardened my heart to Mery. In the end I'm convinced there was nothing there. I held her hand and reflected on its coldness. I willed some warmth between us, a sign from the gods that a glimmer of love remained. I found none, not in my heart.

'It is all right,' she had said. For Mery it was always all right. Not so for me. Her son sat upon the highest throne in all the lands. My son was a poor priest in an obscure Delta town.

Even in Dep the outpouring of affection for Mery

was astounding. Farmers came from towns near and far
to offer sacrifices at the Temple of Horus, and women
flocked to the Temples of Isis and Neith to make their
offerings. For seventy days no business was conducted
in the Delta, nor anywhere else in the Two Lands.

Beginning a month before the funeral was to take
place, caravans began arriving one after another from
lands to the east, men in strange curled beards and
women hidden with veils and decorated with bangles
and silk robes. Foreign kings sent unarmed soldiers to
pay their respects and they carried chests filled with
presents of every sort for the Queen's eternal life and to
mortar their relationship with King Den.

On the fifth day before the funeral, I left with a
fleet of ships containing the princes and nobles of the
Delta. Sailing with me were Menetnashte and Bakht.
Khnum could not sober himself long enough for the
journey.

The scene upon Mother Nile is impossible to
describe. There were so many boats of every manner and
description, if a man were to have fallen overboard he
would surely have been crushed. It took twice as long as
we had anticipated getting to Inabu-hedj, but once we
were within a few hours sail, ships from the King's navy
identified royal guests and ushered them forward. Yet
for hundreds of cubits around the harbor the boats were
so thick we had to walk from the middle of the river on
planks set across their bows to get to the docks.

The scene in Inabu-hedj was staggering to the
senses. The King's Guard captain who escorted us to the
tents set up for guests told us that the priests had
estimated the crowds at nearly a million people. Every
house had rented out space to visitors. Every place
where a tent could be pitched, it was. Visitors camped in
caves in the mountains and the poorest of the poor
simply slept out on the sands of the desert. The smells of
Inabu-hedj were always a rich stew of people and foods,
but now the stench was overpowering for the river itself
was the most available for toileting. The intolerable heat

of Shomu only served to intensify the assault on one's senses.

The noise, too, was overwhelming. Inabu-hedj had always been a noisy city, so full as it was with merchants and trade and all the Kings' workshops. Yet added to that now were the thousands of foreign dignitaries shouting in strange languages, trying to make themselves understood. The army was hard pressed to maintain even a semblance of order.

Due to our delay in arriving, we had only a day to prepare for the funeral. I awoke feeling a strong urge to offer prayers to my patron goddess, so I hired a young boy as a messenger and he returned shortly with two priestesses dressed in white. They, in turn, escorted me through the crowds to the Temple of Isis.

I was greeted at the temple stairs by only a few of the priestesses I vaguely knew. Since my removal as Head Priestess the entire order had been rearranged. The priestesses were polite and took me around to the back of the temple, where they allowed me private access to the inner sanctuary. It had been years since I had set foot in a Temple of Isis. I removed my sandals and as I rounded the corner I began to tremble with fear. What if Isis viewed Apep's newfound presence in my ka as an abomination? For a moment I hoped that the daily prayers of the priestesses lacked fervor and that Isis' spirit would not be in her statue at the present moment.

I entered the sanctuary, keeping my gaze on the floor. The light from the brazier cast a warm, speckled light that played across my feet. I quickly crossed the floor and sat upon the lone bench. I sat for minutes before I realized that my muscles were tense and I had not breathed deeply since I left the tent. And so I tried the meditations that I had so long ago taught to my acolytes. I replayed the stories from our pantheon of gods and slowly retraced them back and still further back to Nun, to the nothingness that existed at the moment of Creation.

The ether of Nun swarmed around me. I breathed

in the sen-sen breaths, deep, slowly, my inner eyes watching my breath mixing with the ether, watching it swirl within my lungs, then exhaling through my nostrils in a continuous stream of life. I sat silently, empty of all thoughts and emotions. I waited for the creative act to come, for my once beloved Isis to visit a new vision upon me, perhaps the creation of a new path, a new lifetime, even a new day.

I waited. I breathed until I became aware of my own breathing. I tried again. Nothing. I prayed for Isis to enter my ka, but my chest felt constricted and I realized that the passage to my ka was too narrow for her to squeeze through. In that instant I experienced clarity. I finally understood. I dropped to my knees and bowed my forehead to the earth before her in gratitude.

The next day was Mery's funeral. There are many events that stand out in a person's life. There are births and deaths, celebrations and formalities, feasts and famines. Yet none will ever stand out in my mind like Mery's funeral. I admit that and I do not regret that my own funeral will most likely be a simple affair, attended by only a few people of little distinction. It was part of the clarity of vision I experienced in the Temple of Isis.

The day began with the blowing of ram's horns from the Temple of Horus and then picked up by horns at the palace and all the temples within Inabu-hedj so that Ra's orb was greeted that morning with the mournful sound of Horus' chosen ready to stand before Anubis' scales.

I awoke and looked out from the tent and saw people scurrying in every direction to greet Ra. People lay prostrate on the ground while others bowed low or sank on bent knees to greet him. He, in turn, showered his people with warmth and light as he rose into a clear, cloudless, blue sky.

We dressed quickly and ate a substantial meal, for the funeral ceremony would last until Ra's disk sank into the western sky. To his credit, Tepemkau had arranged for our contingent to be in the Royal processional, albeit toward the very end. Soldiers came to bring us toward the palace, but the processional was so long we found ourselves many streets away.

We heard the piercing blasts of the ram's horn announcing the start of the procession, but it took fully two hours before our chairs were lifted and we began to move. Ever so slowly did we wind our way through the streets of the city, up the hill and to the royal necropolis. As we went, the common people were pressed together from the houses to the streets so that our carriers had barely enough room to walk past. By time our chairs passed, there were no flowers left for the people to throw at our feet. The carriers before us had trampled the petals to a pink slippery muck that went up to their ankles.

People wailed and flagellated themselves and rent their garments in sorrow. Every so often a commoner or a rekhi would throw himself or herself at our chairs, tears streaming from their eyes. "She sent a physician and saved my child," one said. Another walked side by side with our carriage and relayed to us the tale of how Mery had decided a case in favor of his rekhi family rather than a rich landowner. I wondered whom this man thought was his audience. Yet for hours we listened to these tales from wealthy and rekhi alike.

Finally we reached the necropolis, which stood on a plateau above the city. We climbed from our chairs and walked up the path to the necropolis grounds. Menetnashte grabbed my arm and turned me around and for the first time I had a clear grasp of the immensity of the crowds. Stretched from the base of the mountains, even up the mountain slopes, all the way into Inabu-hedj, was a solid wall of people, all looking intently in our direction. A warm breeze blew over the plateau. Above us Ra burned brightly. The heat from above, combined with the hot air flowing up from the valley floor, was oppressive. Servants circulated throughout the nobility with pitchers of water.

As I turned back toward the necropolis, I was

struck dumb by the building that I confronted. Somehow Den had managed to complete a mastaba, the shear size of which had never before been seen in the Two Lands. It adjoined his father's tomb, but Mery's funerary complex covered an even larger area of land. The building was low and flat, its roof supported by evenly spaced columns that stood outside a thick mud-brick wall. Around the building stood nearly forty much smaller tombs, all joined together. Pits had been dug in each tomb to accommodate the bodies of those loyal servants who would soon accompany Mery on her journey.

The Horus priests began their incantations as Mery's heavily wrapped body was taken from her carry platform. Then teams of priests took off the jars containing her organs. Mery's body was placed in a wood coffin. The priests then placed her gold breastplate, signifying her role as King Regnant, upon her chest. They adorned her body with various other pieces of jewelry, reciting the appropriate prayers for each. Finally, they moved her inside, where they performed the Opening of the Mouth ritual, so that she would be able to breathe and eat in the Afterworld. Then Mery was placed in her stone coffin and buried in the deep pit that waited. The priests exited solemnly and workers covered the coffin and a team of masons was sent in to brick in the coffin and mortar it in place against jackals and thieves. It took many hours for this to be accomplished and during that time servants circulated with light refreshments and water.

When they were done with their work, Tepemkau stepped forward and held his hands high. All in the necropolis silenced themselves. From the rear of Mery's mastaba came a long line of people, all dressed in the finest white linen. At the head of the line was Herihor, dressed differently from the rest, in his finest military uniform. Even at his age he looked trim and fit and my heart pained at the sight of him. Yet I groaned with the knowledge of what he had come forward to do. Bakht and Menetnashte turned toward me and I tried to keep my eyes from tearing, but my efforts were doomed.

One by one the loyal servants entered the outer room of Mery's mastaba, some shaking uncontrollably, others stiff and erect, still others smiling with glorious anticipation. There was her boat maker and chief potter and many of her artisans and handmaidens. Each was carried out moments later on a reed stretcher and lowered into his or her own tomb. They were carefully placed on their sides, facing east toward Ra's rising, so they could wake early each day in the Afterlife to serve their Queen. Their respective tools were placed with them. Thirty-nine loyal, loving servants were buried that day with Mery.

Finally it was Herihor's turn. I had wondered how Amka, Tepemkau and Nekau had positioned him in Mery's Afterlife, for it was beyond question that Mery was eternally wedded to Wadjet in the eyes of the gods. Then I realized why Herihor was the only one dressed formally, in his army regalia, for he was to be Mery's personal guardian during her journey and would serve as Wadjet's and Mery's guardian for all eternity. I imagined that he now prayed fervently to Horus that his friend and master would forgive the liberties he took with Mery.

Then it was over. Herihor was taken from the mastaba and placed in the tomb closest to Mery's and bitter tears rolled down my cheeks at what might have been. I watched, my heart numb, as they placed Herihor's shield upon his chest and closed his fist around his sword. The teams of masons reappeared and sealed each tomb and finally the entrance to Mery's mastaba. With Ra waning in the late afternoon sky, the ram's horns sounded, sending Mery and her servants to their fateful meetings with Anubis. I shuddered.

The crowds began to leave the necropolis. Already businessmen walked in twos and threes, talking animatedly, making deals that they had delayed for the past seventy days. I lingered, watching the priests packing their incense, scrolls and poisons.

I wandered toward Mery's mastaba. Before the mortared entrance I turned around and gooseflesh immediately rose on my arms and back, for Den's architect had laid out the mastaba so that its door looked over Mother Nile and faced directly toward the Gates to the Afterworld, a split in the distant mountains through which the priests tell us the souls of the departed sailed.

Then I saw Den's cortege approaching. Den sat upon his throne, the crook and staff across his chest, the kohl under his eyes smeared and streaked. His carriers came closer and closer and when they were nearly abreast of me Den looked down and saw me there. At first he did not register who I was, but slowly his expression changed. Yet instead of a look of rage I noticed that tears began to run down his cheeks. He looked so pitiful, trying to contain himself. Finally, he could do so no longer and he uttered a pathetic sound between a cry and a cough and began sobbing uncontrollably. Nekau looked up at his master then back to me, then commanded the procession to continue.

Seeing Den's cortege, Menetnashte worked his way through the crowd and arrived just as Den passed me. I was suddenly filled with pride at my son's manly body, his dark, brooding looks and regal bearing. I could not help but draw a comparison between him and the slightly built, effeminate Den.

Below us the crowds appeared like an army of ants. Most headed toward Inabu-hedj to celebrate and hoist cups of beer to Mery's safe journey. I took Menetnashte's hand in mine.

"Look hard at the spectacle below us, my son," I said, sweeping my free arm before me. "This, all of this, could have been yours." I watched Den's cortege slowly retreat from view.

"Could have been... and... and yet may."

AFTERWARD

Meryt-Neith lived approximately 3100 B.C. She is buried in Abydos in a tomb that is situated very much as it is described in the book. Her mastaba complex was the most elaborate of all the First Dynasty kings to that date, an indication of her respected status. The opening to her complex overlooks the Gates to the Afterworld, a revered site in ancient Egyptian religion.

Due to many factors we do not know many details about Meryt-Neith's life. We do know that she reined for approximately seventeen years, which leads some Egyptologists to speculate that she governed as Regent for her son, King Den. There is also debate over whether she was originally from the Delta or Upper Egypt (which the ancient Egyptians called Kem).

For those interested in learning more about Meryt-Neith and her times, I recommend two scholarly books by one of my mentors for this project, Toby A. H. Wilkinson of Cambridge University, England.

Genesis of the Pharaohs, Thames & Hudson, 2003.

Early Dynastic Egypt, Routledge, 1999.

For an expanded list of references, as well as the latest archaeological discoveries about Meryt-Neith, please visit my website: www.lesterpicker.com

Les Picker spent nearly ten years researching and then writing his First Dynasty trilogy, consisting of The First Pharaoh, The Dagger of Isis and the upcoming Qa'a.

ACKNOWLEDGEMENTS

Trite as it sounds, I could not have written this book without the wisdom and time of many generous people. I would like to acknowledge some of them here.

Dr. Gunter Dreyer of the German Archaeological Institute, patiently spent many hours with me in Cairo and Berlin, by email and on the telephone, answering my questions and tutoring me about life in Meryt-Neith's time.

Dr. Toby Wilkinson of Christ's College, Cambridge University, gave me fresh perspectives on early dynastic life and patiently answered my questions. He shared my enthusiasm for this project, for which I will be always grateful. His book, *Early Dynastic Egypt* (Routledge, 1999) is a wonderful, readable resource for those people serious about Egyptian civilization at the time of Narmer. These dedicated scientists toil, often in obscurity and always under trying conditions, to uncover our past so that we can understand ourselves better.

Abdel Zaher Sulimaan, my Bedouin guide, patiently taught me about life in Egypt's eastern desert and, more importantly, about life. Dr. Zawi Hawass, head of the Egyptian government's archaeological program, without whose dedication and passion for his country's ancient past much of the archaeological work that led to my writing this book would not have been possible.

William Cates, John Hurley, Jay Magenheim, Randy Richie and Joel Rosenberg, Dave Jaffe, Sherif Osman, and Scott Brown, my men's teams, have collectively supported my vision, kept me on track and knocked-me-up-side-of-the-head when needed, usually regularly. I owe them a huge debt of gratitude but, of course, not as large as they owe me.

Terry Sexton, my Tuesday-mornings-with-Terry writing companion, brainstorming partner, and personal editor, I can't wait to celebrate publication of your books!

As with any work of historical fiction, there are numerous fabrications and embellishments in this story, although I suspect that there may not have needed to be had we known more about the actual facts of Meryt-Neith's life. For those historical inaccuracies, I take full responsibility.

Finally, and most importantly, I thank my incredible wife, Leslie, without whose abiding love and unconditional support I could never have written this book. She is the love of my life (and my first-line editor).

ABOUT THE AUTHOR

Les Picker has more than 600 writing and photo credits in National Geographic Society publications, Better Homes & Gardens, Forbes, Time, Inc. Publications, Money, Fortune Small Business, Bloomberg Personal Finance, National Parks Magazine, and dozens of other publications. He is a former newspaper reporter, photographer and editor. For three years Les was a columnist for Oceans Magazine and for four years was Editor-In-Chief for a national environmental magazine. Les is a member of the American Society of Journalists and Authors (ASJA), Nikon Professional Services (NPS) and Hasselblad Professionals.

For four years, Les was a weekly columnist for The Baltimore Sun and continues as a freelance feature travel writer. For three years, Les was a regular commentator on National Public Radio's Marketplace, carried on 260 stations nationwide.

Les has an earned doctorate in ecology from the University of Maine, was a faculty member at the University of Delaware and an adjunct faculty at The Johns Hopkins University. His writing website is www.lesterpicker.com. His photography work can be found at www.lesterpickerphoto.com. Les was the winner of the prestigious 2011 Canada Northern Lights Award for Best Travel Photography.

His novels include:

The First Pharaoh (Book One of a three-part

series). The story of the uniting of Upper and Lower Egypt into a dynasty that lasted for 3,000 years.

The Dagger of Isis (Book Two of a three-part series). Traces the life and times of the first female Pharaoh.

The Underground. How does a woman solve the mystery of a murdered mother and a doting father?

Sargent Mountain. A happily married woman deals with the death of her husband... and her discovery of "the other woman."

Les can be contacted through his website or at: lespicker at gmail dot com. You can follow him on Facebook and on Twitter: http://twitter.com/lespicker

THE DAGGER OF ISIS READER'S GUIDE

1. Where does the title come from?

2. Could things have worked out differently for Nubiti's and Meryt-Neith's relationship?

3. Did Meryt-Neith's near rape at the beginning of the book affect her in any way for the rest of her life?

4. How did King Narmer's unseen presence affect the characters?

5. One of the aspects of ancient Egyptian life was the legal rights given to women, including the right to initiate divorce proceedings, to own a business, and to inherit property. Did learning that in the novel surprise you?

6. Would Nubiti have turned out the way she did without her mother's influence?

7. How would you characterize the relationship between Nubiti and Bakht?

8. The mid-East even today is riven by tribal loyalties and conflicts. Much of that cultural influence dates back to the time before Meryt-Neith. How does Bakht's priesthood reinforce that tribal culture?

9. In the preface, Nubit says:

"Anubis, I am Nubiti, half-sister of King Wadjet and daughter of Shepsit and King Djer. Before your scales I swear that my heart is light as a feather. Before you lay the scrolls of my life as told to my scribes. Please do not judge Meryt-Neith's actions harshly. Allow my sister to visit with me in the Afterlife. My words are Truth."

Does this reveal anything about Nubiti's character?

10. In the preface, Meryt-Neith says:

"I am Meryt-Neith, Queen of the Two Lands, loyal wife of King Wadjet and mother of King Den, son of King Wadjet, son of King Djer, son of King Hor-Aha, son of the god-King Narmer. I swear before you, Anubis, that these scrolls are the True Telling of My Life. I was a good niece, a good wife and good mother. I was the caretaker of our beloved Kem until my son, King Den, came of age. I beg you to be lenient toward the sins of my sister, Nubiti, so that she may enjoy the rewards of the Afterlife. I await your judgment."

What does this reveal about Meryt-Neith's character?

11. Who was responsible for the tragedy of Meryt-Neith's and Ti-Ameny's relationship?

12. Did Nubiti gain any lasting lessons from her father's death?

13. Was Meryt-Neith a good mother? Was she overly protective? What were the most important life lessons she imparted to Zenty?

14. Does the Apep priesthood bear any resemblance to modern-day conditions in the Middle East? In what ways?

15. Did Meryt-Neith make the right choice in exiling Nubiti to Abu Island?

16. How would you characterize Herihor's relationship with Zenty? Who gained the most from their relationship?

17. Some Egyptologists believe that the first Egyptians were dark-skinned tribesmen from what is now Sudan. Whether or not that is true, early Egyptians interacted with their southern neighbors frequently. Did any aspects of Nekau's relationship with the Royal Court surprise you?

18. Why did Meryt-Neith call Nubiti to her death bed?

19. What did Meryt-Neith mean on her death bed when she said to Nubiti: "It is alright. I have seen it. All is forgiven"?